LOVE,
ACADEMICALLY

JEN SMITH

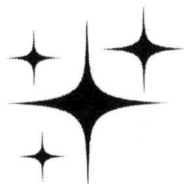

Serendipity, 51 Gower Street, London, WC1E 6HJ
info@serendipityfiction.com | www.serendipityfiction.com

Print ISBN 9781917163378
Ebook ISBN 9781917163385

Set in Times.
Cover design by Bailey McGinn.

Jen lives in the Midlands with her two kids, but dreams of hot footing it down to the south of France to live in a chateau. With an MA in Medieval History, Jen's favourite castle is Caerphilly and her favourite monarch is King John (yes, yes, she knows). Jen loves writing about the trials and tribulations of falling in love, finding your person and overcoming everything that life throws at you, together. She writes for *you*, dear Reader, because everyone deserves a bit of escapism and a happily ever after.

Rhys is just for you, Gemma. *Rudween wedi mal a la tete.*

CHAPTER 1

Pedant *(noun) ped·ant*

1. One who is unimaginative or who unduly emphasises minutiae in the presentation or use of knowledge

2. One who makes a show of knowledge

3. A formalist or precisionist in teaching

(obsolete) A male schoolteacher

LILA

"He said what?"

Lila Cartwright marvelled at the complete and utter arrogance of that man. It was quite impressive actually, the way Rhys Aubrey thought that making people cry was acceptable behaviour.

She stared at the students huddled on her little sofa, one of them clutching a wilted tissue in her hands, another sitting as close to her as she could get, as if sharing warmth for comfort. The boy, DeVon, sitting on the sofa, had wrapped his hands around her delicate teacup so tightly that she was mentally scoping out the first aid box in her bottom drawer in case it cracked under the pressure.

"Mr Aubrey said that if we wanted to be real historians, then we should come up with some ideas of our own and stop wasting his time with regurgitated snippets that we don't understand," DeVon said pensively. The girls nodded.

"I see." Lila smiled, ever the diplomat.

"But it's not just that," one of the girls, Ada, said. "It's the way he talks to us, the way he looks at us. Like we're not worth his time, like we're maggots."

Her heart sank. "Has he ever called you maggots?"

She shook her head. "No. But it's like that's what he thinks."

"So." Lila reached for the tissue box and offered them around again. "Firstly, thank you for bringing this to me, it must have been very difficult. You've been very brave."

"It's not the first time he's made Kerry cry." DeVon waved a hand at the tissue clutcher. "This time it was because he didn't like the font she'd used for her essay."

Never mind his attractive strong jaw and carefully curated hair, Rhys Aubrey was obviously a complete and utter arse. Who cared about stupid fonts?

Lila leaned forward, engaging with the students, like all the good books told her to. "It's not appropriate that you be upset in your seminars by your lecturers, okay?"

The students exchanged watery, relieved glances. Although she desperately wanted to help, she was mentally rearranging her afternoon to ensure she got the work she was actually paid for done.

It served Lila right. If she didn't want people coming into her office and offloading their issues onto her, then she shouldn't make it so damned inviting. She didn't need to throw cushions on the sofa and chairs, or have a teapot with freshly brewed tea and China cups and saucers on the little coffee table. The tempting smell of chocolate chip cookies that she kept in a little tin box didn't make her office any less appealing.

She shouldn't moan. This was her job. Kind of. As the History Department Coordinator, she was there to listen to the students' trials and tribulations, to big-sister them in their first year away from Mummy. Well, it was the unspoken part of her job. Lila's job description didn't technically cover dealing with students, but how could she not, when they appeared in her office stressed and in tears because of how one of her colleagues, one of her lecturers, had treated them in a seminar?

Lila dredged up the memory of the HR training course she'd been on earlier in the year.

"We've got a couple of ways we can move this forward. We can either deal with it formally or informally. It's up to you which route you choose, and I will support your decision." Lila's lips pulled into a comforting smile. "If you want to make a formal complaint, I can email you the process of how to do that. Or you could ask me to deal with it informally."

The students looked warily at each other.

"What would 'informally' mean?" Kerry sniffed.

Lila hesitated, keeping her smile in place. This was the thing. She was full of spontaneous ideas without much to back them up. Like the time she signed up for a charity bike ride, forgetting that she did not actually know how to ride a bike. But it had seemed such a worthy cause! Or the time that she made her friends traipse to Hay-on-Wye for the book festival without booking any accommodation and they had ended up staying in a horrendously expensive suite in a very romantic country hotel just outside of Builth Wells.

"We could move your seminars to here?"

That would be less than ideal, but it would give the students the support they needed, and possibly give Rhys the kick up the arse to sort out his behaviour.

"There's not that many of you and I could fit you all in. I'd be here, but not taking part. It would be part-supervised, I suppose."

She dredged her memory of the university HR handbook. "There are some internal courses I could recommend to Rhys. I obviously can't force him to go on one, but I can do my best to persuade him."

The sharp knock on her open door made her jump. Kerry, the tissue clutcher, flinched as she looked over Lila's shoulder.

"Miss Cartwright, am I interrupting something?" Rhys

Aubrey's soft southern Welsh accent didn't quite hide the terse accusation underneath. What was with the 'Miss Cartwright'? She wasn't a primary school teacher. But it did slide off his tongue very nicely indeed.

"Rhys," Lila said, standing and taking a couple of steps towards him. Her smile widened. It was harder for people to be mean when faced with kindness. That was her philosophy anyway. "How can I help you?"

"What's going on in here?" He took a pointed look at each of the three students in turn.

Lila kicked herself for not shutting the door – rookie mistake. Her old office in the Politics Department had been at the dead end of a corridor, but this new one was smack in the middle of the department thoroughfare.

"Just a friendly chat, Rhys," she said, taking another step towards him, trying to both herd him out of the door and block the students from his view. Rhys just stood there, arms tense and folded over his stupidly broad chest. He must have played rugby or something in Wales. It was their national sport, right?

"A friendly chat? With DeVon and," he gestured vaguely to Kerry and Ada. Christ, he clearly couldn't even remember their names, "two others from my seminar group?"

"Yes," she confirmed brightly. "Are you heading back to your office now? I'll pop in and see you when I'm done here."

It was an obvious dismissal, and Rhys shifted his attention from the students to her, his brown eyes narrowing in assessment. Rhys's dark brown, neatly kept hair was cropped close at the sides, and waved gently over his forehead, the line of his jaw strong and tense as he held her gaze. Lila didn't let her gaze falter, even if her neck was starting to hurt from looking up at him. He was just *bigger* than her in all respects; broad shoulders, thick thighs and big wide hands that could probably crush walnuts.

Rhys Aubrey was obviously used to having the upper hand, used to people backing down if he waited long enough. But he was in her office and she had the high ground, Anakin.

On her fifth count, Lila's cheeks started to hurt.

"Fine. I'll await your visit to my office, Miss Cartwright."

With a dismissive glance at the students, Rhys stalked from the room, moving really rather lithely despite his size.

Lila bristled. What an absolute prick. Yeah, she'd dealt with him before, but it had always been perfunctory and objective. This time, he'd let loose that disparaging conceitedness that simmered under the surface. Was he so blinded by his own sense of self-importance that he lacked all human empathy?

Perhaps he wasn't human. Perhaps he was from a race of slimy frog men that only had the powers of empathy bestowed upon them when they hit forty. Who knew?

Some telepathic conversation seemed to happen between the students.

"We don't want to get anyone in trouble," Ada said, "but something needs to change."

"Don't think of it as getting someone into trouble, and I want to assure you that there would be no blowback on you," Lila said gently, taking her seat again.

If the students wanted to bring a formal complaint against Rhys then there was no way she was going to stop them. Although perhaps Rhys just needed a bit more coffee or sugar before his late morning seminar. Lack of sugar made people grouchy.

"We'd like to have supervised seminars. I don't think I want to be in a seminar with him again without someone there." Kerry's chin wobbled slightly.

"That's something I will strongly suggest Rhys agrees to," Lila said, offering the tin of cookies around.

"Thanks," DeVon exhaled. "You said there's a course?"

A 'How Not to be an Absolute Dick' course would be good for Rhys.

"Yes, of course, DeVon. I'll follow up with you all by email after I've talked to Rhys. Is that okay?"

That's what Lila liked, nods and smiles and happy outcomes all round.

Ada turned to her as the students headed to the door, a mischievous grin crossing her face.

"You know when someone holds eye contact with you for over three seconds it's because they either love you or hate you?"

Lila laughed. "I think it's certainly hate there, don't you?"

"Maybe." Ada shrugged. "But you never know."

Uh, yeah you did. Especially when it was Rhys Aubrey. So what if his bum sat nice and pert in his chinos? So what if his soft accent wormed its way into your very soul? Never mind that she'd imagined that full bottom lip in between hers more than once.

Rhys Aubrey was not in love with her and he never would be.

Lila shoved a cookie into her mouth, needing both fortification and a sugar hit. She grabbed a copy of the staff handbook and thumbed through to the internal courses. Rhys could benefit from all the 'Leadership Skills' courses, but she highlighted a couple that he should start with.

Lila tucked the tin of cookies under her arm, because cookies made everyone happy, right? Rhys could definitely use some chocolatey goodness to perk him up. Perhaps it would make him less of a dick.

RHYS

Rhys slammed his office door behind him.

How dare Lila Cartwright insert herself into his affairs? Meeting with his students without his knowledge. Discussing him and his teaching methods. It was wholly inappropriate. That kind of behaviour would definitely not have been tolerated in his family's business.

But this wasn't Dallimore International, and he wasn't a senior manager anymore.

Rhys refocused on his Word document. He'd allocated an hour before his lunch break to proofread his application to the Royal Historical Society Fellowship, again. It had taken a lot of persuading for Professor Painter to recommend him because whilst his academic contribution to Angevin history was insightful, his body of work could be larger.

He sighed in his frustration and re-read that sentence again. The five years spent trying to force himself into his father's mould after his undergraduate degree had really put him behind, academically. He was now the wrong side of thirty, his PhD amendments still waiting to be ratified, no book in progress, and only a handful of articles and two standalone chapters. He needed a strong personal statement for the Royal Historical Society, otherwise...

Well, he wasn't going to think about the 'otherwise'.

It was no use, he couldn't concentrate. The words were fizzing together on the screen. He sat back and looked at the ceiling. Damn Lila Cartwright and her smells-like-baked-goods office. Now he was hungry, and he had at least another hour before his scheduled lunch break.

"Rhys!" Lila didn't even knock as she flounced into his office in her puffy-sleeved orange top and yellow skirt, tin under one arm, floppy tome of paper in hand.

He struggled to keep his eyebrows down.

"Miss Cartwright."

"Rhys, please, call me Lila." She smiled, probably hoping to make him more amenable to her. Nope.

Lila Cartwright was up to something that involved him, and he wanted to know what it was.

He tried to remember a time that she'd actually been in his office but couldn't. Lila looked around, peering at the photograph of the Aubrey-Dallimore family propped on the top of the filing cabinet.

Rhys crossed his arms across his chest at her obvious lack of urgency. Couldn't she see he was busy?

"Miss Cartwright, what could you possibly have to discuss with my students?"

The quicker he got his answers in, the quicker she could get out of his office and he could carry on with his day.

Lila looked at him like she'd forgotten why she was there. How she had ever gotten the job of Departmental Coordinator, he did not know. She was scatty, a bit dotty, and, yes, he would go as far as to say it, featherbrained.

"Here," she said, flinging the wad of paper on one of his seats and wrestling the lid off the tin under her arm. "Have a cookie." She slid the tin across his desk with a smile.

Rhys held her gaze, because what the hell? Why was she giving him a cookie?

Lila Cartwright was taller than most women of his acquaintance, but they were Welsh and generally shorter, but he doubted she would come much past his shoulder. With her clear, blue eyes and light blonde hair, she was like the dolls his sister used to have sat on a shelf in her room. But dressed worse. She was still standing there with a stupidly beautiful smile on her face, waiting until he did what he was told.

Fine. He rolled his eyes, huffed and grabbed a cookie, taking a large bite out of it.

He raised his eyebrows. Happy now?

"Is that your family?" she asked, pointing at the photograph.

Was she kidding? Since when had this been a social call with cookies and a get-to-know-you chat? She'd be bringing out her needles and wool soon, and they could swap knitting patterns. He must get her advice on 'knit one, purl one', because he just could not get that cable knit to sit straight.

Rhys knew his glare had lost some of its potent effect because his mouth was stuffed with cookie. Which was, by the way, absolutely fucking delicious.

"Oh right, okay." She smiled and sat on a chair opposite him. "So, your students…" She trailed off.

"Yes, that's why you're here," Rhys said pointedly.

"Yeah." Lila scrunched up her little nose. "They're not

enamoured about the way you deal with them in seminars." Her smile thinned apologetically.

Rhys took a steady breath in through his nose. "Meaning?"

"Well, kind of meaning that you can't make them cry over fonts. Or at all, really." Lila gave a little awkward chuckle. Was this really the kind of discussion where a chuckle would be appropriate? Rhys added unprofessional to the list of reasons why Lila Cartwright should never have gotten the job of Departmental Coordinator. "Yeah, not making the students cry in seminars is a really good start."

"Look, I'm preparing them for academia or the world of work, whichever they choose." Rhys narrowed his eyes at her. He hadn't done anything that required a rebuttal, so why was he defending himself to her?

Lila cringed.

"Well, I'm not one hundred percent sure that the 'world of work'," she actually used air quotes, "is really keen for their staff to be reduced to tears."

Rhys just looked. Her blonde hair was messily pulled back into a haphazard bun at the nape of her neck, her glasses were smudged and a little wonky, and was that a toothpaste stain on her top?

What did she expect him to say? It certainly wasn't his experience to hold everyone's hands and sing Kumbaya. How could he get her out of his office so he could continue working on his personal statement? Perhaps if he ate all her cookies she'd leave.

"The thing is," Lila pressed on, "they were thinking of pursuing a formal complaint."

That got his attention.

"What?"

If he had a formal complaint against him, then he would have to disclose it on his Fellowship application and his sturdy, but rather thin, application couldn't bear that strain. Even if not upheld, a formal complaint would haunt him and it would provide all the proof his father needed that Rhys was a failure who not only couldn't cut it in the family business, but couldn't cut it in his ridiculous little academic job.

"Yeah, but I asked them to let me deal with their issues informally to see if we couldn't resolve things." She grinned. "And here we are."

"Here we are, indeed," Rhys said.

Dealing with it informally was better. Then there wouldn't be a speck on his record. Not that there was anything that needed dealing with. It wasn't his fault that his students didn't know one end of an academic argument from the other. He'd given them all the information, told them how to do it – what was he supposed to do? Write their essays for them in the font specified by the student handbook?

"What would dealing informally with their," he cast around for the right word, "*issues* mean?"

"I'm glad you asked, because informally would be so much better. I mean, there's a lot of paperwork and procedure with a formal complaint." She snatched up what he could now see was the staff handbook from the seat next to her and flipped through it, crumpling the pages as she went. He watched her disorganisation with rising ire.

"Where is it? Ah, here it is."

Lila Cartwright shoved the tin of cookies out of the way, sending a spray of crumbs across his desk and flopped the staff handbook in front of him.

"I've circled the ones I think that would be most beneficial," she said, tapping at the page with a pastel-pink fingernail.

Rhys flicked his eyes to the staff handbook with a long-suffering sigh. 'Effective Communication'? 'Coaching and Leadership'? Did she really want him to go through this?

Rhys prided himself on being able to convey a multitude of emotions with the mere narrowing of his eyes and twist of his mouth, and disdain was one of his best.

But Lila just smiled at him. "The students are keen that you do some professional development regarding this issue."

"Fine," he ground out. Anything to not have a blemish on

his record that his father could use against him. There was no hiding from it. His father would find out, he always did. Rhys wondered idly whether his father had planted a camera in his office; he wouldn't put it past him.

If possible, Lila Cartwright's smile grew wider.

"Oh, and there's one more thing," she said, reaching for a cookie. "Mm, these are good, aren't they?"

They were, but he wasn't going to give her the satisfaction of agreeing. Rhys's eye twitched.

"The other thing, Miss Cartwright?" he asked.

She took another bite of the cookie, brushing crumbs onto his carpet.

"Yeah, so the students feel it would be best if they have their seminars with you in my office."

Her throat bobbed in a swallow and a pink blush stained her cheeks as Rhys looked at her. His seminars? In her office? Supervised?

"I require supervision?" he asked quietly, dangerously.

"No, no, it wouldn't be supervision," she said lightly. "It would just be having them in a different space, a different environment. You won't even notice me."

"Am I to expect constructive feedback at the end of each session?"

Lila shrugged. "Well, only if you want it, but I didn't think you would."

Rhys raised an eyebrow. Was she so naive that she didn't understand sarcasm?

"I would actually be working, but I'm sure I can rearrange my days to make sure I can attend properly, if you want me to?" Her voice raised slightly at the end of her sentence, and Rhys could actually see the cogs in her mind working.

"I'm sure that won't be necessary, Miss Cartwright."

She frowned slightly before plastering that annoyingly beautiful smile on her face again, as she stood and grabbed the tin from his desk.

"Here," he said, offering her the battered and dogeared staff handbook back. He did not want it.

"You keep it, I've got loads. I'll book you on those courses." She turned to leave. "Oh, and Rhys?"

"Hmm?" His eyes were on his screen already because now this ridiculous conversation was over, he could get back to what he was supposed to be doing. What more could she possibly want?

"What's with the whole 'Miss Cartwright' thing? Call me Lila."

He cut his eyes to her, surprised. Was she trying to be his friend?

"Okay, see you later!" She hugged the cookie tin to her chest and swept out of the room, leaving rainbows and sweetness in her wake.

Rhys scowled at the door she'd left open.

LILA

By about four, Lila had finished her tin of cookies and had made a significant dent in checking the student intranet log-ins that had been inputted incorrectly by the previous coordinator. But she was flagging as she watched the students stream past her door, heading home or to the pub, clustered together, laughing and joking.

Grabbing her phone from her bag, she pulled up the group chat she had with her two best friends.

To: Girl Group Chat

> Hey, I am in desperate need of fun on Friday night, so please please don't cancel on me! It's been too long since the three of us went out!

Jasmeet text back immediately.

i am covered in glitter and i will NEVER manage to wash tit off. the kids have been FERAL this week. im doing shots Friday night

*it fucking autocorrect

Lila smiled. For all her toughness and no-bullshit attitude, Jasmeet loved her job as a primary school teacher, and her kids loved her. Yes, it was all snot and tears and scraped knees, but Jasmeet's fridge was covered in beautifully scribbled, colourful cards and pictures from her students, past and present. More were added every year.

Don't let me do more than two shots, you know I can't handle it! Sorry the kids have been trying. It must be a full moon or something.

what's full mooning you

Oh, just having a stressful week dealing with students and a petulant lecturer who thinks he's above everything and everyone.

is that possibly the lecturer with the good bum that has been the bane of your life since you moved department

Who? What? xx

Maddy was always late to the party and couldn't remember anything, but she was one hundred percent forgiven because she had the most adorable, squidgiest, giggliest seven-month-old baby that Lila had ever seen.

don't you dare cancel friday night, maddy. ruby can watch ellie, she'd probably love tit if you gave her some time alone with her

*it ducking autocorrect

FUCKING

Friday is in the diary, I'm coming. But I may leave by ten. I can't drink like I used to, and I've only been able to pump one bottle of milk recently, so I can't be too tired on Saturday. xx

That was a long message for Maddy, so Ellie must be sleeping. Ruby, Maddy's wife, was probably desperate to get Maddy out of the house. She could be ever so slightly helicopter-y.

good. i might see if i can find someone to go home with, but i won't leave before 11.

Lila sighed. So much for girls night.

Really? You're planning on ditching me on girls night? I'm mortally wounded!

And Maddy, that's perfect, I'm so looking forward to seeing you out.

i'll only leave if you're happy and i probably won't find anyone anyway

Who was she kidding? Jasmeet was the beauty of their little threesome, all sultry, large chocolate eyes, glossy black hair and the longest legs Lila had ever seen.

> You definitely will find someone, and of course I'll be happy, I'll have spent the evening with my best girls!

Jasmeet, Girls Group Chat

> don't think you're off the hook. i want to hear all about mr sexy bum and his petulance

Telling Jasmeet that she found Rhys the teeny, tiniest bit attractive, and possibly that his arse was like a little round peach, was probably not one of her brightest moments, because Jasmeet had hung on to it like how a snowy owl grabs a vole. But she had pushed and pushed and Lila had to give her something, some indication that she was over Jason.

And she was over Jason. Completely. It was just hard to put herself out there again.

Her phone buzzed in her hand. She clicked on the email alert and sucked in a breath.

The bright blues of the job website filled the little screen, with 'We've found the perfect job for you…' at the top. Yeah right, like they had. Lexicography jobs were few and far between, especially for someone as lowly qualified as her ('lowly', meaning not at all). She scrolled down, and what would you know. They had found the most perfect, gold-dust, flawless job in the entire world.

Lexicographer/Editor at Oxford University Press.

Actually writing and editing the dictionary, her dream job. She scanned through the requirements quickly. Undergraduate degree in a relevant field; her English Literature degree would do nicely. Preferably a postgraduate degree in Linguistics, Language or Translation or appropriate professional experience.

That meant that every man and their dog with a postgraduate degree vaguely connected to the field would be applying.

That was that then.

Lila didn't have a postgraduate degree, and she didn't have 'appropriate professional experience'.

Really, clicking on the "yes, show me job alerts for 'lexicography'" was the most wishful of all wishful thinking.

The agreement had been that when Jason finished his medical training and became a doctor, it would be his turn to support her and she would go back to university to do a Masters in Linguistics, because who didn't love finding out where words came from? But of course, that never happened.

She very rarely opened up the knitting basket in her mind marked "Feelings Left Over from Jason", never unwinding the purple ball of anxiety, the yellow one of self-doubt, or the massive bright red ball of fluffy, unworkable wool labelled "missed opportunities and self-pity", because quite frankly, they did nothing to help her. All they did was make her feel bad. Lila pushed down those feelings deep and hard into her stomach, because no. He was not her life anymore. She was happy and carefree and she could do what she liked. She was "Kenough".

She read through the job listing again. The closest she would ever get was her job in the university, adjacent to, but never touching, the world of words and language.

In Lila's dream, she would be surrounded by words all day, discovering where they came from, how they developed. She'd be writing new meanings of words as they changed through modernisation of usage. It was the archaeology of language, the uncovering of forgotten pieces of history, the deciding of how the world was viewed through the most important form of communication: words.

Queen lexicographer, Susie Dent of Dictionary Corner, was (of course) Lila's rock star.

Lila clicked through to the MA in Linguistics on the university's web page. It would be the absolute perfect course, but there was no way she could afford it, not even part-time or even with the discount the university would give her because she worked there. She still had that loan to repay from her time with Jason.

Besides, she'd have to explain it all to her boss, Sue, and that would mean letting people know that she had a desire to do something, putting herself out there for someone to laugh at and tell her that she wasn't worth it, and wouldn't be able to do it.

Lila clicked back onto her list of student logins for the intranet with a sigh. Dreams were all well and good, but not when they got in the way of putting the food on the table, and keeping the roof over her head, as well as the cookies in her tin.

Besides, she'd never be good enough for a lexicography job.

> Girls, I am really looking forward to Friday night, I really need some cheering up.

CHAPTER 2

Spurious *(adjective) spu·ri·ous*
1. Something that seems to be genuine, but is false

LILA

The bar had never been so busy.

They'd been lucky enough to get a four-seater table with high stools near the bar, and Lila was definitely ignoring the stroppy glances of people coveting their extra space.

"No, Mads! You can't go just yet! The night is young and look, I'm ordering shots!" Jasmeet waved her phone in front of Maddy's face. Table service by app was one of the best things to come out of the pandemic.

"Go on, Mads, have one more," Lila wheedled. It had been too long since Maddy had been out with them, and she was enjoying having her best girls around her.

"I need a wee, then I have to fight my way through the crowd to get outside and wait for my Uber. Sorry girls, I just want to go home." Maddy turned to Lila, her brown eyes pleading, and ever so slightly tiredly sunken. Lila's heart went out to her, because she was obviously exhausted and desperate for bed.

"Go on, Mads, go have a wee and go home," Lila said, offering her a comforting smile.

"I'm so sorry to leave you, I've had such a good night though, thank you for getting me out of the house." Maddy hugged Lila.

"Don't let that little prick Rhys wind you up. You're good at your job. And you," she said, pointing at Jasmeet, "keep me up to date with all the gossip at school please."

Jasmeet had been Maddy's mentor teacher when she'd been fresh out of teacher training and heading into her first primary school classroom, and they still worked in the same school. Maddy had firmly cemented her place in Lila's heart when she had turned up to Jasmeet's fancy dress twenty-seventh birthday party as a five-year-old, complete with a finger painting for her favourite teacher.

"Of course, my little grasshopper," Jasmeet said. "Text us when you get home so we know you're safe please."

"Yep, will do. Love you girls."

Maddy blew kisses to them both as she forced her way through the crowd to the toilet in the corner of the bar.

"Don't give her a hard time, Jas," Lila said, leaning over the table to her friend.

"I'm not, I just want to make sure her life isn't all baby, baby, baby," Jasmeet said, making sure her hair sat just right over her shoulder, and adjusting the top of her dress so her boobs were on show to their fullest effect. "Ooh, shots are here."

The harried waiter slid the tray onto the table and they grabbed their shots quickly. Jasmeet downed hers in one, but Lila was more cautious.

"What actually is it?" Lila sniffed, and reared back. That was one strong drink.

"It's a Kamikaze. Vodka, triple sec and lime juice." Jasmeet laughed.

Lila's face pinched and her throat burned as it went down. How did people drink this stuff? She would not be having another one of those, thank you very much.

Jasmeet gazed around the busy bar, her eyes snagging on what would probably turn out to be her prey for the night. "Ooh, look at that one."

Lila followed Jasmeet's gaze to the most beautiful man

she had ever seen. Tall, well built, angular jaw with a hint of stubble, black hair closely cropped. How did he get his black skin so smooth and soft? He was heading towards them, his sparkling eyes fixed on a flushing Jasmeet.

"Close your mouth, Jas," Lila whispered as he got closer.

Jasmeet snapped her mouth shut and averted her gaze back to Lila. "Is he still coming over? Is he still looking?"

Lila flicked her eyes to him, and nodded.

Jasmeet took a sip of her drink. "Okay, act natural."

The only one acting unnatural was her friend, but Lila nodded with a smile anyway.

"Hey." Even his voice was smooth. Lila watched Jasmeet melt under his attentive, molten eyes.

"Do you mind if my friend and I join you? Perch on the end of your table?"

"Sure," Jasmeet breathed, and Lila pressed her lips together to stop the smile from escaping. "I'm Jasmeet." She offered her hand like she was Lady Jasmeet of 'Let's Hook Up Tonight-Ville'.

"Dan," he said, squeezing her fingers lightly and flashing a smile at Lila. Oh, was he… she recognized him vaguely from the Engineering Department.

"Dan, I've got the drinks. Oh," his friend appeared, "it's you."

Lila's heart sank, because who else would it be other than the one person she did not want to think about tonight? That's right, ten points! Rhys Aubrey.

Why was he here? She was trying to get away from him and his mess, and here he was, looking at her like he was surprised she even existed outside of the History Department.

Dan slid onto the stool next to Jasmeet. "You two know each other?"

"Yes." Lila pasted a smile on her face. "Jasmeet, this is Rhys Aubrey, one of my lecturers."

She heard him huff behind her. Jasmeet's eyebrows flew

up her forehead so quickly it was a surprise they didn't fly off her head.

"Dan, this is Miss Cartwright," Rhys said stiffly.

"Rhys, how many times? Lila, Li-la," she said, enunciating each syllable.

"Lila Cartwright. Oh, I see," Dan said, exchanging a knowing glance with Jasmeet.

So, Rhys had been discussing his obvious dislike of her with his friend who just happened to work at the University as well? Just brilliant.

Her smile turned taut. "Are you going to sit down, or just stand there like a lemon?"

"Fine." Rhys scowled, sliding his large frame onto the stool next to her and taking a swig of his beer. He'd changed into a dark, well-fitting shirt, rolled up his really rather non-academically muscular forearms, and chinos that hugged his legs.

Jasmeet gave her a smirk, which meant that she had somehow managed to check out Rhys's arse and yes, it was a delicious, round little peach.

Dan turned to Jasmeet, leaning close, and she practically swooned. Lila rolled her eyes in frustration. Yes, she knew that Jasmeet would probably meet someone (because who wouldn't want her – she was beautiful), but so early on in the night? And when Rhys was sitting next to her, frowning at his friend? He was probably having exactly the same thoughts as she was.

If Jasmeet and Dan were going to be gazing into each other's eyes all night in some kind of mating ritual, then she was going to have to talk to Rhys, or just sit there like a lemon, staring into space.

Lila turned to him. "So, Rhys. Good night?"

Rhys shrugged his broad shoulders. "Yeah, fine. Just didn't really want to come here."

"Look, you're not the first person that I would have chosen to spend my evening with either, but here we are," she said

27

bitterly, taking a small sip of her wine. Gosh, that shot had gone straight to her head.

"No, I didn't mean that." He frowned at her. "Dan wanted to come here. I prefer somewhere less," he cast around for the right word, "people-y."

"Sorry, I didn't mean to be rude, I've had a shot." As if that was an excuse. "Boys' night out?"

"Kind of, we haven't caught up for ages, and Dan really likes the cocktails here. Although I'm not sure he cares about them tonight." Rhys nodded at Jasmeet and Dan, sitting close in flirtatious conversation.

"Looks like we've both lost our friends," Lila said, despondently.

Another sip of wine, and a beat of silence between them in the loud room. Lila straightened. She would have a good night if it killed her, and if she had to drag Rhys along for the ride, then so be it. Anyway, perhaps Rhys Aubrey wasn't as haughty as she thought. Only one way to find out.

"Tell me, Rhys, what do you do for fun?"

"Research Henry II," he said immediately.

"I mean for fun fun. Not for work fun."

"Work is fun, that's why I do it. It's fun." Was that a little blush she saw creeping up under his rather snugly fitting navy shirt? Was he embarrassed? It hadn't gone unnoticed by Lila the way his chinos hugged his rather thick thighs, and the way his hair was deliciously dishevelled. No, it would do no good to notice how attractive Rhys's jaw was. "Well, not all of work is fun."

He met her eyes and raised his eyebrows. No, it would appear he did not enjoy every aspect of work at all, and she smiled.

"Dan and I do kickboxing. Does that count?" Rhys said, directing the conversation away from work.

"Yes, that counts. Wow, kickboxing?" That's why his arse looked so firm. Yes, definitely hard. More like a conker than soft like a peach. "So, you could fell a giant with a few well-placed kicks?"

"Yeah, perhaps." His eyebrow creased, amused.

Her phone buzzed urgently on the table, and Lila snatched it up.

"Maddy, what's the matter, you can't be home already?" She waved her hand at Jasmeet to get her attention and mouthed 'Maddy', pointing to her phone.

"No, I'm fine, my Uber's nearly here." The words rushed out. "I've just seen Jason and that skank getting out of a taxi and they are heading into the bar. Right now."

Lila deflated even more. This was the worst girls' night ever.

"Thanks Mads, I'll be okay. Make sure you text when you get home." Lila hung up the phone.

"What is it? Is she okay?" Jasmeet asked.

"She's fine. Jason and Leanne are here," Lila said, shrinking on her stool.

"For fuck's sake," Jasmeet said under her breath, pushing her long hair over her shoulder.

First, having to make small talk with Rhys, and now her ex and the girl he had an affair with? Great. She couldn't let Jason see her like this, tired and despondent. She didn't want his pity.

She needed to be Fun Lila, Exciting Lila, Moved-On Lila – which she had, completely. But Jason always had that knack of making her feel small, worthless, a bit pathetic. Somehow, he managed to unwind those balls of wool and wrap them round her like a weighted blanket, and it was so *so* easy to slip back into Doormat Lila, Downtrodden Lila. Black-and-White Lila. She could feel gloom pushing up like a cool wave from her stomach, turning her from colour into black and white, and she didn't want it. She liked being Technicolour Lila.

Not today, thank you very much. She straightened her shoulders and lifted her chin.

Jason thought she was pining for him, wasting away

waiting for him, and she would prove that she wasn't. She would prove... what? Lila bit the inside of her cheek. Jason would back off with his bullshit if she had a boyfriend, wouldn't he?

Black-and-White Lila would be sad and lonely. Technicolour Lila would have a boyfriend.

Lila took a sly glance at the handsome man across the table. He would be ideal, because who wouldn't want Dan as a fake boyfriend? But that wouldn't work. Why would he be sitting next to Jasmeet and not Lila, his girlfriend? Besides, Jasmeet was nearly sitting on his lap and it would be easier scraping off limpets than prying her away from Dan. She turned her eyes slowly to Rhys. He was attractive, yes. Broad-shouldered and taut, and that scowl could intimidate anyone. Even her douche doctor of an ex-boyfriend.

"Look Rhys, I know you don't like me. But please, please, please, pretend be my boyfriend?" She turned what she hoped was a winning, desperate smile on him. A smile that said, *PLEASE*, in bold and italics.

"What? No." Rhys shook his head with a huff.

"Rhys," Dan interrupted, his voice cashmere-smooth. "The lady obviously needs help. Be a gentleman. Help her out."

Jasmeet placed her hand on Dan's forearm and gazed at him adoringly. Lila could almost hear her saying 'What a hero! What a lovely man!' She worked hard to keep from rolling her eyes.

"Just for tonight Rhys, just for my ex. He's nearly here. Please?" He wasn't looking convinced. "I'll do anything."

Rhys opened his mouth.

"No," she said, before he could get any words out. "Anything other than getting you out of that course."

Rhys gazed at her for three long seconds, eyes narrowed.

"Anything?" he asked.

"Anything."

RHYS

Lila Cartwright was looking at him like her life depended on it, trademarked smile tucked away and her pink lips pressed together tightly. She'd actually done something with her hair tonight, and it waved over her shoulders all glossy and shiny. And she'd put more make up on; the mascara made her eyes soulful and deep.

Anything... except getting him out of the ridiculous course he had to go on.

He glanced at Dan, who was watching expectantly, the curve of his eyebrow saying 'if you don't help out her best friend, I don't have a chance with this girl, so be a good wingman and do it'.

Rhys sighed heavily.

This was the last thing he wanted to do. He'd just come out for a few quiet drinks and a catch-up with Dan. So why did he feel like he couldn't say no? Although 'anything' was a good thing to have on her. What he could ever need from her, he didn't know, but he would think of something. Eventually. That 'anything' would be there until the end of time, waiting for him to use it.

"Fine," he said quietly, hitching his stool closer to hers and laying his arm across the back of her chair. That's what boyfriends did, right?

"Rhys, you are an absolute lifesaver. I cannot thank you enough." She leaned into him slightly, smelling of honeycomb and obviously full of nerves.

"Who is he? Why am I doing this?" Rhys asked.

Lila tucked her hair behind her ear and dipped her head. Was she nervous of him, the ex-boyfriend, or the awkwardness of this weird situation?

"Jason is my ex, we've been split up for ages and I am completely over him, but he always makes me feel," she swallowed, "I don't know, a bit pitiful. That's it, he pities me, and I hate it."

"I can understand that," he told her. "Do you think you could put your smile on? Surely, you should be enjoying yourself with your boyfriend."

Lila laughed, and it put Rhys at ease a little. Not a lot, but certainly a little.

This would be fine, he could pretend to be Lila's boyfriend for a couple of hours or so. Just because he hadn't been a boyfriend for a while, didn't mean that he had forgotten how to do it.

She looked different outside the harsh fluorescent glow of the History Department, attractive with big blue eyes and plump pink lips. The duck-egg-blue sleeveless dress complemented her peachy skin — even if the big cameo brooch she was wearing was hideous — and her legs were shapely and lithe. Wasn't she cold with bare legs? It wasn't summer. But yes, Lila was objectively attractive.

Dan caught his eye and grinned, before turning back to Jasmeet. Now, Jasmeet was a gorgeous woman, but that high-maintenance, Instagram perfection was completely not Rhys's type anymore. However, Dan was pulling out all the stops for her. Rhys had been here before, watching Dan give that playful smile to girls, asking them where they got their dress from; he was a masterful flirt.

"So tell me, Rhys." Lila put on the smile like he'd said, and settled back against his arm, sipping her wine. "Why Henry II?"

Now this was a subject he felt comfortable with. He could talk about Henry II and his sons for hours, days, weeks.

"The Angevins are the medieval version of a soap opera," he started.

"What's the Angevins?" Lila asked, and Rhys blinked at her. She worked in the History Department, and she didn't know one of the most influential medieval royal families? Actually, he would go as far as to say they were one of the most influential dynasties in the whole of history, not just the medieval period.

"The Angevins were a dynastic house, being Henry II and his children, who included Richard I and John," Rhys explained.

"Richard the Lionheart? And evil Prince John?" Lila asked, watching him intently. Rhys eyed her warily. He wasn't used to people taking an interest in his work, especially outside of his close-knit circle of friends. Okay, it was more like a single friend. Dan. And even Dan got bored of it.

"Are you sure you want to talk to me about this? I can go on and on." Rhys offered her an apologetic grimace.

"Yes, of course. I wouldn't have asked otherwise," she said blithely, lips turned up in a little smile.

"Okay then," he said, shifting slightly in his seat. His thumb nudged the softness of her arm and she twitched. "Sorry."

"No, it's okay. Sorry."

Lila moved slightly, and her arm came to rest against his thumb. Touching was fine, wasn't it? Touching is what girlfriends and boyfriends did.

Rhys smiled and started at the beginning.

Lila's smart insights and intelligent questions showed just how much she was taking an interest, and Rhys fully appreciated that. She'd even laughed when he'd told her about Henry II's professional farter, Roland le Fartere, going as far as making him spell his last name. He was just getting to the Thomas Becket debacle in Henry II's reign when he was rudely interrupted.

"Hey Lila."

This must be the ex. What was with the way he sang her name? Rhys took an instant dislike to the tall man with the floppy blond hair stood at their table.

"Oh, Jason. Hi," Lila said with a smile, her voice high enough to feign surprise. Rhys shifted the hand behind her to cup her upper arm. "How are you?"

"Yeah, good thanks," Jason said, peering at Rhys, who looked straight back at him.

"This is my boyfriend, Rhys. Rhys, this is my ex, Jason."

"Nice to meet you," Rhys said. He reached over Lila, holding out his hand. Jason's grip was weak and insipid, like a dead fish. If there was one thing he'd learned from working at Dallimores, it was how to shake hands properly.

"Yeah, and you," Jason said, a frown across his forehead. "Jasmeet," he greeted her.

"Dickhead."

Okay, so no love lost there then.

Rhys watched Jason expectantly. He'd come over, but did he even have anything to say? Jason looked again between him and Lila.

"Where's Leanne?" Lila asked, breaking the awkward silence.

"She's over with our friends," Jason said, waving a hand over his shoulder. "Li, can I speak to you," he hesitated, "in private?" Jason jerked his head, indicating a quieter area by a corner.

Li? What kind of stupid, unimaginative nickname was that?

Rhys could see the cogs working in Lila's mind as she glanced at Jasmeet, whose eyes were impressively hard, boring drill holes into Jason's face.

"Sure," she said, sliding from the stool and adjusting her dress. That colour blue really did suit her. "I won't be long," she said to Rhys, squeezing his forearm. Good, that was an excellent boyfriend/girlfriend interaction.

Rhys turned back to his drink as Lila wandered away with Jason.

"What?" he asked, feeling Jasmeet's scowl turn on him.

"What type of boyfriend are you?" She leaned across the table at him, nostrils flaring.

Rhys was unimpressed. "Uh, the fake type."

"A real boyfriend wouldn't let Lila deal with that wanker by herself." Rhys wondered vaguely what Jason had done so Jasmeet wouldn't even say his name. "You should go over there. Now."

Rhys frowned. "Lila can handle herself." And he certainly wasn't going to jump in the middle of whatever that was.

"She may be able to deal with twatty lecturers at work," Jasmeet said pointedly, confirming Rhys's suspicions that Lila Cartwright had been gossiping about him. "But she can't deal with Jason. He has a habit of crushing her confidence and destroying her self-esteem. So, be a good little boyfriend and go over there." Jasmeet flicked her fingers at him. "Now, please."

Rhys scowled at the woman across the table, but she just held his gaze. She was Eleanor of Aquitaine, the She-Wolf of France, and he couldn't fault her in trying to protect her friend.

"Fine," Rhys grumbled and stood.

Looking around, he spotted Lila and Jason. He had both hands on her shoulders and his mouth was moving quickly. Rhys could practically see him sucking the life out of Lila.

"Hey," Rhys said as he approached them, sliding his arm around Lila's waist and pulling her to him, away from Jason's grip. "You okay?"

Lila nodded, her lips pulled into a tight line, a poor semblance of a smile.

"Are you done here?" Rhys asked Jason, eyebrows raised, not really expecting an answer.

"Look, man, I'm just telling Lila that she shouldn't take too much on. You must know how she gets, she doesn't do well with a lot on her plate, and this new job..." Jason trailed off with a worried look at Lila.

What was he expecting? Some solidarity in putting down a woman he supposedly used to love? What the hell was this guy's problem? Besides, Lila's life was none of his business.

"No, I do not know 'how she gets'. She's doing amazingly in her new job, and has been for the last couple of months." He looked at Lila with a confused frown. "I'm not really sure what your point is?"

"Hey, man, I'm just looking out for her," Jason put his

hands up defensively. "Lila shouldn't take too much on. She can't cope."

"Look man, I don't know who you think you are, but you don't talk about her like that." Because what the actual fuck. Rhys knew full well that was not how you talked to, or about, people. He'd learned that through horrible experience. "We're done here," he said, turning Lila away from her ex.

"I'm just looking out for her," Jason called after them as he led Lila back to the table.

"Thank you," she whispered.

"That's what boyfriends do." Rhys bristled. "Why does he put you down all the time? What's all that about not being able to cope? I think you cope just fine."

Lila rewarded him with a beautiful, bright smile. "Do you?"

It was a real question; she was looking for affirmation as she climbed back onto the stool, smoothing her dress over her legs.

"Yes, of course I do." For all her scatty featherbrained ways, he begrudgingly had to admit the department ran much more smoothly with Lila as coordinator.

He settled his arm across the back of her stool and let his thumb graze the skin of her arm again.

"You don't have to keep your arm round me, Rhys," she said kindly, letting him off the hook.

"Jason might be looking," he replied simply. If he was going to be a fake boyfriend, he was going to damn well do it properly.

LILA

Lila was comfortable with Rhys's arm around her, but she couldn't push away that crushing self-doubt that always came after a conversation with Jason. The 'don't do too much', 'you know how you get', 'you can't cope'. It had been true, she couldn't cope when she had been with him. She couldn't have taken this new job in the History Department, she just *couldn't*. Past tense.

"What did that knob want?" Jasmeet asked, as soon as Lila had taken a fortifying gulp of wine. "Does he not have a girlfriend to get back to?"

"Oh, you know," Lila said, waving a dismissive hand. "Just to say hi. He's worried about me, am I sleeping enough, I look tired – you know, the usual,"

"I don't think you look tired," Rhys said with a frown. Bless him.

"And?" Jasmeet knew Jason all too well.

Lila sighed. "He doesn't know who this 'Rhys' guy is, and is worried whether he's good enough for me," Rhys choked a little on his drink. "Jason just feels that I shouldn't overstretch myself with this new job."

"Fuck boy over there deserves my heel up his arse," Jasmeet said, knocking back another shot. "What a dick. Why can't he just bugger off and leave you alone?"

Lila knew better than to argue with Jasmeet. But Jason was only trying to look out for her, perhaps out of guilt, but now they'd broken up, it felt misplaced. She'd put herself and her life back together in this past year and a half after Jason. New house, new car, new job, new clothes. New, happy, positive, Technicolour Lila.

"He's your ex, right?" Dan asked. "I bet his girlfriend isn't best pleased that he's running over here to talk to you."

"Probably not." Lila cringed. God, what must Leanne think? Probably that Lila was so desperate and so much of a mess that she needed Saviour Jason to come and make sure she was okay.

"I bet he told that skank that he is the only one who can help you and that he needs to keep an eye out after what *he* did," Jasmeet said, shaking her head. "Wanker."

"What did he do?" Rhys asked, and she caught Dan shake

his head slightly at her fake boyfriend. "Oh, am I not supposed to ask?"

Rhys looked between her and Dan quickly, confused.

Lila reassured him with a smile. "No, it's fine." She bumped him slightly with her shoulder. "He cheated on me with Leanne for about a year." She shrugged again.

Rhys's frown deepened. "Why would anyone do that? If you don't want to be with someone, you split up with them."

She looked at him. It was so black and white for Rhys, and she didn't know how to explain it. Not that she should *have* to explain Jason's reasoning. Actually, Rhys was one hundred percent right. If you didn't want to be with someone, you break up. The end.

"He didn't want to split up with her because Lila was supporting him through his medical qualifications. She was working two jobs so he could 'study', supported his lazy ass, paid all the rent, and then—" Jasmeet shut her mouth quickly with a snap. "Sorry Lila, it's your story to tell. That man just grips my shit."

"It's okay, Jas." Lila swallowed. "We were together for years and years, from university, and Jasmeet is right. I supported him throughout his medical training, then it was supposed to be his turn to support me to go back to university to do a postgrad."

Rhys nodded, eyes pinned on her.

"He was on student rotation at the hospital over my birthday one year, so Jasmeet and Maddy—"

"Who's Maddy?" Rhys interrupted. "The lady on the phone?"

"Yeah. So Jasmeet and Maddy took me out to a posh restaurant. We were just about to start our main course when Jason walks in with Leanne, arm around her, kissing her. There was no way they weren't together. Turns out it was her birthday as well." Lila smiled sadly. "What are the odds, eh? Two women, same birthday?"

She'd replayed the moment she'd seen them over and over

in her mind, especially in the first few months after Jason had moved out and before she'd moved to a house closer to the university. She'd replayed it so many times that the sharpness had faded and it lost its colour, like an old VHS tape. Sometimes there were replays of things that hadn't happened; throwing her drink over Jason, making all the scathing arguments that she thought of three days after the fact, sweeping out of the restaurant on the arm of a dashing young man.

What actually happened was that Jasmeet had thrown her drink over Jason, Maddy had laid into him, and she had slunk out of the restaurant into the late March rain and waited in the taxi rank by herself.

The stabbing pain whenever she thought about him with Leanne had dulled into a slight ache, and then, after a few more months, into nothingness. She mourned her time with Jason, but not because of him, but because of *her*. She'd wasted so much time supporting him, living for him, that it had been difficult to find herself again. They'd been together for so long, it was hard to know who she was without him.

"Oh," Rhys said, and there was little else for him to say.

"I'm sorry you had to go through that, Lila," Dan said, those sparkling eyes settling on her earnestly.

She smiled at him across the table. "That's kind of you to say, Dan."

"She's just too damn nice to tell him to fuck off," Jasmeet said, not so under her breath. "And she hates that goddamned Oasis song that Jason sings at her every time he sees her. Pathetic."

"Never mind, it's over and done with. He just makes me feel stupid when I see him. So really, Rhys," she turned to him, and his face was closer to her than expected, "thank you so much. I really appreciate you helping me out."

Rhys's lips turned up into a small smile and he nodded. "You owe me though, Miss Cartwright."

She laughed, and Rhys's smile spread.

"Anything. But not the course."

"Another round?" Dan asked the table, while only looking at Jasmeet. She blushed prettily and nodded.

"I'll have a lemonade please," Lila said, and Rhys nodded.

"Make that two."

"Okay, and done." Dan ordered on the app and put his phone back onto the table.

"Enough about my dismal love life, is there a girlfriend or boyfriend who is going to be upset with you, Rhys?" Lila mentally slapped her forehead. Why hadn't she thought about this before? He was an attractive early-to-mid-thirties man – of course he would have a significant other. And here she was pressuring him into being her fake boyfriend.

"No."

"Okay…" She stretched out the word, pushing for more information. She'd just laid herself bare in front of a colleague and his random guy friend, so the least he could do was return the favour.

No, he'd already gone above and beyond, and still was pretending to be her boyfriend.

"What Rhys means to say is that, no, he's not seeing anyone at the moment, and his last serious relationship was a few years ago," Dan said, giving Rhys a meaningful stare. "You'll have to excuse Rhys, sometimes he lacks social etiquette."

Rhys's neck flushed.

"That's all right, people are hard to read sometimes," she said.

Rhys cut his eyes to her as if checking that she wasn't making fun of him. Lila gave him a smile.

"It's been a while since I've had a girlfriend. There's no one to be annoyed at me."

It was Lila's turn to flush a little, and she swung her eyes away from Rhys before he could see.

"What about you, Dan?" she asked, draining the last of her wine. Lemonade was definitely a good choice, otherwise she would be good for nothing tomorrow. Jasmeet took a sip of her fruity cocktail and tried not to look overly interested (but the gratitude came down the best friend telepathy line). Excellent wing-womaning.

"I'm free and single," he said, turning to Jasmeet.

"Well, that's good to know," Jasmeet crooned, cocking an eyebrow at him. Dan smirked.

Well, that was that then.

What had been the possibility of them leaving together was now a strong eighty-five percent. Lila and Rhys exchanged exasperated glances as Dan and Jasmeet continued their conversation, voices too low for anyone else to join in.

"So, Rhys, tell me, what would be your worst date ever?" Lila asked. "If you say pretending to be a work colleague's boyfriend, I'll be mortally wounded."

Rhys laughed. A proper, throw-your-head-back, truthful laugh and Lila laughed with him.

"Karaoke." He shuddered. "I will never, ever, do karaoke. I cannot imagine anything worse than putting yourself up there for everyone to see you sing terribly. Where's the fun in that?" Rhys said, taking both his and Lila's lemonade off the tray held by the young waitress.

"That's the whole point! You're not supposed to be good at karaoke, you're just supposed to enjoy it." Lila said. "Karaoke is fun, especially when you're with friends."

"No, you're wrong." Rhys sipped his lemonade, secure in his assessment. "What's yours?"

"I'm pretty much up for anything," she said, tilting her head in thought. "I just like to know that someone has thought about spending time with me, but…" She hesitated, thinking.

"Yes?" he prompted, his fingers grazing her arm.

"If I had to choose, I despise those high ropes places, you know? Where you're all hooked up and you climb around the trees?"

Rhys's face twisted, like he had just eaten the sharpest of lemons. "Oh God yeah, no. I am not good with heights."

"Me neither." She wet her lips and took a long look at him. "You know, you're not all bad, Rhys Aubrey."

He narrowed his eyes at her. "Neither are you, Miss Cartwright."

CHAPTER 3

Paladin *(noun)* *pal·a·din*

1. A Knight renowned for heroism and chivalry

RHYS

Dan had missed kickboxing once already this week, and Rhys wasn't holding his breath that he would turn up for class tonight either. It was great that he and Jasmeet were getting on so well, but seriously? Rhys had already had to partner someone he didn't know earlier that week, and he didn't really want to do it again. He pulled out his phone to text Dan.

> Are you coming tomorrow night?

Rhys put his phone down on his desk and lined it up next to his keyboard. He glanced at his computer screen, but the email still sat accusingly on his screen. He read the one line for the twelfth time.

> Aubrey-Dallimore, if you don't come, I will never forgive you.

The annual Dallimore family dinner and drinks was coming up, a celebration of All Things Dallimore.

It was really for the senior management of all subsidiaries of Dallimore International, but Rhys still got an invite, even though he no longer played an active part in the Dallimore businesses. Probably to 'show him what he was missing', or to 'prepare him for his return'. He had avoided it for the last couple of years, but with this email from his little sister, Elin, he really didn't have a choice. He had to go and be paraded around, pointed at, judged, and more than likely, laughed at. Forging your own way in life was what his father had expounded, but only when that forging happened through the lens of Dallimore International. You were expected to 'do your duty' to the family, 'be part of the team', and flog your guts out working your way up before starting your own business, under the umbrella of Dallimores, and *heaven forbid* if you wanted to do something else.

He glanced at the date, even though he knew full well that there was only another eight months left in the agreement between him and his father. Rhys had been given five years to 'make something of himself' in this academic field.

'It's long enough in business, why not in academia?' his father had said. There was this awful looming spectre of daily suits and glass offices and stakeholder meetings and working every minute of every goddamned day in a business that was so mind-numbingly boring, plus all the endless family politics.

Some people (e.g., Elin) thrived on that. Rhys did not. He did not want any single part of it, and the prestigious Fellowship was what he had set up to his father as a measurement of 'success'. Because his father needed something *tangible*, something *measurable*, something where he could say, 'no, my son Rhys doesn't work for the family business, but he's the youngest member of the Royal Historical Society' to his buddies over expensive whiskey, or when pretending to like golf.

But also, Seren would be there.

Seren, with her sleek black hair, her fitted dresses, her French-manicured nails.

Rhys simply could not turn up without screaming 'success' in all aspects of his life.

He tapped his top lip in thought. Lila Cartwright *had* said 'anything.' A woman on his arm would prove he was successful in his private life, if not his work life. That he didn't need the Dallimore name to enable him to be happy and successful.

Rhys's mother had set him up on precisely three ill-fated blind dates before he'd stamped his foot and firmly told her to butt out. This could be his way of proving that he was perfectly capable by himself.

Lila was friendly, pretty, and she would be able to glitter and dazzle with that smile of hers.

The more he thought about it, the better it seemed. There would be no sympathetic glances, there would be no veiled 'are you okay' comments and arm squeezes when Seren walked in.

Yes, decision made.

He would take Lila Cartwright to the Dallimore family dinner and drinks as his fake girlfriend. Well, assuming she agreed. But again, she had said *anything*.

It was gone one, so Lila should be on lunch. He'd tell her now, so she could prepare. It was in a couple of weeks, so there was plenty of time.

Rhys stopped by her office, but she wasn't there. He checked the little cafe downstairs, glancing over students' pumpkin-spiced lattes or (if they were pretentious enough) espressos, heads buried in books and phones. Nope.

When he didn't need her, Lila Cartwright turned up like a bad penny, but now he actually wanted to speak to her, she was missing, like John from his father's (Henry II's) first will. Rhys smiled at his own private joke. That was funny.

Becoming increasingly frustrated, Rhys headed outside and took a long look around.

She was definitely at work today, it was a Wednesday and

she'd been in her office when he'd passed it that morning on the way to a lecture.

He stalked toward the middle of campus. Where was she? The university was nice at this time of year, fresh and crisp, hopeful and clear, full of new undergrads and dreams. But Rhys didn't see any of that as he stormed past the Engineering Department, sweeping his eyes across the lake on his left. A lone figure sat at the other side of the water, and Rhys would recognise that blonde hair, barely kept back in its bun, anywhere.

Finally, Lila. Her sky-blue coat bright against the dull autumn mist.

Rhys wished he'd brought his jacket as he strode around the lake towards her, because being outside for longer than three minutes on this dreary day was chilling his bones. Why was she out here by herself staring into nothing? And why did she look so morose, so lost? He slowed his steps.

Should he ask her? Should he comfort her?

Yes, they'd spent a few hours last Friday night being 'friends', if you could put it that way, but they weren't *real* friends, and he certainly wasn't qualified to offer any help, unless she was contemplating Richard I's capture in Austria.

But he should check that she was okay before he asked for a favour. That's what people did. But it wasn't a favour though, it was her end of the bargain, her part of the deal.

"Hey," he said, when he was close enough. "What are you doing out here by yourself?"

He was more brusque than he would have liked, but it was chilly without his jacket and he was scouting outside like a truffle pig.

Lila turned, her usually playful eyes hollow and dull. When she saw who it was, she plastered a smile on her face, but Rhys wasn't fooled. He may not be great at reading people, but he'd seen… yes, despair.

"Oh, hey Rhys, what are you doing here?" she asked, shuffling up to make room for him. He eyed the old wooden bench carefully, before perching in a space that looked the least damp.

"Looking for you," he said.

Lila had chosen a good spot. It was nice out there with the ducks paddling lazily, away from the bustling university.

"What do you need? I'm due back at two, but I can help now if it's urgent," she said, all signs of sadness gone.

"Oh, no, nothing work-wise." He paused. This stuff really was not his forte. What would Dan do? Dan would ask. "What's wrong? You don't look very happy."

"It's nothing, it's just I always start questioning my life choices when I see Jason." Lila sighed and her shoulders slumped. Definitely not happy. "I'll be all right in a couple of days."

He'd asked what was wrong, and she'd told him, but Rhys had absolutely no idea what to do with the information. He nodded.

"Anyway, if it's not work, what do you need me for?" she asked, her real smile back. How did she pull that brightness from the depth of her soul when she was feeling so down?

"Uh, well, I've got this thing coming up and I," he hesitated, "well, I need a girlfriend, and since I was your boyfriend last Friday…" Rhys trailed off. This was harder than he thought it would be. Why was he nervous? It wasn't like he was asking her out for real, this was just her 'anything' part of the bargain.

"Oh, right! Yes, I can do that, you just tell me when and where." She smiled warmly, putting him at ease. "What kind of thing is it?"

"It's dinner and drinks with my family." Rhys swallowed, trying to keep the distaste from his face. It's not that he didn't like his family, it was more that he didn't want to socialise with them. Actually, not the family, it was just his father. And Seren.

"There's a story there, and I can't wait to hear it." Lila checked her watch and stood up, eyeing him shrewdly. "Walk back with me?"

Rhys was chilly and set a brisk pace, forcing Lila to hurry to keep up.

"So," she prompted, "why do you need a fake girlfriend for family dinner? I'm sure someone would love to go out with you, for real."

He shot a look at her, wondering if she was making fun of him, but her eyes were fixed on the damp ground. It had been a long while since he'd had a real date, not just a quick roll in bed to release some frustration.

Thinking of an excuse was taking too long.

"I don't know if you've noticed, but I'm not a big fan of people," he said wryly. "I find it hard to trust, especially with—" He cut himself off with a snap of his jaw. She'd have to find out sooner or later anyway, he was just so used to hiding this part of himself. He didn't want to be tarred with *that* particular family brush. People treated him differently when they found out he had money. Or, at least, his family had money and were (there was no sugar-coating it) extremely influential.

"Especially with what?" she said, waiting patiently for him. It was nearly a minute before she huffed dramatically. "Good lord, Rhys, it's like trying to do origami with tissue paper."

What did that mean? He looked at her blankly.

"Which is really hard," she clarified.

"Oh right." He looked down at the leaves lying sodden on the ground. "My family are the Dallimores, of Dallimore International. My full name is Rhys Aubrey-Dallimore. Aubrey is my mother's name, Dallimore is my father's."

Silence.

Yeah, it didn't matter what Lila thought of him, whether she was just after his money or not, because they weren't dating. They weren't even friends, not really. This was just a business arrangement.

"Who?" Lila turned to look at him, confusion creasing her pretty forehead. "What's Dall-more International?"

Rhys blinked. He was so used to people knowing who he was, or at least having heard of the biggest construction company in Europe, it was actually quite refreshing that she didn't. Or it meant that she didn't watch the news.

"Dall-i-more," he corrected. "It's a consortium of businesses centred around the construction industry. Except Aubrey Legal, that my sister runs, which is, like it says, legal work."

"Oh." Lila's eyes widened. "She sounds important."

"She is and my cousins are too," Rhys said, shoving his hands in his pockets and picking up the pace a little. Couldn't she walk any faster?

"Wait, are you the only one who—" Her sentence finished in a high-pitched scream. She suddenly disappeared from Rhys's peripheral vision, leg skidding out in front of her and arms flailing like windmills. Lila landed heavily on the ground on the ground with a damp squelch and another screech. "Ow! Oh my God, it *hurts*!"

Rhys looked down.

How had Lila Cartwright managed to *fall over*? Was she a child? She was lying on the ground, pale blue woollen coat splayed around her, hair tie doing absolutely nothing to hold back the mess of blonde hair getting damp on the ground.

"Ow, ow, ow," she whined, sitting up and bending her leg gingerly.

God, this was embarrassing. If she couldn't walk in a straight line on a normal day, how would she manage at the Dallimore dinner? Perhaps taking Lila as his date didn't scream 'success' like he wanted it to, but was more of a liability.

"What did you do?" He grabbed her arms and hoisted her to her feet.

"I slipped on the leaves. No, no, no! Stop, stop!" she cried and he held completely still.

"What's wrong?" he asked, searching her face.

Christ, what had he done?

"It's my ankle, I've hurt my ankle," Lila said, digging her fingers into his forearms for support.

"Should we take off your boot?" Rhys suggested, bending down and reaching for the zip. They weren't too tall, so he couldn't remonstrate that they were inappropriate for slippery autumnal leaves.

"Don't you dare, Rhys Aubrey-Dallmore," Lila screeched. "It's really, really sore. Let's just leave it on, yeah?"

"Dall-i-more," he corrected under his breath. "Okay, okay. What do you want me to do?"

"Just," she put her arm around his shoulder, "put your arm around me and *help*, Rhys."

"Yes. Right, yes." Rhys slid his arm around her waist, bending to make sure he got his shoulder under her arm properly.

Lila took a couple of stuttering hops before stopping to wipe her brow. He looked at her incredulously. Really? They wouldn't get back to the office before nightfall at this rate, and by that point he'd probably be nearly dead from hypothermia.

With a huff, Rhys swept her up in his arms.

LILA

"Rhys! What are you doing? Put me down!" she shrieked.

She wasn't usually the shrieking kind of girl, but she was hoisted so swiftly and confidently by Rhys that the high-pitched squawk just kind of, well, escaped.

"I'm carrying you, because it will take forever otherwise."

Could he be any more annoyed? It's not like she *made* the leaves slipperier than a thousand banana skins.

"How are you so strong? Is this all the kickboxing?" she asked, as he jostled her in his arms.

"Yeah, not that strong. Can you hold on or something?"

Rhys frowned, glancing at her. "You're not heavy," he said quickly, "but you're a dead weight if you don't hold on."

Lila smiled. He was so awkward, so aware of his own perceived shortcomings. She slipped her arms around his neck and held on for dear life. He was a strange mixture of minty shampoo and cedar aftershave. It shouldn't really go together, but it did, and it suited him. His strong jaw was covered in a slight dark stubble, and his dusky eyelashes were thick and full.

"What?" he said, flicking his eyes to her.

"I'm just looking at you. Who knew your eyes were more hazel than chocolate brown?" She grinned.

"Okay, whatever." But there was a flush to his cheeks. She supposed that could have been from the cold, the exertion, or a particularly bad lunchtime taco.

Students scattered from their path, looking on with comical stares. Some of them snapped photos or videos on their phones, but Lila didn't care. Never in her wildest dreams did she think she would *ever* have her Richard Gere moment, even if her ankle was throbbing painfully.

"It's like *An Officer and a Gentleman*, Rhys! Do you have a hat?" She laughed, throwing her head back.

"I obviously don't have a hat. Can you stop wriggling?"

Lila pressed her lips together to keep a smile inside. It was ridiculously fun, being carried through the university with *Up Where We Belong* streaming through her head. Rhys probably wouldn't appreciate her bursting into song.

He looked less than impressed, his jaw clenched and his hazel eyes fixed ahead.

"You don't have to carry me, you know," she said as they passed the Engineering Department. Although she didn't mind in the slightest.

"How else are you going to get anywhere?" His voice was stern, and his eyes singularly focused straight ahead of them. "You'll need to call your manager – who is it? Sue?"

"Why?"

He flicked his eyes to her, those eyebrows drawn neatly together. "Because you have to go to the hospital."

"What? No, I don't." She tapped him on a muscular shoulder. "Rhys, just put me down."

"Fine." He stopped and lowered her slowly to the ground. "Go on then, walk."

Lila wobbled, and braced her good leg, throwing her arms out wide to keep her balance. He was all challenging and confident, so sure that she wouldn't be able to move. Well, she'd show his arrogant conker tush.

"Fine," she echoed, and put her foot gingerly on the floor. It would be okay if she didn't put her heel down and if she just hopped a bit, surely? She took a couple of pathetic steps. Good lord, she needed some painkillers. The pain shooting up the side of her calf was not a featherlight tickle. She grabbed his shoulder for support.

"See, Rhys, it's fine," she whimpered.

"Don't be ridiculous, Lila," he said. "Get your phone out and call Sue. I'll take you to the hospital."

"Rhys, it's fine" she said. "I'll get a taxi, or call Maddy." Or, more likely, wait until Jasmeet was finished and could come and get her after school.

"Stop, Lila. You cannot walk." His voice was louder than it had been, and his lip curled in frustration. "Call Sue. Now."

"You are so bossy, Rhys Aubrey-Dallmore," she grumbled, dragging her phone out of her pocket.

"It's Dall-i-more, not Dallmore," he snapped. "I've corrected you three times now."

Everything about him was tense and taut, and a tiny vein was pulsing frantically in his temple. That flush across his cheeks had dropped into a deep red, and he'd indignantly forced his shoulders down and chin up. God, she knew exactly how his students felt – lower than maggots. More like amoebas on maggots. Her stomach was hollow and her mouth dry, but he was expecting a reply.

"Oh, I'm sorry, Rhys. Sorry," she mumbled.

He'd told her *repeatedly*, and she had *repeatedly* got his name wrong. She'd been concentrating on not slipping (didn't do a great job), and trying to take in everything else he was saying about needing a fake girlfriend and 'Dallimore' just hadn't stuck in her head.

He sighed and passed a hand across his chin and his face softened. Was that a bit of contrition?

"Are you calling Sue? Or am I?"

Lila tapped her phone quickly, and Sue answered on the second ring.

"Sue, it's Lila. I've got to go to the hospital. I've hurt my ankle," she said, trying to keep her voice light, but feeling rather brittle after the dressing-down from Rhys.

"Oh gosh, Lila. Is it broken?" Sue asked.

"No. It's not that bad, but Rhys is making me go. He's taking me, but I'm sure he won't be long."

Rhys scooped her up again, bouncing her against his chest.

"Oop," she huffed. "Sue, it's like *An Officer and a Gentleman* out here!"

Rhys made a rough, disparaging noise in the back of his throat.

"Oh my God, is Rhys carrying you?" Sue gasped, and she could hear the squeak of the wheelie chair scuttling along the floor, probably to the window. "I can see you! Look up!"

Lila waved at Sue's silhouette in the first-floor window.

"I hope there's not going to be a sexual harassment complaint. I don't have time for that," Sue said.

"Gosh, no. I think I'm annoying him more than anything." Lila smiled sweetly at Rhys's profile. His mouth was pressed into a firm line.

"Tell Sue I don't have any lectures this afternoon, but could she email my students and move my office hours." Rhys was breathless as they entered the car park. Good. A breathless Rhys couldn't tell her off again.

"I heard. Let me know how it goes at the hospital, Lila.

Hopefully you'll be back tomorrow," Sue said, before ending the call.

Thanks for the sympathy, Sue.

"Rhys, you know you don't have to do this, but thank you. I appreciate it," she said, resisting patting his shoulder again. He did have nice shoulders, and probably sleeping on them would be incredibly comfortable. Uh, why was she thinking about sleeping on Rhys Aubrey's shoulder? No.

He gave her a glare out of the corner of his eye, but the tips of his ears coloured pink.

"Petunia is that one over there." Lila pointed to a sky-blue, teeny-tiny Fiat 500 that Jason would have never agreed to let her buy. But it was one of the first things she did when they split up, get this pretty little car on finance at the cheapest deal she could. Petunia was beautiful and freeing.

Rhys looked at her quizzically.

"My car, the little blue one, with the rainbow sticker in the back window," Lila said happily.

"Uh, no." Rhys stopped in his tracks. "I'm not driving that."

"Don't say that, she'll hear you," Lila whispered dramatically. "She'll be offended!"

"Lila, it's a car. It doesn't *hear* me," Rhys rolled his eyes so hard she was unsure they'd ever come back round. "I cannot fit in that car. Neither can you with your leg out. It's too small, and—" he snapped his mouth shut.

"And what?" Lila pushed.

Rhys let out a long-suffering sigh. "It's got a pink steering wheel."

She let out a cackle of a laugh; the idea of posh, double-barrelled Rhys Aubrey-Dallimore squeezed in behind the pink wheel of her teeny-tiny car was utterly ridiculous.

He took her in the wrong direction.

"We'll take my car."

Like Rhys, his car was stoic and black, shiny and new, parked next to rust-bucket student cars and staff family saloons with Peppa Pig sunshades in the rear windows. It was sleek and nearly triple the size of tiny Petunia. He let her down gently onto her good foot and fished the keys from his pocket, keeping his arm around her waist for support.

"This is a posh car, Rhys. I feel like I'll get it dirty just by sitting in it," she said, because she probably did have wet leaves stuck to her arse where she'd fallen.

"Don't be ridiculous, it's not like you're covered in filth." He opened the door for her and helped her in, fussing like a particularly put-out mother hen.

"Rhys," she said quietly as he pulled the seat belt around her. He was close enough for her to see his eyelashes flutter against his cheeks. The column of his throat bobbed in a swallow and his arms bumped her thigh, her stomach, her arm.

"Rhys." More pointedly this time, as she stilled his cold hand with hers. Rhys's brown eyes flicked to hers. "I can do it," she said, working his fingers from the seat belt.

He nodded and extracted himself from the passenger side, closing the door with a soft click.

Lila let out a breath. The car smelled of Rhys, of woodsmoke and strength. The dark stubble across his strong jaw lingered in her mind. She had to get a grip. He was just dropping her off at the hospital in the quickest way possible. He'd carried her, not because he wanted to (because who would *do* that), but because it was the quickest way to get her to the car park.

She was fine, all fine. That little crush on Rhys Aubrey's arse could stay exactly where it was.

Rhys folded himself into the driver's side and pressed the button to turn the car on. Nothing so basic as an actual car key for Rhys Aubrey-Dallimore. He pressed a couple of buttons on the dashboard and the seat warmed under her legs. He rubbed his hands together.

"Oh Rhys, I'm so sorry. You're cold," she said. He'd been outside all this time without a coat. It wasn't *cold* cold, but it was chilly enough that a jacket would be preferable.

"I didn't expect to be traipsing around outside to find you."

The car slid forward silently.

"Do you want to go back and get your coat?" She'd wait.

Rhys's jaw tightened. "No. The sooner we get there, the sooner we can get back to work."

Okay, fine.

RHYS

Why they had to wait, Rhys did not know. Surely there should be *someone* available? He'd never had to wait for any kind of medical service before, but then again, he'd always called the private health care provider and swung the considerable weight of his name around. There were some bonuses that came with being a Dallimore. This, however, was a whole different world.

Lila shifted in the uncomfortable plastic seat, her leg out awkwardly in front of her.

"You can go, you know. You don't have to wait with me."

Rhys sighed. Dan wouldn't just leave her here, so he couldn't either — no matter how much he wanted to — because he had no lectures and just the sweet bliss of Henry II's Charter Rolls waiting for him.

"How are you going to get back?"

She shrugged. "I'll get Jasmeet to come and get me when she finishes work. Or Maddy. Or I'll get a taxi."

Ridiculous. She should have someone to sit and wait with her, make sure she was okay. A taxi? No. He should be plotting Henry II's movements over the first five years of his reign, but for some reason, he couldn't bring himself to leave her by herself. She needed someone with her.

"Do your parents live close?" Perhaps they could come and sit with her. She'd be much more comfortable with that.

"They live in Italy. So no, not that close. They moved about ten years ago. We video chat sometimes." Lila smiled sadly. "Seriously, Rhys, I'm okay. You go, you've probably got stuff on."

He took a long look at her, trying to discern whether she was teasing him or not. Would she even be comfortable by herself? Would she be annoyed if he left her? Would it jeopardise his fake girlfriend for the evening of the Dallimore family dinner? There was a minefield behind those guileless blue eyes.

He couldn't take the risk. "Nothing that can't wait."

Lila opened her mouth, probably to argue with him, but he cut her short.

"Stop. I'll stay and give you a lift home."

End of discussion.

These stupid, joined-together plastic chairs were too small for any normal sized person to fit into, and he jostled and shifted to see if he could squeeze himself in a bit better. If they were going to make people wait here, the least they could do was provide chairs people could actually sit in. This wasn't a waiting area, this was a punishment area for having the audacity to need medical attention. In the end, he gave up, and leaned his head back against the wall and closed his eyes. The awful yellow lighting hurt them.

This afternoon should have been another couple of hours working out the logistics of moving an entire household so quickly and efficiently in the twelfth century. If there was one thing that Henry II was, it was restless. He was always on the move, holding together his 'federation' of states (Rhys refused to call it an empire because that indicated some sort of homogeneous community, and Henry II's lands were anything *but* homogeneous) by sheer force of personality. After that, he would have had yet another pass at his Fellowship application pencilled in, read through some inane student essays and then gone straight to kickboxing.

Shit, kickboxing. It was unlikely he'd get out of the hospital in time.

Not going to make it tonight, mate.

Dan

Hot date?

Rhys scoffed. This was the antithesis of a 'hot date'.

No. See you later.

"Is everything okay?" Lila asked, wincing as she moved her ankle.

"Is it sore?" he asked, pointlessly. Of course it was sore, that's why they were there.

Lila nodded with a grimace. "And cold."

Did he have a blanket in the car? No, of course he didn't. Why would he?

"Put your foot up here." Rhys gestured to his lap. "You should elevate it."

"You want me to put my leg on you?" Lila asked, surprised.

"Well, you don't have to if you don't want to. But you should elevate it."

Why was she making this so hard? He was only trying to help.

"Oh, should I?" she asked, forehead creasing.

"Yes," he said firmly. Surely, everyone knew that you had to elevate a twist or a sprain.

Rhys watched her throat bob in a swallow before she said, "All right," and put her hands under her thigh, lifting her leg gingerly and resting it over his legs.

Ah. He hadn't thought this through. What was he supposed to do with his hands? He couldn't put them on *her* leg. That would just be weird. He had said that she could put her leg up there, so the least he could do was not maul her. With a lack of anywhere else to put them, he just kind of squished them across his waist.

"Thank you," Lila said, facing him, sitting sideways on her seat now. "It is more comfortable this way."

Rhys just nodded. Lila had managed to get some glitter on her face (where did it even come from?), and it glinted in the fluorescent light. That's it, the car would have to be valeted. There was no way he could cope with glitter flashing at him when he was trying to drive.

She was looking at him expectantly.

"Do you bake cookies every night? Is that why you always smell of vanilla and sugar?" He blurted the first thing he could think of. And he was hungry.

"I hate baking, but I like the end result, and they taste so much better than any from the shop. Believe me, I've tried them all."

There was a lot to unpack there. The whole goddamned History Department smelled of cookies and sweetness and she didn't even like making them? Eating them was a different matter, and he fully appreciated their appeal. Rhys would lay a wager that she had pushed a shopping trolley full of different brands of cookies and a head of broccoli around a supermarket, with just the barest nod to five-a-day.

"So if not baking, then what do you want to do with your life? Not that running the department isn't a worthy thing," Rhys added quickly, tightening his jaw, because could he be any more condescending? Sometimes his words didn't come out right. They didn't sound the way they did in his head.

"I don't know what you lecturers would do without me. You wouldn't even know what lecture halls you need to be in, regardless of the rest of the stuff I do for you all," she chided lightly.

"I didn't mean that your role wasn't important."

"I know, I'm teasing you." She nudged him with her shoulder.

But she hadn't answered, she'd deflected. Rhys waited, but Lila looked down at her fingers, fiddling with one of her sparkly rings.

"I don't want to tell you, you'll laugh."

"Why would I laugh?" Unless it was something he was

59

supposed to laugh at? Although he didn't think it was, not the way her cheeks were flushed with what he presumed was embarrassment. He would be the last person to laugh at anyone following their dreams.

Lila shrugged and crossed her arms over her chest. "Jason always thought it was a bit silly."

"Oh right, did he?" It wasn't a question. He'd already established that Jason was a bit of a self-centred dick. "I think denigrating someone because of what they want to do, what their passion is, is an awful thing to do."

He should know.

"Personal experience?"

"We're not talking about me." But they would have to before family dinner and drinks.

Lila blinked a couple of times and wet her lips, deliberating. Rhys waited.

A soft sigh, and then she answered. "My absolute best, biggest dream job, would be lexicography. It's—"

"I know what it is," he interrupted. "Writing the dictionary, the history of words."

Lila's smile was small and hesitant, looking for approval.

"I don't think it's silly. Dictionaries are the cornerstone of the English language. Words are the basis of all learning."

Her face lit up, a beacon of excitement and happiness.

"Yes, that's it exactly," she said, blue eyes sparkling. "The history of words, their etymology, bringing new words and usages into our everyday language. I love it. I can't think of anything better."

He drank in all her passion. That was exactly how he spoke about the Angevins to his father when he told him he wanted to pursue history and not corporate business anymore. Dreams deserved to be nurtured, not squashed. He knew how it felt to be disparaged for wanting to follow your dreams. The least he could do was encourage her.

"So, why aren't you doing it?"

It wasn't as easy as all that. There were always things that held you back, always things to overcome. You couldn't just say to someone 'just do it!', because changing your life like that was hard, and it was scary as hell.

Lila looked around the waiting room, pale lips turning down at the corners. Her leg was a comfortable, warm weight across his thighs. Her eyes rested on her fingers, twisted together in her lap, before meeting his.

"I'm not good enough. I don't have the right qualifications or experience." Lila scrunched up her nose.

Rhys frowned and opened his mouth to say that she could get the qualifications, she could get the experience, but changed his mind. Not everyone had the luxury of money or time.

"It's just a weird, silly little thing that I like. That's what Jason always used to say anyway." Her knuckles were white in her lap.

"I don't think it's silly or weird and I'm pretty sure you would be good enough."

It was the truth. She was meticulous and detail-orientated, if a little fluffy and glittery. He didn't see why not.

"That's kind of you to say," she said, tilting her head.

"Not really, it's just my opinion." Rhys shrugged. "You should have people in your life who believe and encourage you, not people who put you down."

"I've got Jas and Maddy. But no more men. I've sworn all of you off completely," she said with a brittle laugh.

"I don't blame you. Jason sounds like a right dickhead."

Men like Jason gave the rest of them a bad name.

"Yeah, well," Lila said quietly, tucking loose strands of hair behind her ear. "But never mind about all of that."

Rhys studied her. There was much more to his colourful Departmental Coordinator than met the eye, and he was surprisingly enjoying this little chat with her. She hated baking but liked the end result. She loved words. She'd had a not-very-nice relationship, and she was dealing with the aftermath. Lila was admirable. And yes, with her pink cheeks and elegant sweep of her neck, she was quite pretty.

CHAPTER 4

Cocksure (adjective) cock·sure

1. Feeling perfect assurance, sometimes on inadequate grounds

2. Marked by overconfidence or presumptuousness

LILA

They had been waiting for hours. Well, two. But it was still a plural.

"Here," Rhys said, handing her a plastic cup of hot chocolate. He sat down next to her again and pulled her leg onto his lap.

He really wasn't all that bad. Sure, he could be a bit direct, but this was the second hot chocolate he'd bought her and he had stayed with her all this time.

"Kit Kat? The vending machine didn't have any cookies, not that they'd be any good anyway," he said with a wry smile, offering her a Kit Kat Chunky.

"Rhys, I would kill for chocolate," she said, snatching it out of his hand, barely getting it ripped open before she stuffed it into her mouth. "What? I missed my afternoon cookie."

"You have an afternoon cookie?" he asked, his eyebrow crawling up his forehead.

"Yes, and a morning cookie. It's what makes me so sweet."

The corner of his mouth ticked up in a tiny smile before he caught himself and forced his eyebrows together in a frown.

"Is it going to be much longer?" Rhys checked his swanky watch for the thirtieth time. "It's been hours. I'm going to ask."

"Rhys, don't. They're doing their best. They're just overworked and under-resourced," Lila said, gripping his strong arm. Which was very strong.

He was probably used to private health care, GPs and A&E staff at his beck and call, with all his international business money. Well, now he could experience how the other half lived, with waiting rooms and hot chocolate from vending machines.

"Fine." He huffed and sat back.

"It won't be much longer." Dealing with Rhys was like dealing with an overgrown child.

She really hoped it wouldn't be much longer because she was absolutely starving. There was only so big a hole chocolate could fill.

They sat in silence. At some point over the last two hours, Rhys's forearms had rested on her shin, which was only fair as she was using his lap as her leg prop. He rubbed the fabric of her pink trousers absently between his fingers.

Lila sighed. She should probably text her mother.

> Just to let you know, I slipped on leaves and am in hospital. It's probably just a sprain and I'm okay.

The waiting room had filled, and more important cases had been seen before her; a couple of kids, two extreme bleeders and a projectile vomiter.

It was an hour later when her mother texted back and even then it wasn't really much of a text.

Mum

> Okay, text me if you need anything.

She may be an adult, but what she needed was a big hug, a soft blanket and someone to stroke her hair. Instead, her parents were busy living their own lives, and Lila should get on with living hers.

In the end, it was nearly three hours before she was called through to triage.

"Finally," Rhys grumbled under his breath, helping her up. He wrapped an arm around her waist and guided her to the triage room. For a well-built man, he was really quite gentle.

"Are you coming in?" she asked as they reached the triage room door. Suddenly, she really wanted him to.

Rhys frowned, his eyebrows drawing in. "Uh, sure?"

It was definitely a question.

Lila swallowed and nodded. She was vulnerable and tired and so hungry, and for some reason, having a warm body next to her helped.

"Okay then."

She sat in the slightly less uncomfortable chair and Rhys hovered behind. The doctor took off her sock and boot and poked at her ankle with cold fingers.

"Does this hurt?" he asked, perfunctorily.

Lila sucked in a breath. "Yes, it hurts." Like a bitch.

"And to move it?" The doctor bent her foot up and down.

"Yes," she said, grinding her teeth together.

"Should you actually be moving it like that if it's sprained or broken?" Rhys asked pointedly. The doctor flicked his eyes to Rhys disdainfully before turning back to his paperwork.

"Right, we'll need to X-ray it. I don't think it's broken, but we'll have to see."

"And how long will that take?" Rhys asked, voice laced with tension. She sighed; if he didn't want to be here, he should just go. She'd given him an out time and time again.

"We work as quickly as we can, Mr Cartwright," the doctor snapped, obviously overworked, scribbling something on a pink sheet of paper.

"We're not—"

"I'm not—"

Rhys spoke at the same time she did, and they exchanged a strained glance.

"He's not my husband. We're not together," Lila clarified.

The doctor obviously didn't care and didn't bother to look up. Rhys cleared his throat behind her. It was fifteen long seconds of silence before the doctor shoved the pink form at her.

"Follow the yellow line to the waiting room and the X-ray technician will be there soon."

That was it, they were dismissed.

Rhys's face was like thunder, probably at having to wait again for an X-ray. He looked like he was going to open his mouth, probably to have a go at the doctor for God knows what.

"Thank you," Lila said with a smile, trying to balance the scowl on Rhys's face.

"Is there any way," Rhys started, supercilious and saccharine, "that we could have a wheelchair? It's not like she can walk, is it?"

"Ask the nurse," the doctor said, scanning his computer screen. "I've got another patient to triage now, so if you could…" He indicated the door with his head.

"Yes, of course. Thank you, Doctor, thank you," Lila said, offering him one of her best, people-pleasing smiles .

The doctor softened a little. "You're welcome."

It took Rhys ten minutes to source a wheelchair for her and another ten minutes for them to navigate around the hospital because the yellow line to the X-ray department faded in and out and was not particularly helpful.

She tried not to giggle at Rhys's increasing frustration, because that would go down well whatsoever. It was just that he was so ridiculous with his huffing and puffing every time they went the wrong way. He even growled at an old woman with a Zimmer frame when she got in the way. Did he expect people to be racing around as if it were the London Underground?

It was another hour (and another hot chocolate) in the waiting room before Rhys wheeled her to the X-ray area, trailing a harassed technician. A few scans later and they were back waiting again.

"Why does all of this take so long?" Rhys groaned and adjusted his position on his seat. Again. "And why, for the love of God, are these seats so uncomfortable?"

"Rhys, please. Just go home. You've been here long enough. It's," she looked at her phone, "nearly half-six now. Surely you have better things to be doing on a Wednesday night?"

"I've wasted the afternoon here, what's a couple more hours?"

Lila looked at her hands and bit her cheek. How rude. It was not like she hadn't told him to go, time and time again, and he had insisted on staying.

She was perfectly capable of looking after herself. She had Maddy and Jasmeet. She could call a taxi. She could cope. Lila didn't need Rhys Aubrey, especially not a stroppy Rhys Aubrey.

Lila took a breath. "Rhys, you don't have to—"

"Don't say it, Lila," he snapped, holding his hand out to stop her talking. "I'm here and I'm not going until they let you go."

Rhys Aubrey-Dallimore, with his stupid double-barrelled name, couldn't possibly be understanding, couldn't possibly be empathetic. The only reason she kept going on about him leaving her there was that he blatantly didn't want to be there.

"I was only going to say that you don't have to be so grumpy. Waiting is just what happens in the NHS." It was one hundred percent not what she was going to say. "They haven't got enough funding or enough staff."

"Yeah, well." He visibly deflated.

Lila cast around for something else to say. Sure, they could sit in awkward silence, but if she was going to pretend to be his girlfriend, then they had to at least get on. Otherwise, it would be obvious.

"Did you start that online course? How's it going?" Perhaps not the best subject, but she'd said it now.

"I did start it, yes. You told me I had to." His eyes cut over to her. "It's fine, it's just annoying."

"Why?" How could an online course be annoying?

"It's telling me stuff I already know. It's getting in the way of my research."

Lila snorted a laugh. If that wasn't the epitome of the petulant academic, she didn't know what was.

"Really? Stuff you already know?"

Rhys glared at the floor, colour shooting up his neck. His jaw twitched. Oh Christ, now she'd upset him, and that was the last thing she wanted to do. She was crabby and hungry, and they had been waiting for what seemed like six years, but there was no need to take it out on the one person who was actually here, looking after her. Even if he had been an arse about it.

He shifted to look out of the window and the darkening sky outside.

"Rhys." Her fingers reached for the sleeve of his crisp shirt, buttoned neatly at the cuff. She had the intention of apologising again as she'd obviously touched a nerve, but the door swung open and they were ushered by a different nurse into a different office to wait for a different doctor.

RHYS

This could all have been dealt with in about thirty minutes at his private service. As it was, he had wasted the entire afternoon and half of the evening. They were now in another room, waiting for a doctor to give them the results of Lila's

X-ray. Rhys hadn't even asked if she wanted him there, he'd just wheeled her in and sat down in the chair with the rip in the padding on the seat.

The nurse left them. Again.

His fished his phone out of his pocket.

Dan

> I have to cancel anyway, I'm seeing Jas. Why can't you go? What's happened?

What had happened is that he was trying to be a good person (What Would Dan Do?) and help out a colleague. Now he was missing not only his research, but kickboxing as well.

> I had to take Lila from work (Jasmeet's friend) to the hospital and I'm stuck here.

Dan

> Is she okay? Will Jasmeet be worried?

> I have no idea whether Jasmeet will be worried. She's had an x ray on her ankle. We're waiting on results.

Quite frankly, Dan seemed to be more interested in whether this would interfere with his date than the suffering Rhys was going through. He put his phone back in his pocket.

Perhaps it wasn't a complete waste. He had 'engaged' with Lila, asked her about her hopes and dreams and all that rubbish – exactly what that stupid online course had suggested. For the life of him, he couldn't work out why she wasn't doing a lexicography job. She said she needed qualifications and experience. Well, she worked in a university with an English department, so surely, *surely* there would be some kind of course she could do? Some experience she could get?

She was obviously competent (except for the cookie crumbs on his desk and possible glitter in his car), otherwise she wouldn't have got the Departmental Coordinator job. He took a look at Lila out of the corner of his eye and she wasn't smiling. Her eyes were on the sparkly rings on her fingers, twisting them this way and that. She was tired, and (he presumed) hungry, even though he'd tried to keep her fed with chocolate. Waiting was fucking tiring.

Rhys shook his head. Things weren't that simple for people, there were barriers –financial or otherwise – that he didn't know about. He shouldn't press the issue, and he certainly shouldn't judge. But, if there was one thing Rhys knew about, it was following your dream, even if it meant disappointing everyone around you.

Then, one of Lila's issues slammed open the door. Jason.

"Lila, are you all right? I've only just heard. I've taken you as my patient," he said, putting his hand on her shoulder and looking down at her as you would a child. Rhys rolled his eyes.

"Oh, Jason. Hello," she said nervously, those wide eyes glancing at Rhys.

If Lila had been desperate for him to be her fake boyfriend at the bar then, now her expression was positively begging him. He'd best be her boyfriend again, especially if he wanted her as his fake girlfriend at the Dallimore family dinner.

This day could *not* get any worse.

"Jason," he said, standing.

This fucker thought he was a pretty boy Chad Michael Murray, but he was a weak imitation at best. In fact, his features were more weaselly than anything. Rhys glared at him and shoved his hands into his pocket. No way was he shaking hands with that dick again.

"Rhys," Jason replied tersely, before turning back to the woman in the wheelchair. "What have you done to yourself, Li? Are you okay?"

"I'm okay, I fell," she said, sheepishly. "Slipped on some leaves."

Jason took a long accusing look at Rhys, who just held his stare.

"Let's take a look at your X-rays." Jason pulled out the black and white photographs and held them up to the light, despite the fact there was an X-ray box *right there* on the wall behind him. What a pretentious douche.

"Hmm. Yes, I see."

Jason sat down on the office chair and wheeled himself too close to Lila, touching her ankle, which was propped up on the leg rest of the wheelchair.

"It's not broken, it's just a bad sprain. I'll give you some painkillers and wrap it up for you, but you have to rest, okay?" he said, looking up at her from under his floppy hair. Could Dr Dickhead try any harder? It's like he'd read an article on how to flirt and was putting everything he could remember into action.

"Right, okay. Thank you," Rhys said, his voice clipped. Jasmeet's 'be a proper fake boyfriend' speech ricocheted around his head.

Jason looked up at him, leaning back in his chair when Rhys's glare pinned him.

"Where were you when Lila fell?" Jason asked, more than a hint of accusation in his voice.

"Jason," Lila warned softly.

"I was right next to her, Jason," he said tartly. There was something about this man that really got under his skin. Perhaps the fact that he was an absolute fucking knob.

"Right," Jason said, turning to the desk to fill out some paperwork. "I see."

If Jason was trying to antagonise him, then he was doing a damn good job.

"What is it, exactly, that you see?" Rhys bit out.

"Good job you're doing at looking after her," Jason murmured under his breath.

Rhys looked at Lila, who had her eyes fixed firmly on her fingers in her lap. Why wasn't she saying anything to him?

Why wasn't she standing up for herself? Fine. If she wouldn't do it, then her 'boyfriend' would.

"Lila doesn't need anyone to look after her, Jason. We established that the other day. She is perfectly capable of looking after herself," Rhys snapped.

"Rhys," Lila said quietly and he sat down abruptly. He may only be her fake boyfriend, but he was damned if he was going to let this guy, with his big dick energy, treat her like that.

Jason smirked at him and Rhys ground his teeth together. Kickboxing sounded really good right now.

"Li, here's a prescription. I'll take you the pharmacy after I've wrapped your ankle," Jason said.

"Rhys can take me, but thank you," Lila said quietly. Jason nodded graciously and rummaged around in a drawer to find some dressing.

He took his damned time wrapping her ankle up, all sly glances and little smiles up at Lila. If Rhys was really her boyfriend, he would be getting seriously pissed off by now. Not to mention the fact that Jason had a girlfriend. How would she feel if she knew Jason was mooning over his ex? Because that's what he was doing. Mooning like a fucking teenager.

"Li, if you need anything just text me," Jason said, opening the door for Rhys to wheel her out. "I'll always be your friend, ready to hold your hand."

"For fuck's sake." The words just burst from his chest. "You mustn't know her very well, because she doesn't *need* anyone to hold her hand, *Jason*."

"I think I know her better than you," Jason snorted. "We were together for seven years."

"Yeah, and you messed it up, boy," Rhys snapped, his anger getting the better of him, Welsh accent stridently cutting across his vowels. Christ, he hadn't used the word 'boy' in that derogatory tone for years.

Jason took a step closer to him.

"Guys," Lila pleaded.

This was absolutely ridiculous, Lila wasn't even his girlfriend. Jason had made his choice and was seeing someone else, and here he was squaring up to him? What the actual fuck?

"Guys, please stop arguing. I'm tired and hungry. I just want to go home," she said quietly, her blue eyes imploring him to just wheel her away. "Rhys, can we go home?"

Rhys looked at her and frowned. Lila was on the verge of tears, her voice choked and her throat working hard to keep all her emotions in. Why was she upset? It wasn't as if she still cared about Jason. Or did she?

Regardless, he felt like a right dick, letting her ex-boyfriend get under his skin, making her upset.

"Yes, of course," he said, turning the wheelchair.

"Call me, Li, if you need anything," Jason called after them, a fucking smirk in his voice.

Rhys's knuckles were white on the handles of the wheelchair as he navigated the winding corridors to the pharmacy.

He positioned her and passed the prescription for painkillers (and, he hoped to God, crutches) to the pharmacist behind the counter.

Rhys was genuinely baffled. She was so *Lila*, so vibrant and alive in work. Then Jason rocked up and she turned into a meek little serf, needing someone to tell her what to do. That wasn't the Lila who'd pushed him into doing that stupid course.

"Why do you let him think you can't do anything by yourself?" he asked when he sat down next to her.

Lila turned her sad eyes to him. "Because sometimes I can't."

She shrugged helplessly and tears she had obviously tried so hard to keep down started to escape down her cheeks.

She was *crying*.

What was he supposed to do with that? How did you comfort someone who was crying? Dan didn't cry, and his sister always had their mother and other people to look after her when she was upset (not that Elin was a crier). That was one of the things his ex, Seren, didn't like; he just wasn't very good with emotions, his own or other people's.

He reached over and patted her hand awkwardly.

"There, there, it's okay," he said. "You're okay. You're okay."

The words sounded stupid but Lila snorted a laugh, so they must have done something.

"Thank you for pretending again." She turned a watery smile on him. "I was really hoping I wouldn't see him here."

Rhys shrugged and looked away from her outpouring. "It's fine. It would have been weird if I wasn't your fake boyfriend."

"I'm sorry. I've ruined your day and now I'm crying." She sighed. "I'm just hungry. I need to be fed regularly."

His day had been ruined, and yes, she was crying, but it was all right. He'd done a good thing.

"I can stop and get you fish and chips if you like. But you can't eat them in my car."

Why had he said that? His car would stink of vinegar.

"Can you? Would you? Thank you! Thank you so much," Lila said, putting a hand on his forearm.

"Yep," he said, folding his arms across his chest, waiting. Again.

LILA

It's a good job they hadn't taken Petunia, because it would have been a struggle to get the crutches in.

"Don't worry about stopping, Rhys. I've ordered some fish and chips to be delivered on Just Eat." God, she was starving. "I've ordered you cod and chips okay? Oh, and gravy." That was the least she could do for all his help today.

"Oh. All right," Rhys said. He stopped at the main road and looked at her expectantly. "I don't know where you live."

"Oh sorry! Left here."

Lila massaged her hands as he drove. The five minutes it had taken to get to the car park were the longest of her life (well, not really, but still). Her palms burned. Perhaps she had some blanket fabric at home to wrap around the handles to make them softer. All the better if it was rainbow sparkly.

Rhys obviously didn't feel the need to talk and turned the radio up a couple of notches from a button on his steering wheel. Nothing so dull as a knob on the dash for Rhys Aubrey. It was some kind of politics talk show, with a bonging clock to signify changes in topic. His dark eyebrows pulled together in concentration as he listened, making a 'hmm' noise in agreement every now and again. He was still in his shirt sleeves. He'd literally dropped everything at the office to look after her.

"Rhys." She put her hand lightly on the bend of his elbow. He glanced at her. "Thank you for today."

"Yep. I'll have to pick you up in the morning."

"I appreciate it and I'll make it up to you. I can bake cookies!"

Rhys didn't quite laugh, but she'd take that little curve of his lips as a win.

It was about twenty minutes in traffic before Lila directed Rhys down into the new build estate and onto her little cul-de-sac.

"You can park in the driveway," she said, indicating Petunia's parking space. "Don't hit my plant pots."

He gave her a disdainful side-eye, as if questioning his driving skill was sacrilegious. She pushed down a smile because Rhys wasn't half as scary as he thought he was.

Opening the car door, she swung her legs out, hovering her injured one just above the ground as she levered herself up, securing her handbag over her shoulder. Lila took two tentative shuffle hops and waited for Rhys to appear with her crutches. Instead, he rounded the car and swept her up in his arms. Again.

His jaw ticked with effort, and dark smudges had appeared under his eyes.

"Rhys, it's literally four steps. Pass me my crutches," she protested, but making absolutely no move to get him to put her down. She could get used to this.

"Lila, those four steps will take you half an hour and I can't cope with the slowness." He stopped at her front door for her to dig her keys out of her handbag. Tissues, pens, book, phone, oh that's where that nail varnish was, ah, keys.

"Okay," she said, but he didn't put her down.

Rhys marched her into her tiny house, right into the open-plan room on the right and plopped her on the sofa, wiggling his arms out from under her. He angled the ottoman so she could rest her ankle on it and pulled a blanket with a unicorn on it onto her lap. There was something strange but comforting about Rhys helping her, trying to get the unicorn blanket just right. She pressed her lips together and frowned to keep the giggle from coming out.

"Stay here, I'll get your crutches."

She could not sit there in her work stuff. Having a sprained ankle and sitting on the sofa called for warm, comfy lounging clothes and her house wasn't *that* big. Throwing off the blanket, Lila hobbled her way to the cupboard under the stairs and pulled out some fleecy bottoms and an Oodie from the tumble dryer. She lowered herself gingerly to the floor and wriggled out of her work trousers, shoving them in the washing machine and dragging on the softest bottoms ever made.

The front door slammed.

"Where are you? The fish and chips have arrived," Rhys called from the front room, the sharp tang of vinegar (double, just as she liked it) filling the house.

"Don't come in the hallway. I'm getting changed!" Oodies were the best things ever invented, but a little unwieldy and who knew having a sprained ankle was so debilitating? Finally, she levered herself up from the floor and shuffle-hopped back to the living room.

"I'm not even going to ask why you're getting changed in the hallway."

Rhys stood behind the sofa, clutching the bag of fish and chips. "Can I move now?"

He was such a drama queen.

Not waiting for an answer, he headed for the kitchen. Grumpy, conker-assed Rhys Aubrey-Dallimore definitely needed something to eat.

Lila positioned herself on the sofa (leg up) and found *An Officer and a Gentleman* to buy for £5.49 on Amazon Prime. So worth it. How had Rhys gotten to his mid-thirties without seeing Richard Gere and Debra Winger in this 1980s *masterpiece*?

> I'm home, it's just a sprain. I've got crutches.
> I'm going to watch An Officer and a Gentleman.

Mum

👍

"Here." Rhys reappeared as the opening credits came on, putting a tray of fish and chips on her lap. "I've left the gravy on the side for you, because chips and gravy is an abomination."

"Abomination? You wound me, Mr Aubrey."

Rhys sat next to her, a tea towel across his knees so he didn't get his trousers greasy. Bless him.

"What is this?" He gestured vaguely to the TV with a chip.

"Since you are a heathen, I thought *An Officer and a Gentleman* would be essential viewing to start your education."

"Fine," he grumbled.

He looked at her carefully and opened his mouth to stay something, but quickly snapped it shut again.

"What?" she asked.

He looked around the room. "You've got a lot of stuff."

"Mmm hmm. I like things."

She liked pictures of tropical birds and oriental fans. She liked having her cross stitch where she could reach it from the sofa. She liked having a choice of blankets, depending on her mood. She liked buttons and shiny brooches and carved wooden boxes. She liked her piles of books.

"That's so not what you were going to say, Rhys."

Her words were a bit muffled, because eating was much more important right now.

Then the floodgates opened.

"What is with your ex, Jason? Why is he such a prick?" Rhys asked. Lila opened her mouth to answer his question but Rhys ploughed on. "I mean, how *dare* he suggest that you're incapable? He doesn't have any right to talk to anyone like that, let alone his ex-girlfriend of seven years. In case he forgot, *he* cheated on *you*. He doesn't get a say in how you live your life. You don't need anyone to 'hold your hand', you don't need to be looked after. You're a capable adult, and it fucks me off that he treats you like a child and you just revert to being one. You don't act like that at work."

Wow. That was probably the most she had ever heard Rhys Aubrey speak in one go.

"Um right. Well…" Lila swallowed. All she really wanted to do was sit on the sofa, watch Richard Gere, eat her chips and go to sleep. She shouldn't have pushed.

"Sorry," he muttered, stuffing too much fish in his mouth to stop any more words coming out.

"No, no, I asked. It's okay." Where to start? What to say? Lila shifted on the sofa. "We were together for ages and I guess he felt guilty that I was supporting him. So, he tried to help in other ways, like looking after me, making sure I was okay." Lila shrugged. "That kind of turned into him making most of the decisions, dealing with the finances. He was jealous if I ever did anything for myself. He was insecure and narcissistic."

Rhys put his empty plate on the ottoman in front of them and looked at her.

"I couldn't see it. I thought ours was a normal, loving relationship. I support him, he supports me. I didn't know those were toxic traits until afterwards. Jasmeet tried to tell me time and again, but I wouldn't hear it. I suppose the cheating was the last straw."

She tucked her hair behind her ears.

"Oh," Rhys said, eyes not leaving her face. He was trying to work her out, like she was one of his historical documents that needed deciphering.

"I kind of revert back to that person when I see him. I don't see him a lot. In fact, I hadn't seen him for months until we bumped into him last week," Lila explained. "But there we are."

She forced a cheery smile on her face and turned back to the film, because there was absolutely nothing worse than laying yourself bare to someone. Except perhaps crying in front of them. Oh wait, she'd already done that today.

"Lila, no one can make you feel that you're not good enough. Only you can do that, and you shouldn't," Rhys said quietly, leaning back against her purple throw cushion and linking his hands across his stomach. His stomach that was still way too flat after scarfing all those fish and chips.

She watched his pulse jump in his neck, the unhurried rise and fall of his chest, the calm blink of his eyes, and she believed him.

"Okay," she nodded.

"You finished?" he asked. Not waiting for an answer, he whisked the empty plates into the kitchen and returned with a glass of water for her. Settling himself into the sofa again, he crossed his ankles on the ottoman next to her blanket-covered legs, plain grey socks and all.

CHAPTER 5

Foofaraw (noun) foo·fa·raw

1. A great fuss or disturbance about something very insignificant

RHYS

The film was terrible, but the sofa was comfortable, and he was full after the fish and chips and really didn't want to move. Besides, the least she could do was let him sit in her warm, cosy house, which was filled to the brim with fabric scraps, an old typewriter with half the keys missing and balls and balls and balls of wool. Why someone would need so much wool, he did not know. It wasn't just that though, it was the haphazard stacks of books everywhere, the overflowing bookshelves, the open paperbacks face down on every surface. How many books was she actually reading? Some piles were so precarious that they were likely to collapse and crush whatever happened to be underneath them at any moment.

At least the kitchen was clean and tidy.

The living room, however, was lived in. Full of Lila Cartwright.

By the time Richard Gere courageously abandoned his attempt to break the obstacle course record, Rhys was completely done with *An Officer and a Gentleman*.

"Is there something else we could watch?" he asked.

"You wound me, Rhys! Wound me!" Lila threw dramatic arm across her eyes. "Here." She tossed the remote control on his lap. "You choose. Not the news."

He looked at the remote control in his hand, the power she so easily relinquished to him. She had wanted to watch this film and he was a guest. Jason had probably been all over their TV choices, forcing her to watch fucking douchey stuff like *Man Versus Machine* or *How It's Made*.

"No, it's fine. I'm actually getting into it," he said, putting the remote control between them.

That knowing smile again from her.

"You're lying, but I appreciate it. Thank you."

How did she know he was lying? Was it so completely out of character that he would like this ridiculous storyline and the stilted acting? Or did he have a tell?

"It's getting late. I should go," he said, making no attempt to move.

"After the film, though." She bumped him with her shoulder, teasing. "Because you're into it and desperately need to know how it ends, yeah?"

He rolled his eyes, but couldn't help the little tug on his lips. The two-seater sofa suddenly seemed a lot smaller than it did five minutes ago.

"Besides," she continued, "I've told you way too much about me, you've seen me cry and you're in my house. It's your turn."

What could she possibly want to know about him? He was particular, he was Welsh, he liked the news, and he liked everything in its place. But she knew all of that already.

Lila's expectant blue eyes stared back at him.

"Fine. What do you want to know?"

She clapped her hands like an excited child and shuffled on the sofa to face him better, adjusting her ankle on the ottoman.

"What do I want to know? Hmm." Her eyes lit up as she

settled on a question. "Okay, raspberry ripple or caramel swirl?"

"What?" He blinked. "Uh, raspberry ripple, I guess."

"Correct!" she beamed.

"Why are you asking me about ice cream?"

Was there some kind of ice cream social etiquette that he'd missed?

"Do you want to talk about your family and why you've hidden your real name from everyone at work?" Lila asked, tilting her head accusingly. He scowled and clenched his fists. "Did you always want to be a historian?"

That was all too entwined with his family, and Rhys hadn't mentally prepared himself to explain everything just yet. It was just all so difficult, so stressful, so *not* what he wanted to be talking about in the comfort of Lila Cartwright's sofa.

"Um…" he started.

"Okay, an easier one, although I thought that one was easy enough," she said under her breath. "Kickboxing. Tell me about kickboxing."

Rhys looked up at her apologetically.

"I will tell you about my family before we go for dinner. I just wasn't prepared for it to be today."

Rhys was amazed at the variety of her smiles, because this one was understanding and sympathetic. Ah, that was a revelation. That smile must be part of the reason students were always in her office. That, and the cookies.

"That's okay, there's plenty of time. Isn't there? When actually is it?"

Rhys nodded. "Yeah, not for a while yet."

"Okay, good. So, kickboxing?" Lila prompted.

"Kickboxing," Rhys echoed, and smiled at her. She was remarkably easy to talk to. She understood that he didn't want to talk about certain things, *couldn't* talk about certain things, and she didn't push. It seemed like she was interested in him for him, not for his money or name. And that was rare. "Dan persuaded me to go a few years ago. Work out some of my, what did he call it, oh yeah, 'massive anger issues'."

"You?" she said lightly. "Anger issues? I would never have guessed."

"Miss Cartwright, are you making fun of me?" He scowled at her. He guessed that she was, but sometimes it was best to check rather than make assumptions.

"Yes, Rhys Aubrey, I am."

"Oh." Fair enough, asked and answered. "Yes, apparently I have 'massive anger issues'."

"Did it help?"

Her blonde hair was escaping around her face, curling over her collarbone. It looked like silk.

"So much."

It really had. That two hours twice a week had got rid of his pent-up energy and allowed him to release his anger in a healthy-ish way. He also enjoyed beating up Dan.

Her plump pink lips formed a shocked O.

"Wait, so you used to be *more* angry?"

"I know you're taking the piss now." He narrowed his eyes at her, but it didn't have the full force of his usual glare. Not that he wanted to scare her. No, he was enjoying answering her questions.

"What else? Tell me more." She flung her head back against the sofa theatrically and he suppressed a smile. Overly dramatic was something he would have to add to the list of reasons why Lila Cartwright shouldn't have got the job as Departmental Coordinator. Although, it was becoming less and less pertinent.

"Um…" What else was there? "Oh, I'm applying for a Fellowship at the Royal Historical Association."

Rhys felt his face heat. It was a big deal and if (no, *when*) he failed, he didn't want people knowing and laughing at him behind his back.

"Shut up!" She sat upright and slapped him on the arm. "You are not! That's amazing, Rhys!"

He smiled shyly at the exclamation marks in her voice. He hadn't even told Dan.

"When is the application due in? How does it work? Tell me all." Lila sat forward, Richard Gere completely forgotten.

"A few weeks yet. My statement is nearly ready." He hesitated. "I don't think I'll get it. It's a bit of a long shot."

"What? Why?" Lila said, her eyebrows drawing in.

"I don't think I have the body of work needed. I came to academia relatively late, and I've not had the time."

God, that felt good. It was a boulder that had rolled off his shoulders. Just that verbalisation that he might not get it, that he might fail, felt so good to say. It didn't quite get rid of the nagging, twisting feeling in the pit of his stomach every time he thought of having to explain it to his father, but it released some of the tension in his shoulders.

"But you've got to be invited to apply, haven't you?"

Rhys gave her a searching look. "How do you know that?"

"Uh, I think you'll find I know lots of things, Rhys," she said primly. "Is your coming to academia later than others something that we're not going to talk about right now?" she asked astutely.

"It's just that I haven't really talked about it with anyone before. I'm not sure how to," he said, honestly. What was it about Lila that drew everything out of him? "I just need to process it and then I will work out how to tell you, because you should know before you meet my family. It's not actually a major thing, it's just hard for me to—" He paused. "I'm quite a private person."

"Okay." She gave him a smile that set him at ease and turned back to the TV.

Easy. That was the right word. Lila was easy, comfortable. It was easy being in her space. There was no pressure to be anyone other than himself. She accepted him just as he was. He didn't have to pretend, he didn't have to talk. This was nice.

He should go home, but her house was so warm and homey

and, he realised, he was actually quite enjoying himself. There was no expectation here.

Richard Gere had finally carried Deborah Winger through the factory floor, and *now* Rhys understood what Lila had meant when she asked him about a hat.

He turned to Lila to say that exact thing, but her eyes were closed, lashes resting against her pink cheeks, breathing deeply. She was fast asleep. He should leave, go back to his grey flat with its grey walls and hard sofa. He'd just check the news first.

LILA

"Put your arms around me. Come on, Lila, help me out a little," Rhys said, his voice a groggy whisper on her cheek.

"What's going on? What time is it?" Lila rubbed her hand across her forehead and put her arms around Rhys's neck automatically. He worked his arms under her legs and lifted her from the sofa.

"It's gone two. You fell asleep." He paused sheepishly. "I fell asleep too."

"What are you doing now? I'll just sleep on the sofa," she whined. It was comfortable, the blanket was soft and she was fine right there.

"The sofa isn't big enough for you to sleep on, and you'll have a sore neck when you wake up," Rhys said, navigating the stairs so he didn't bash her ankle.

Her eyes drifted closed again, her head lolling against his crumpled collar. He was comfortable and smelled of, well, Rhys.

"On the left," she mumbled, her forehead falling against his stubbled jaw.

Lila heard the door swing open and Rhys cursed quietly

when he kicked a stray shoe. He lowered her so she was sitting on the bed and unwrapped her arms from him.

Snapping on the bedside light, he said, "I'll get your painkillers."

Forcing her eyes open, Lila changed quickly into a vest top and shorts snatched from her bedside drawers and threw her lounging clothes on the floor. They were way too warm to sleep in, even when it was cold.

"Here." Rhys reappeared and put her phone, a glass of water and two tablets on her little bedside table, stepping over her discarded clothes. "Okay, I'll be back to pick you up in the morning. Well, later in the morning."

"Rhys," she said wearily.

"Lila." He swung round to face her, eyes slightly pink and hair just that right side of dishevelled. Rhys looked devilishly sexy when tired, but, also he looked damned tired. "Don't say you'll get a taxi. I've already said I'll come and get you."

"I wasn't going to say that," she snapped, before smoothing her face into a sleepy smile. "It's gone two in the morning. By the time you get home and get to bed it will be nearly three and then you'll only be back here in a few hours."

Rhys shrugged and passed a hand over his face.

"It's too dangerous for you to drive when you're this tired. Why don't you just stay here? That would make sense."

"Where?" He barked out a laugh. "The sofa is too small for you, let alone me. Your spare room, which I managed to find instead of the bathroom earlier, is the size of a matchbox and is full of books and, and, I don't even know what else."

She sighed and plugged in her phone before snuggling down in the bed, carefully moving her leg.

"I know all of that, Rhys, it's my house. I meant here. This bed is perfectly big enough. We're two adults. I'm sure we can sleep next to each other."

Rhys hesitated. His shoulders drooped and his eyes blinked so slowly she thought he may have fallen asleep standing up.

Everything she'd said was true. He would have to be back here in a few hours if he insisted on coming to get her.

"Lila, I—"

"Rhys Aubrey, I'm not going to hear anymore from you. If you won't stay here, then I will hold a Mexican themed day in your office, invite all your students and make you sing Mexican karaoke."

Lila yawned and waited.

She was one hundred percent not about to jump Rhys – she was far too tired for all that. Besides, she had sworn off men. Rhys just had a nice arse. He had looked after her all day and now it was her turn to look after him. What if he got in an accident because he'd fallen asleep at the wheel? What if he overslept and missed the entire day at work? Lila didn't know which would be worse for him. Besides, if he slept at her house (and therefore had more sleep because of lack of travelling), she would be doing her best to diminish the rattiness that he surely would have tomorrow.

In essence, she was doing the world (and Rhys) a favour.

"Fine." He sighed and moved to the other side of the bed, hesitating before undoing the buttons on his shirt. Bless him, Rhys was shy of her.

She made a show of taking a sip of water so he knew she wasn't ogling him, because she wouldn't want him ogling her if their positions were swapped. She did not, however, fail to notice the muscles in his back moving as he draped his shirt over the back of her dressing-table chair. He sat on the edge of the bed and put his phone on the bedside table.

"I need to be at work early. Can you please set an alarm, my phone is dying," he said quietly.

"You can't sleep in your trousers, Rhys," she murmured. "I've got some really big fluffy pyjama bottoms if you want them?"

"No," he said, obviously too tired to make any other comment.

Rhys stood, the trousers slid off and he folded them quickly over his shirt on the chair before practically diving into bed. Lila deliberately didn't look at his dark boxers that highlighted the excellent curve of his arse, but she couldn't help catching a glimpse. She was only human.

"Okay. Goodnight, Rhys." Lila, finally satisfied, switched off the bedside light.

"Goodnight, Lila," Rhys replied. "The alarm?"

"My alarm is set, Rhys," Lila muttered. "Go to sleep."

"Your bed is lumpy," he grumbled, shifting his weight.

"It is not. You're just so close to the edge if you took a deep breath you'd end up on the floor," she said, turning on her side and putting a hand under her pillow.

The whole bed shook as Rhys shuffled further onto the bed with a huff.

"Are you happy now?"

"Are you comfy now?"

"Goodnight, Lila," he snapped.

Lila smiled to herself, because she had won, and he was comfortable now.

"Goodnight, Rhys."

It was nice, having another person's weight on the other side of the bed, even if it was Rhys Aubrey. Lila's eyes closed, and she drifted off listening to Rhys's even, deep breaths.

RHYS

That had been the best night's sleep Rhys had had for a very long time. It didn't hurt that he was so absolutely, desperately tired after waiting round all day at the hospital and then eating grease-laden fish and chips.

But he was surprised his alarm hadn't gone off yet. Never mind, that meant he had a few more minutes. The bed was so comfortable, so vanilla-pod warm.

Rhys tightened his grip on—

Oh God.

His heart stuttered in embarrassment because he was wound like an octopus around Lila Cartwright.

Rhys's arm was tucked around Lila's waist, but that wasn't the worst part. Oh no, he apparently didn't do unconscious sleep cuddling by halves. His head was nestled on her chest, his nose touching the underside of her jaw, the softness of her neck mere breaths away from his mouth. In the night, he'd managed to hook his leg around the one of hers that was closest to him. He was limpeted to Lila Cartwright like a fucking barnacle.

Rhys groaned inwardly and blinked. He was barely wearing any clothes, just his boxers, and they were twisted so much that if he didn't move soon, he ran the risk of never having children. Lila, it seemed, wasn't wearing much either. Her leg was bare and warm under his. He swallowed.

With any luck, she'd still be asleep and he could untangle himself from her without her even knowing, and then they could put this whole sordid thing behind them.

That would be the best thing.

"Rhys?"

That plan was scuppered then.

"Are you awake?" Lila's voice was soft and sleepy. "Rhys?" She shook his arm lying across her waist gently. "Rhys, you're like a radiator. I'm boiling to death."

He had to move now.

"Oh, hey," he said, clearing his throat. He started to disentangle himself. "Uh, sorry, I don't know—"

"Don't worry about it," she said, pulling her leg from his. Even first thing in the morning, she had a smile.

"What time is it?" he asked, lying on his cold side of the bed, covers pulled up to his chin.

As if summoned, Lila's alarm went off, all tinkly dew drops and promises of sunshine.

"It's seven fifteen," she said, reaching for her phone. "Ugh, so early."

"Seven fifteen?" He sat bolt upright in her bed, the duvet falling around him.

He'd overslept by an hour and fifteen minutes. He was usually on his way to work by now. It would take at least twenty minutes to get to the university from here, and Rhys would take any bet that Lila Cartwright did not rush in the morning, especially with a sprained ankle.

"We've got to get moving," he said urgently, reaching for his trousers and trying to adjust his underwear discreetly before pulling them on, not caring if Lila caught more than a fleeting glimpse of his boxers. He thrust his arms into his shirt.

"What do you mean? Work doesn't start until nine, Rhys. We've got plenty of time," she said, the duvet falling away from her as she sat up.

"I like to be in by eight by the absolute latest. I have things to do," he shot back at her, and ran a hand through his hair. Fuck, he sounded like a dick. She'd been kind to him. "Sorry. I just have a routine."

"Okay, well so do I, and it involves a cup of tea and a slice of toast." She swung her legs out of the bed.

Rhys blew out a breath as she stood up, testing her weight on her ankle.

It was okay. He didn't have any lectures until ten. So what if he wasn't there at eight? Once didn't matter, did it?

"Do you want a cup of tea?" Lila asked, shuffling to the door. She pulled her tangled blonde hair over one shoulder.

"I'll do it." Rhys moved quicker in three seconds than she had in twenty. "How's your ankle?"

"It's much better, although it'll take me a while to get anywhere without crutches."

He should carry her downstairs again, shouldn't he? That would be quicker.

"Go put the kettle on. I can make it to the bathroom and bum shuffle down the stairs."

He nodded and escaped her bedroom.

It hadn't been that long since he'd been in a woman's

bedroom, but it had been an awfully long time since he had woken up in one the morning after. Staying over wasn't something he generally enjoyed. He didn't have any of his stuff, he didn't usually sleep well and other people didn't know his routine.

Not that this was the morning after. It wasn't, because nothing had happened. Except he had made a complete twat out of himself.

Rhys put the kettle on and made sure his shirt was tucked in, doing his best to pull the overnight creases out, despite it hanging neatly on the back of Lila's chair. The toilet flushed and what felt like half an hour later, Lila flopped onto the sofa, still in her pyjamas.

"Do you take sugar?" Rhys called to her, putting a slice of bread in the toaster.

"Yes, two in the morning, please."

He made both cups (his black, hers less black) and brought the hastily buttered toast into the front room, balancing them on the squidgy ottoman in front of Lila. She was watching some morning TV show that he had never seen because he was usually nearly at work by now.

"Here you are," he said pointedly.

"Thanks, Rhys," she said with a smile, and nibbled at her toast. He practically downed the scalding tea in one go. His knee bounced.

"Don't you like breakfast TV?" Lila asked, indicating with the remote control.

He glared at her.

"Or perhaps you're not a morning person," she said, turning back to the TV. "Or a *person* person."

Watching Lila Cartwright eat toast was not the best use of his time this morning. He should be in work, he should be charting Henry II's movements, going over his lecture notes, checking his emails. The hangover from corporate business and the urge to always do more was strong.

"What is it, Rhys? What's going on in that head of yours?" Lila sighed and sat back on the sofa.

"I'm just used to being in work early. It's stressing me out not being in work early."

He ran a hand through his hair and wondered if Lila had a spare toothbrush.

"Why didn't you say it was stressing you out?" She shoved the rest of the toast in her mouth. "I'll do my best. I can't guarantee I'll be as quick as you want, but I'll try."

"Lila, you…" He started to say that she didn't have to, but he changed his mind. "Thank you."

What a relief. To know she was making an effort was enough. Well, it would help if she was quick, but he couldn't expect much more from her.

It took her about half an hour before she called for him to bring her crutches. She was sat on the bottom of the stairs, one flat shoe on, the other foot encased in a fluffy purple sock. The wide emerald green trousers and equally flashy lime-coloured shirt somehow made her eyes bluer. Her crutches were already in the car.

"Rhys, I can walk," she protested as he scooped her up, although she didn't protest very hard, and settled her arms around his neck.

"It's quicker. You have everything?" Rhys didn't really care as he bundled her out of the door and into his car.

He settled in the driver's seat and cranked up the heated seats, because despite the sun shining, it was firmly autumn.

"Too hot?"

"Not as hot as you," Lila replied and he looked at her, just to check that she was teasing, and she flashed him a smile, before digging in her handbag for something.

Was that an embarrassed pink flush creeping up her neck? Perhaps he should just joke about the whole winding himself around her?

"Because I'm 'like a radiator'?" He popped a wry smile on his lips.

"Yes, that's exactly it." Lila retrieved a lip balm and pulled down the sun visor to apply. "Now, Jeeves. To work please."

Yes, madam.

"I need to stop at the Sainsbury's on the way, get some new underwear and a shirt. They're not brilliant shirts, but they'll have to do."

"Oh, yeah, fine."

He caught her smile out of the corner of his eye. It must be her default setting.

"Yeah, just so people don't think I spent the night with you." He glanced at her. "As in, *spent the night* with you."

"I get it, Rhys."

"No, no, I didn't mean—"

"I know what you meant," she said, her lips in a tight smile.

He was making this worse.

"Lila, you'd be a catch for anyone."

"Just not you, yeah?"

Lila pulled out her phone and started tapping away on it.

"That's not—" he started, but she just waved a hand at him.

It was best he shut his mouth. Right now.

LILA

So people wouldn't think he'd spent the night with her? What did he think she was, some kind of brazen hussy? Well, she had invited him into her bed, but it wasn't like that. Besides, what was wrong with spending the night with her?

Sure, she wasn't as attractive as Jasmeet, but she was nice enough. And calling her 'a catch'? Who even says that? Perhaps a ninety-year-old grandmother in a rocking chair talking about her granddaughter's first real boyfriend.

But she was obviously not 'a catch' for Rhys Aubrey-Dallimore. Why did he even want her as his fake girlfriend if he was so repulsed by the idea of people thinking that he had 'spent the night' with her?

> Much better today ladies, got crutches. Ankle like a purple marshmallow.

Maddy, Girls Group Chat

> Aw babe! Do you need anything? I can help! xx

Lila scoffed lightly. Maddy couldn't help, she had too much to do.

> No, I'm fine, thanks though Mads!

Jasmeet, Girls Group Chat

> she's fine because the hot lecturer is looking after her

> Uh, no, I'm fine because I'm a strong independent woman who doesn't need a man to look after me.

She sneaked a look at the man currently looking after her. He was definitely looking harassed.

> Okay, so he is driving me to work.

Jasmeet, Girls Group Chat

> hahahahahaahahaha! yes you are a strong independent woman who does not need a man. he does have a nice bum though!

Lila put her phone back in her handbag. Jasmeet was right. But no, she wasn't a perv, and yes, she would definitely erase the image of a shy Rhys Aubrey's muscular back from her mind. And she would one hundred percent stop thinking about the warm weight of his arm across her stomach, his soft breath across her collarbone.

"Do you want anything?" Rhys asked, pulling smoothly into a parking space.

"No, thanks."

She'd have to hope that Sue would take pity on her and get her lunch from the cafe downstairs, so there was no need to bother Rhys 'spent the night' Aubrey anymore.

> Everything okay there?

Mum
> All fine. I take it your ankle is okay?

> Yes thanks. Are you coming home for Christmas this year?

Mum
> England hasn't been home for ten years! You can come here if you want?

Obviously, her mum had forgotten that she thoroughly disliked milder Christmases. No hot chocolate, no snow, no frosty windows? No, thank you.

Mum
> We've actually got Joyce and Peter staying for Christmas this year, but you're welcome to come as well.

> Thanks Mum, I'll think about it.

Lila spent the next few minutes staring out of the window feeling sorry for herself. Her ankle wasn't that sore at the moment (thanks to lovely painkillers), but Jason was there, picking at that locked door in her mind where she kept all the feelings of uselessness, smallness and pathetic-ness. She really didn't want to let those out because they were so difficult to put away again.

Rhys had, unknowingly, brought back harsh memories of 'you won't find anyone else who loves you for who you are' with his graceless comment, and the memories of other pinpricks slowly started to deflate the balloon of her self-esteem.

When Rhys reappeared in a crisp, light-blue, short-sleeved shirt that was definitely not his slim fit, long-sleeved style, she plastered on a smile. That was enough meandering around the streets of Put Down Town for one day.

"Hey," he said, closing the door with a soft click. "I got you these."

Rhys rummaged in a bright orange Bag for Life and produced a suspiciously cookie-shaped package from the in-store bakery.

"I know they won't be as good as yours, but I thought..." He trailed off awkwardly, watching her face with confused brown eyes.

Lila accepted the package and the unspoken apology.

"Thanks, Rhys." She smiled, and this time it reached her eyes.

"I didn't mean—"

"Don't ruin it." She cut him off.

He nodded once and started the silent car. It was actually quite sweet. Rhys was not nearly as inept at reading people as he might think. Well, not her anyway.

They drove in an amicable silence. Rhys parked as close to the pedestrian exit to the car park as possible so she wouldn't have to hobble so far.

"Give me your car keys. Dan and I will drive your car home on our lunch break."

He was so bossy.

Lila handed them over dutifully and started what felt like

an eighteen-mile trek to the History Department, Rhys falling into step beside her.

"You don't have to snail it to work with me. I've already made you late," she said, giving him yet another out.

"I can't very well leave you by yourself, Lila, can I? How would that look?" Rhys retorted, shoving his hands in his pockets, his breath pluming out in the cold air.

Oh. That's right.

It was all about how he presented himself, not that he actually wanted to walk with her. Graceless wasn't the word. Possibly maladroit, bungling, oblivious or downright rude.

"Hmm."

Rhys visibly forced himself to slow down to wait for her on her stupid crutches. Her bag fell off her shoulder down to her elbow and Rhys hoisted it back up for her. He brushed her hair carefully over her shoulder, his cold fingers flitting over the skin of her collarbone, so the strap of the bag didn't rest on it, a crease of concentration between his dark eyebrows. She swallowed.

Should she explain to him that most people didn't like being treated as a chore, or that his what other people thought was more important that being a decent human being. Or was his precious reputation going to be tarnished by her glitter if he was seen with her? How on God's green earth was he going to have her as his fake girlfriend, if he couldn't bear to be seen with her? Perhaps that was it. He'd changed his mind and was being extra hurtful so she would cry off. Well, that's not how she worked. She'd made a deal and she intended to hold up her end of the bargain.

Lila pulled her eyes away from the stubble across his jaw.

"I've done it again, haven't I?" He sighed. "I don't do well with people."

"That's not true. You just need to think before you open your big fat mouth."

Wisely, Rhys did not open his big fat mouth again until they got out of the lift on the second floor of the building that housed the History, Classics and Anthropology departments. The lift journey was too long, it was all too close and Rhys smelled vaguely of her house, her washing powder, her bedding. Of her. And Lila didn't hate it. Not one bit.

"Okay, see you later then," he said awkwardly. He was a greyhound, desperate to get away from her.

Lila swallowed hard and gave him a smile.

"Go to your office, Rhys. It's fine."

With a brisk nod, Rhys was gone and she shuffled to her own office. Plonking herself in her wheelie chair and resting her foot on a pile of folders, she started work for the day and tried not to think of the soft touch of Rhys's fingers across her collarbone.

Lunch was a meal deal from the cafe downstairs brought by Sue, who was more interested in a potential claim against the University than the fact that she was hurt.

"I think we'll need to do a risk assessment," she said.

"For leaves? Sue, it was my own fault."

Sue shifted on her feet. "And you're comfortable with Rhys?"

"Yes, it's fine, Sue," she said. "We're friends."

Or, at least she thought they were something like friends. Especially after how she had woken up practically pinned to the bed by Rhys's strong arm pulling her close to him. She definitely did not stroke his hair and let him sleep until he started to stir, because he must have been shattered. Besides, she had been snuggly warm with an extra person's body heat. A flush crept up her neck, because that practically naked person had been Rhys Aubrey pressed against her and she had felt everything. Everything.

"Okay. Make sure you get TurnitIn sorted for the end of semester undergraduate essay submissions. Oh, and I'm going to need you to produce a PowerPoint for my meeting with the Vice Chair on Friday." Sue heaved herself off her desk, snagged a couple of cookies and trudged back to her office and her Solitaire game.

Lila checked the WhatsApp group chat.

Maddy, Girls Group Chat

I've got baby yoga, but I can see if Ruby can get you? xx

Jasmeet, Girls Group Chat

no can do chickadee dan's coming to pick me up from work

Oooh! Date night! I need all the gossip please, Mads, don't bother Ruby, she's on nights this week isn't she – don't want to get her up early! I can get a lift from someone at work!

Jasmeet, Girls Group Chat

rhys of the good arse

Haha. No.

Resigned, she clicked online and ordered a taxi to take her home. There was Amanda in Admissions, but she didn't know her well enough to ask for that kind of favour.

The only other person was Rhys, but she couldn't ask him. He'd already done so much for her, and besides, it seemed like he needed a break from 'people'. And by 'people', he meant her, because he hadn't been with anyone else. He'd practically sprinted down the corridor to his office, couldn't wait to be away from her. Okay, he could have some leeway because he'd looked after her. He was full of contradictions; desperate to get away from her, but insisting that he stay. Huffing and puffing about missing work and having to wait in the hospital, but then staying on her sofa all night and literally curling up with her in bed.

Oh Rhys, if a girl wasn't careful, she would get sucked into that world of dichotomies. Good job she was careful. But best to keep it business-like, professional, efficient. By email.

Lila span her wheelie office chair around and stared out the window at the lake. She'd missed her sanity break looking over its stillness (and her favourite red-leaved trees) because it was too dangerous with her crutches. Besides, it would probably take her half an hour to get to her bench and then she'd have to turn around and come back to the office. Positive thinking. She'd be having lunch out there again sooner rather than later.

Without Rhys Aubrey.

CHAPTER 6

Tsundere

1. (chiefly Japanese fiction) A fictional character who fits the archetype of being cold or even hostile towards another person before gradually showing a warm and caring side.

RHYS

It was the day he had been dreading.

His first seminar with the students who hated him. Supervised. In Lila's office.

He wasn't sure which was worse; having to do his job in full view and scrutiny of someone else, or the fact that it was Lila, who he had wound himself around like ivy last week.

Why had he agreed to this again? Oh, that's right, because a formal complaint on his record would never be erased. Even if it wasn't upheld, the allegation would still be there. There would still be a record. His slim chance at the Fellowship would slip from his grasp. And his father would find out. Somehow, in some way, his father always found out.

He'd replied to Elin and called his mother to say that he would be at the dinner and drinks party, and that he was bringing someone. He'd then avoided the calls from Elin, and put a quick stop to the questions from his mother. What was he supposed to say? Yes, she's coming as a favour to me because I pretended to be her boyfriend once. Well, twice. No, she's not my real girlfriend, not really even a friend.

Rhys was slowly articulating in his mind how to explain his family to Lila. Logically, it wasn't a difficult thing to understand. He'd just left the family business. There we are, done. But the iron band wrapped around his chest tightened whenever he thought of verbalising what a disappointment he was to everybody. The disparaging curl of his father's lip whenever anyone asked Rhys about his work. The gleam in his eyes whenever the five years that Rhys had been given to make a success of himself was discussed. Because that five years was very nearly up. Then he would be enveloped back into the family machine, the unrelenting corporate grind. He'd be expected to toe the line, work every hour God sent, be embroiled in the awful family arguments that pitted siblings and cousins against each other.

Not unlike today's seminar topic; Henry II's relationships with his sons, starting with Henry the Young King. They'd move on to Richard, John and other children later on in the semester.

Rhys gathered his paperwork, because he always gave out source material to encourage the students to actually read original texts, or the closest translations thereof and to make up their own minds, not just regurgitate something someone else had made up their own minds about.

That's what teaching was all about, getting them to think properly. It was so frustrating when they couldn't be bothered to give it some proper, independent thought. But teaching was a means to an end, a means so he could study and do what he wanted to do.

He didn't know why his stomach dropped as he walked to Lila's office. It was like he had to perform in front of her, to make sure that she thought he was good enough. He really didn't need any academic validation from her, of all people. She was not an academic.

Rhys hadn't exactly been avoiding Lila. No, it was more like if he didn't have to see her, he wasn't going to go out of his way to see her. Most things could be dealt with via email. Besides, the awkwardness had grown. How was he supposed to act around the woman he had spent the night with? Especially after so suavely disparaging her and putting her down. Like Jason.

Just so people don't think I spent the night with you.

But he hadn't meant it like that. It was more that he didn't want it to be awkward for her, people thinking that she was sleeping with a lecturer (which, technically, she had). But it hadn't come out like that. Well, she certainly hadn't taken it like that. He should have been more tactful, but it was so hard to understand what people thought sometimes.

He'd noticed she was walking without crutches now, but he hadn't seen Petunia in the car park.

Petunia. What a ridiculous name for a car.

"Hello, Lila," Rhys said, waiting to be invited to her little sitting area rather than overtaking her office completely.

"Rhys, why hello. How lovely to see you," she said, and a small smile touched her lips. Her blonde hair was trying to escape, and she dutifully tucked a strand behind her ear.

"Nice to see you as well," he replied, a little confused. Did she not have this seminar in her calendar? Did it not pop up as a reminder an hour before?

Lila grinned. She was teasing him. Again.

"Go on, make yourself at home," she said. "There are cookies on the table."

He frowned. This wasn't a social call, it wasn't a mother's gossip group, there should be no need for cookies. But the aroma of vanilla sweetness in her office was making his mouth water.

"Thank you." Rhys put his coffee and papers on the table, making sure they were nice and neat. "How have you been?"

Lila blinked at him.

"Good, thanks. How are you?" she asked, turning her chair to face him and clasping her hands in her lap.

"I'm fine."

He sat back in the chair by the coffee table, trying to be calm, but his shoulders and jaw were way too tense for any kind of 'relaxed'.

Lila tilted her head to the side, narrowing her eyes at him. "Are you?"

No.

"I really don't want to do this."

"What about it in particular do you not want to do?" she asked gently.

He took a long look at her, and she looked straight back with her guileless blue eyes.

Rhys found himself increasingly annoyed that he noticed what she wore every day. Sometimes he appreciated it. Sometimes he noticed how her clothes would look ridiculous on anyone else, but on her they fit perfectly, hugged her body and made her eyes bluer. Sometimes the colours clashed and gave him a headache. Either way, he always noticed. Today, it was the objectively horrible tight, silver trousers and oversized red and blue patterned shirt, and she made it look good. Really good.

She was still waiting for an answer, and honesty was best. Surely?

"I'm not sure if you'll take this in the way I mean it, but I don't want to hold my seminar in front of you."

"In front of me? Or in front of anyone?"

Her. In front of her. So she could see all of his vulnerabilities, everything he lacked. So she could see how bad he was at reading social cues.

He didn't answer.

"I get that it's difficult. It's like you're under supervision. But honestly, I won't even be paying attention. I've got so much work to do." Lila gestured towards the computer.

"But the fact that the students need—" He dragged a hand

through his hair roughly. That was too much. He didn't need to talk about how disappointed he was.

"Look, think of it as a new environment," she said. "They want to learn. They want to be here, okay?"

Rhys nodded. They may want to learn, but he didn't feel they wanted to learn from him. At all. And that was his own fault.

"Have a cookie, Rhys." Lila gestured to the plate on the table. "Get your blood sugar up."

He took a long look at her. She'd obviously tried to make this as easy as possible for him.

"Thanks." He nibbled at a cookie. It was good.

She smiled warmly and turned back to her computer. There was a pink flush creeping up her neck. As if she could feel him watching her, she tucked her hair behind ear and ducked her head, a tight little smile curving her lips.

Was she self-conscious? Perhaps she was. But why? His forehead creased in a frown as he studied the tilt of her head towards the computer and that errant lock of blonde hair that always seemed to escape from her bun.

For the first time, Rhys wondered whether taking her to the Dallimore dinner was the best idea. What if she hated it? What if his completely corporate-driven family cut her down to size? Would Lila's happy smiles be enough to cut through the harsh business talk? He'd just have to make sure that she wasn't left alone and protect her from the prying eyes and accusatory tones of his family.

"Hi, Lila."

Rhys jerked his eyes away from her to the cluster of his smallest seminar group, huddled together in the doorway of Lila's office.

"Hey, DeVon." Lila gave them that bright smile. "How are you, Kerry? Ada?"

She knew their names.

They nodded and gave her a mumbled "fine thanks" before shuffling over to the coffee table. Rhys stood from his chair and forced a smile to his face, the floral cushion falling to the floor. Lila's office was less than ideal, because whilst it was cosy and comfortable for a nice chat, a seminar should have more of a formal setting. There was no need for blankets draped over the back of the sofa, or for plump cushions with tassels at the corners to welcome the students.

"Hello. Thank you for coming to this seminar in a different venue. Lila has very kindly provided cookies," he said, gesturing at the coffee table and inviting them to sit down. Why he had to behave like he was a butler in a country house when he was just here to teach them, he didn't know. He had better things to do than pandering to students.

They sat warily on the edges of their seats, the girls on the little sofa huddled together as if for warmth, and DeVon on the other chair opposite him. Their eyes kept flicking over to Lila tapping away on her keyboard.

Might as well get this purgatory started.

"So, what can you tell me about the relationship between Henry II and his son, Henry?" Rhys forced lightness into his voice.

The three students glanced at each other before DeVon piped up.

"I think Richard was obviously Henry's favourite, not Henry the Young King," he said, lips pinching tight, waiting for whatever Rhys had to say.

"Okay." Rhys swallowed and tried to keep the disdain off his face. This was going to be a long seminar. "What makes you say that?"

DeVon launched into a ramble about how Richard was the most like Henry, and how he was a warrior, blah blah blah. Henry was an administrator, not a warrior, and whilst DeVon had obviously done some reading about Henry II and Richard, he had obviously not ventured very far into reading about any of the other sons.

"I see." Rhys nodded and tried to frame a question that wasn't a put-down. "What about John? He was an administrator, like his father, Henry II. Or Geoffrey, one of Henry's illegitimate children. Could they possibly be the 'favourite'?" Yes, he air-quoted.

DeVon looked at his notes and one of the girls shuffled on the sofa.

"It's a good conclusion to have drawn, DeVon, and there is certainly some evidence to support that." Some, not a lot. "I think 'favourite' is a difficult word. I see Henry II as acting less as a father to his legitimate sons. He treated them more as rivals. It's my opinion that Henry's relationships with his illegitimate sons were less fraught, precisely because they were illegitimate."

DeVon nodded and scribbled something in his notes. The girl who was always using the wrong font opened her notebook in front of her.

"But we're talking about Henry II and his son, Henry the Young King in this seminar. What other aspects of their relationship have you found?"

Rhys opened the floor and sat back. The two girls were tentative at first, but he kept asking open questions, giving non-committal answers rather than telling them straight 'you are wrong' and pushing their line of thinking in different directions.

He kept an eye on Lila. She was most definitely listening and every time his voice scratched in his throat, the tapping of her keyboard stuttered, even though she never took her eyes off the screen.

When he (gently) pointed out the gaping holes in his students' knowledge and suggested they should do some more reading with phrases borrowed from a Google search on 'how to give constructive feedback' such as 'have you considered', and 'I take your point, but...', he was sure that Lila's mouth curved into a proud smile. A small smile that wasn't meant for anyone, but one that he caught himself wishing she would use only for him.

Rhys blinked.

This was new.

LILA

Lila learned a couple of things that afternoon.

The first one was that Henry II was not a very good father. The second was that she didn't concentrate very well when Rhys was in the room.

It probably wasn't Rhys himself. There were so many other people in the room and it was much easier to listen to them rather than do her finger-numbing, soul-crushing work. It was important that the department had up-to-date records, the students needed access to the intranet and quite frankly, it was completely frustrating that everything was so higgledy-piggledy. If she'd known it was going to be this much work to sort things out into a basic semblance of organisation – and that she'd have to do half of Sue's work as well – she would have asked for more money. Well, she would have thought about asking.

It wasn't that she could feel Rhys Aubrey's hazel eyes flitting across her cheek and down her neck, or the slightly confused look he gave her when he left. No, it was just the fact that her office was the new seminar venue. Nothing to do with who was in her office.

Yep. Definitely not that.

Lila's phone buzzed on her desk and she checked the notification from her personal email account, opening the marketing email quickly. Susie Dent, Queen of Dictionary Corner, was going on tour? Talking about the surreal origins of everyday words? What an absolute dream of a show to see.

There were dates across the next few months, and she scanned the venues to see which was closest and how much it was. God, who cared how much it was? She'd pay a lot of money to see Susie Dent talk about words.

> Jasmeet, do you want to go and see THE QUEEN with me?

Susie Dent, not Beyonce or Camilla.

Surely Jasmeet would come. She'd suffer through a word-based gig with her best friend, especially considering how many shopping trips Lila had gone on for art supplies and how many times she'd been her guinea pig for craft projects for five-year-olds.

She left two tickets in her basket and waited impatiently for Jasmeet to text back. Not that she would for a while, she was teaching. There was no use asking Maddy. If she was having a rare night off, she wouldn't want it filled with what was the most 'boring' (EXCITING!) thing ever, i.e., the origin of words. Besides, they wouldn't be home early enough, and there would be no leaving before the end to miss the crowds.

"Lila?"

A knock on her open office door interrupted her wondering about how appropriate her 'origins of swear words' t-shirt would be for Susie Dent, and she smiled at Rhys's students.

"Hey guys, come in. Have a cookie."

Lila reached for the cookie tin on her desk. DeVon took two, shoved one in his mouth and one in his pocket. Kerry nibbled on the smallest one she could find and Ada shook her head.

"We wanted to come by and say thank you for facilitating the seminar," Ada said. "It was so much better. We feel like we actually learned something rather than stressing over whether we were saying the wrong thing."

Kerry nodded, hugging her books to her chest.

"Oh guys, I am so glad," Lila said. "That's fab."

Lila took a sip of her tea. Kerry nudged Ada with her elbow and raised her eyebrows.

"Oh yeah," Ada said, exchanging a sly smile with DeVon and Kerry. "Is there something going on between you and Mr Aubrey?"

108

The tea was suddenly too hot in her mouth, too milky, too sugary, too much.

"What?" she coughed. "Me and Rhys?"

Kerry cracked a smile and Ada giggled. DeVon was distinctly uninterested, and shoved another cookie into his mouth.

"Yeah, you and Mr Aubrey. He kept staring at you, and," Ada shrugged one shoulder, "we just wondered if it was you who had made him a bit less *him*."

Lila blinked rapidly at them, swallowing down her surprise. She'd thought the seminar had gone surprisingly well and if he carried on like that, there was no reason for them to hold it in her office. He had measured his words and considered his responses. There were no put-downs, no scathing comments, no pregnant silences. It had been a good, constructive seminar, even if his voice had tensed just a little now and again.

"There is nothing going on with me and Rhys. He wants to be the best lecturer he can. But even if there was," she said gently, with a wry smile, "I'm not sure that it would be any of your business."

Kerry's face dropped and her already pale cheeks lost even more colour. Ada looked at the floor and DeVon stopped chewing.

"I'm sorry, guys. I don't mean to be horrible and I really appreciate your," Lila cast around for the right word, "interest. But perhaps we'll leave the personal lives of staff to those staff members, yeah?"

"Told you we should have just said thank you and left," DeVon murmured.

"Have another cookie. My door is always open for whatever help you need. But we won't talk about my private life, okay?"

Lila gave them what she hoped was a reassuring smile. Boundaries were needed, and she was absolutely right in setting them. They weren't friends, they weren't even colleagues. She was there to support them in their further education.

But she did worry about hurting their feelings. They were only trying to look out for her. Or were they really just looking for gossip? Perhaps she shouldn't have said anything, just bumbled something about 'don't be so silly' and waved them off. She thought of Jasmeet, she thought of her therapy. Standing up for herself and not getting drawn into a discussion about her and Rhys (not that there was even a 'her and Rhys') was the right thing to do, no matter if it hurt their feelings a little bit.

Lila shook her head and turned back to sorting the intranet system for Professor Freeman's masters students. She'd only checked through two students before she had to stop.

What did they mean, Rhys had been staring at her? Surely they'd got it wrong. Just because she'd imagined Rhys's eyes on her, it didn't make it true. The feeling of a dragonfly wing over her collarbone was the slight breeze coming through the open window. The urge to smooth her hair behind her ears and make sure her make-up was perfect, that was just her being vain.

Hers wasn't exactly the biggest of offices, so it would be highly likely that Rhys's eyes would land her once or twice in the course of the hour-long seminar. 'Staring' was a particularly strong word for what was more than likely a fleeting glance.

Yes. That was it.

Thinking of Rhys (not that she had been thinking of Rhys), she would have to check when his family dinner was. She didn't want to have to cancel and rebook Susie Dent when she could easily go to a different show.

Lila hobbled down the corridor to Rhys's office. Yes, she could walk without the crutches now, but she was a smidge nervous about driving. Besides, Anika (her Uber driver's sister) was about to give birth in South Africa and she really wanted to know the sex of the baby.

Lila knocked and opened the door without waiting for an answer.

Rhys was standing at the window with his back to her, hands in his pockets, pulling his trousers tight around that conker-like little bottom of his. Not that she was looking.

"Rhys?"

He jumped, snapped out of his reverie.

"Sorry." Rhys turned to her and sat down, face blank. "I was lost in thought."

"Henry II being the poster boy for bad parenting?" she asked, giving him a smile.

"Something like that." He lined up some papers on his desk. "What can I do for you?"

Okay, straight down to business.

"When is your family dinner? I need to put it in my diary."

"Oh, yes," he said, tapping on his phone. "Two weeks on Saturday and I think we should get together soon. I'd like to tell you about my family, if you are going to be my girlfriend." He huffed slightly. "Well, my pretend girlfriend."

Two weeks on Saturday? Goodness, that was soon. Just as well she didn't book those Susie Dent tickets, they would have clashed.

"Yes okay," Lila pinched her lip between her teeth. "What do I wear? What's the dress code?"

Unless it was skinny jeans and a nice top, or a sundress (in which case she'd be freezing because it was late autumn), then she would definitely need to do some shopping.

He sat down behind his desk and looked at his computer screen. So dismissive. Lila raised an eyebrow.

"We'll go for dinner after work and I'll tell you everything you need to know."

Firstly, that was not an answer. Secondly, that was most definitely not a question. Rhys was making an assumption that she would just go along with him, literally dismissing her like a minion. Uh, no thanks. She'd had enough of that.

"Rhys?"

He turned his head towards her, but his eyes were still on his computer screen. "Mmm?"

"Rhys!" she snapped. There was no way she was talking to his side face. "Attention over here, please."

His lips parted in shock, as if no one had ever talked to him like that. He was probably so used to having everyone do his bidding that any kind of pushback was a shock.

"Look, I know you've done a lot of people-ing today with the seminar and all, so I'm going to give you another chance to get this right." Her smile was a stretched non-smile, because there was no way Rhys deserved a real smile right now. "Think about what you just said and how you said it, and try again."

She must have lost her ever-loving mind to have said that to Rhys. But here she was, clutching her hips tightly to stop her hands from shaking. He wasn't that scary, he was just a man. Like he said the other day, the only person who could make her feel worthless was her.

The muscles in Rhys's jaw bunched together as he snapped his mouth shut, his emotions so easy to read on his face. Anger, with his eyebrows drawn in and those pouty lips turned down. Then confusion as his eyes skirted his desk. The relaxation of his forehead and jaw into realisation and then the slow slump of his shoulders in defeat.

He passed a hand over his face and his throat worked as he swallowed.

"I'm sorry. Would you like to come for dinner with me tonight, if you're not busy? We could talk."

"That would be lovely, thank you. I'll cancel my Uber." She rewarded him with a tiny, satisfied smile.

"You're getting an Uber? Where? Do you have plans?" Rhys asked, his eyebrows screwing together.

"No, no plans. I don't feel quite up to driving yet,"

He leant back in his chair, assessing her. "And your friends couldn't help you? Sue?"

"Jasmeet is working and busy. I can't ask Maddy or her

wife, they've got the baby. Sue lives too far away." And Sue wouldn't. Lila rubbed her ring finger and her thumb together. Explaining herself to Rhys Aubrey was not on her schedule for today.

"Why didn't you ask me?"

"I've put you out too much already. I can't ask you to ferry me back and forth to work as well. I'm sure I'll feel able to drive in the next couple of days."

"Don't be ridiculous, you must have spent a fortune on taxis." He pursed his lips. "You should have said."

"I'm not going to argue with you about this, Rhys."

"I'll dri—" He stopped and tried again. "Please may I drive you home after dinner tonight?"

Lila's heart stuttered ever so slightly, because Rhys was trying. He was really, really trying.

CHAPTER 7

Adumbrate (noun) ad·um·brate

1. To foreshadow vaguely

2. To suggest, disclose, or partially outline

RHYS

There was a nice pub about thirty minutes from the university and then only about ten minutes back to Lila's house, so that worked. But he was tense and a bit frustrated. How could she not have asked him to help her? Surely, *surely*, he had proved himself capable of helping?

She could have asked him.

She should have asked her friends for help, and they should have helped her, regardless of whether they had a baby or not.

It was his own shortcomings that he was mostly angry about. The simple fact was that he should have checked on her. Not via email, but in person. He had been so wrapped up in his own stuff that he wouldn't let himself think about her, and when the thought of walking down the corridor, leaning on the doorframe to her office and checking on her *in person* popped into his head, he quickly dismissed it. He didn't think about her at all. Not one bit. Except when he was sitting in her office, surrounded by her vanilla glittery-ness. Then he couldn't *stop* thinking about her, couldn't stop watching her throat bob in a swallow, the crease of her forehead as she tried to do something on her computer. After the seminar, he couldn't concentrate on his work, so he'd resorted to staring out of the window, hoping for divine inspiration. Instead, he'd had an interruption from the distraction herself.

Now she was sitting next to him, in his car, leaving her sweet cookie smell all over his soft leather.

What was happening to him? He had *never* been so distracted before.

"Rhys?"

Lila jerked him out of his thoughts.

"Sorry, what? I was lost in thought."

"You've missed the turning. We are going to the Grape & Olive, aren't we?"

"Shit," he said under his breath.

"It's okay, no rush."

Rhys turned the car at the next roundabout and pulled into the pub car park, rushing to the passenger side to open the door for her. Because that's what you were supposed to do, right?

"Who knew you were such a gentleman?" She grinned, heading over to the entrance of the pub, only limping slightly. Rhys jammed his hands into his pockets. She'd already made it quite clear that she neither needed nor wanted his help.

They were guided to a table and handed an over-sized card menu.

"Would you like any drinks?" the waitress asked.

God yes.

"I'll have a pint please. Lila?"

"Um, Aperol Spritz please," she said with a smile.

"I'll give you some time," the waitress said, and left to sort their drinks.

Aperol Spritz? What even was that? Her pastel purple nails skimmed lightly over the menu and he couldn't stop looking at the big sparkly yellow ring on her right hand.

"What are you going to have?" Lila asked.

"Um." What he always had. "Probably hunter's chicken."

"Rhys." Lila sighed and folded her hands on the table in front of her. "What's wrong?"

"What do you mean?"

"You're all frowny and you've barely said two words since we left work." Her head tilted, and something flashed in her eyes. Concern? For him? His stomach tightened just a little bit. It was nice having Lila be concerned for him.

"I'm sorry," he said.

"You don't have to be sorry. Just tell me what's going on," she said, leaning further over the table towards him.

Her hair fell over her shoulder, pink lips parting as she watched him, imploring him with those cloudless sky-blue eyes to say something. Anything. But he couldn't, words wouldn't form because he was just staring at her. He couldn't free himself from her eyes, which pinned him.

What did she want to know? About this warm coil in the base of his stomach? About how he couldn't concentrate because of the sugary glitter that seemed to exude from her? How he, Rhys Aubrey-Dallimore, who had been at the top of the corporate ladder, the hard-nosed businessman, couldn't stop thinking about how soft her unicorn blanket was?

What *was* this?

"Rhys?"

Her voice was a wisp of wind, a dusting of snowflakes.

"Here you are." The waitress plonked his pint in front of him.

Thank fuck.

He took a long, long gulp and nodded his thanks at the waitress. She'd be getting a good tip.

"Did you Google me? Google the Dallimores?"

His voice was too hoarse. The family. That's what they were here for. The family, the story, the fake girlfriend. Yes.

"No? Was I supposed to?" She bit her bottom lip.

"You're not a student, Lila. I don't give you extra reading," he snapped, shaking his head.

Her face hardened, and her eyebrow raised.

"I'm sorry." He leaned his elbow on the table and covered his mouth. This was not going well. He was too tense and this was all too much.

"Look, I get telling me whatever you want to tell me isn't easy for you, but that isn't my fault. Don't take it out on me," Lila said, leaning back in her chair. "If you don't want me to be your pretend girlfriend, then that's fine. I don't have to come."

Rhys frowned. He'd only vaguely considered that possibility. He quickly shook his head. Explaining to Elin (and worse, his mother) that he was no longer bringing someone was a circle of hell best left unvisited. It was certainly much, *much* worse than having to tell Lila about his dysfunctional family. Besides, Lila would distract them from his all too apparent failings, and perhaps it would be nice to have someone on his side. If indeed she *was* on his side, if he could *let* her be on his side.

"My family run businesses. They're rich." He took a breath, looking around furtively.

"All right," Lila said slowly, a crease marring her forehead. She spread her hands like a 'so what' gesture. She obviously didn't get it.

"My father and uncles are Croesus-rich, and my sister and cousins aren't far behind," he said, holding her eyes, watching for a reaction. "Croesus was—"

"I know who Croesus was, thank you Rhys." She raised her eyebrows at him. "You told me that they work for the family business, but you don't?"

"That's right." Rhys nodded. "I did work for the family business. I started part-time on a building site at sixteen to 'experience everything', as my father said."

Lila's eyes skittered across his shoulders and she pressed her lips together.

"I worked holidays and weekends in all the different departments and divisions. Filing. Doing the post. Answering the phone. Customer service. You name it, I did it. We all did."

She held up a finger in question. "When you say 'you all', you mean your sister and your cousins?"

"Yeah, all of us. It's to find out what your strengths are. Then you're expected to go and build a division or a business around what most interests you. Except," his shoulders slumped forward, "nothing interested me."

"Oh." Lila tilted her head to the side, a sympathetic smile tilting her lips.

This was harder than he thought, laying himself out naked and vulnerable for her to see. He swallowed and continued.

"After my undergraduate degree, I worked full time at Dallimores for a few years, skipping from one department to another. I hated it," Rhys said with a dry half laugh. "There was absolutely nothing I enjoyed about corporate business. So, I decided to do my Masters part-time whilst I was working. I liked history, so thought, why not?"

Lila watched him avidly.

"I can't explain it. It felt like home. It felt… right. The smell of the library, the Latin, the thrill of *understanding* people from so long ago. That's when I realised I didn't want to be at Dallimores, I didn't want to *be* a Dallimore." He shrugged. "So I left."

"That's why you were 'late' to academia."

"Yes. My father was not happy about it. Academia, that is. 'What a waste of time', 'I'm cutting you off', 'you'll never be a success', 'what's wrong with the family business?', 'you're wasting your life', 'I've given you everything'." Rhys looked at the table, those words still causing a dull ache in his chest after all this time. "He gave me five years to make a success of myself."

Lila's eyes darkened as if she was personally affronted.

She reached over and laid her hand on his arm. He couldn't meet her eyes, couldn't risk the rawness of his throat betraying his emotions, but nodded in what he hoped she took as thanks for her comfort. He had never *ever* said those things out loud before.

The softness he knew would be in her eyes would ruin him.

"What does 'success' look like?" Lila's voice was smooth and warm.

Rhys swallowed the pain in his throat.

"The Fellowship. That's what we agreed on. I was cocky and arrogant. I didn't fully understand how academia worked."

"Oh Rhys," she said, squeezing his arm.

"We didn't speak for three years, not even birthdays or Christmas. It's only recently, probably because of my mother, that things have been less... well, we've talked once or twice," Rhys finished.

He took another long gulp of his pint, Lila's hand falling away from his arm.

"I see," she said quietly.

"It's not just work." Rhys twisted his mouth into a semblance of a smile. "If you're there as my girlfriend, I can show that I'm successful in my private life as well. With someone who doesn't just want the Dallimore name and money."

"Surely, you can get a girlfriend, Rhys. You're an attractive guy," Lila said and a pink flush crept up her neck. "Even if you are a bit prickly."

He jerked his eyes to hers.

"I'll take that as a compliment." His smile this time was less a semblance, more a real one. Lila Cartwright thought he was attractive, she'd just said so, and now she was blushing.

He took another drink, bolder now.

"I mean, I've not been celibate for the last five years. But people find out my name, my family, check the *Sunday Times* Rich List and it all changes. People don't like me for me, they like me for what they think I can give them. Connections, money, a certain lifestyle." He shrugged and looked into his pint. "I don't want that anymore."

"That's why you're an Aubrey."

"That's why I'm an Aubrey."

Lila sucked in a long breath.

"Well, Rhys Aubrey," she said lightly. "I can't guarantee that I won't use you for your connections in the construction industry and, uh, Parliament or whatever 'connections' you rich people have."

He snorted into his drink.

"But I will charm the pants off your family. They'll all see you've made the right decision for you."

Rhys looked up at her and his heart lifted.

Apparently, affirmation from Lila Cartwright was exactly what he needed to soothe his anxious mind.

LILA

Lila's heart went out to Rhys because, bless him – all he was doing was chasing his dream, which his family should have encouraged. Instead, they put him down, made him feel small and unworthy. She'd been there. She knew how it felt, and luckily had Jasmeet and Maddy to pull her out of it. Rhys had, what? Kickboxing? Dan?

Perhaps not all of his family felt that way, though. It seemed his father was the biggest culprit. But still, who would want to work in boring corporate construction anyway?

"You don't mind?" Rhys asked, glancing at her before assessing the menu again.

"Mind? Why would I mind?" she asked. "Hang on, *what* would I mind?"

Rhys squirmed in his seat.

"Coming with me. Being my fake girlfriend. After everything I've just said? It won't be easy." He offered her a wan smile. "By that, I mean, *I* probably won't be easy."

Lila blinked at him, because that was excellent self-awareness from Rhys Aubrey.

"I'll help. We'll get through it together." Her voice was quiet, because it seemed that was exactly what Rhys needed.

Rhys narrowed his eyes at her, searching her face for any sign of her making fun of him. Poor, hurt, untrusting man.

"Anyway, shall we order?" Lila asked, as the waitress headed in their direction.

It didn't take long for their food to arrive, but Lila's stomach was grumbling by the time she shovelled the first forkful of her lasagne into her mouth.

"What time will we be eating? If it's late, I'll have to have a snack beforehand. Otherwise, I'll expire and you'll have to catch me as I faint," she said, putting the back of her hand to her forehead and fanning her face with the other.

Rhys snorted a laugh.

"I don't know, eight-ish? There'll be canapes I would imagine," he said, picking at his hunter's chicken.

Shit. In all of the Rhys-o-Drama, she'd forgotten.

"Um, Rhys?" Lila laid her knife and fork down carefully on the edge of her plate.

"Mmm?" he said, not looking at up her.

"Rhys, this is important."

He must have noticed the urgency in her voice because he stopped chewing, swallowed heavily and looked at her intently.

"What is the dress code?" she whispered. The super rich? Canapes? Boring business-y type people? It could only be one thing.

Please be smart casual. Please be smart casual.

"Oh," Rhys said, screwing his face up. "Black tie."

Black tie. Oh, good lord.

"And what will you be wearing?" she asked, keeping her voice calm and low.

"Um, a tux? That's what black tie is."

Lila took three deep breaths. In through the nose, out through the mouth, but it was no use.

"Oh my God, Rhys," she said, burying her face in her hands. What, in the name of all that was holy, was she going to wear?

"What's the matter?" he asked, calmly cutting up his godforsaken chicken.

"What's the matter?" she squeaked.

How could he be so stupid? Rhys Aubrey-Dallimore would be wearing a tuxedo and there was nothing more attractive than a man in a well-fitting tuxedo. It probably was designed especially for him, clinging to his pert little arse like a wasp on picnic food.

Lila pushed out a breath and laid her hands flat on the table.

"What does black tie mean for women, Rhys?" she asked, but he just looked confused. "Is it a long dress? Is it a cocktail dress? Is it sweeping? Oh my god, is it *Met Gala*?"

"Um," Rhys said, obviously dredging his memory. "The last time I went, Elin wore a long dress. So did my mother and Seren."

He calmly looked back to his chicken.

"That's a pretty name," Lila murmured, poking at her pasta. "Sister or cousin? You're going to have to draw me a family tree. There are too many of you."

"Seren, um." Rhys's mouth turned into a cringe. "I kind of forgot about her. She's my ex-girlfriend..."

"Oh, lord me."

"Well, actually, ex-fiancée…"

"Pardon?"

"And she's married to my cousin, Ieuan."

What fresh hell was this? "You're joking me."

"Nope," Rhys said, stabbing at his chicken like he wanted to kill it again.

"No wonder you avoid going. She's tall and blonde and super model-y, isn't she? Oh no, she's actually a super model and I'm going to be dowdy and frumpy and ridiculous in a twenty-pound maxi dress from Matalan."

Lila knocked back her drink for fortification. She was going to a black-tie event as a fake girlfriend, with a supermodel ex-girlfriend who was married to said fake boyfriend's *cousin*?

If this was an American soap, there would be a person with amnesia and a secret baby. Also, her twenty-pound maxi dress from Matalan (the only long dress she owned) was not going to cut it, was it? It was a summer dress with sunflowers on it. That would *not* go down well with Rhys I-have-a-custom-tux Aubrey-Dallimore.

Something crushing and hot rose in her. She wasn't going to be good enough for this. She couldn't just sprinkle some glitter and make herself acceptable to rich people.

"What's happened to you? You were all calm and helpful. Now you're," Rhys waved a hand at her, "panicky."

"Rhys, do you know any women? At all?" She stuffed pasta into her mouth. Eating would help. Eating was her safe space. "Some of us like to not look ridiculous in front of her fake boyfriend's supermodel ex-fiancée, and his rich list family," she said, trying to slurp the dregs of her drink. "You are not being very helpful. I'm liable to not make a good impression and probably make things worse if you. Don't. Help. Me."

Rhys pressed his lips together, but his eyes sparkled. If he laughed, she would stab him with her fork.

"It's not funny, Rhys!"

But if she couldn't laugh then she'd just worry and very possibly cry, because it was all so ridiculous.

"It is a bit funny," Rhys corrected, letting a smile come out. "Besides, I'm sure a twenty-pound maxi dress from Matalan will be fine."

"Oh no, I don't think so, Rhys Aubrey-Dallimore. There will have to be shopping. You'll have to come."

Rhys's face slackened.

"You can help me pick something appropriate, okay?" It was more a beg than a question, because she desperately needed help. How was she supposed to know what to get? "Please?"

His eyes shuttered and he let out a long-suffering sigh. The silence between them stretched taut.

"Fine," he said, turning back to his food.

Lila sat back in her seat and blew out a breath. "I thought you were going to say no for a minute then."

"Why would I say no?" he said, shaking his head. "You're helping me. The least I can do is help you help me."

She made a strangled noise that could have been a laugh in her throat. Did Rhys just make a joke?

"Okay, tell me about Seren and your cousin Ian," Lila said, stabbing at her food.

"Ieuan," Rhys corrected.

"That's what I said."

"No, you said Ian. It's Yigh-an." Rhys shrugged haughtily. "Sometimes English people struggle."

"Ha, ha. Yigh-an, Yigh-an," she tested.

"You've got it, Ieuan." He smiled that smile again, and she looked to her food, swallowing quickly.

"Please tell me the rest of your family have more easily pronounceable names?" she begged.

"Bleddyn, Myfanwy, Angharad, Myrddin. You know, standard Welsh names."

Lila took a breath. "I'm going to have to practice. I can't have your family thinking I'm some uneducated heathen."

What if they hated her? She wasn't rich, she wasn't of good breeding stock or whatever rich people said and she certainly wasn't Welsh. The least she could do was get their names right. What if they thought she was just too plain next to Rhys? What if she let him down? What if—

"I'm teasing, Lila," he said, raising his eyebrows at her. A small smile crossed his face.

"Is that the first time you've made a joke? Ever?"

Rhys sat back in his chair and crossed his arms across his chest, assessing her. "Lila, you'll be absolutely fine. I wouldn't have asked you if I didn't think you could do it."

High praise indeed.

"Thank you, Rhys," she said. "I promise, I'll be the best fake girlfriend you've ever had."

RHYS

Rhys's car still smelled of cookies and vanilla long after he'd dropped Lila home. Her smell got literally everywhere. He'd have to vacuum the car, because if there was the remotest chance that there was *glitter* in the car (and there was always that chance with Lila), then he had to get rid of it.

He'd been tempted to linger in Lila's house, accept the proffered cup of tea, but Dan had texted as they were leaving the pub, wanting to meet up, so now he was on his way. It was surprising that Dan had asked him to meet up so spontaneously; he knew that Rhys preferred to make plans rather than have things sprung on him. Since Dan had been missing in action, he felt he should see him. Even if only to show how displeased he was with Dan missing kickboxing all the time.

"Dan," he greeted, putting his lemonade on the table. Why was it that small, local pubs always had the most uncomfortable wooden chairs, second only to plastic hospital chairs?

"Rhys, hey man," Dan said, looking up from his phone. "I got you a pint."

"I've already had one and I'm driving," Rhys said, pushing the beer towards Dan. "Everything okay? Your text was quite cryptic."

All it had said was:

Pint. The Cross Rifles. 8pm.

Rhys was not used to being ordered around, he was usually the one doing the ordering. He clenched his jaw, because now he knew how Lila had felt when he'd ordered rather than asked earlier. That was a whole new level of empathy that he really didn't want to slide into.

"I haven't seen you. I wanted to catch up," Dan said.

Catch up? Rhys raised an eyebrow because that certainly did not sound like Dan.

"Jasmeet cancel on you?" That would be the most obvious explanation.

"No, we didn't have plans tonight," Dan said, sipping his pint.

"Are you planning on ever coming to kickboxing?" Rhys asked pointedly. "Because I hate going with different people."

"Yeah, sorry I've been a bit AWOL," Dan said with a grin. "But Jasmeet is amazing."

Dan obviously wanted to talk about her. This was not 'catching up'. Rhys settled back into the uncomfortable chair.

"Tell me."

"Man, she's incredible. We've been out a few times and texting constantly." He grinned. "I really like her."

"Really like her?" Rhys repeated. He'd learned that repeating what Dan said as a question made him sound interested. It's not that he wasn't interested, it just sometimes didn't come across very well.

"Yeah, *really* like her." That dopey grin on Dan's face wasn't going anywhere. "She's funny, clever, passionate about her job."

Rhys stifled down a sigh.

"I cannot get enough of her. I think this might be a long-term thing."

"Long-term?" That was new for Dan. He was more a 'two months and move on' kind of guy. Rhys grinned. This was good for Dan, so he pushed down the frustration that he'd cancelled kickboxing. Twice.

"Yeah. Long-term." Dan nodded.

"And you know this after a couple of weeks and a few dates?" Rhys asked, genuinely interested. How did people decide who to spend their time with and whether a relationship was going to be 'long-term' or not?

"Yeah, I do," Dan said, suddenly serious. "When I'm not with her, I want to be."

Rhys nodded. "Okay."

"You've not felt like that before?" Dan asked.

"No, I can't say that I have." Not even with Seren, and he

was supposed to marry her. Good job he didn't then, if he was supposed to feel like that.

"You just haven't found your person yet." Dan leaned back in his chair.

"And Jasmeet is 'your person'?"

A slow smile spread across his face. "I'm pretty sure she might be, yeah."

"Good for you, Dan," Rhys said. "But you can't keep skipping kickboxing."

"Hang on, you cancelled the other day when you were with Lila."

Rhys rolled his eyes and launched into a wide-ranging rant about the current state of the NHS.

"So, you spent all afternoon and most of the evening with her? At the hospital?" Dan asked.

"Yes. Her fucking twat of an ex-boyfriend was the doctor that dealt with it." Jason *was* a fucking twat, there was no getting away from it.

"Tell me you pretended to be her boyfriend again and that you didn't drop her in the shit."

Rhys narrowed his eyes at his friend. "What do you think I am?"

"I know you, man," Dan said, eyebrows raised, and he did. They'd been friends since their undergraduate days. Dan had seen him struggle through his years at Dallimores and helped him get the job at the university. He'd been there with him, through it all.

"Of course I did." He'd quite enjoyed rubbing Jason's face in it.

Dan looked at him speculatively. "What happened when you took her home? What aren't you telling me?"

Sometimes, Dan was way too astute for his own good.

"Nothing. We had fish and chips," Rhys said, taking a gulp of his lemonade. He was not about to tell Dan that he fell asleep on Lila's sofa, slept in her bed and practically suctioned himself to her.

"Hmm," Dan said, draining his beer and pulling the other one closer to him. "You like her."

"What?"

He hadn't really thought about it, but yeah, perhaps he did like her. Lila was okay to be around, once you got past all the rainbows. She hadn't had a clue what his family did, she hadn't googled him, she hadn't checked the *Sunday Times* Rich List, and that was refreshing.

"I suppose I do like her," he said, nodding.

"Hmm mmm," Dan smirked. Rhys chose not to follow up on that ambiguous noise.

"I helped her out, she's helping me out," he said. "We have a transactional relationship."

"Right," Dan said. "And how is she helping you out?"

"She's being my fake girlfriend for a family dinner."

"Woah," Dan said. "She's meeting the parents already?"

"It's no big deal," Rhys said with a shrug.

"Yeah, it is. It's much bigger than fake-boyfriending for an ex," Dan said, leaning his arms on the table. "Why do you even need a fake girlfriend?"

"It'll just be easier. My parents expect it, Seren will be there as well and I just want to prove to them that I'm succeeding at life."

"Ah yes, Seren and Ieuan," Dan said, voice hard. Rhys had gotten over Seren a long time ago, and her marrying his cousin, Ieuan, whilst weird, wasn't the end of the world for him. He didn't love her, had no claim on her, and if they were happy together, who was he to stand in their way? "I get it, man. Lila's cute and I bet parents love her."

Dan was right; Lila was cute, with her little nose and clear eyes. His mother would love her and so would his sister. But his father? Who knew what he would think. He'd just have to make sure Lila wasn't left to fend for herself with his father's scathing, penetrative questions. Whatever Lila said, his father would find some fault with her. There was no pleasing that man and he wasn't about to subject Lila to an interrogation. No one deserved that, especially not someone who was helping him out.

She would be there as a prop. A physical manifestation of the success of his life. They could have an amicable fake break-up at a suitable time in the future.

It was time for a subject change.

"Tell me about work," Rhys said. If this was supposed to be a 'catch up', he wanted to make sure he covered all aspects.

Dan launched into staff politics in the Engineering Department and Rhys was once again glad that he didn't have to share resources or machines, or whatever engineers used, with other lecturers. It was bad enough having to share the departmental library where they kept the Charter Roll publications and not for the first time, Rhys wondered why he couldn't just have them in his room. But rules were rules and they were made to be followed. Something about 'being available for all staff and students'. Like his students were going to look for primary source material without having it shoved under their noses.

It was nearly ten before they left. Rhys dropped Dan home, ignoring the question as to why his car smelled of vanilla.

> To confirm, I'll pick you up on Saturday at 9.30 and we'll go shopping for a dress for you to wear.

> If that's okay.

Lila

> Sir, yes sir! Confirmed. We'll go for lunch. I know the cutest cafe!

Lunch? How long would it take to buy a dress? If they were there for about ten, he should be home by midday. Shouldn't he?

CHAPTER 8

Oniomania *(noun) onio·ma·nia*
1. An uncontrollable desire to buy things

LILA

Rhys was on time, precisely on time. Of course he was.

"Sit on the sofa. I will be two minutes," she said, grabbing her handbag from the floor and plonking it on the table. She just needed her heels to try dresses on with (especially now she could walk properly again), and her sunglasses, because the weather had promised some sunshine.

"Are you not ready?" Rhys asked, arms crossed in front of his rather pleasant chest. Casual Rhys was looking especially edible today. Worn, dark blue jeans and a plain, long-sleeved beige Henley with the two buttons undone at the neck had never looked so good.

"I am ready, I just need two minutes to get a couple of extra things."

"So, you're not ready then."

She pinned him with a look. "Rhys, are you going to be like this all day? Because I need to know whether to bring extra cookies or not."

"You're taking cookies on a shopping expedition?" he asked, eyebrows drawn together.

"Expedition? It's not like we're trekking through the jungle. It's just the Bull Ring." On a Saturday. So it pretty much would be like a jungle. "And yes, I will have to bring cookies if you are going to continue to be the most pedantic person in the entire world."

"I don't think—" he started, but snapped his mouth shut. "Okay."

Lila rewarded him with a grin. He was learning.

"Also, I have a request," she said. Rhys gestured for her to continue. "Can I be in charge of the radio? I don't want to listen to the news this morning."

Because the news was depressing, people were awful, and she didn't need that kind of energy when she was preparing for dress shopping.

Rhys narrowed his eyes at her, and she gave him the sweetest smile from her arsenal.

"Fine."

There was nothing in the first shop, or the second. There was more selection in the next few, but nothing that screamed 'wear me to a posh family dinner whilst pretending to be a work colleague's girlfriend'. Trying stuff on in high-street shops with their unflattering lighting and tiny changing rooms, and then parading herself around in front of Rhys-Tuxedo-Aubrey was not her idea of fun and Rhys certainly didn't look as if he was enjoying it.

She'd managed to pry out of him the type of thing that his sister would wear, so hopefully she wouldn't look like a complete idiot. With a couple of good accessories and maybe a couple of alterations, she could make a dress look less high street and more high end.

"So?" she asked, as she pulled at the satiny fabric around her hips. "What do you think?"

The thin spaghetti straps would need shortening and

possibly a bit off the length. The green-y colour wasn't great, but it fit all right across her boobs and hips.

"It's fine," Rhys said with a shrug.

Her shoulders drooped. 'Fine' was not what she was going for.

"I'd take the hem up a little, so it would fall here," she said, pulling it up slightly so it wasn't draped on the floor. "Would that be okay?"

"Yeah, it's fine," he repeated.

"That's what you said about the last one and the one before that," she said, pushing a despondent half smile onto her face.

"They're all fine, Lila," he said with a huff.

"Okay," she said quietly, stepping back into the changing room to scrape her ego off the floor and put on her own clothes again.

It was the best so far. She snapped a photo of the dress on her phone, just in case she couldn't find anything better. Hanging it, and the other three that she'd discarded on the 'not today' rack at the entrance to the changing room, she gave a wan little smile to Rhys.

"Not that one, then."

"Maybe, if I don't see anything else."

"Okay."

Shopping sometimes was like purgatory. A purgatory full of dresses that were too tight, too loose, too long, too short, didn't fit across her boobs, didn't fit around her hips, too cut-out-y.

She sighed as they headed out of the shop and into the bright lights of the shopping centre. Despondency was creeping in, and her feet were starting to hurt.

"What about that shop?" Rhys stopped and pointed at one with tall, skinny mannequins in the window.

Lila shook her head. "I don't fit into clothes there."

"What do you mean?"

"Rhys, women come in all different shapes and sizes and

I'm telling you, that shop does not make clothes that fit my body shape."

"Oh."

He probably waltzed into the Rich-Boy-Jeans-Shop and picked up a thirty-two-inch waist, regular and they fit like... well, like good-fitting jeans. That's just not how it worked for her. If jeans fit her arse, they did not fit her waist. If they fit her waist, it felt like her legs were squeezed in like sausages.

"Sorry," she murmured.

"It's okay." He was peering at her as if he was doing some incredibly hard maths in his head. "Shall we stop for coffee?"

A break from this horror? Yes please.

"And cake?" she asked in a small, pathetic voice.

"And cake," he said, giving her a small smile.

She took him to Bumblebee Cafe because it had the best (and biggest) cake, where she ordered a raspberry milkshake, a millionaire shortbread and a huge slice of chocolate cake.

"You have so much sugar there, Lila."

"Shopping is stressful, I need comfort sugar."

The fortification was definitely needed, especially with Rhys's crumpled up mouth saying 'it's fine' etched into her brain.

"Why is buying a dress so difficult?" he huffed, closing his hands around his black coffee. Because of course Rhys drank boring black coffee. He poked at the muffin she'd forced him to buy. "Seriously, why is it so hard? I don't see what was wrong with those other dresses. They were fine."

Lila stared at him incredulously. He actually didn't see it, did he? How could he have gotten to early thirties without having *any* kind of shopping experience with a woman?

"Look Rhys, I get that shopping is boring and you'd much rather be doing pretty much anything else with your Saturday morning, but I'm doing this to help you," she said. "What would your posh, rich family think if I turned up just looking 'fine'?"

Rhys had the decency to look a little bit ashamed. Just a little, mind you.

"I don't want to make a fool of myself." The words came out quietly. Trying new things often didn't work out for her and she really should just stick in her lane. But Rhys had done her a favour and she did say 'anything'.

"Okay, I understand," Rhys said, breaking off a bit of muffin and forking it into his mouth.

A sad smile pulled at her lips.

"I'm not super rich, I work at a university, I've still got some debts from Jason, and I can't afford hundreds of pounds to spend on a dress I'm only going to wear once." She stirred her thick milkshake with the straw. "It's a waste."

It was embarrassing, talking about what little money she had. Well, it wasn't like she was poor, she was just a normal person who couldn't fork out about a million pounds for a dress.

"You have debts from Jason?" Rhys tilted his head towards her. "Why?"

She snapped her eyes to his and raised an eyebrow. That was a bit much, wasn't it?

"Too personal. Rhys, not answering that." She flashed a smile. Rhys let out a breath and closed his eyes for longer than a blink.

"Sorry," he mumbled. There was a tension around his mouth that wasn't there before and she took pity on him. Societal niceties were sometimes a bit beyond him, but he was learning and that was good.

"Perhaps I'll rent one. Put it on the credit card, and send it back when we're done." She tapped her chin with her finger. "Or I'll just get that green one and alter it."

Rhys stared off into the distance and she busied herself with her cake. Both cakes. Sugary fortification for yet more crappy dresses. Perhaps they could go somewhere expensive and she'd put it on her credit card. But she'd been so good with the credit card, and it was nearly paid off. Things had been tight when Jason was in medical school; he hadn't been earning and her salary didn't go very far. Joint credit cards and a loan had helped get them through some really tough spots, but the repayments came out of her bank account. She was so close to being free of the last vestiges of her relationship with Jason.

RHYS

Life wasn't fair for some people. It just wasn't. Jason had a lot to answer for. Lila, for all her rainbows and ridiculous pink steering-wheeled car, was kind. Perhaps she was too kind and dickwads like Jason took advantage of that.

Rhys took a quick look at her, sliding her second cake towards her. Two cakes. She must really need sugar if she was having two cakes. The muffin was all right, but he would have preferred one of her cookies that she'd threatened to bring but ultimately didn't.

Although, as he watched her attack the chocolate cake, he realised he was just as bad as Jason. Here she was, helping him out when she really didn't have to and he was asking her to spend her hard-earned money on something she'd only wear once.

Spend her money for him and his stupid family. Yeah, they'd made a deal, this was her end of the bargain, but if she'd said no, it's not like he could have forced her to do it, was it?

He pulled out his phone and scrolled to Elin's number, holding his finger up at Lila's questioning look. His sister answered on the second ring.

"*Shwmae* big brother, to what do I owe this tremendous pleasure?"

Rhys rolled his eyes.

"*Shwmae* Elin, I need your help,"

"Wait, let me press record. Right, say it again."

Why couldn't his sister just do what he needed? Why the snarky comments?

"Elin," he said shortly.

She laughed. "Go on, what do you need?"

"I'm shopping with Lila—"

"Your girlfriend!" she interrupted. "Lila is such a pretty name."

"Yes, well," he said, shooting a quick glance at Lila, catching her polishing off her cake. "We're looking for a dress for the family dinner. Where do you go?"

"Oh my God, if you'd have told me, *I* would have gone shopping with her!"

He could not imagine anything worse. The two of them gossiping about the only thing that they had in common – him.

"Elin, please." He pinched the bridge of his nose.

"The top floor of Selfridges has personal shoppers. Ask for Miquita, she's the absolute best. Tell her you're my brother and she'll sort you out. Put it on my account, you can pay me later," she said quickly.

"Okay, *diolch yn fawr* Elin. That's a big help." *Thanks very much.*

"Anything for you, *brawd.*" *Brother.* "I have to go, I've got a meeting."

"Bye, Elin."

That was another reason why he no longer wanted to work at Dallimores; Saturday meetings. Rhys hadn't wanted to be there on the weekdays, let alone the weekends. But of course, that's what was expected from the family. *Dedicated to the family, dedicated to the business* was another favourite saying of his father's and Rhys had not missed that little nugget.

"Elin? Your sister," Lila clarified.

"Yes," Rhys nodded. "Are you ready to go?"

"Yeah, sure," Lila said, slurping up the dregs of her ridiculous milkshake. "Did she give you some ideas, because I'm at a bit of a loss now, I'm afraid."

With her shoulders slumped and chocolate cake smudged on her chin, Lila Cartwright looked like a sad child. This was his responsibility now and he would sort this out.

Before his brain caught up with his body, he was leaning across the table and reaching for her. His fingers curled underneath her chin and his thumb swiped at the cake on the corner of her mouth gently, his eyes laser-focused on the softness of her skin. There was a bob of her throat as she swallowed, and her lips parted with a puff of breath. He found himself looking at those lips, thinking how easily he could press his thumb to the bottom one, see if it was as velvety smooth as it looked.

Rhys darted his eyes up to hers, which were wide and surprised by his touch. A noise came from her throat, a small, wispy, breathy hum that he was almost positive she didn't know she'd made. Heat flushed up his neck and he pulled away. What was he even thinking? She could wipe her own face.

"Come on," he said, pushing his chair back. "Let's go."

Rhys guided her to Selfridges, but she stopped before going in.

"Rhys, weren't you listening?" Her voice was almost pleading. "I can't afford Selfridges."

"Lila, you're helping me out. I do not expect you to spend your money on a favour to me." He should have made that clear before they even went on this stupid, mind-numbing, stick-pins-in-his-eyes shopping trip.

"Rhys, I can't expect *you* to—"

"You're not expecting anything. You've made that abundantly clear," he said, softening his face so his words weren't as abrasive as they sounded.

"Abundantly clear?"

Apparently, his 'face softening' didn't work.

"Look, Rhys—" she started, but he held his hand up to stop her.

"If it makes you feel any better, this isn't for you. This is for me." He pulled a hand through his hair. This was a transaction. "You're right. If I want this to work, my 'girlfriend' can't be dressed in something that looks just 'fine'."

Lila's soft smile faltered a little and her clear eyes clouded. Had he said the wrong thing? It was essentially what she had been saying for the entire time they'd been in those horrible shops with their tiny changing areas and nowhere for him to sit.

"Okay," she said, giving him a smile that didn't reach her eyes. "But we can take it back afterwards."

Take it back? Would they even accept it back once it had been worn? He'd think about that another time.

Rhys led her through the packed bottom floor and up two escalators to a much more sedate, much quieter top floor. She kept lagging behind him, and eventually, he stopped.

"What's wrong? Why are you all slumped?" That was the right word. Her shoulders were drooped, she was dragging her feet and clutching her back like it was a life jacket.

"Rhys, I…" she started, eyes darting around the store. "I don't belong here," she whispered.

For fuck's sake.

"Lila Cartwright," he said, snippily. "*I* don't belong here either. I have an online shop who have my measurements and they send me clothes. They'll send me a tux." Lila went to say something, but he wasn't finished yet. "I don't belong teaching students. I don't belong in corporate business. I don't belong in my family."

Lila's head tilted and her eyes softened in sympathy, which was precisely not what he was going for. Regardless, he carried on.

"But that doesn't matter, because I do what I want." Well, mostly, and at the utter detriment to pretty much everything in his life. Family relationships were stretched thin and his teaching was so awful he had to have supervised sessions in Lila's office. In his darker moments, he wondered how he would survive working with his family again, with his father, when he failed. Not *if*, but *when*.

"I can't force you to do this, Lila. I don't want to force you. It would help me, yes, but not at the cost of you not wanting to do it at all."

"Oh, Rhys."

Lila started forward as if she was going to wrap her arms around him and smother him in a hug, but he took a quick shuffle backwards and she stopped. Nope, no hugging, thank you very much.

"Come on," she said, hoisting her purple stegosaurus handbag onto her shoulder and squaring her shoulders. "Let's go and buy a stupid dress."

Thank fuck that little pep talk had worked because it would be infinitely worse if he didn't have a girlfriend to present when he had already told his family he did.

Rhys wielded his name like a rapier and soon they were in a private room, with a cup of herbal tea (for her), sparkling water (for him) and a plethora of finger sandwiches. Miquita had practically asked 'how high shall I jump' when he'd said he was Elin's brother, and he wondered how much his sister actually spent in this shop. How many handbags and dresses could one woman need that made Miquita's eyes flash with pound signs when she heard his name?

Thinking of money, he'd have to work out how he was going to pay Elin back. Perhaps it was so expensive that he'd have to wait for his dividend payments from the shares he had in Dallimores. His savings were small; 'Lecturer' did not pay excellently.

The dresses here were so much better than those fluorescent-lighted shops that Lila had dragged him into, and he had a comfortable chair.

"That one is great, Lila," he called as the door shut behind her and Miquita after the second dress was demonstrated.

No answer. Rhys rolled his head back. How much longer was this going to take? Waiting, again. Always waiting for Lila.

"Yes, your boyfriend will love you in this one," Miquita said loudly from behind the closed door. He snapped his head up. If this was the 'one', then he would gush and swoon and say whatever he needed to say so they could leave.

The door opened and Miquita came out first, giving him an extremely pointed look. Right, he could get on board with this.

Lila followed and he stood, the serviette on his thigh falling to the ground.

Miquita was telling him about the dress, fluttering around Lila and making sure that the skirt fell properly, but he couldn't focus on her words. He raked his eyes from Lila's hair, where she'd pulled it into a low knot at the back of her head, across the one shouldered dress that flowed out from her hips and pooled gently on the floor.

It was perfect.

"Yes," he interrupted Miquita, clearing his throat because his voice didn't work well.

"May I suggest shoes?" Miquita asked, giving him yet another pointed look.

"I have shoes," Lila said, lifting the skirt with both hands and poking her toe out.

"It would be better if you wore something else with that gown." Miquita was full of tact.

"Shoes," Rhys said roughly. "Yes."

Miquita strode out of the dressing area and Lila looked down at the dress.

"Rhys, I feel like a princess," she said with a giggle.

Gently walking to the mirrored wall, she twisted and turned so she could see all angles. There was something in the way the dress shimmered softly when she moved, the line of her neck and curve of her bare shoulder and Rhys could not tear his eyes away.

Henry II could be reincarnated and ask him to go on Crusade with William Marshal, and Rhys would still be here, his chest expanding, staring at Lila Cartwright.

"What do you think?" she asked, catching his eyes in the mirror.

"Yes," he said, nodding. His eyes wandered across her collarbone. "You look..."

There were no words that would do justice to how she looked.

She ducked her head with a shy smile and a flush crossed her cheeks. He hadn't seen that smile before and he filed it away for future reference.

It was difficult to sit down when Miquita came back into the room and bent down to change Lila's shoes, because surely he could do that. It was even more difficult when Lila stepped back into the dressing room and he couldn't see her anymore.

His mouth was dry and his hands were not.

His heart stuttered.

LILA

Rhys was indecipherable as they drove home. Something had changed in him when she'd walked out of the dressing room in *that* dress. A softening around the eyes. A slight slackening of his jaw. The intensity with which he didn't take his eyes off her for one second.

He had said she was beautiful.

Yeah, she looked nice, but who wouldn't in a dress that practically came with its own entourage? Would it be too much to think that Rhys Aubrey, on some level, had stopped seeing her as an annoyance or an opportunity to prove something to his family and possibly as a woman?

Yes. It would.

She wasn't the type of girl that men wanted. She was the fun girl next door, the buddy, the pal. There were no dramatic grand declarations of love for her. Lila was not Jasmeet, and she was okay with that. And she wasn't looking for a relationship. Not at all.

Lila hadn't lied when she said she had felt like a princess. What girl wouldn't? It was the most perfect dress she had ever set eyes upon and Miquita had earned every part of her commission, including the shoes and the bag that she'd gently pressed into her hands, with another terse 'yes' from Rhys.

Shame that she'd have to sell them all after the evening and give Rhys the proceeds. There was absolutely no way she could possibly keep them. Where, pray tell, would she wear them again? Oh, perhaps every now and again for the hoovering.

"Do you want to come in for a sandwich?" Lila asked when he pulled up behind Petunia.

"Uh," Rhys swallowed and looked awkwardly into the distance.

"You don't have to," she said quickly, unclipping her seatbelt and putting her hand on the door handle. "I'll see you at work on Monday."

"No, uh." Rhys's throat worked and she waited. "I'd planned to tell you more about my family today. If you're happy to hear it."

It should have been a question, but she let it slide because The Family Discussion was a big thing for him.

"Yeah, great." Because surely a girlfriend would know these things. Also, how long had they been together? Where did they meet? Who chased who? This was going to be a lot more complex than randomly bumping into Jason.

"Okay."

It didn't take long to give the new dress a home in her sewing room, opening the bag to let the skirt hang nicely, just how Miquita had shown her. Before long, they were sat at the breakfast bar in her little kitchen picking at a small helping of beans on toast, because Rhys had eaten about ten thousand tiny sandwiches in the shop and she'd had two cakes. And a milkshake.

"So, Elin is the power in the marriage then?" Lila said, wishing she had a notebook. It would be a bit weird, though, if she sat there taking notes on his family as he blurted it all out. Because that's what he was doing, blurting and trying to get it over with as quickly as possible.

"Yes. James is…" he searched for the right word. "He's not as ambitious as Elin, which is a good thing. I think he'd be quite happy not to work, but my father wouldn't allow that."

Oh.

"Dad isn't happy with my life choices," Rhys started.

This, she knew.

"It's difficult for me to be in a room with him," he said, stabbing at some stray beans on his plate. "He's narcissistic, manipulative, scheming."

Rhys shrugged and a rueful smile tugged at his lips.

"I know I can be," he hesitated, "difficult sometimes and I've had to spend time learning social niceties. But, as you know, I don't always get it right."

Well, that was a lovely bout of self-awareness from Rhys, and for that she gifted him a little smile.

"But I really try. That's the thing with my father, he doesn't try. I could forgive him if he learned from his mistakes, learned how to deal with me, Elin, my mother. But he doesn't. To him, we're commodities."

"Oh, Rhys," she said, feeling a sudden tightness to her throat.

Rhys stared over her shoulder, as if it were easier to talk about this without looking directly at her.

"I'm allowed this 'sabbatical' as my father calls it, because he's so sure I'll fail and be back in the family business, ready to take over from him when he dies."

"Is that what he's said?" Horrified wasn't the word. Why would you force your child to do something they hated?

Lila schooled her face, because there was nothing worse than pity. But Rhys wasn't looking at her.

"Oh yeah, it's fully expected. But Elin would be much more suitable. Or my cousin Madoc."

"The one who married your ex, Seren?"

"No, that was Ieuan," he mumbled, stabbing stray beans. Definitely should have a notebook. "Dad liked Seren. 'She'll always look good on your arm, son.'" Rhys snorted. "As if I care about that."

Lila raised one eyebrow at him. He'd just bought her a God-knows-how-expensive dress and now he was essentially confirming exactly what she thought; that she was not, and would never be, good enough for his family. Her shoulders drooped.

"No, I didn't mean," he passed a hand over his face. "I'm sorry, Lila. This is hard."

She let her face soften.

"Keep going. You're doing well."

"My father thinks that the partner of a Dallimore should look good and not interfere. Unless you amuse him, then you move up the pecking order."

"And your mum? She looks good on his arm?"

Sometimes, a rewind button would be lovely. It would be excellent if those words, so easy to come out of her mouth, would just hop, skip and jump back into her big, fat gob.

But Rhys just smiled softly.

"My mother tempers him. Mostly. He likes to think that she has no influence, but she does," he said, tipping his head forward. "Well, sometimes."

"But not about you?"

"Not about me." His voice was a whisper.

Lila looked at him, his broad shoulders hunched, his eyes tired and hollow, mouth tight. Behind that abrasive, solid, coldness was a sweet, vulnerable little pickle, just trying to go his own way. Like Fleetwood Mac.

Right, enough of this wallowing.

"Rhys, don't you worry," she said, her voice full of all the cheeriness she could muster. "We've got this."

He assessed her carefully, looking for any kind of guile. But Lila had no guile.

The man across from her straightened, put his shoulders back and set his jaw. Yes, this was good. She needed him to be Fighting Rhys, because there was no way she could face his family, without him being one hundred percent aloof, snarky, 'Miss Cartwright' Rhys.

"Okay."

Rhys didn't leave after lunch. She didn't mind him sitting on her sofa while she read Susie Dent's *Interesting Stories about Curious Words,* patiently watching *The Great British Sewing Bee*, or asking about the difference between French seams or normal seams. When he stood up to rescue some papers from his car to mark, he had off-cut wool stuck to his jeans and she smothered a giggle.

It was comfortable.

Jasmeet, Girls Group Chat

> please don't make me go and see susie dent. she is not the queen of anything and I really don't want to go

Lila frowned at her phone. Thanks for the reply days and days after her question. It would have been nice for Jasmeet to do something that *she* wanted to do for once.

> Okay! No worries!!

Rhys didn't leave until early evening when she stretched and yawned and snuggled into her unicorn blanket.

"I need to go, Lila," he said. "But before I do, can I ask you something?"

She shot him a narrow-eyed look.

"If it's anything to do with my secret cookie recipe, then no. I will take that to the grave," she said, slightly teasing but mostly serious.

He didn't seem to register this and his face crumpled in a frown.

"Why are you paying Jason's debts?"

Well, that was direct. Lila rubbed her ring finger and thumb together.

"It's not really Jason's loan. We both signed the agreement," she said, not meeting his eyes.

"Is he paying half?"

"No."

"Did you take the loan out?"

"I signed the paperwork, yes."

"Lila," he started, with a head tilt that was all disappointment.

"Okay, fine!" she said, throwing her arms up in the air. "It was his idea, he did it all and said it would be much easier if it came out of my account because I was the one earning."

If Rhys's face was any harder, it would have been made of granite.

"And now he's earning and you're still paying it off?"

"That's about the size of it," she mumbled.

Rhys sighed heavily. "Lila, you can't—"

"No, stop." She snapped her eyes up to his. "You asked. I told. I didn't ask for your advice."

"But—" He just couldn't help himself, could he? He had to push and push and push.

"No, Rhys! This is my life and I will do what I want to with it. If that includes having to pay off a loan so I don't have to interact with Jason for the sake of my mental health, then that's what I'll do."

Lila flopped back against the sofa and swallowed hard. That was another tick in the 'stupid' box. She'd bet her silk kimono – the one that Maddy and Ruby had brought back from their honeymoon – that Rhys thought she was pathetic for continuing to let Jason walk all over her, paying his debts.

But it was so nearly done and in the next couple of years she could put those payments towards a linguistics course and she'd be on her way. She just had to bide her time and hope she didn't have any major issues, like a boiler breakage or a car failure or anything else that would wipe out the scant bit of money she'd have after she repaid the loan.

She glanced at Rhys, and that frown hadn't moved from his face. His jaw worked as if he was trying to figure it all out. Figure *her* out.

"I'm sorry, Lila," he said eventually. "I shouldn't have asked."

"It's okay, Rhys," she said automatically.

"No, it's not. I apologise." He took her hand in both of his warm ones. "I am sorry."

"It *is* okay. I forgive you."

A small smile flashed across his face, but didn't reach his eyes.

"I really should go now."

"Oh, all right," she said with a smile. "I'll walk you the four steps to the front door."

A huff of a laugh escaped his chest and he shuffled his papers together and put them in his bag.

"Thanks again," she said, leaning against the door frame. "For the dress."

"You're welcome. Besides, it's for me really. You know, the 'personal success' part of my life."

Mr Dallimore Senior had really done a number on him if 'personal success' was measured by a relationship with the opposite sex. But now was not the time to get into that.

"See you on Monday," she said. Rhys looked as if he wanted to say something, so she waited. In fact, he even opened his mouth to say something, but clamped it shut again.

"Rhys, don't worry about it, okay?"

"Okay," he said, his smile tight. He was definitely still worrying about it. "See you on Monday."

CHAPTER 9

Anagnorisis *(noun) an·ag·no·ri·sis*

1. *The point in the plot at which the protagonist recognises his or her or some other character's true identity or discovers the true nature of his or her own situation*

RHYS

The seminar was hell. There was no other word for it; hell.

Not only was he stuck on a merry-go-round of 'but Richard I was a *good* king' with his students who had watched one too many Robin Hood adaptations, but he was distracted. Couldn't concentrate. Things like 'pay more attention' never once graced his school reports and he prided himself on his ability to single-mindedly focus on whatever he was doing. In fact, even his father had praised his machine-like ability to work.

But his brain was failing him today. There was little to no concentration and certainly not in Lila Cartwright's office. Because he had already eaten two cookies from the tin that sat on the little table, and he wanted another. Because of the lemon cake smell coming suspiciously from one of Lila's desk drawers. Because of the way the light from the window made her hair seem to glow.

"Mr Aubrey?" the sniffler asked, although she was much less sniffly today.

He tore his eyes away from Lila's fingers dancing on the keyboard of her computer and focused on the student in front of him.

"Yes?"

"Do you think he did?"

Rhys raised his eyebrows expectantly at Sniffly Girl. He wasn't going to ask her to repeat herself, but if she wanted an answer, she was going to have to. What would that stupid course that he'd dragged himself through have told him to do?. He sighed.

"I apologise, I was distracted. Can you repeat that, please?"

The students exchanged glances.

"Do you think John had Arthur of Brittany killed?" DeVon asked, leaning forward. At least they were engaged, but when on earth did they move on to Richard's successors?

"I think we will never definitively know," he said vaguely. "But it is highly likely that Arthur died in captivity in Rouen Castle and that John did indeed have a hand in it."

"But he was his nephew," DeVon commented.

Rhys smiled. The Angevin family tree was convoluted and difficult to get to grips with, but DeVon had obviously done some work for this seminar.

"Do you think that mattered to John?" Rhys probed.

He could be doing so much more with his time than coaching students through the ups and downs of medieval kingship. After his two lectures this afternoon, he had forty minutes scheduled to, once again, fine-tune his statement for his Fellowship application. As a reward, he could lose himself in Henry II's impressive administrative structure for an hour and twenty minutes. Then kickboxing, dinner, and home.

That was his orderly day and he liked it.

What he didn't like was Lila, with her welcoming smile and her horrendous yellow dress with the blue splodges on it, worming her way into his mind and taking attention away from his important things.

The students' voices faded to a murmur as he watched Lila

talk quietly on the phone, the handset propped under her chin as she tapped at her keyboard, a smile on her face. She had a smile for simply everyone.

Even fucking Jason.

Lila replaced the phone and glanced up at him. She nodded towards the students and mouthed 'pay attention', before turning back to her computer screen.

Oh right. Great. Like he could concentrate now when all he could think about was the way her lips formed words and all the filthy things that he could use that mouth for.

What the *fuck* was wrong with him? Rhys couldn't be in her office anymore. It was too suffocating. This was not good. Perhaps he was ill. That would explain everything; the lack of concentration, the tightness in his chest, his hands clammy on his papers.

Rhys stood abruptly.

"I think that's enough for today," he said, interrupting Other Girl halfway through whatever she was saying.

"Oh, okay," DeVon said, confused.

He could see Lila frown at him from the corner of his eye, but he couldn't look at her.

"I'll see you in the lecture tomorrow and we'll discuss Arthur of Brittany in more detail next week," he said, already halfway across the office to the door.

Escaping to the sanctity of his office, he closed the door behind him. It was cool in there, and smelled of nothing. There were no crumbs in here, no cookies, no cushions. Nothing. It was calm and orderly and safe.

He stared at the papers on his desk, ready and waiting for him. He had exactly twenty minutes before his lecture. Alone and safe. But he wasn't safe from his own fucking traitorous thoughts. Lila's soft giggle was *not* part of Henry II's movements in 1174.

Fuck.

"What's with you today, man?" Dan asked, offering his hand.

Rhys was panting, staring up at the florescent lights flickering on the ceiling of the kickboxing dojo. Dan had knocked him on his arse with a sweeping leg that Rhys should have seen coming; the same sweeping leg that Dan had been trying on him every single kickboxing lesson for the past two years.

"Whatever it is, I'll take it." Dan hauled him up. "I am *never* letting you forget this."

Rhys glared and shook out his arms, bouncing on his toes. When the sun shone on the corrugated iron roof in this unseasonably warm week in late October, it was positively melting.

"I don't know," he said, throwing a punch at his friend. "I'm distracted."

"By what?" Dan asked, bobbing under his arm and jabbing him in the ribs. "Or, by who?"

"Whom," Rhys corrected, trying to get a kick in to force Dan back and give him a bit more space.

Dan stopped bouncing and grinned at him.

"What?" Rhys grumbled. "Get your guard up."

Dan did as he was told and Rhys landed a solid round kick to his mid-section.

If anyone could help, it was Dan.

"It's Lila." Rhys threw a jab. "Miss Cartwright."

"I know who she is." Dan smirked.

"She's just in the way all the time. I can't stop—" Rhys bit down on his words.

"Thinking about her?" Dan offered. "Looking at her?"

Rhys's eyes closed and he tightened his jaw , hanging his head.

"What the fuck is wrong with me?"

"There's nothing wrong with you. She's a pretty girl."

"Woman," he said, absently.

"What?"

"She's a woman, not a girl."

Dan laughed, and headed over to the side of the mats to swig on his bottle of water. There were more breaks than normal because of the copious amounts of sweat that dripped down their faces. A cold shower would be incredibly nice (and fucking welcome) when he got home later.

"So, you like her, yeah?"

"She's nice. Yes, I like her."

"You know what I'm asking," Dan said, lifting his eyebrow at him.

Rhys stared over Dan's shoulder. He wasn't so socially inept that he didn't know what Dan was asking. He knew, all right.

Sure, he was attracted to her. Who wouldn't be? But Dan was wrong; Lila was more than pretty. She was beautiful. Even in that yellow and blue dress that she was wearing today, which was perfectly hideous, but somehow suited her smile. Although how anything could suit a smile was beyond him.

Rhys had enjoyed sitting with her at the weekend. It was nice, with no expectation of conversation, no expectation of anything really. She was comfortable and she had listened to him so well. Lila had made an extremely uncomfortable situation almost palatable. Best of all, she didn't judge, she encouraged. Whatever path he chose, whatever he decided to do with his life, the only thing that Lila wanted for him (and for everyone, it seemed) was for them to be happy.

Selfless. That was a good word to describe her. Generous with her smiles and selfless to a fault. Otherwise, she wouldn't still be paying the loan that prick took out with repayments coming from her account. Something would need to be done about that at some point, because it wasn't right. Was it even legal? If she'd signed it, then yeah. But now they weren't together any longer and he was a big-shot hospital doctor, he could damn well pay for his own fucking loans.

"You've got it bad," Dan said with a laugh.

"I haven't got anything," he mumbled.

But Dan was right. Having a bit of a thing for Lila would

explain his sweaty palms and his inability to look anywhere else when she was near him. A bit of a thing. Yes, that was it. A thing. But only a bit.

"It's all right, man. Don't worry about it," Dan said, pushing his water bottle top down to close it. "I saw it coming a mile off."

"What?"

"You were protective over her that night we met her and Jasmeet," Dan said with a shrug.

"Uh, hang on, I was just doing what Jasmeet told me to," Rhys said.

"Yeah, but you didn't have to, you know," Dan said, "be *protective* protective."

Okay, so Rhys had no idea what '*protective* protective' meant and he wasn't about to ask. He followed Dan back into the middle of the mats, grabbing a kick shield on the way. As Dan practiced his round kicks, Rhys analysed some more. If he could understand what was happening inside of him, then he could live with it.

This was an arrangement, a fake date, she was a fake girlfriend, and for one night only. He couldn't get attached. She was his box-ticking item for 'successful personal life' without input from the Dallimore family. Regardless of how he felt, she didn't want any kind of relationship. She'd made that clear.

But he couldn't help remembering how good it felt waking up next to her. When he was with her, it was like the stone that lived in his chest, the crushing anxiety of expectation, just... dissolved.

"Your turn," Dan said, gesturing for the kick shield. Rhys moved into his fighting stance.

After the end of their arrangement, he'd tell her that he wanted to see her again, spend more time with her. It didn't have to mean anything, not if she didn't want it to. They could at least be friends, couldn't they? The way his stomach curdled at that thought, and how his heart stuttered just a little in his chest told him that he didn't want to just be friends with Lila Cartwright.

He wanted to kiss her, hold her, wake up with her.

Do things to her that were certainly more than what friends would do.

LILA

Jasmeet had pulled herself away from Dan long enough to make it to girls' night. Well, girls' night was a bit of a stretch because Maddy had cancelled. The baby had a temperature, and she and Ruby were all aflutter, bless them. Lila pushed down that little niggle that this had been in the diary for ages because they couldn't help it if the baby was ill.

"Is that Dan texting you now?" Lila asked, nodding at Jasmeet's phone.

"Yeah, but I've told him it's girls' night, so that's the end of that," she said, putting her phone face down on the ottoman.

She'd see how long that remained there.

"It seems like it's going really well between you two." Lila tried to keep the bitterness out of her voice.

Not so much bitterness, but wistfulness. Yes, that was a better word. What she'd told Rhys was true; she didn't want a boyfriend. She didn't *need* a boyfriend. Lila was quite content by herself, living on her own terms, doing whatever she wanted to do.

True, it had been nice to wake up with Rhys's arms around her that time and nice to spend time with him shopping and sitting and talking. But that's all it was. Nice.

The truth was, her little heart was still fragile and cautious, and would prefer to hide in a cocoon of sparkly wool rather than venture out and get pin-cushioned once again.

So, no, not bitterness. Not jealousy. Wistfulness.

"It is. I really like him," Jasmeet said, with a dopey grin on her face. "What?"

Lila schooled her features to wipe the scowl off them.

"Oh, sorry," she said with a little wince. "I just don't want you to get hurt."

"Oh Lila." Jasmeet's head tipped sympathetically to the side. God, she hated that head tilt. "I know you're wary, but not every guy is Jason."

Did Jasmeet realise how condescending that was? Lila took a sip of wine.

"Anyway, enough about me," Jasmeet said, slipping a lock of hair over her shoulder. Even in jogging bottoms, a dirty t-shirt, no makeup and hair pulled up into a loose, messy bun, Jasmeet managed to look like a supermodel. Lila picked at the hole in her own dirty t-shirt.

"Did you get a dress in the end for that thing with Rhys?" Jasmeet asked, flicking through Netflix.

That thing didn't really feel like it did it justice. But it wasn't really her place to tell Jasmeet about the inner workings of the Dallimore family. She wasn't even sure she could tell Jasmeet that Rhys was *part* of the Dallimore family. Did Dan even know? He must do, it seemed like they'd been friends for ages.

"You have, haven't you? When is it again?" Jasmeet asked.

"Next week." Lila trained her eyes on Netflix. "Yeah, I've got one."

"Let's see it then." Jasmeet clicked on the description of a thriller and quickly clicked off it again.

"It's hanging up in the craft room." Craft room was a tad excessive for describing the tiny box room that was overflowing with junk.

"Bring it down then." Jasmeet tried another film.

"Best if you come up to see it," Lila said. She'd one hundred percent trip over it as carried it down the stairs and then it would rip and that would be the absolute end, and she would never be able to face Rhys ever again, especially after he'd spent so much money on it. Not that she knew how much money he'd spent. There had been no price tag, which meant it was a *lot*. And shoes. And a bag.

Jasmeet frowned, but set her wine on the little side table next to a half-finished crochet octopus.

Lila chewed the inside of her cheek as she led the way upstairs. She was a bit nervous about showing Jasmeet The Dress – that's right, The Dress needed capital letters, because it felt expensive enough to have them.

"Why are you being so weird? And why is it in your spare room, not your wardrobe?" Jasmeet folded her arms across her chest as Lila hesitated in opening the door.

"Okay, look, just don't make assumptions, okay?"

"Assumptions about what?"

"About this."

Lila flung the door open and ushered Jasmeet in to see The Dress hanging on a hook she'd put up for a picture that had never made it to the wall.

"Oh my God," Jasmeet whispered, taking a step forward. She ran her fingers over the delicate lace flowers. "This is beautiful, Lila. Absolutely beautiful."

"Yeah," she said.

"Have you shown Maddy and Ruby?"

Lila shook her head.

"Are those *shoes*?" Jasmeet exclaimed. She grabbed the shoe box on the floor and Lila winced when she wrenched it open.

"Jas, please be careful."

"And a bag! Lila, you've really outdone yourself," Jasmeet said, turning one of the shoes to look at it from all angles. "This is perfect and so *you*. You'll look spectacular. Rhys won't be able to keep his hands to himself."

"No Jas, it's not like that," she said, wringing her hands in front of her. "What are you doing?"

"What do you think I'm doing? I'm calling Maddy and

Ruby," Jasmeet mumbled, tapping away on her phone. Maddy answered the video call after a few rings.

"Mads, check out this dress that Lila's got for her weird date with Rhys," Jasmeet said, flipping the camera.

Weird date? So they'd been talking behind her back, no doubt about how desperate Rhys must be to take someone as plain as her as his fake girlfriend.

No. Stop it.

These were her friends, they loved her. If they were talking about her then it was out of concern. Not putting her down or belittling her or laughing at her.

"Lila," Maddy was saying. "How did you afford that? And the shoes and bag?"

"It looks expensive, Mads," Jasmeet said.

"It is expensive. I've spent enough time walking around shops I can't afford trying to get Ellie to sleep to know." Maddy's voice was quiet, but urgent.

"How is Ellie?" Lila asked, hoping to distract them.

"She's sleeping on Ruby now, dosed up with Calpol," Maddy said. "You're not getting out of this. Have you over-extended yourself? Is your credit card completely maxed out?"

Jasmeet looked at her expectantly.

"Did you know Susie Dent has been awarded an OBE?" Lila asked, perkily.

Jasmeet scowled.

"Okay, fine." Lila glanced down at the frayed t shirt and jogging bottoms she was currently modelling. "Rhys put it on his family's account."

There was a beat of silence.

"Rhys put it on his family's account," Jasmeet repeated.

"Yep." Lila grabbed the shoes and reverently put them back in the box.

"Crap. I've got to go, the baby's crying. Jas, get the details." Maddy ended the call.

"Spill," Jasmeet raised an eyebrow. "Why do you look so

shifty? Oh my God, something's going on between you two. I knew it!"

"No, Jas. Not at all," Lila said, pushing the shoe box closed.

"What is it? Is he a drug dealer? The mafia? Because I've seen how Dan lives on his lecturer salary and it's good, but it doesn't enable him to drop—" Her phone buzzed in her hand. "Oh my god, Maddy has found the dress. Look!" She held out her phone.

It was like a bruise that you can't help but poke, and Lila couldn't *not* look.

"Shit," she whispered.

"Yeah, shit," Jasmeet agreed. "So?"

"Okay, but you *cannot* bring it up in front of Rhys. It's not my place," Lila said.

"I mean, if he's dealing in rare animal bones or is actually a drugs lord, I am honour-bound to report it to the police," Jasmeet said, only half joking.

Lila sighed and launched into a rather short and choppy explanation of Rhys's family history. There was an icky, sludgy feeling in the bottom of her stomach because she was telling secrets that weren't hers to tell. There was a reason why Rhys was an Aubrey, not an Aubrey-Dallimore. He had confided in her and she was breaking his confidence by telling Jasmeet. But she had to, there was no other way to explain it. And she had to explain it.

CHAPTER 10

Recogitate (intransitive verb) re·cogitate
1. 1. To think over again

RHYS

Lila

Rhys, I'm so sorry, I've had to tell Jasmeet about your family. Not ABOUT about your family, just that your family are rich.

I'm so sorry Rhys. She saw the dress and wanted to know how I afforded it and I panicked.

I made her promise not to tell anyone. I'm really sorry Rhys, please don't hate me.

Rhys?

Okay.

It wasn't really okay, but what else was he supposed to say to that? Oh, thanks for telling everyone the one thing I have tried my hardest to keep a secret. Thanks, Fake Girlfriend, for betraying me.

Realistically, he was surprised that he'd managed to keep it hidden for as long as he had. It had been years and no one had worked it out. He'd not been close enough to anyone except Dan, for them to have worked it out.

Here was Lila, who had wormed her way into his life with her messy, comfortable house and wide, unguarded smiles, blabbing his family name to anyone who would listen. How was he going to get through the Dallimore dinner with someone who had betrayed him?

These were his intrusive thoughts as he pressed the handbrake button in front of Lila's house. He would have parked behind Petunia, but a little black car was in his spot.

Rhys tugged at his collar as he waited for Lila to answer the front door. His bow tie was suffocating.

"Rhys, hi."

It wasn't Lila who answered the door, but Jasmeet, looking entirely too smug. He narrowed his eyes as she blatantly perused him up and down.

"Well," she said with a grin, opening the door wider. "You scrub up quite well."

"Is she ready?" Rhys asked, pulling at his collar again. He should probably redo it so he stopped fiddling with it, but he'd already done it four times and this was the best one yet. Besides, was it tight, or was he just nervous about seeing his family?

"Nearly," Jasmeet said, scuttling upstairs.

Elin would have to be his safe space. His sister, for all her annoyances and issues, supported him and his decisions, even if she didn't understand them. Lila was already doing so much, coming with him tonight. He couldn't put any more of his nervousness on her.

Even if she had told Jasmeet his secret.

A noise and a shuffle came from upstairs. Rhys's shoulders tightened even more. It was nerves about seeing Lila in *that* dress. The dress that made her feel like a princess.

Fuck, he was like a teenager on his first date. This was fucking ridiculous.

His head whipped up at the merest hint of a sound on the stairs, but it was just Jasmeet and a twinge of disappointment pulled at his insides. He needed to get a grip of himself.

"Two minutes, Rhys."

Jasmeet narrowed her eyes at him.

"She's really nervous. She's worried about letting you down, about not being good enough for—" She snapped her mouth shut.

Ah. Right.

"For my rich family," he finished for her.

Jasmeet flinched slightly and waved her hand dismissively.

"I think she's more nervous about the whole Welsh thing than the rich thing." She lowered her voice. "They're your family, Rhys. She never met Jason's family."

"What, never? In seven years?"

Jason was a fool and delusional to boot. Rhys could think of two explanations as to why Jason had never introduced her to his parents. Firstly, he hadn't told them that they were even together. Or, that they did know about her and he was ashamed to take her to meet them. Either thought left a sour taste in his mouth, because of what a disgusting fucking human being Jason was.

"Never. In seven years," Jasmeet repeated.

Using Lila's beautiful nature and willingness to help to his own ends was despicable and demonstrated by his free use of Lila's wages for *his* motherfucking loan. It boiled Rhys's blood. But destroying her esteem by never introducing her to his family was something else. Jason had more than likely removed every ounce of self-esteem that Lila had. He started to understand why she fell back into old habits around Jason and why it took her a few days to get over seeing him.

Protectiveness surged through his chest and his hands clenched involuntarily. Rhys was a lot of things, but he vowed there and then to be the best person that he could for Lila. She deserved the world and he would do his best to help her get it.

"So, yeah, she's worried that she's not good enough. She'll never say it, but that's the problem," Jasmeet said.

"That's ridiculous."

"That may be so," Jasmeet took a step into his personal space, "but if you make her feel in any way less than your richy-rich family, I will break you. I won't do it quickly, I won't do it easily. It will be painful and you will rue the day you ever thought about hurting my friend."

Jasmeet's big brown eyes bore holes into his face with laser precision.

"Do you understand?"

"I have absolutely no intention of making Lila feel less than anything," he said, bristling. "In fact, Jasmeet, I resent the fact that you are equating me with that absolute fucking dishcloth, Jason."

Jasmeet grinned.

"Well said, Rhys."

A smile pulled at his lips. They were on the same page. Good.

A little "oh shit" reached his ears and Rhys turned to see Lila gripping the banister with both hands, shuffling down the stairs slower than an ant with two legs.

Rhys found it difficult to get a full breath into his chest because regardless that Lila was bent almost double, the skirt of her dress thrown over one arm and her brows pulled tightly together in concentration, she made him forget how to breathe.

"Oh, for God's sake, Lila, we practiced this," Jasmeet said, rushing halfway up the stairs to take her hand.

"It's all right for you, Miss-I-Wear-Stupid-Shoes-All-The-Time," she grumbled.

Rhys's muscles tightened with the effort of not pushing past Jasmeet to scoop Lila up from the stairs and depositing her safely on the floor. If she fell and hurt herself, then it would be his worst nightmare, spending all night in the hospital (again) in a goddamned uncomfortable bow tie. Because of course he wouldn't leave her by herself.

Lila huffed out a breath as she reached the bottom of the stairs and unhooked her dress from her arm.

"There aren't any stairs at this place, are there?" she asked, looking up at him with those big, trusting eyes.

How would he know? If there were, he would carry her. He shook his head slightly.

"You look..." he started, but his voice didn't work very well.

"Hang on," she said, dropping her gaze to his bow tie. She reached up to tug lightly on it, even though it was perfectly straight because he'd seen to it in the mirror.

Pressing her lips together, she glanced up at him.

"There," she said. "Much better."

His body reacted to her being so close and there was a distinct tightening in his crotch area. Fucking hell, she'd tugged on his bow tie. What would happen if she tugged anywhere else?

Rhys swallowed and took a step back. A semi wouldn't be a good look.

"So?" Jasmeet said, jerking her head towards Lila.

"Yes. You look..." He cleared his throat. "You look..."

Why were words so fucking difficult? With Jasmeet glaring at him, and Lila looking like *that* in front of him, a blush staining her cheeks, her eyes bright, he could not think of one single word to say.

"It's okay, Rhys," she said, with a smile. "Come on, let's go."

Lila headed towards the door.

"Lock up, would you, Jas?"

"Yeah, of course," she said. "Text me if you need me."

He frowned. Why would Lila need her? Perhaps it was because he couldn't string a sentence together, because his mouth was too dry and his brain was mush, all from seeing Lila Cartwright done up. For him.

But it wasn't 'for him'. It was her end of the bargain. If he wanted to see her done up *for him*, then he had to tell her that was what he wanted.

After tonight. After their bargain. When they could start afresh. It was unfair to put that pressure on her now, tonight.

Rhys opened the car door for Lila and ushered her in, closing the door softly behind her. She wasn't wearing a coat, and it wasn't warm. Perhaps he should have bought her a coat as well? Jasmeet watched with a warning glare on her face as he settled behind the driving wheel, and pressed the 'Start' button.

"Hey," Lila said, her fingertips grazing his hand as it rested on the gearstick. "It'll be all right tonight, Rhys. I promise."

Rhys wasn't so sure. Whether or not he had Lila beside him, looking earth-shatteringly beautiful and being a well of bounteous support, it was going to be a difficult night. A night that, apart from Lila, he had tried not to let invade his thoughts. Because that dark hole of doom was never fun to head down.

LILA

It was only a dinner and they were just people.

That's what Lila was telling herself as Rhys pressed his hand to the bottom of her back, guiding her through throngs of people who parted like Rhys was the second coming. He was tense, his shoulders bunched and jaw locked tightly.

"Rhys, you need to stop scowling at everyone," she whispered with a smile.

She couldn't be nervous. That was pretty much the whole point of her being here tonight; to support, to be calm, to prove to Rhys's family that he was a successful human being. Although, how a person like Rhys could be unsuccessful, she didn't know.

"I don't know if I can," he said under his breath.

Lila stopped and turned to face him.

"Look, I know this isn't easy for you. I know you're out of your comfort zone," she said, doing her best 'kind counsellor' voice. "But if you keep being so tense and robot-y, people are going to smell a rat."

Smell a rat. What an interesting phrase. Lila shook her head slightly. *Think about that one later.*

"Robot-y? From the woman who loves words?" he asked with a wry smile.

Lila's own smile grew.

"Yes, Rhys. Robot-y," she said. "Come on, let's get a drink, shall we?"

Rhys nodded. Instead of woodenly guiding her through the crowds, he grabbed her hand and gave her a light tug.

"Better?" he said over his shoulder.

"Better," she said, trying hard to keep her blush down. Because not only was she holding hands with a very attractive Rhys Aubrey, who looked a little like James Bond in his tux, but he had probably caught her having a good look at his arse.

The mail order tux did wonders and must have been altered and fitted within an inch of its life, because it was practically moulded to his little conker bum. Which was delightful. His dark, wavy hair was more slicked back than usual, giving him a more formal (but no less attractive) look. Rhys certainly looked the part, but Lila was under no illusions as to the strain on him, only noticeable in his tight jaw and the dart of his eyes around the room.

Rhys let her hand go to smoothly lift two champagne glasses from a passing waiter and pressed one into her hand. She took a long, fortifying draw.

"Well, that's not five-quid prosecco, is it?" she said.

Rhys laughed deeply and throatily, and he was beautiful when he laughed.

"You should laugh more," she said with a smile.

"I laugh," he defended.

"Not as much as you should."

Rhys swallowed and looked over her shoulder.

"My mother is making a beeline for us," he said. "So is my sister and her husband, James."

"Okay, okay. How do I look?" Lila asked, running her fingers over her hair to make sure it was still pinned back as Jasmeet had done it. Of course, with enough hairspray to make even the 80s do a double take, it wasn't going anywhere.

"You look—"

"Rhys!" a soft female voice called. Perfume swirled around her as Rhys's mother hugged her son tightly, with a stream of Welsh. She was tall and slender, but the curve of Rhys's lip, and the strong line of his nose were exactly the same as hers. Rhys hugged his mother back, his eyes squeezed shut like a little boy. He obviously loved her very much and they probably didn't see each other as much as he wanted, especially with the fraught relationship he had with his father.

"*Saesneg os gwelwch yn dda*, Mam," Rhys said, letting her go.

"Of course, English," Rhys's mother turned to her with shining eyes. "You must be Lila, it's so nice to meet you."

"Hello Mrs Aubrey-Dallimore. It's lovely to meet you," Lila said, mentally giving herself a fist pump because all the practicing of 'Dall-i-more' not 'Dall-more' in the mirror had paid off.

Rhys's hand snaked its way to the bottom of her back and it was thoroughly reassuring.

"Oh, call me Cerys. Don't you look stunning?" she said, gripping Lila's hands in both of hers. "Oh, don't you make the perfect couple?"

Lila batted her eyes up at Rhys adoringly and his lips twitched, trying to keep his grin in.

"Hi," Lila said, locking eyes with a younger, female version of Rhys. "I'm Lila."

"Elin," she grinned, barely able to conceal her delight, just like her mother.

The only words to describe Elin were 'stonkingly

glamorous'. With her high cheekbones, long neck and impossibly sharp bob cut, she could have walked off a catwalk. Well, if she was a good foot taller. The black floor-length dress that she wore was accentuated with a red fold over collar – definitely, one hundred percent designer – and Lila wondered what Jasmeet and Maddy would think.

"Rhys, we'll talk later, yes?" his mother said, desperate hope written across her face.

"Of course, Mam," Rhys said with a soft smile, before watching his mother continue to work the room. This was a room in which people 'worked'.

"Don't you look divine! Miquita?" Elin was saying.

"Miquita," Lila agreed with a grateful smile. "Thank you so much for helping. I had no idea what to wear. I've never been to a black-tie thing before, certainly not anything like this," she said, words just falling out of her mouth.

Rhys squeezed her waist and she took that as a signal to remain calm.

"You are a delight, Lila, an absolute delight. How did my awful brother manage to snag someone so beautiful?" Elin said, raising an eyebrow at Rhys. Good, if Elin bought it, then everyone else would.

"Oh, and this is James," Elin said, flicking her fingers over her shoulder at the man standing just behind her.

"James, hi," Rhys said, reaching past Elin to shake his hand.

"Rhys, it's been a while," James said with a bright, handsome smile.

If there were two people more opposite than her and Rhys, it was Elin and James. Where Elin was hard, ruthless edges with sharp eyes that never rested on one place too long, James was a laidback little cinnamon roll who was protecting his wife's handbag like his life depended on it. Perhaps that's what these Dallimores needed, a little fluffy unicorn to soften their hard points.

"I'm so glad Rhys has found you," Elin said, stepping

closer to Lila. "We're not the dragons that he likes to make out. Well, I'm not, at least."

"Oh, um," Lila said. What could she say to that? *Oh yes, Rhys is so stressed out about seeing you all that he's enlisted me as a fake girlfriend.*

"Elin, you're making Lila uncomfortable," Rhys said smoothly, stepping closer, pressing against her.

"Oh, you worry too much, big brother," Elin rolled her eyes. "No, in all seriousness, regardless of what he's told you, I love him. I miss him. I'm so proud of him for standing up for himself, doing what he wants to do. And now he has you as well, and you both look so happy."

A lopsided smile tugged at the corner of Elin's mouth as she looked between them.

"In fact, I don't think I've ever seen Rhys with that sparkle in his eye."

"Elin," Rhys said, pulling at his collar.

Something caught Elin's eye behind her. "James, can you see Madoc?" Elin asked, craning her neck. "He's over there talking to dad and Rhydian."

"Is Rhydian your uncle?" Lila asked.

"Yes, and Madoc his son, our cousin," Elin said, eyes on the cluster of men on the other side of the room. "He's probably plotting my downfall, trying to get on Dad's good side so I'll be cut out of the Spanish merger."

Elin spared a sardonic smile for Rhys.

"Seriously big brother, thanks for taking yourself out of the equation. I can deal with Madoc, you taught me well."

She swept away, only turning to give James a nod as if to say 'you're coming' and for him to follow.

Lila smothered a laugh.

"Poor James."

"Nah, he loves it. He loves her," Rhys said with a grin. "Oh, and uh, just so you know, Seren is on her way over."

"Seren your ex?" Lila whispered with a nervous smile.

"Yes, apparently everyone wants to meet my girlfriend."
Rhys smiled back at her and linked his fingers with hers.

"Rhys, hello."

"Seren, how are you?"

Rhys performed the introductions, and *wow*. How would anyone believe that Rhys had gone from this absolutely stunning woman to dowdy old her, probably with something stuck in her teeth. Because Seren was *perfect*. Hair, poise, face, figure. All perfect. She was sleek and elegant, petite and lithe and Lila's face grew warm at her own inadequacy. Especially when Seren ran her assessing gaze over every inch of her.

"It's lovely to meet you," she said, her honey voice low and smooth.

"Yes," Lila managed to squeak out, "and you."

"Rhys, you're looking terribly well," Seren said, stepping ever so slightly too close to him.

Uh, no thank you, back off lady. Lila shifted in her heels and Rhys moved with her, because she was gripping his arm tighter than the Spanx she was wearing. Seren's eyes flicked to her.

"Your new life suits you," she said, almost wistfully.

"Yes, Seren. It does," Rhys said with a satisfied smile and a quick glance down at Lila. Gosh, Rhys was good at this fake girlfriend/boyfriend stuff.

"I'll catch up with you another time," she said, giving them both a warm smile, before gliding away. Yes, she *glided*.

"She won't," Rhys murmured. "I've got absolutely no desire to catch up with her."

Lila watched as Seren started to look back over her shoulder and jumped into action. She had to hold up her part of this bargain. Shifting towards Rhys, she put both hands on his chest, smiling up at him. Rhys's hands fell to her hips, tightened ever so slightly, and pulled her flush against him.

Yep, flush against him. Body to body. She could feel *everything*. Every flex of muscle, every shallow breath. Every. Single. Thing.

"She's looking," Lila whispered, by way of explanation.

"I don't care," he whispered back.

A giggle escaped Lila's throat, but glancing up, she could see that he wasn't joking. Not in the slightest. He was looking down at her, earnestly, a slight pink flush creeping above the collar of his pristine shirt.

Something shifted between them. Something hot and deliberate uncoiled itself low in her belly and she became so *aware* of every stitch of fabric on her skin, of how it pressed into her where Rhys's hands held her possessively.

Breaking eye contact with Rhys, she focused on his bow tie, tugging at it gently, even though it was already straight.

Seren the supermodel. Elin the powerhouse businesswoman. Cerys the commander of the room. And her, Lila, a little goldfish, who felt like she was dressing up in Jasmeet's clothes. Let's face it, Rhys couldn't even bring himself to tell her she looked nice.

Lila let out a sigh.

"What?" Rhys asked, squeezing her hips gently.

Lila pasted a smile on her face. Tonight was about Rhys, not her, so she would put all that aside and wallow in ice cream tomorrow.

"Nothing."

RHYS

It was going extremely well. Rhys had managed to avoid his father at all costs, avoided his uncle Rhydian and his insipid cousin Madoc.

His mother was overjoyed that he was there. Elin had been excellent. James had been, well, James.

It was all down to Lila, he knew it was. Lila, with her perfect dress, secret smiles, and unwavering support next to him, was literally propping him up.

Pulling her against him had been a mistake but he couldn't help it. A mistake because his dick didn't realise that was as much as he was going to get and was making its displeasure known by being particularly troublesome in his tight-fitting tux trousers. They were just a fraction *too* tight.

"Here," Rhys said, as he refilled Lila's water glass. They were sat at the ridiculous round table, filled with low glass vases overflowing with pink and white flowers. His mother must have thought they were at a society wedding, because the white covered chairs and gauzy bows were just too much.

"Thanks," Lila took a sip. "Everything okay?"

"Everything is perfect, Lila," he said, shuffling his chair closer to hers. He rested his arm across the back of her chair, just like he had on that first night he had pretended to be her boyfriend, and rested his leg against hers.

"Is this okay?" he whispered, leaning towards her.

"You're my boyfriend, Rhys," she said, with a tight laugh. "Of course it's okay."

Rhys frowned. Okay, there was definitely something going on with her. Shit, he'd been too forward, all but dry humping her in the middle of this stupid hotel function room (no matter what his mother said, it was *not* a ballroom). He went to move his arm, not wanting her to feel uncomfortable.

"No, no, Rhys," she said, putting a hand on his thigh, causing a soft heat to build up in the pit of his stomach. "I'm sorry, it's absolutely fine. Of course it is."

"Is everything okay, Lila?" he asked. "Are you all right?"

If she wasn't, he would take her home right now, family be damned.

She bumped him with her shoulder.

"I'm fine, Rhys."

"Shit, you've got—" There was a piece of hair snagged under the one strap of her dress, "hang on."

Rhys carefully pulled it out, his fingers gently grazing the curve of her shoulder, raising goosebumps on her skin.

"*Pwy wyt ti*?" *Who are you?*

Fuck.

The table went silent as Llewellyn Dallimore's voice boomed across it. Rhys breathed an "I'm sorry" before straightening up to face his father. The rest of the table was silent, his mother picking at the tablecloth in front of her. Elin took a long drag of her drink.

"Dad, this is Lila," Rhys said. "My girlfriend."

His hand tightened around her shoulders.

"Hello, nice to meet you," Lila said with a bright smile.

"*Saesneg?*" English.

"Dad," Rhys said, a warning clear in his voice, at the same time as Lila spoke.

"I'm afraid I don't know any Welsh except, now let me get this right," she said, taking a breath. "*Cymru yw gwlad y dreigiau a Tom Jones.*"

Wales is the land of dragons and Tom Jones.

"You learned that?" Rhys asked, gobsmacked. Welsh was *hard*, there were no rules, no vowels, lots of sounds that just weren't there in English.

The table fell silent. This could go one of two ways. Either his father could laugh and all would be well with the world, or he would be upset at the absolute mangling of his beloved language.

"I've been practicing all week. Did I say it right?"

Those big blue eyes looked up at him, and even if she had said *Wales is the land of sheep and shit*, he would have been fucking impressed that she'd taken the time to learn it.

"We got the gist of it," he said with a genuine, wide smile.

Llewellyn Dallimore threw back his head and laughed, a big, belly laugh that shook the table, shook the room. Fuck, it must have shaken the entire building.

"Well, shit," Elin said. "Colour me impressed."

"Language," his mother chastised.

"Where did you learn that, my girl?" his father asked. "Lila, is it?"

Well. His father had managed to both call her a term of endearment, *and* her actual name in one breath.

She nodded.

"Google translate. I was worried that it wasn't right? It's really hard to find a sentence that didn't involve spitting or hawking spit or..." Lila was saying. "Why is Welsh so spitty?"

"I think we can all agree it is the effort that counts," he said, with a sparkle in his eye. This was the father he wanted. The one that was proud of his son, that wanted the best for him. Not the bitter, angry old man who wanted an exact replica of himself; a power hungry, money-grabbing robot.

Rhys couldn't be that anymore, and he didn't want to be.

"Right, Rhys? It's the effort that counts," his father said pointedly, his smile turning downwards as he looked at his son across the flower arrangements.

"Yes," Rhys said coldly. "The effort, indeed."

"Speaking of effort." His father placed the glass of whiskey down on the table. Rhys had learned at a young age that his father didn't actually like whiskey, but he felt it made him look distinguished. "How is *your* effort going, *bach*?" *Boy.*

Now, whilst 'my girl' or 'my boy' was a term of endearment, 'boy' by itself was most definitely not. Especially the way his father spat it at him, attempting to make him small and meek.

"My *effort,* as you so correctly put it, is going extremely well," Rhys said.

"Hmm," his father waited for Rhys to fill the silence, but he knew this trick. He just waited, keeping his face blank, serene, unbothered. Lila's hand pressed on his leg, stopping it from bouncing uncontrollably. "When can I expect an update? You don't have long left."

A not so veiled threat that if his Fellowship application was rejected, he was due back at Dallimore Headquarters to fall into the bleak corporate void and lose every part of himself that he had worked so desperately hard to find.

"Soon," Rhys said.

"I'm ever so proud of him," Lila interrupted, throwing

him a warm smile. "It's such an achievement to even apply for Fellowship at the Royal Historical Society. Especially considering Rhys is so young."

"Young?" his father challenged with a sneer. "He's not young. He's over thirty. I'd made my first million by twenty-five."

Rhys's shoulders tensed. No matter what he did, he hadn't made his first million by twenty-five and therefore he was a failure. He would never make a million, not unless he sold his shares in Dallimores. Frankly, he was happy *not* making a million. That was absolutely fine by him. As long as he could spend his days tucked in the library, working out the motives of people who were long dead, wondering about the logistics of moving an entire household so many thousands of miles, then he was happy.

"Gosh, that's impressive. But I meant in academic terms," Lila said. "Thirty is young in our world and many people don't even have the capacity to apply for a Fellowship, let alone actually be accepted. Did you know there are only twelve applications accepted each year? You have to apply to apply. It's ridiculously competitive." She looked up at him. "I've never seen anyone work harder than Rhys. Even if he doesn't get the Fellowship this year, I'll still be incredibly proud of him."

Emotion clogged his throat. Lila didn't have it in her to lie, so those words of pride, of support, were real and true. He reached blindly for her hand under the table and held on to her tightly.

LILA

The death grip he had on her was beginning to make her fingers numb.

"Rhys, you're crushing my hand," Lila whispered as the

plates were cleared. Rhys had only let go of her to eat and then had greedily reached for her again, interlocking their fingers on full display for his entire family. He loosened his hand, but didn't let go.

"So Lila, you're a lecturer too?" James asked, leisurely leaning back in his chair.

"James," Elin said, patting his arm. "She's the Departmental Coordinator."

"I manage all the lecturers. They wouldn't know how to tie their shoes without me," she told James with a smile.

"You need a woman to tie your shoes?" Llewellyn put in.

How rude was he? Firstly, interrupting a conversation between her and James, and then insinuating... well, she didn't quite know what he was insinuating, but it didn't feel good.

"I need Lila to do a lot more than that, Dad," Rhys quipped, raising his glass of water to his lips.

Oh. My. God.

Elin nearly choked on her drink.

"Rhys," she hissed, but her fake boyfriend just smirked and raised his eyebrow.

What in the blessed Countdown Conundrum was that? Because whatever it was, it made her insides melt and her mouth fall open. A little eyebrow quirk made her clench her thighs together in need? For *Rhys Aubrey*? Apparently so.

"Oh yeah? Do you have quite a large job description?" James asked from beside her, completely oblivious and innocent. What a pure, naive little penguin.

"Oh, shut up, James," Elin said, with a snort.

Llewellyn stood and held his hand out to his wife, looking around the room with his eyebrows drawn together in a frown so much like Rhys's. His big frame bristled with importance. Rhys was a perfect mix between his fine-boned mother and the air of authority exuded by Llewellyn Dallimore. They had disappeared to 'work the room', and the tables were being cleared and the lighting dimmed. A string quintet set themselves up in the corner as Rhys leaned close to her.

"I'd like to dance with you," he said, his warm breath ghosting across her cheek.

That was a no. Firstly, she could not trust herself in the heels that had been strapped to her feet, and secondly, she couldn't trust herself pressed up close to Rhys Aubrey.

This was an arrangement. This was fake. Yes, they had to make it convincing, she supposed, but that didn't mean that she had to put herself in a position to... what? Have him bend her over the nearest chair and give her a jolly good seeing-to?

Well, that was a picture she couldn't seem to shake out of her mind and it was making her extremely warm. It had been quite a while since she'd had an orgasm that wasn't by her fingers or her trusty bedside drawer friends.

"No, I don't think dancing would be a good idea," she said slowly, "what with my ankle and all."

"Is it hurting?" he asked with a frown.

"No, it's just," Lila looked to the ceiling for inspiration, "I'll show you up."

"Okay," he said with a smile. "Let's get a drink."

"Do you reckon they'll have non-alcoholic sparkling? I don't want any more champagne," she said.

Lila did want more champagne (who said no to expensive champagne), but more champagne would lead to reckless decisions.

"Probably, let's find out," he said, slipping an arm around her waist and guiding her to the bar.

"You're not bad at this, you know," she said.

"At what?" He glanced at her as he manoeuvred them through the crowd to the bar.

"At being a boyfriend," she said, wincing. This was one of the times where she wished she thought before spouting nonsense.

"You're enjoying me being your boyfriend," he said with a coy look at her. Statement, not question.

"That's not what I said. But it is... a nice evening."

Lila leaned against the bar and did not, whatsoever, look at Rhys. But she did spot his grin out of the corner of her eye.

"You *are*," he accused. "You're enjoying me being your boyfriend."

"Oh for God's sake, Rhys," she said, accepting a non-alcoholic sparkling wine from the bar staff.

But he was still waiting for a reply, his smile tucked just under the surface.

"Okay, fine," she said, with an eye roll. "I'm having a good time."

Rhys took a small step closer and grazed his fingers over her bare shoulder. She willed herself not to react, or throw herself at him. Either one.

"Surprisingly, I am also having a good time," he said, voice low.

"Oh, well thanks. That's a compliment I'll pop in my memory book," she said, trying to lighten the mood.

"No, that's not what I meant," he said quickly. "I meant I was surprised because I didn't think I would have a good time here, with my family. Not about enjoying my time with you."

"I know what you meant, Rhys," she said. "I was teasing."

The intensity in his gaze struck her, and he shook his head slightly, his shoulders sagging.

"I thought I was getting better at reading you. I'm not, though, am I?"

"Oh Rhys, I'm sorry. I didn't mean to make you feel bad," she said, putting a hand on his sleeve. "I was only joking."

He made a noise in the back of his throat.

"I think you do a pretty good job actually. You're doing a good job at being a very..." What was the word she was looking for? "...attentive boyfriend. And I am having a good time."

"Are you sure? I know you're only here because of our deal, but I do want you to have a good time and if you want to leave, you can," he said solemnly.

Her heart throbbed for him because he was so earnest, so delightfully focused on her. Probably because if he focused on her, then he wouldn't have to focus on his family.

"Rhys, I wouldn't leave you here," she said, her voice a little unsteady. The hazel of his eyes flared brightly and he angled himself closer towards her.

She wouldn't. He'd made the massive, life-changing decision to leave his family business and his father never let him forget it.

"I hate this stuff," he whispered. "All the flowers, the mingling, the stupid networking. Look." He nodded over her shoulder at Elin, with James holding her handbag close behind, talking with a group of older men, turning her shoulder so his cousin Madoc couldn't get into the Circle of Trust.

"I just don't get it." His eyebrows raised in question. "Who would want to spend their time cultivating other people to get ahead in a dull and dreary business? All that politicking, manipulating, trying to work out what people want and how to exploit that for your own means." Rhys shook his head. "It's much easier to discern motivation when all bits of the puzzle are there in front of you. It's why I like history. I can see it all. You can track motivation, see what changes someone's personality. Understand why people changed their minds about things. It's all there, it's all documented. You've just got to look hard enough."

Rhys's eyes wandered over the crowds.

"You've got time to work it all out, no pressure to make snap decisions on what someone wants. Helps that the Angevin period is a bit Game of Thrones-y."

Rhys's mouth twisted into a wry smile and he lifted one shoulder in a shrug. That was a lot of admitting that he'd just done, a lot of introspection that he didn't have to share with her, but he had.

"Are you happy?" she asked.

"At work? Or now?"

"At work. Do you regret leaving Dallimores?"

"No. I don't regret it one little bit," he said, eyes not leaving hers. "I'm feeling the pressure now. I have to get that Fellowship, otherwise I'll have to go back."

"Why?" Lila asked. "You're a grown-up. You're self-sufficient. Even if you don't get the Fellowship, why do you have to give up everything you've worked for?"

Rhys gritted his teeth.

"I'm sorry," she hurried to say. "I didn't mean to overstep. It's just you seem truly terrified of having to do all *this* again."

"I am."

"So, don't," she whispered.

This poor man, weighed down by the expectations of his high-flying, ridiculously wealthy family. Scorned for wanting his life to go in a direction different to the one already mapped out for him. Ridiculed for wanting to do something that he loved. Even if she didn't understand his love for dusty old medieval kings, Lila could see the hot passion in his eyes when he told her of John's military disasters, or William Marshal's cross-channel land holdings, or the beauty of Henry II's Orford Castle (circular on the inside, hexagonal on the outside. Apparently).

Rhys was a dictionary torn down the middle, with a rosemary and garlic focaccia of interesting adjectives on one side, and the supermarket wholemeal sliced bread of boring conjunctions on the other.

Lila wound her arms around his neck and slowly pulled him into a tight hug. Solid arms slid around her waist and he inhaled deeply against her neck. Okay, that was enough, because if she didn't let him go now, then she never would, because this hug was *everything*.

It was warm and secure, but as his nose slid down her neck, she felt a coil heat in her belly. There was no denying her attraction to Rhys, with his delicious eyes and broad shoulders that she fit so snugly into.

But this was just the deal. She was his 'girlfriend' and this was what girlfriends and boyfriends did. Although that fuzzy little bumblebee buzzing at the back of her mind said that Rhys couldn't possibly be that good an actor.

Hang on. The last thing she wanted, or needed, was a real relationship. A messy, difficult, highly-strung man who put way too much stress on himself was not something she needed in her life.

CHAPTER 11

Imbroglio *(noun) im·bro·glio*
1. An acutely painful or embarrassing situation

RHYS

Fuck.

He could not hug this woman anymore. Well, he could, and do a lot more with her, make her moan and whimper and scream his name. That's very *patently* what his body wanted and it was overriding his brain, because why on earth would he bury his face in the softness of her neck, or encourage her hips towards his, moulding her curves to his frame?

This was *not* a date. This was not a *relationship*.

This was a deal, a bargain. Two people helping each other. He had been her fake boyfriend for the ditchwater equivalent of a person (Jason), and she was here being his girlfriend for his family to show them how much of a success he was.

But it had become more than that. He hadn't quite intended to bare his soul, just tell her the bare minimum so she could get by. But no, his stupid mouth had other ideas because this woman in his arms made him feel so damned comfortable, so accepted, that it was easy to let all his tension and stresses go.

His emotions (and for that matter, his dick) hadn't been this difficult to control since he was a teenager.

Rhys was glad when his uncle, Daffydd, interrupted when he did because otherwise it would be painfully obvious to everyone exactly where all the blood in his body was heading, especially in these stupid trousers.

He really needed to measure himself and update the website. Perhaps Lila would help? No, that was not the thing to be thinking about right now.

"Get a room you two" came a loud and rather slurred voice from over Rhys's shoulder and he quickly disentangled himself from Lila.

"Fuck. Sorry," he said. Whether he was apologising for nearly mauling her, or for whatever was going to come out of Uncle Daff's mouth now, he wasn't entirely sure.

"Daffydd, nice to see you," he said, holding out his hand.

"*Rydyn ni'n deulu,* we're family, Rhys!" Daff batted away his arm and pulled him in for a sloppy, swaying hug. Pulling away, his uncle went to hug Lila, but Rhys put a hand on his chest.

"No, Daff," he said with a smile. "No hugging my girlfriend." It slipped out of his mouth so easily.

It wasn't that Daff was handsy or whatever, but Lila hadn't even said hello and this epitome of the 'Drunk Uncle' wanted a hug? Nope.

"Of course, and you're *Saesneg*, aren't you?"

"Yes, I am," she said with a smile.

Rhys was getting used to deciphering the many nuances of Lila's smiles and this one was indulgent and amused. If it was strained and wary, then he would have turned her right around out of that situation and taken her home to her comfortable sofa, her myriad of blankets and whichever insipid old romance she wanted to watch.

"Ah well, *cariad*, you two make a lovely couple," Daffyd said, sloshing amber liquid around his glass. He was decidedly worse for wear, his eyes not quite pointing in the same direction, his bow tie crumpled and his face ruddy, but he was happy and smiling.

Daffydd had aways been his favourite uncle. It was Daff who Rhys called when he missed the last train home from nights out in Cardiff. It was Daff who made sure he had a much more in-depth sex talk than the perfunctory one his dad gave him. Daffydd was the one he called, overwhelmed with emotions, when he didn't want to work at Dallimores anymore and wanted to be a historian.

"What you should do, my boy," Daff said, his pointing finger swaying slightly, "is give your beautiful girlfriend a kiss."

Daff knowingly winked at Lila, a ridiculous, over-exaggerated wink that Betty Boop would have been jealous of.

"Daff," he warned.

"What?" Daffydd shrugged, mock hurt. "I'm just saying, 'young love'."

Yes, air quotes from his pisshead of an uncle.

"Daff, I'm not going to—" he started, but Lila interrupted.

"Oh, Rhys," she admonished, with a swat on his arm. Then, turning to Daffydd, "He's so shy."

Grabbing both his lapels, Lila turned her face up to his and tugged him down towards her. The softness of her lips pressed against his and she leaned into him. His hands snaked around her hips, pressing her harder to him. It was chaste and hot, and Lila's hands flattened against his chest, aligning herself to him just right,

"All right now, you two! Break it up!" Daff crowed.

Lila pulled back, blinking, but he wasn't ready to stop, and greedily pressed his lips to hers again for another fleeting kiss.

She looked up at him, her big ocean eyes unsure and confused. That was a look that he would have to decipher later because Daff was laughing loudly and slapping him on the back. She wet her lips, as if seeing if she could still taste him and fuck, that was hot.

"Happy now?" He turned to his uncle, but pulled Lila tightly to his side.

"Yes, I am," Daff took a large gulp of his drink. "Seriously though, my boy, I don't think I've ever seen you look so happy."

Smiling, Daff squeezed his shoulder.

"You seem to be very content in your job and you've got this wonderful girlfriend who obviously adores you."

Lila rested one hand on his lower back and the other on his chest, folding herself around him. His breath caught. As he glanced down at her to check she was all right (because Daff was being *way* too much, as he always was), she smiled up at him warmly. A smile that said she was fine, she didn't mind, before turning back to Daffydd.

"Well done, my boy. I'm proud of you," he said, eyes warm and wistful. He shook his head lightly and looked at his drink. "Oops, glass is empty! *Wela'i di wedyn.*" *See you later.*

Daff sauntered off, presumably to the bar to replenish.

"Oh my God, I'm so sorry, Rhys," she said, pressing her hand to her mouth. "I shouldn't have, I didn't mean to…" she trailed off.

He frowned at her. What had he missed?

"Shouldn't have what?"

Lila stared up at him with wide eyes, as if the police had come in and arrested everyone and he was blissfully unaware.

"I shouldn't have kissed you," she whispered, her cheeks the most beautiful shade of fuchsia.

Rhys grinned, remembering the way she wet her lips to taste him again.

"You never need to apologise for kissing me."

Lila eyes widened and a long breath escaped her lips. She swallowed, and took a small step back. Rhys's hand dropped from her waist. This was a show, a pretence, and he didn't need to be pawing her every second. He played with his shirt cuffs for something to do.

"Do you think we were convincing?" she asked.

Fuck yes. He more than thought so, he *knew* so.

"I think so." He nodded.

"He's really nice," Lila said, gesturing towards Daff.

"Yeah, he is."

Rhys took in the room, the relentless networking and handshaking his family did. They were all the same; always looking for the next opportunity, uncaring about who they stepped on to get higher up their greasy little ladder. He loved Elin, but there she was with their father and Rhydian, probably throwing Madoc under the bus, whilst Madoc scowled from the other side of the room, talking with a new COO of some division or other.

Daffydd's business circles were smaller, having decided early on that he would be a more silent partner in the brothers' business. That wasn't to say that his division of Dallimore International, Dallimore Shipping, wasn't successful. Daffydd was extremely good at reading people and had hired a very capable CEO and management team.

"He's the best one. I love him."

"Never married? No kids?" Lila shifted on her heels.

"No, never married. No children."

Rhys took a breath. Daffydd's wasn't his story to tell, but it felt so good to be able to talk about his family. He'd spent so long keeping it all bottled up inside, afraid that people would find out who he was and judge him, only want him for his money, that he didn't realise how much of a relief it would be to finally talk to someone.

"He's gay," Rhys blurted out. "He told me when he was drunk once. I tried to bring it up again, but he didn't want to speak about it. I don't think he's ever told my dad and my other uncle. I think that's why he drinks so much."

"That's why he's so keen on you living your own life."

"Yeah, I guess it is." He had never connected the two before.

"That's really sad," Lila said, with an uncharacteristic crease in between her eyebrows. "Your uncle living his life in hiding, not thinking he'll be accepted for who he is."

Rhys nodded slowly.

It was a different generation. A hard generation with

remnants of mining and striking in the South Welsh valleys. The Aubrey-Dallimores were nothing if not traditional, and Daffydd didn't quite fit the traditional mould.

"Do you think your father knows?"

Rhys considered how his father would react to the news his brother was gay. The hope was that he would nod and say 'all right, when can I meet your partner?' because Uncle Daff's sexuality really was a non-issue.

"I think he does, if he thought about it hard enough. But I don't think he will ever want to do that."

"Poor Daffydd."

Yes, poor Daffydd.

LILA

Lila reapplied her pink lipstick in the bathroom mirror, thankful that her excruciating blush had finally died down.

Grabbing Rhys by the lapels and kissing him had seemed like a good idea at the time, but now? In the cold fluorescent lights of the ladies toilet? Not so much. They hadn't ever discussed kissing or anything like that. She'd taken matters into her own hands and just run with it. But with closed lips. Not even the hint of tongue. That fact alone saved her embarrassment ever so slightly.

But...

Rhys had kissed her again. Rhys had leaned forward and put his lips on hers. He had instigated it, it wasn't just her. He'd also looked genuinely wicked when she'd apologised.

You never need to apologise for kissing me.

Even just the memory of his intense eyes, solely on her, made her hot and needy.

They'd both played this fake girlfriend/boyfriend thing excellently.

After tonight, that would be it. There would be no more

lunches, shopping, hanging out, car journeys. There would be no need. This was the end of their bargain. She could put that pesky desire in a non-existent basket, cover it with offcuts of fabric and it would eventually fade away to nothing. Which was exactly the right thing to do.

That bratty little word '*but*' kept pushing at her brain.

But... she would miss spending time with Rhys. She liked the simpleness of him, the straightforwardness. He said what he meant and did what he said.

It had also been an awfully long time since she'd had sex.

Rhys was attracted to her, wasn't he? He'd kissed her that second time. It was the way he always seemed to reach for her, as if he couldn't stop touching her back, her waist, her hands. The way his eyes had darkened when he talked to her, the not so subtle glances towards her lips, the way his eyes tripped across her collarbone.

Lila had been around long enough to know the signs.

Perhaps a no-strings-attached roll in the hay (*I wonder where that saying came from?*) would be the perfect way to end their bargain. Then they could go back to only seeing each other at work, in passing. Rhys would be finished with his course soon. He wouldn't be holding seminars in her room forever.

The thought of having sex with *Rhys Aubrey* made her mouth dry. Yes, okay. Good.

A waft of perfume came through the bathroom door and Seren glided in as if she were on rollers. When her eyes met Lila's in the mirror, she tilted her head and altered her trajectory, rolling to a stop next to her.

"Why, hello. Lila, isn't it?" Seren's voice was smooth and honeylike, and she exuded confidence in the way of someone who has never been told 'no' in their life.

"Yes," she said, trying to hide the shake in her voice. She was strangely nervous, being with the ex-girlfriend without Rhys as a buffer. "Hi."

"Your dress is nice," Seren said, giving it the once-over.

"Thank you," Lila said, with a grateful smile. She was going to leave it at that, but she'd had some bubbles and before she knew it, her mouth was open and words were just falling out. "You look like a princess."

It was true. With her delicate tiara (yes, *tiara*), matching diamond necklace and white satin dress that skimmed her body, pooling on the floor, she did indeed look like a princess.

A small smile accompanied a slight eyebrow lift, as if Seren was scared to make too many facial moments in case they ruined her Botox or gave her wrinkles.

"I'm going to give you a piece of advice," she said, turning to the mirror to assess her make up.

Perhaps it would be something trivial like, 'make sure you have that drycleaned rather than put it in the washing machine', or 'you should really wear the Chanel eye shadow'. What she did *not* want was advice on her fake boyfriend or his family.

"No, no, that's okay. You don't have to," Lila said.

Seren ignored her.

"Please remember that *this* is Rhys's world, whether he wants it to be or not. He *will* end up back with his family. No matter how much he rebels, he will come back or be dragged back. And when he does, will he bring you with him?"

Was that a challenge in Seren's eyes? It was hard to tell when her face was so blank and motionless. The old Black and White Lila would have bowed her head, curved her shoulders inwards and nodded softly. But she was Technicolour Lila now, with a couple of glasses of champagne in her.

"Is that what you think he's doing? Rebelling, like a child? He's a grown man, Seren," she said. "I don't know what the future holds for him, for *us*, but I trust Rhys to make the right decisions for *him*. The Rhys I know isn't easily bullied."

"You don't know Llewellyn." Her perfect lips pursed. "I'm not your enemy here, Lila. In fact, I've never seen him so happy. I'm glad someone got through to him." Seren turned back to Lila and offered her a tight smile. "Anyway."

Then she wafted into a cubicle.

Lila stared at the closed cubicle door for a second or two. That was a healthy reality check Seren had just dropped, and she didn't have the brain power to think about it right now.

Instead, she grabbed her clutch bag from the side and headed out to meet Rhys, giving her best 'Seren walk' a go.

Oh Christ.

He was leaning by the main door, hands tucked into those tight trousers, bow tie loosened, looking just like frigging James Bond. A hot one, not that one in Her Majesty's Secret Service. Except instead of the trademarked sexy smirk James Bond usually wore, he was frowning in confusion.

"Why are you walking like that? Do your feet hurt?"

"I was *trying* to walk like Seren,"

"Why?"

"She's so elegant and perfect."

"That she may be," Rhys said, shrugging out of his jacket. "But I prefer someone a bit messier."

Rhys swung his jacket over her shoulders, tugging at the lapels to make sure it sat straight. A flash of a frown smudged his eyebrows as he reached to tuck a wayward lock of hair behind her ear. As his fingers grazed her cheek, her lips parted and a puff of air escaped. They were close enough that one deep breath would have her against his chest.

"Come on," he said, his voice a little rough. "Let's go."

Rhys intertwined their fingers and led her outside.

The car drive home was… anticipatory. Rhys didn't let go of her hand, except to change gear, and then took it again, running his thumb over her knuckles, circling the softness of her palm. It was like he couldn't stand to let her go.

This boded well, because Technicolour Lila had decided that tonight was indeed the night, and she was going to invite him in and get down and dirty with Rhys Aubrey.

"Come in for a moment," Lila said, as he walked her the

five and a half steps to her door. She squeezed his fingers that had conveniently found hers.

Rhys followed her into the front room and she deposited her handbag on the table and reached to unbuckle her shoes.

"Let me," Rhys said.

He dropped to his knees in front of her and looked up expectantly. That warmth in the bottom of her belly that had been present all night, expanded and heated. Because he was on his knees for her, and her mind was doing all kinds of filthy things.

"Oh, yeah," Lila hoicked up her skirt rather ungracefully.

Rhys carefully unbuckled one shoe, slipped it off her foot and motioned for her to lift the other.

"Lila," he said, eyes focused on his task.

"Hmm?" she didn't trust her words. The tips of his ears were pink.

"You were perfect tonight," he said, depositing the other shoe by the first and standing in front of her. "Absolutely perfect."

A soft smile tilted her lips. She reached for his hands, and linked their fingers together. His lips parted and she lifted her face towards his, pulling him gently closer.

"Lila," he whispered when his mouth was scarcely a breath from hers. "You are so beautiful."

She thought of all the times when he was going to say how she looked earlier, he couldn't get his words out.

He thought she was beautiful.

Pushing up on her toes, she kissed him.

It wasn't soft and chaste like before. No, she pressed her body against his and his arms went around her tightly. Her hands found their way into his hair and he staggered slightly, pushing her back against the table. A pile of books toppled somewhere, but she didn't care. He opened his mouth and it was wet and hot and she couldn't get enough. He hitched her up onto the table, running his hand from her ankle, pushing up the skirt of her dress as he gripped the soft underside of her thigh, the same thigh that had magically wrapped its way around his hip.

She could feel him hard and straining and she ground against him, trying to get some friction where she needed it most. Because she was needy and desperate. The evening had been one of tantalising looks and touches and now she was being thoroughly seduced.

Rhys's tongue was in her mouth, caressing and taking and her nipples pushed against the fabric of her dress.

She reached for his trousers and undid the button quickly. Slipping her hand inside, she gripped him outside his boxers and he groaned into her mouth. She ran her hand up and down his length. The noise he made in the back of his throat had her smiling against his lips. She had her fingers under the waistband of his pants when he grasped her wrist, stilling her.

He eased her hand out of his trousers and took a small step back, adjusting his hardness in his pants.

"Are you okay?"

"I, I don't," he started, gulping a breath. "I don't want—"

Holy fuck.

She scrambled her skirt down. She'd read this completely, utterly, devastatingly wrong.

"Oh, right. Yeah," she said, pushing her hair back from her face with both hands and shuffling off the edge of the table. "Yeah, no, of course."

She was just saying words now, words that didn't make any sense.

"I just think—" he started.

"Yep, yes. I get it," she said, blowing out a hard breath.

She was hot and tingly all over and *not* in a good way. In the absolutely mortified, 'wish she could change into a squirrel like Mad Madam Mim in *Sword in the Stone* and disappear up a tree forever' kind of way.

"No, not that I don't—"

"Please Rhys, stop talking," she said, not meeting his eyes. "You're making it worse."

"Lila, can I just—"

"You should probably go."

Lila walked carefully over to the front door (it would *not* do to trip now) and held it open.

"Lila," he tried again. How was he not getting the idea here?

"Goodnight, Rhys," she said firmly and when he finally, reluctantly made his way outside, she closed the door firmly behind him.

The embarrassment was so strong that not even Kevin Costner and Christian Slater (and, of course, Brian Blessed) in *Robin Hood, Prince of Thieves* could dull it. After a fitful sleep, and not one, but two, bacon sandwiches this morning, Lila rushed around big Sainsbury's getting her groceries for the week.

No one knew that she had been rejected last night, how could they? But she felt it was written across her forehead. 'NOT GOOD ENOUGH TO SLEEP WITH'. Because that's what it was, wasn't it? She wasn't good enough, he didn't like her enough, it was all an act and he had been damned good at it.

Just so people don't think I spent the night with you. He'd said it when he'd stayed over after the hospital and here she was, thinking that all the touching, the handholding, that *kiss* meant there was… what? Something more? Well. Obviously not.

Tears had pricked at her eyes in the washing powder aisle when she couldn't find the Fairy Non-Bio for Sensitive Skin because they'd rearranged the bloody supermarket. Why weren't things simple anymore?

It was now three o'clock and she'd eaten her bodyweight in chicken nuggets and was well into a pint of ice cream. Her knitting lay on the floor because she kept dropping stitches. She'd messed up her cross stitch and did not have the patience for crystal painting, and certainly could not concentrate on Susie Dent's latest novel (which, by the way, was amazing).

Restless, that's what she was. Yes, restless. If she were the exercise-y type, she'd go for a run, or to the gym, or... whatever else exercise-y people did.

Rhys hadn't texted and she absolutely refused to text him. Absolutely. He had made it incredibly clear where he stood, and it was not next to her. She'd gotten too carried away with the evening, the hand-holding, the longing looks. The kiss. The kiss*es*, plural.

Checking her phone for the millionth time, Lila sighed. Neither Jasmeet nor Maddy had texted her and they knew it was Rhys's thing last night. The least they could have done was asked how it went. She always remembered their stuff. But she couldn't take it out on them, this was just the hot burn of rejection talking. Her friends loved her, they just had their own lives.

What she should do is channel some of this anxious, embarrassed energy into something beneficial and stop stressing about what she was going to do tomorrow when she saw him at work. Oh God, work. She could call in sick, but then she'd have to lie to Sue and she was terrible at lying. And he'd know she wasn't sick. He'd know she was avoiding him.

A plan of action was required for dealing with Rhys Aubrey-Dallimore tomorrow. A plan of action that she must *not* deviate from. There was no reason why seminars had to be held in her office anymore. If he finished the last module of his course by Wednesday morning (which he should), then seminars could go back into his own room. There was no *need* for her to have direct interaction with Rhys, and she would be professional and helpful as always. But by email. Not face to face. Impersonal, digitally sanitised email.

Channelling her energy into something vaguely productive, Lila sat on the floor and sorted out her wool basket, throwing away scraps and balling up strands that were long enough. It took her nearly forty minutes to become frustrated with the rats nest of wool that was tangled at the bottom of the basket. She shoved it all back together and practically threw the basket under the table. It bashed the table leg and the whole thing juddered, papers falling to the floor.

Lila let out a frustrated groan. Could *nothing* go right today?

Scooping up the paperwork, she recognised her loan statement. Well, it wasn't *her* loan statement, was it? It was Jason's. Or, charitably, it was *theirs*.

She gripped the paper tightly in her fingers, crumpling the edges. It was high time that Jason paid his own frigging way.

Grabbing her phone before she lost her nerve or talked herself out of it, she scrolled to Jason's number and tapped the green button.

He answered on the third ring, and there was the sound of a door closing behind him. She'd bet anything that he was with Leanne and then scarpered quickly to answer the phone. What a dick.

"Hey Li, are you okay? Is everything all right?" His pathetic attempt at concern really pissed her off.

"I'm fine, Jason. I'm calling to let you know that the loan that *you* took out when we were together is nearly paid off. You owe me half of it, Jason. I'll take a lump sum payment. I'll text you the details."

Standing up for herself was terrifying and thrilling, and well overdue.

"What? Lila, what's wrong? Do you need money? Are you short of cash?" Jason said, and she could imagine him pushing his stupid floppy hair out of his face.

"No, I'm not short of cash," she said, balling up the statement. "But you took that loan out in our joint names and I have been paying it. Now I'm asking for you to pay half of it. Which is fair."

More than frigging fair.

There was a silence at the end of the line. Perhaps he was in shock. She had never, ever spoken to him like that before.

Never been forceful or demanding. She had been Black and White Lila with him, but Technicolour Lila was not to be trifled with.

"I'll text you the exact amount and my bank details. If I don't receive it within fourteen days, I'll go to a solicitor. You owe me this Jason. Don't make it difficult."

Yes, a solicitor could probably help if Jason wouldn't give her the money back. She didn't care how much she had to pay for a solicitor to write a letter, Jason was not getting away with this.

"Come on, Li. You're being unreasonable," he said with a huff.

"I'm being unreasonable? *I'm being unreasonable?*" Was he fucking serious? After *everything* she'd done for him, everything he did to her, *she* was being unreasonable? Uh, no. "If anything, I'm being pretty goddamned reasonable by only asking for half, and only asking for it now, when you're earning the big bucks."

"That's not true, I'm not," he said half-heartedly.

"Yeah, well, you're well versed in loans and I'm sure someone will give you one if you don't have the money." Jasmeet would have been so proud of that scathing tone.

"Lila, please, let's talk about this," he pleaded.

"No, thank you," she said. "Fourteen days, Jason."

Lila ended the call and quickly tapped out a message with her bank details and the amount and sent it to him, then stared at the phone in her hand, waiting for Jason to call her back to try and persuade her to change her mind. True to form, it took about fifteen seconds for her phone to ring. She sent his call to voicemail. Twice. She didn't bother replying to the WhatsApp messages he sent.

Lila felt good. Empowered, on top of the world, like she could do *anything*. She wanted to tell someone, anyone, how excellent she had been but no one knew about the supposed 'joint' loan. Not her parents, not Jasmeet or Maddy. It was too embarrassing to tell them.

Oh, by the way, whilst Jason was gaslighting me and cheating on me, I've also been paying off the loan he took out in our joint names! Well, yes, of course I know it was stupid and I shouldn't have signed it, but I did anyway...

Only Rhys knew and she, one hundred percent, was not calling Rhys. She also wasn't going to think about Rhys either because he, like Jason, didn't deserve her time or her thoughts.

> Jasmeet, what are you doing right now? Shall we do something?

Jasmeet, Girls Group Chat

> babe. would love to but I've got to prep for school today. catch up on Wednesday. Okay?

Lila smiled sadly. Jasmeet just expected her to be free on Wednesday, or if not, change her plans so she was free. Okay, so she had no Wednesday plans, but that wasn't the point.

> Mads, you up for a visit? We could take the baby out for a walk?

No answer. Not even blue ticks. Nothing. Nada.

Sunday was, strangely enough, a busy tourist day for her parents and of course they were an hour or so ahead, so they were slap bang in the middle of a vineyard tour. She texted their group chat in the vague hope either of them would be free.

> Hi, are either of you around for a chat?

Determined not to waste her excellent feeling after the call with Jason, and desperate to keep her mind busy and not contemplate the excruciating embarrassment of last night, Lila decided on a walk. A long walk around the reservoir, a walk that would tire her out. A walk with a very interesting podcast to keep her mind busy. If people were busy, that's fine, she could do it by herself.

Technicolour Lila.

CHAPTER 12

Expound (verb)

1. to make known (as an idea, emotion, or opinion)

2. to make plain or understandable

RHYS

Elin

I like her, don't fuck it up.

Mum

Rhys, it was so wonderful to see you last night. Lila is lovely, we'd love to have you both over for dinner some-day.

Daffydd

Let's go for a drink soon, my boy.

Dan

I want to hear about last night. When you free?

To: Dan

Tonight? I think I've fucked up. I need your help.

Dan

Shit. I'll be over at eight. Get some beers in.

To: Dan

Yeah okay.

Dan would know what to do. Well, Dan would take the absolute piss first, and then tell him what he should do. Because once again, he had not managed to articulate himself very well and in the process had probably done exactly what Elin had said not to do. Fucked it up.

Last night had been so perfect. *Lila* had been so perfect. She had charmed his family, been on his side one hundred percent with his father, played the dutiful girlfriend to perfection.

Rhys cringed. He'd run away like a scared teenager and hadn't explained himself. She hadn't *wanted* him to explain himself. That was fair enough, because she must have felt so rejected. *He* must have made her feel so rejected.

The wait for eight o'clock was interminable. He tried working, but the words all merged together and he couldn't get the taste of her out of his mouth. His dick had been in a state of near permanent semi-hardness since he'd gotten home last night and release in the shower had been unsatisfying and pointless. The memory of Lila's leg wrapped around his waist plagued him and was catnip to his not-neglected dick. He went for a run, but ended up running in circles because he couldn't concentrate, so he cut it short after half an hour.

Come over whenever you're ready.

Dan

That bad? I'll try to get there earlier.

Thanks man, I appreciate it.

199

It was just after seven when he buzzed Dan into his flat. Rhys handed him a beer. Dan took a long look at him in his pathetic jogging bottoms and faded t-shirt worn thin around the neckline.

"You look like shit," Dan said.

"I didn't sleep well."

Yeah, because every time he closed his eyes, all he saw was a red-faced and glassy-eyed Lila on her doorstep, slamming the door in his face.

"So." Dan took a swig of beer. "What did you do wrong?"

Rhys clenched his jaw. Fuck, talking about this was hard. But Dan understood him and the situation. Dan had the insight that he sorely lacked.

"Did you tell her you want to take her on a proper, non-fake date?"

"No," Rhys looked at the bottle in his hands. "I didn't get the chance."

"Because?" Dan prompted.

Rhys slammed the bottle on the table.

"I spent the entire night looking at her, touching her. I took her back to hers, we kissed, she undid my trousers and I stopped her." Rhys's voice was too loud, and echoed around his sterile grey kitchen. Lila had different coloured glasses and floral tea towels and he had dull white plates and perfunctory cutlery.

"She practically had her hands on your dick and you stopped her?"

Dan's lips were pressed tightly together, but his eyes sparkled with mirth.

"Dan," Rhys warned. He did not need to be laughed at right now.

"I'm sorry, man," Dan said. "And then she kicked you out?"

"Yeah. That's about it."

Dan tilted his head. "She was obviously up for it. Why did you stop her?"

It was a question he had asked himself a million times, in a million different ways, since Lila's door closed in his face.

"Did you not want to? Because that's all right, man," Dan said, his eyebrows pulling together in a concerned frown.

Rhys gave him a *look*.

"All right, just checking! You've not had a girl for so long, I thought perhaps—"

"Perhaps what?" Rhys raised an eyebrow at him. Where was he going with this?

"That you were ace or aro or whatever," Dan said, draining his bottle of beer.

"No," he said, looking at the table. "I wanted to, Dan. I really fucking wanted to."

Dan grabbed another beer from the fridge and passed it to Rhys.

"Then why didn't you?"

"Because I didn't want her to think it was expected. I didn't want her to think that the fake date stretched to sex. I didn't want to take advantage," he said.

Dan leaned against the kitchen counter and crossed his arms.

"Did you treat it like a real date?"

"Did I hold her hand, put my arm around her, stare at her all fucking night?" Rhys said, voice rising again. "Yeah, I did."

"Did you tell her that you wanted to go out for real? That you actually liked her?" Dan's voice was quiet.

"I was going to, but then we were kissing, and…" Rhys glanced out of the window.

"So that's your next move. You explain," Dan said, like it was the most obvious thing in the world.

"She probably won't answer the phone to me."

Dan assessed him. "Tell me you've called her? Texted her?"

Rhys shook his head.

"I thought she wouldn't want to talk to me." His voice was small.

"She probably doesn't. But if you don't try to talk to her, she'll think you don't want to," Dan said.

Why were people so complicated?

"So, I should text her?"

"Yes."

To: Lila

> Hey, I really enjoyed last night with you, a lot. Can we talk about what happened? Can I explain? It wasn't you at all. It was me.

"No! Don't fucking send that!" Dan cried.

"I've already sent it," Rhys said, bewildered. "But what's wrong with that? It's true."

"It's not you, it's me? That's what you say when you want to break up with someone," Dan said.

"We're not together yet. I'm *trying* to get us together," Rhys explained, like Dan was the most stupid man in the world.

"Fuck me, Rhys. You really are dense sometimes," he muttered, tapping at his phone. "Let me call Jasmeet, she can run interference for you."

"No! Don't do that, Dan," Rhys said, reaching out to cover his phone. "I don't want Lila to think I've been gossiping about her behind her back."

"I'll ask her to be discreet. I can be discreet."

Rhys scoffed.

"Can you? Can you really be discreet?"

"Yeah, course I can," he said. "Look, I'll just tell her the truth, that you're even more miserable now that Lila won't talk to you. I won't give her any details. She won't be able to help but get involved. You know how she is when it comes to Lila."

Jasmeet had indeed threatened him, but he still had both his balls, so he could only imagine that Lila hadn't told her best friend what happened.

But that was the kind of stuff women told each other, wasn't it?

Rhys blew out a breath. He didn't have anything to lose.

"Fine."

"I think the words you're looking for are 'yes please Dan, that would be a great help, thank you'," Dan said.

Rhys rolled his eyes.

"Thank you for your help, Dan."

Dan grinned.

"You're welcome, lover boy."

"Yeah, don't call me that," Rhys said. "Besides, you're one to talk."

They migrated to the sofa and Rhys found some football on TV.

"I'll have to see her at work tomorrow,"

"Ask her if you can talk. Make an arrangement to see her. Don't corner her. If she says no, she says no." Dan pointed his beer bottle at the screen. "That was a free kick."

They sat in an easy silence for a few minutes. That's what he liked about Dan, they'd known each other long enough that silence was just as easy as words.

"Besides, she might need some time to get over the fact that you led her on and then pulled her hands off your dick and ran away."

"Fuck you." There was more venom in his voice that he'd really meant.

"What else is going on, Rhys? This is more than you falling out with Lila, isn't it?"

Rhys blew out a breath.

Telling Lila about applying for the Fellowship had made him warm inside. She'd been so excited for him, and perhaps Dan would as well.

"I'm applying for the Fellowship at the Royal Historical Society," he blurted. "The application is due in soon and it's just so weak. I don't have a big enough body of work."

"That's fucking amazing, Rhys!" Dan said, but his grin

soon turned to a frown. "Why are you applying then? Why not wait until next year or the year after, when you've published more?"

"You know what my father is like. I promised him I would do five years in academia and if I hadn't made a success of myself, I would go back to the family business."

"But you hated Dallimores. You've never been so miserable than when you were there after uni," Dan said, pointing at him with his beer bottle. "What's this 'five years' shit all about?"

"It was to 'get it out of my system', unless I became a success," Rhys said. "Now I'm nearing the end of it and my Fellowship application isn't likely to be accepted. I'll have to go back."

"Why?"

"Because I promised."

"So? Don't do it if you don't want to. You're a grown up." Dan shrugged. Obviously, he had never met Llewellyn Dallimore. Rhys had staunchly kept him as far from his family as he could. The Dallimores had a tendency of flashing power and money, pulling you in and then using you to further their own agenda. He'd wanted to keep Dan as far away from that as possible.

"It's not that easy, Dan," Rhys said, and Dan nodded. There'd been enough conversation across the years for Dan to get it.

He turned back to the football. "Lila took your richy richness all right then, I take it?"

"She didn't care at all," Rhys said, with a little laugh. "It was refreshing, actually."

"I think you'll find most people don't," Dan muttered staring at the screen.

LILA

If Lila was in a spy movie, she thought, she'd be one of those glamorous film noir heroines with a pencil skirt, a slash of red lipstick and a long cigarette. Perhaps a French accent. As it was, she was wearing a deep purple woollen dress, tights and flat boots, no lipstick and certainly no cigarette. Sneaking through the History Department like she was in the French Resistance was both exciting and terrifying.

Exciting because peering round corners with her heart in her mouth *was* kind of exciting. Terrifying, because what if she saw Rhys? Worse, what if she had to *talk* to Rhys? She'd explode from mortification.

Not that she'd let him see that, oh no. After her call with Jason (and the seven missed calls, fourteen unread messages and three unopened emails later) she was empowered. If Rhys didn't want to sleep with her, then it was him who was missing out, not her.

And that was fine. Absolutely fine.

She did not need stupid Rhys Aubrey-Dallimore in her life.

Peeking around the door to the staff kitchen (you know, just in case), it was a relief to see that she could make her pot of chamomile tea without the presence of the devil himself. Well, you know. Rhys.

"Lila, what are you doing?"

"Oh, good lord, Sue! You scared the living daylights out of me!" Lila said, clutching her teapot dramatically to her chest.

"Okay," Sue said, her face twisted in confusion. "But what are you doing?"

"Making a pot of chamomile tea," Lila said, pretending that she wasn't a French Resistance spy. "Do you want a cup?"

"Uh no. Chamomile tea tastes like drinking flowers," she said.

Hate to break it to you, Sue...

"I'm glad I've caught you, Lila." Sue pushed her glasses up her nose. "I'm going to need those intranet issues fixed before tomorrow. I've had more than one complaint and it's getting quite bothersome."

Two complaints were bothersome? Yeah, it is 'bothersome', Sue, and if she had been on her predecessor as much as she was Lila, then it wouldn't have been an issue in the first place.

"Nearly there," Lila said with a smile, praying she would be finished by five so she could go home. Her legs hurt from her quick march walk around the reservoir yesterday. Twice.

"Good," Sue said, scrunching her nose up as she watched Lila pour hot water into her chamomile teapot. "Okay, well."

She turned to leave.

"Oh, Sue," Lila said, catching her arm gently. "As I've got you, can I have a quick chat about the Linguistics Master's course?"

"In the English department?" Sue frowned hard at her. "What about it?"

"I'd like to do it."

There was a beat of silence and Lila's courage faltered. She hadn't even planned on asking Sue, because it was just a pipe dream. But she was buoyed with adrenaline from her French Resistance fantasy and her assertive conversation with Jason. Actually, Jason's half of the loan should be able to fund most of it. Fingers crossed.

"Why?" Sue asked, before waving her hand dismissively. "I don't know if I can release you for the required lecture hours."

Without checking, Lila wasn't sure that Sue could ask her why she wanted to do a course and she wasn't about to disclose her lexicography dream to her just to be ridiculed. Recently, Sue had been so... prickly.

"I think the handbook says that staff can be released for up to six hours per week for university courses," Lila said with a smile. There was no 'think' about it. She'd checked it ten million times and the Linguistics course was four hours a week.

"Oh, right," Sue said, shifting uncomfortably.

"The handbook also says that there's a discount. Do you know how much it is?" Lila continued. She might as well get it all out.

"No."

"Could you find out?"

"I suppose I can ask Finance."

"Great, if you could let me know by Wednesday, that would be amazing. Applications are due soon and I want to make sure I've got mine in." Lila popped the lid on the teapot and gave Sue the biggest grin she could find. "Thanks, Sue!"

Lila scuttled back to her office, clutching her teapot nice and tight so she didn't spill any of her precious flower water.

Who the crap did she think she was? Managing upwards? That was some really ballsy stuff and Sue had been left a bit shell-shocked. She checked her phone again while the tea was steeping.

Nothing. It was times like these, when she'd had no replies, no check-ins, that she felt a bit like a burden to her friends and family. They were all busy. Jasmeet was doing whatever she was doing with Dan, Maddy had Ruby and their baby, her parents were living their best lives.

She couldn't complain. She was glad for them all. They were happy, they were growing, it was exactly what she wanted her for her friends and family.

It was just that Jason had kind of isolated her. Okay, no 'kind of' about it. He *had* isolated her. If it hadn't been for Jasmeet being able to see what Lila couldn't (that Jason was a manipulative piece of shit) and forcing herself into Lila's life, then she would be completely alone.

Hey ladies, you both okay? Good weekend?

What she did *not* do, however, was look at the stupid message that stupid Rhys Aubrey-Dallimore sent last night.

It's not you, it's me.

Okay fine. Maybe she did look at it. Several times. Could he get any more clichéd? Yeah, he sometimes struggled with social niceties, but was that really the best he could do? It was now well into the afternoon and she still hadn't seen his pert little conker arse, so everything was good. If she could just make it through the next two hours, then she would be golden and perhaps by tomorrow, the mortification would have lifted a little.

Who was she kidding? The embarrassment of rejection wouldn't leave her until she was dead in her grave, and then she'd be resurrected just to remember Rhys's words. *I don't want...*

Yep. Brilliant. Great.

Lila knew she'd have to see him sooner or later, but surely later was better than sooner, when it wasn't so... raw. Yes, raw. When she could laugh it off and say 'oh that? Oh, never mind *that,* Rhys!' and give a sophisticated, tinkly chuckle, as she imagined Seren would.

It was ten past four when the inevitable happened.

"Lila?" Rhys stood in her doorway, having the good grace to look at least a little bit abashed.

"Oh. Hello Rhys," she said, flicking her eyes to him and then straight back to her computer where she typed and deleted, typed and deleted. If she looked busy, maybe he would leave.

"Do you have a moment?" He took two steps into her office. His hands were clenched inside his pockets.

"Not really," she said, eyes fixed on the fake words in her new Word document. "Drop me an email with anything you need and I'll deal with it at my earliest convenience."

That was good. No complaints about not being professional and she *was* busy with all that stuff for Sue.

"I was hoping we could have a chat."

A chat? No, thanks. That did not sound in the least bit desirable. Especially not in the middle of the office. She could say, 'Bear with me Rhys, just hold that thought about how

I nearly got into your pants and then you ran away, whilst I deal with the students you make cry.' Okay, so that was uncharitable, but that was the gist of it.

"Sorry," she said, tapping away at her keyboard. "Like I said, put it in an email and I'll be able to help with any work-related issues."

Rhys sighed.

"It's not work-related, Lila. You know that."

"Then it's not an appropriate conversation to have right now," she said, nearly flippantly. Her leg was bouncing with nerves. She was well and truly in her big girl pants era.

"Can I see you after work?"

"I'm busy after work." She glanced at him, and his eyebrows were pulled into a sharp frown. "And for the foreseeable future."

"Lila," he snapped. "I can't make it up to you unless you let me explain."

She blinked incredulously at him. Who did he think he was? Coming into her office and snapping at her like that about a private, personal matter when she had made it clear that she did not want to talk about it.

"I think you'd better reassess your tone, Rhys."

Lila had absolutely nothing to lose today. He'd already rejected her once, so how much more embarrassment could he cause? Answer: not a lot.

"I'm sorry." When he spoke again, his voice was more measured. "I'm just frustrated, because I want to explain what happened the other night."

"I don't think there's much to explain," she said, meeting his eyes with a taut smile. It wasn't a question.

"There really is, Lila." Rhys took a step towards her, his face guileless and eager. "I really do need to talk to you. To explain."

There seriously was nothing to explain. *It's not you, it's me* and Lila didn't want to have *that* conversation where he would say 'Oh you're so nice, you're so special, I just don't feel like that about you, let's just be friends.' She could cope without having that mortifying discussion when the outcome would be exactly the same if they didn't have it – just friends. Which was fine. Absolutely fine.

"Well, it won't be today." She looked back at her computer screen.

RHYS

Lila Cartwright was an annoyingly stubborn woman. He'd gone to her, cap in hand and she'd turned him away like there was nothing to discuss, when there most certainly was. But she was determined, and he was not going to force her. That would make him no better than Jason, overriding her opinions, making her feel less-than.

Unable to sleep well, Rhys took to running in the morning before work and had smashed his 5k personal best. The eleven o'clock cookie had become something of a ritual, as had the afternoon sugar boost. But Lila was right, the cookies from Big Tesco weren't half as nice as hers.

The Fellowship application sat accusingly on his monitor. He hadn't made any alterations to it for a week and it was due soon. It needed some final tweaking, but he couldn't work out what. It just didn't have enough *stuff*, because he hadn't done enough. If he didn't absolutely have to apply for this, he would never put himself through it.

What Lila said sprang up in his mind, not that it was buried particularly deep.

So don't. You're a grown up. You're self-sufficient. Even if you don't get the Fellowship, why do you have to give up everything you've worked for?

He didn't have to give up academia. He could live his own life, not worrying about what his father said. Couldn't he?

CHAPTER 13

Quixotic (adjective) quix·ot·ic
1. *Extravagantly chivalrous or romantic*

LILA

The need to keep Rhys at arm's length was tiring. Fighting the urge to pop into his office to ensure he had his mid-afternoon sugar pick-me-up, tell him about her day and ask about his, was hard. But he had brought this on himself by making it extremely clear that he didn't want *that* kind of relationship with her. The kind of relationship where they had sex. Hot, needy, desperate sex. Because that's what she wanted, and it was difficult pretending that she didn't. Her lips remembered the taste of his, and thinking about his hand squeezing her thigh, his length pressing against her core made her *hot*. Wet. For him.

But she wasn't about to go crawling to him. She did enough of that with Jason and Technicolour Lila did not crawl for anyone, unless she chose to crawl towards Rhys Aubrey's unclothed dick.

God, where had that thought come from? That wasn't like her, she was normally so, well, *nice*.

In the post-Jason stage of her life, she was starting to look at what *she* wanted, and take that very same thing. It was time to embrace herself, her needs. Not put other people ahead of her so much.

Eventually, when Jasmeet called on her lunch break that crisp, autumnal Tuesday, she didn't answer. Neither her nor Maddy had texted her back at the weekend. She knew that they both had lives et cetera, et cetera, but going out with Rhys on Saturday had been important to her.

When Maddy had desperately wanted to go and see that strange art exhibition in Bristol, who had hot footed it down there and paid the extortionate fee to get in? When Jasmeet had said she'd bake a hundred cupcakes for the summer fete, who was it that had stayed up all night doing it because Jasmeet didn't actually know how to bake cupcakes?

That's right. Lila.

So, was it too much to ask for a little bit of interest in her own life? In something that was important to her? Maddy hadn't even replied about Susie Dent and Jasmeet had dismissed it out of hand.

As soon as Jasmeet's name stopped flashing on her phone, she felt guilty. No one should do something they didn't want to, she fully got that, and Jasmeet had been the best person on the planet when she was with Jason, and when they'd broken up. Maddy had talked (whispered) with her every night when she had been up with Ellie and Lila couldn't sleep.

Snatching up her phone from the desk, she called Jasmeet back quickly.

"Sorry I missed you, I was on a call," she lied.

"That's okay, babe," Jasmeet said. "I wanted to catch you whilst you were at work because it's about Rhys."

Lila was silent for a beat. "Rhys? Why are you calling about Rhys?"

"Because Dan told me he's miserable because you're ignoring him," Jasmeet said, hurriedly. "And if Dan is telling me he's miserable, it's because he wants me to do something about it."

Lila's mouth dried up. Had Rhys been shouting his mouth

off about how she practically forced her hands down his pants and was wholly unwelcome?

"What else did he tell you?" she asked, trying for indifference but fully aware that she sounded a little desperate.

"Nothing, and that's not for me not trying to find out," Jasmeet said, pointedly. "Why are you ignoring him?"

Lila sighed.

"Okay, scratch that. I'll come over tonight and you can tell me then," she said.

Lila was tempted to say that she was busy tonight, because Jasmeet had demanded rather than asked, but that would have been petty. Besides, she did want to see her friend.

"Babe, also I realised I never asked you about how Saturday night went. I'm such a bad friend," Jasmeet said with a hitch in her voice. "There's this thing at work, and I…" she trailed off.

"You can tell me about it tonight when you come round," Lila said gently. "Shall I cook?"

"Yes, please. Can you make Comfort Carbonara?"

"Oh shit, it's a carbonara kind of night, is it?"

The buttery, creamy, mushroom and bacon-filled pasta wasn't *really* a carbonara, but it was the best comfort food in the entire world, saved only for the direst of occasions.

"But only after I hear all about you and Rhys."

Lila's throat thickened with emotion. God, she was awful. Her friends did love her. It's just that she was so used to being last, to being let down, to being swept under the carpet. Technicolour Lila went a bit overboard. She was new and bright and fresh, and not restrained or refined at all.

"Jas, are you okay?"

"Of course, babe. What time are you home and sorted out?"

"About six?"

"See you then," Jasmeet said. "Oh, and Lila?"

"Yeah?"

"Talk to Rhys. He's miserable and that makes Dan weird," she said. "I've got to go. Love you."

Lila stared at the phone on her desk. Fuck.

Firstly, she was a grade A bitch for thinking solely of herself when Jasmeet was obviously going through something bad enough to require Comfort Carbonara. Maddy was struggling with the baby and also had a relationship to maintain.

Secondly, she was going to have to talk to Rhys. It was inappropriate to drag their friends into the situation, but somehow a niggle in the back of her brain told her it was her fault. If she had just talked to him when he came to her yesterday instead of being all aloof and professional, then no one else would have brain space taken up by their little spat.

But that could wait until after a little trip around the lake. It was bright and fresh and soon it would be dull and wet and not nice enough to get out in her lunch break, so she'd make the most of it now.

Autumn was by far her favourite season. It was all reds and oranges, comfy wool dresses and ankle boots, crunchy leaves and low, bright sunshine. The trees around the lake were exploding with colour, still some bright greens clinging to the branches, lush evergreens, but maroon and yellow ochre were simply everywhere. Nature made her smile.

She was so fixated on getting to the lake that she didn't see Rhys until he was right in front of her.

"Oh, hi," she said, her lips stretching into a tentative smile.

"Hi," he said, eyebrows rising in surprise that she'd not blanked him.

"Um..." She gestured to the lake. "Walk with me?"

A slight look of hope crossed his face and he nodded, falling into step with her, his hands clenching in his pockets. They walked in silence until they were halfway around the lake. Yeah, she'd invited him to walk with her, but he was the one that wanted to talk to her, so she'd let him take the lead.

"I'd like to take you out on Saturday," Rhys blurted, a faint blush colouring his neck.

Lila stopped and jerked her face up to his.

"Why? We've already been out. The deal is done. There's no need."

Rhys's eyebrow rose.

"I would like to take you on a date. A proper date."

Wait a second. He'd gone from not wanting her to touch him, to wanting to take her out on a date? Oh, perhaps he was a virgin. Perhaps he didn't do one-night stands. Perhaps she had moved too fast for him.

"You want to take me on a date?"

"A date where there is no obligation to..." Rhys winced slightly and let his sentence hang.

"*Oh.*"

He didn't want there to be any *obligation*. They'd only been together because of their bargain and having sex wasn't part of it. If they had, he would probably feel it was forever tainted by the overhanging agreement they had. It was actually quite gentlemanly. Damn him.

"Is that why—"

"Yes," he interrupted.

"But I didn't feel that there was any—"

"There wasn't," he said quickly. "But I prefer not to be ambiguous."

"You could have told me,"

"Oh yeah?" Rhys said, an amused smile playing across his face. He took a step towards her. "When would I have done that, Lila?"

Her tongue darted out to wet her lips. They were close now, close enough for her to make the sudden desire to climb him like a tree a reality. Because he wanted to take her out.

"So you did want to?" Her voice was barely more than a whisper. Her eyes skittered up the column of this throat to his eyes, dark and ravenous.

"What? Fuck you?" A smirk played across his lips.

She nodded, swallowing hard. God, the harshness of that word '*fuck*' and the easy way he said it made her stomach tighten.

"Say it, Lila. Ask me properly." His voice was low and gravelly.

She wet her lips again. Christ, he was going to make her say it, here where anyone could hear her. There was a couple of girls sitting on a bench, but they were quite a distance away.

Lila took a deep breath.

"Did you want to have sex with me?"

Leaning forward to whisper in her ear, Rhys's cheek brushed hers and she stopped breathing.

"I wanted to fuck you perched on that dining table," he said, his breath hot against the shell of her ear. "I wanted to make you come on my fingers, I wanted to eat you until you exploded on my face, and then I wanted to fuck you exactly the way you like it."

Her lips dropped into a shocked O.

Lila sucked in a breath, fully aware that she was poppy-red and desperate for him to touch her, to make good on his words. He pulled back and she stared at his throat, the small hint of skin just above his loosened tie, the smugness in the twist of his lips. The desire in his eyes.

"Can I take you out on a proper date on Saturday?" he repeated, his voice hoarse.

She nodded, speechless.

"Thank you," he said, turning to walk back around the lake. He stopped, and turned back. "You're so pretty when you're thinking about what I could do with you."

Lila's eyes went wide in shock. How could Rhys – calm, collected *Rhys Aubrey* – have such a filthy, dirty mouth? A mouth that he obviously wanted to put on her. A mouth that she was desperate for.

Lila had to go round big Sainsbury's three times to get everything she needed for Comfort Carbonara, while concentrating on anything other than the shape of Rhys's lips when he had told her he wanted to fuck her.

Goodness. Jason had *never* done anything like that. Minimal foreplay and then he was all about getting his kicks. He'd flop back and say 'shit, that was great, wasn't it?'. Then she'd say 'yeah, it was', and snuggle on his chest whilst planning her next evening in by herself.

Rhys actually seemed to want her to... well, come. A lot. With him. *On* him. On his face, his fingers, his dick. *Well.*

She was home for about ten minutes before Jasmeet arrived, had chopped everything and put the pasta on to boil.

"Babe, have you got any wine in the fridge?" Jasmeet called, using her key and slamming the door behind her.

"Yep, pouring now," Lila called from the kitchen.

Jasmeet threw her bag on the sofa and grabbed the large glass Lila had poured from the side.

"Babe, I'm sorry. I've been so preoccupied," Jasmeet said, sipping her wine. "God, I needed that."

Lila balanced the wooden spoon on the edge of the saucepan and hugged her friend.

"I'm sorry," she said.

"What are you sorry for? You haven't done anything!" Jasmeet said, hugging her back.

The hug was tinged with guilt because she had done something wrong. She'd doubted Jasmeet. She'd been so selfish when frankly, there were other, more important things going on.

"Tell me what's going on," she said to Jasmeet, her arms still tight around her.

"Oh god, it's just a horrid kid and a horrid parent," Jasmeet said, extricating herself. "I want to hear about Rhys."

Rhys. How was she supposed to tell her best friend about the filthy things Rhys had said to her. Answer: she wasn't going to. No way.

"The evening went well, really well," she said, turning back to the pan.

"And...?" Jasmeet pressed. "Why was he miserable? What happened?"

"Oh," Lila said. "Well, we came back here, and we were, you know…"

This was so awkward. Lila was not used to talking about this *stuff*.

Jasmeet, however, did not have any such issues with talking about sex.

"You were getting down to it, you dog," she said, clapping her hands gleefully. "I'm so proud of you! Well done! Was he good? I bet he was good, that tight little ass—"

"Uh, you've got a boyfriend."

"Doesn't mean I can't look!" she said. "Was he?"

"Didn't get that far. He stopped it before we could."

Jasmeet raised her eyebrows.

"Is that Comfort Carbonara ready? I feel this is a story we need it for."

Lila smiled and dished up.

Over a bottle of wine and the creamiest, most garlicky pasta ever, Lila told her everything. Well, not *everything* everything. Certainly not repeating Rhys's words from earlier in the day. She couldn't even think them without blushing hot-rod red.

"Lila's got a boyfriend," Jasmeet sang, her eyes slightly wobbly after two large glasses of wine.

"You're silly," Lila said with a tipsy laugh. She most certainly did not. It was just a shag she was after, wasn't it? Someone to fill the coldness of her bed now and again, because Rhys's touch would be infinitely better than her own.

Obviously, Rhys wanted to sleep with her, he'd said as much. Taking her out on a date was a courtesy. He hadn't said anything about a *relationship*, he'd said 'fuck'. He'd said it a lot.

"Dessert?" she asked, changing the subject.

"I usually have Dan for dessert," Jasmeet said, wiggling her eyebrows.

"Oh God, I do *not* need to know that."

Lila cleared the table and served vanilla cheesecake, with

the remnants of the cream. Calorie counting was not on the agenda tonight. They decanted themselves to the sofa and curled up under blankets.

"Can I stay tonight? I don't want to get a taxi and then come back for my car tomorrow," Jasmeet said.

"'Course you can," Lila said. She'd anticipated as much. "Tell me what's happening at work."

"Well," Jasmeet said, launching into a story about a tantrumming child disrupting the entire class for hours on end, and a parent who – after having an equal tantrum – felt that Jasmeet, as Miss Patel, should effectively parent this child to the exclusion of all other students.

"Stupid parent went to the Head. Had to have a meeting with her."

"What happened?"

Jasmeet rolled her eyes. "I have to ensure that all students are treated equally. There may be additional learning factors for this child and I need to assess him. Which is damned hard to do with a class of thirty-two already, and only one teaching assistant for two children with Special Educational Needs."

"That's shit. What did your Head say?"

"Nothing. There's no more funding for any extra help. I just have to do my best. But if my best isn't good enough, I leave the school open to 'further complaints' and there will 'therefore be consequences'," Jasmeet said.

"Oh Jas, that's awful," Lila said, patting her friend's leg.

"It is what it is, and that's why I've been a bit distracted," Jasmeet grimaced. "I'm sorry."

"There's nothing to be sorry for," she said, gifting her friend her most sincere smile. Jasmeet nodded.

"Can we watch something easy?" Jasmeet asked, pouring more wine into her glass. "I don't want to think."

"Sure." Lila automatically handed the remote controller over to Jasmeet, who flicked *Love Island* on.

"I love this," she said. "It's utter trash, but so addictive."

Lila grinned. She actually didn't like it and had only

watched it when Jasmeet was here, but if that's what her friend needed, that's what she would do.

> **What do I wear on Saturday?**

Rhys

Whatever you want. Whatever you feel comfortable in.

I'll want to fuck you no matter what you wear.

> **Rhys!**

Rhys

Are you that pretty shade of pink again?

> **I'm not having this conversation!! What time on Saturday?**

Rhys

I'll pick you up at 5.30.

> **What are we doing?**

Rhys

It's a surprise.

> **I LOVE surprises!**

Rhys

I thought you would.

"Who is more important than *Love Island*?" Jasmeet, curled up on one end of the sofa, nudged her with her foot. "It's Rhys isn't it? You're texting Rhys!"

"Look, I'm just trying to find out what we're doing on Saturday so I can dress correctly."

"It seems like all you need is a pair of edible underwear."

"Jas! Shut up!" If she hadn't already turned fuchsia pink, then she was now. "Edible underwear? Is that even a thing?"

"Lila, you haven't *lived*!" she crowed. "I'll get you some!"

"Don't you dare, Jas." She slapped her on the leg. "Don't you *dare*!"

RHYS

He shouldn't keep teasing her, he *shouldn't*, but the way she wet her lips when she asked him if he wanted to have sex with her was his undoing. He liked her flushed and wide-eyed. More than liked it. The floodgates had opened, quite literally, and he couldn't keep his cock down. The unsatisfactory tugs in the cold showers that he had started taking every morning and every evening since seeing Lila in that dress, were becoming less and less effective. Especially when she texted him asking what she should wear to their date, because it had him envisioning all sorts of lingerie, like silken tops that clung to hard nipples.

Fuck.

Thing was, it didn't matter what she wore (yes, even that awful fucking dress that hurt his eyes), because she was so unabashedly *her* in all her clothes. And that's what Rhys wanted. Her. Not just for a shag, not just to relieve his blue balls. He wanted her vanilla smell wrapped around him like a goddamned snuggly blanket. But mostly, he wanted to collect each and every one of her smiles and to be the reason for them.

She gave him the courage to be the man he wanted to be. She believed in him, and that was something that had been sorely lacking in his life.

God-fearing Llewellyn Dallimore believed in the best steel

girders, the strength of your concrete, and the Welsh rugby team. He and, come to think of it, literally every person in his father's orbit, were just pawns to be moved around his Welsh Monopoly board.

Whereas Lila offered so much belief and trust and, well, happiness, that he nearly couldn't bear the thought that she might not want to offer it to him. Why would she? Lila had given all of that away to Dickhead Jason and look where that had got her – a load of debt, a diminished sense of self-worth and serious trust issues with men (which was absolutely fair, given the way that wanker had treated her).

He was just going to have to prove to her that he wasn't like Jason, that he wanted all of her, just how she was. Because she was perfect. Yes, she was too glittery by far, too saccharine, too *smiley* but that, apparently, was exactly what he needed. No, what he *wanted* in his life. The realisation expanded in his chest and he placed a hand to his ribs to keep it all in.

There was something he could do for her.

Rhys sat at his kitchen table with his laptop and googled the hospital and 'Dr Jason Douchebag'. On second thoughts, 'Douchebag' probably wasn't his second name and most likely wouldn't show up on the hospital staff list. Fine. Delete.

Rhys sat in his car behind the friendly sky-blue Petunia at twenty past five on Saturday, ten minutes before he was due to pick Lila up. She wouldn't be ready, but he couldn't sit in his dull flat anymore. Restless cleaning only took an hour because he'd been doing it for the past two fucking weeks to try to keep his mind from tracking back to the softness of her lips, the eagerness of her kiss.

It wouldn't be tonight. No, he was going to take his time. Lila deserved savouring, she deserved *dating*. Showing that he was there for more, not just taking what he wanted and fucking off.

It was one of those October afternoons that was nearly

summer warm, but with a biting wind that promised if you forgot your coat for any time after six, it would rob you of all feeling in your fingers.

Right. He couldn't wait anymore. Knocking on her door, he shuffled the flowers in his arms. Flowers were definitely too much – he should just put them in the boot of the car and forget he'd bought them. Lila would like them though, wouldn't she? Rhys had spent way too long in three different florists before he settled on a bouquet, so he couldn't very well put them in the boot and write off the afternoon as a waste.

"It's open, Rhys!" she called from behind the door. "Come in!"

He pushed the door open and was hit with honey-sweet warm air.

"You're early! I'm going to be another ten minutes!" she shouted from upstairs. "Have a cookie! I tried something new. Let me know what you think."

Without waiting for a reply, either a hairdryer or a vacuum cleaner started up and Rhys couldn't really see Lila hoovering right now.

How did she know it was him? It could have been anyone banging on her door. An axe murderer could be unashamedly stuffing his face with the most delicious cookies with a hint of honey (and was that mint in there?).

Fifteen minutes, three cookies and a glass of water later (and some clattering from upstairs), Lila hobbled down the stairs in a knee-length pink dress, bare legs, one boot on and the other in her hand, a handbag slung across her chest and two jackets over her arm.

"I'm sorry, I didn't—" she stopped. Her eyes tripped across his chest to his hands, gripping the flowers way too tightly.

She looked back up at him, eyes wide and soft. There was a confused question buried in her eyes, as if no one had ever bought her flowers before. Perhaps they hadn't.

"Here," he said, holding them out like a bomb.

"Rhys," she said, voice quiet. The boot bumped on the soft

carpet and her jackets fell from her arm. Lila accepted them reverently. "What are they?"

"They're protea. South African flowers," he said, watching her eyes dart around the bouquet, trying to look at all of them at once.

"They're so, uh—"

Her eyebrows drew in, trying to find words to describe the alien-looking flowers.

"I know. I thought you'd like them," he said, suddenly concerned. "It's okay if you don't like them."

"I love them. Absolutely love them!" Lila said, squashing them to her chest. "I've never seen flowers like this before."

A smile tugged at his lips as her eyes flicked between him and the flowers in her arms.

"I can't remember the last time someone bought me flowers," she said earnestly. "Thank you, Rhys."

She was so easily pleased by something so simple, it hurt his chest a little to think that no one had ever cared enough before to give her gifts. Just something small to say that someone was thinking of her. Which he was, all the fucking time.

He watched her find a vase that looked like a large toucan, and she plonked the flowers in, wrapper and all. What the fuck?

"I'll do them properly later. I want to study them and give them some time," she explained.

Rhys was absurdly pleased with that. He had spent hours (and an awful lot of money) looking for flowers that matched her. It seemed that no one else had ever thought about what she'd like, what she'd appreciate.

"You look…" he hesitated and she tilted her head, waiting.

Obviously, he took too long because she glanced down at her one booted foot.

"You don't have to tell me I look nice just because that's what people do," she said.

"What? No. I was looking for the right word," he said,

reaching for her. His finger slid under her chin and he tinted her head up so he could see her. "I think you look beautiful. You always do."

He was rewarded by a pretty, warm blush across her cheeks, before she smiled and stepped away, dragging on her other boot haphazardly.

"I bet you say that to all the girls, Rhys Aubrey."

He didn't like the way she said it so flippantly, so dismissively. Who had made her feel so unpretty? Oh yes, Dr Jason McTwatFace.

"No, just you," he said, just as flippantly as her. She gave him a curious smile and pulled on a purple jacket, pairing it with a yellow scarf.

"Right, I'm ready. Take me to your noble steed, kind sir."

He chuckled, because she was so dramatic and he kind of loved it.

The last time she had been in his car it had been tight with anticipation, but this time it was so easy. That's how he should feel about being around people, easy and free. Lila made him not worry about whether he said anything wrong, whether he'd misinterpreted her. He could just ask and she would tell him. And that was a relief.

"So," she said, after about ten minutes. "Where are you taking me? If it's out to some dark copse so you can murder me, let me know so I can tell Jasmeet where to go to find my body."

"It's a surprise," he said, a smile tugging at his lips. "But it's not a murder copse."

"Damn it, I've lost my bet with Jas and Maddy," she said with a grin. She was teasing him and he liked it.

It was another fifteen minutes before Rhys pulled into a busy car park and opened the door for Lila, leading her through a short alleyway and onto a main road. She put her hand through the crook of his arm and he bent his elbow, pulling her closer so they were walking hip to hip. Well, his hip to her waist. Ish. He slowed his steps so her shorter legs could keep up. Legs that had wrapped around his waist.

"Rhys," she breathed, coming to an abrupt stop. Someone grumbled and walked around them, but he didn't care. Lila's eyes were on the sign up ahead. She turned her face up to his, eyes wide and wondrous. "Have you brought me to see Susie Dent?"

CHAPTER 14

Fervent *(adjective) fer·vent*
1a. Having or displaying a passionate intensity

LILA

Who was this magical man who had bought the most beautiful alien flowers and surprised her with tickets to see The Queen?

"Rhys, you shouldn't have."

"Have you already seen this tour? I wasn't sure..." he trailed off.

"No, no, I haven't," she said quickly. "Jasmeet didn't want to go and Maddy didn't reply. I was going to go by myself, but by the time I got round to getting tickets, they were all sold out."

"I see," he said, the muscle in his jaw ticking.

"This is absolutely perfect," she breathed and she could feel the sheen of wetness over her eyes. Reaching up on her toes, she pressed a quick kiss to his stubbled cheek. "Thank you," she whispered. "I mean it. I really appreciate it."

Jasmeet had made it very clear she would never put herself through two hours of Susie Dent and Jason *never* would have taken her. But here was this stoic Welshman, who sometimes wasn't sure what to do with his hands, leading her down the road to go and see her hero talk about words on stage. She squeezed his arm.

"When did you get these? They've been sold out for ages," she said. A pink flush crossed his neck.

"I got them before we went to my family thing. I was going to give them to you after as a thank you, but I didn't get round to it," he said, weaving them through the quiet throng of word lovers, all heading to see their leader. "Then I thought it would be nice to go together."

She looked at him curiously, again. He actively wanted to spend time with her, doing things that she wanted to do, regardless of how boring he'd find it. Lila's stomach tightened, because this *feeling* wasn't supposed to happen. This feeling of being wanted, of someone thinking about her and what she would like. It was strange and new, and she loved it.

And it was Rhys who made her feel like that.

Rhys Aubrey, who was watching her like she was the only person in the entire world at that moment, waiting patiently for her to say something.

She didn't trust her voice because of the hot swell of emotion clogging her throat, so she just nodded with a weak smile. After a frown flickered across his face, he grinned and tugged her along.

"Come on. Let's soak up all of Susie Dent," he said.

A giggle came from her throat, followed by a sinking realisation that if Rhys Aubrey kept being thoughtful and kind and looking damn sexy in his clothes, then she was going to be in trouble. The past year and a half had taught her that she didn't need a man in her life, she didn't need anyone for a goddamned thing, but perhaps she wanted one. Perhaps a full night of discovering just what was under Rhys's clothes and how every inch of him tasted was exactly what she needed to get him out of her system.

One night of hot, rampant sex and she'd be done.

Lila was a terrible liar, even to herself.

Susie Dent was EVERYTHING.

But it was the man sat next to her who stole her attention. No matter how many hilarious origins of words Susie posited, Lila had one eye on Rhys. He filled the fold-down velvet chair in the theatre, but kept his elbows and knees in, so as not to hog the entire space with his maleness. She had never seen anyone so *aware* of their body and the impact it had on people in his vicinity.

Rhys laughed in the right places (a huff of air and a low rumble from his chest), nodded when he found something interesting, and smiled knowingly when he caught her staring at the crinkle of skin by his eyes when he narrowed them in concentration.

The intermission came and went. Lila gave herself a stern talking-to when Rhys went to the toilet, because this was *not* about stupid emotions or stupid feelings. But all that went out of the window when Rhys came back, balancing the biggest tub of bubblegum ice cream and three different bags of chocolate in his arms, because *they didn't have cookies and I didn't know which you liked so I got all of them for you to choose.*

What a sweet, thoughtful man. Sweet, thoughtful, and damned hot in that shirt with the sleeves rolled up just below his elbows. What was it about the movement of muscle in men's forearms? Well, not 'men', just Rhys, because she had never noticed the way the muscle tightened when he lifted his water to his lips (condensation running down the bottle like a frigging Diet Coke advert from the 90s) in any other man before.

Halfway through the second act, Rhys shifted in his seat, angling towards her a little and reached for her hand, lacing their fingers together. Tilting his head towards her, he raised his eyebrow in a 'is this okay' kind of way.

It was more than okay. In fact, holding Rhys's hand made her feel like a teenager again, aware of every slide and movement of their palms together. Rhys sat back in his chair with a satisfied hum and drew circles on the sensitive part of her palm with his thumb. Well, if that wasn't a wave of heat straight to her core. How was even *this* sexy?

Lila glanced at the man holding her hand. His lips were tipped up in a small smile as he listened to Queen Susie wax lyrical about 'thunderplump' (19th century, to be so rained on so as to be soaked). He'd brought her flowers, he'd driven, he'd taken her to somewhere she wanted to go, he was holding her hand. It was like he had read *The Idiot's Guide to Going On A Date* and was ticking off the checklist slowly but surely, making sure he covered all bases, and Lila's heart squeezed.

It was hard to reconcile this version of Rhys with the one that so candidly told her that he wanted to fuck her. Her face grew warm and she shuffled in her seat, earning her a frown from Rhys and a mouthed 'are you okay?' She nodded quickly and turned her attention back to Susie Dent.

"That was the most amazing show, Rhys," Lila said, again, in the car as they drove home. "Thank you so much."

"I'm glad you enjoyed it," he said, pulling out onto a main road.

"I didn't know about kennings, like 'wave-horse' for boat or 'sky-candle' for the sun. And Susie Dent is just so beautiful, the absolute best."

Lila pressed her lips together and gripped her hands tightly in her lap as she caught Rhys's grin out of the corner of her eye.

"Sorry, I'm prattling on and waving my hands about like a lunatic." But she couldn't help adding, "from the word 'luna', moon."

An amused laugh burst from his chest. "I'm glad you enjoyed it. I like hearing you talk."

No one had liked hearing her talk about what she loved before. Jasmeet and Maddy would generally listen, but they weren't that interested. Jason would roll his eyes and ignore her when she tried to talk to him about pretty much anything that she enjoyed. Eventually, she stopped. His comments wore away at her, making her more and more black and white. She was a secondary character in her own life with Jason.

"You like hearing me talk?" she whispered.

"Yeah. Surprised me as well," he replied, his eyebrow rising.

This time, it was her who reached for his hand settled on the gear stick and slid her fingers in between his. If he kept up with this, then she was dangerously in trouble of letting her heart get a little bit carried away here.

This was just leading to sex.

She didn't need a relationship.

It wasn't long before his big swanky car was pulled up behind teeny-tiny Petunia and he was opening her door and walking her to her front door. Like a gentleman.

"I had a really nice time tonight, Rhys," she said, facing him like a teenager in an American film. She half expected her parents to be twitching at the front-room curtains. Not that they ever did that when she was an actual teenager.

"Me too," he said, taking a small step towards her so she had to tilt her head up to look at him.

Slowly, as if he was testing her boundaries, he lowered his mouth to hers. Her eyes fluttered shut as his lips pressed against hers in a soft kiss. Then he was gone, stepped back from her, hands shoved in the pockets of his well-fitting jeans, distinctly tight around the crotch area. He looked at her, all wickedness and anticipation, waiting for her to make the next move.

"Thanks, Rhys," she said, unlocking the door. "Bye."

She shut the door without looking back over her shoulder.

Lila stood behind her front door, hands braced on the wood for a count of three before she wrenched open the door. Rhys was still standing there, hand still stuffed in his pockets, head down, but she could see his cheek curve with the hint of a smile. He looked up at her in surprise.

Grinning, she grabbed a fistful of his shirt and dragged him in through the front door, kicking it shut behind them. Then they were a tangle of ferocious kisses as he pushed her over the wayward shoes to press her against the wall.

"Rhys," she whispered. His hips moved against hers and he dropped hot, wet kisses down her throat. "Did we do it all?"

He pulled back from her, his lips red and swollen and eyes half-closed. Her hands were still threaded through his hair.

"What do you mean?" he asked, his hands on her ribs.

"Did we do everything you wanted on the date that you'd planned?" she asked, running her fingers across his cheekbone. A bashful smile crossed his lips and he glanced at her lips, wet from his mouth.

"Yes," he said, hands sliding onto her hips. "Is this okay?"

His jaw tightened, holding back and waiting for permission and she loved it. *She* had the power here, and she knew that he would do whatever she wanted, whether that ended up with sex or not.

"God yes," she said and crushed her lips to his again, not giving him time to reply.

Rhys's hand moved, exploring the fullness of her breast. She moaned into his mouth as he rubbed her hard nipple over the thin fabric of her dress. The friction through her scanty lace bra was both delicious and not enough against her. His thigh pushed between hers and she manoeuvred her dress out of the way so she could grind her core against his leg. Fuck, she was dry humping him like a horny teenager. He pinched her nipple in response and grinned against her mouth.

One hand hitched her dress up and slid to squeeze her ass and she bucked against him.

Yes, please.

"You're very needy," he mumbled.

"Yes." She pressed down harder against his leg and shuddered as she got the angle just right. "I am."

Lila let out a noise of dissatisfaction as he extricated his leg from between hers. He stroked her tongue with his as his fingers splayed across her thigh, running down the back of her leg and drawing it up around his waist.

"Fuck, I've wanted this," he said, burying his face in her neck, licking at her pulse point. His hips notched against her and she could feel just how much he wanted it.

Rhys slid his other hand up to her hip under the skirt of her dress, his mouth stilling. He looked almost feral as he drew back from her, eyes impossibly dark.

"Lila," he said, his voice a growl. "You are incredibly naughty."

Tilting her head, she blinked innocently. "What do you mean?"

A slow, wicked smile stretched across his face.

Her breath grew shallow with anticipation. Sliding her hands over his shoulders, she gripped his shirt tightly in her fists.

"Rhys," she whispered, "please."

He smirked and bent to her neck, dragging his teeth along her sensitised skin.

"You want me to touch you?" he whispered, his breath hot against the shell of her ear. "That's why you've not worn any underwear, because you want me to fuck you?"

Colour shot to her cheeks, because that's exactly why she had foregone her knickers today. She wanted Rhys to fuck her, good and proper. She was going for what she wanted.

"You wear no underwear all night, but you blush so prettily," his thumb pressed into the crease of her hip, making her gasp, "when I say I want to fuck you," he finished in a whisper. "Tell me what you want. You're in control."

Her stomach clenched. Knowing it was her in control was one thing, but him saying it? Him asking what she wanted? *Hot.*

"Rhys, please," she gasped, as his mouth was hot and wet just behind her ear. "Please, touch me."

A noise came from the back of his throat and he gripped her jaw, tilting her head back. Like he couldn't hold back anymore, his mouth fused against hers, his tongue sweeping hard through her mouth.

His fingers trailed across the softness of her thigh, not urgently enough for her liking and a pathetic, mewling noise came from her throat. His smile was wicked.

"Like this?"

Rhys moved the skirt of her dress so he could watch his fingers swipe through her wetness. "Fuck, Lila."

He brought his fingers up to his mouth and sucked, his eyes closing.

"You taste so good," he murmured, fingers trailing out of his mouth.

"Rhys," she begged, incapable of any other words. She needed this.

His eyes snapped open and a feral grin spread across his face.

"Hold on."

She yelped as he grabbed her other leg, wrapping it around his waist. Her arms went around him and she pressed her face into his neck, breathing in his aftershave. Rhys took two steps and set her down on the stairs.

"Rhys," she started, "what—"

But she couldn't finish her sentence because he was on his knees between her thighs, pushing her dress up greedily.

"Fuck, Lila," he whispered, "tell me what you want. This is all for you."

She was bare in front of him, too turned on to care. He dragged his eyes away from her wetness to her face, his jaw clenched viciously, hands tightening on her thighs. Waiting. Waiting *for her*.

Raising her head she met the desire in his eyes with her own.

"I want your mouth on me," she breathed, delighted when his eyes lit up like he had been given the greatest present on earth. Another wicked, feral grin and he buried his face between her legs.

There was no build up, no teasing. Rhys's tongue dove straight into her, dragging through her wetness, his hands pressing her knees wider so she was completely open to him. Her hands fisted in his hair, wanting *more*, and her hips jerked against his face of their own accord, desperate for release.

"More, Rhys," she gasped, her head dropping back against the stairs.

A rumble of satisfaction reverberated against her core. He worked his way persistently, relentlessly to her clit. A finger pressed inside her, working her over, in and out.

"Another," she moaned.

A second finger joined the first, curling inside her, rubbing harshly against her. A suck and a flick of his tongue against her clit made her trembling legs tense and hard around his head.

"Oh God, Rhys."

She couldn't stop her hips grinding upwards into his face, keeping time with his fingers fucking her.

"I'm so close."

Yes, teetering on the edge of the biggest orgasm that she had ever had. He didn't stop, his tongue and fingers working her until her body couldn't take any more.

Lila cried out as she shook with pleasure, her back arching up, fists holding Rhys's head in place as he relentlessly attacked her clit, pushing her over the edge, keeping her orgasm alive for as long as possible.

Only when Lila's legs slackened around his head did he slow, slipping his fingers out from her and licking up everything she had given him, gently grazing over her incredibly sensitive, throbbing clit.

Fuck.

"Rhys," she whispered, her arm thrown across her eyes.

"Mmm," he answered, not stopping his mouth on her.

"Rhys, you can stop," she breathed. "That was..." There were no words to describe how amazing that orgasm was to the man who was still licking gently between her legs.

"I don't want to stop," he said. "You taste so good."

"I need," she started, gulping for air, "I need—"

"Tell me, Lila," he said, kissing the crease of her hip. "Tell me what you want."

"I want you inside me."

There was no fear, no embarrassment in her, because he was literally on his knees, worshiping her, and she was one hundred percent okay with that.

"Thank fuck," was all he said.

RHYS

Having Lila's legs wrapped around his head as she came on his fingers was the best, sweetest torture. Whilst he was desperate to get inside her, he was more eager to give her control, do exactly what she wanted. What she *needed*, because he had a feeling that she'd never told anyone what she wanted. Perhaps she didn't know. Perhaps no one had asked before.

He wasn't going to take her on the uncomfortable, impractical stairs, not when she was sated and relaxed.

"Come on," he said, sliding his arms under her and lifting her to standing. "Upstairs."

She returned his wicked grin and scuttled up the stairs in front of him, her dress riding up enough to give him teasing glimpses of where he had spent the last moments; with his face buried in her pussy. They were still hurrying in through the bedroom door as he unzipped her dress and pushed it to the floor. He couldn't wait any more and grabbed her ass to him, running his hands across her stomach and up to her hard nipples, barely covered by her lacy bra. Lila's head rested back against his shoulder and he bit down on the soft part where her neck met her shoulder.

Rolling her nipples through her lacy bra, she pushed her ass back into his groin and fuck, he was like steel. It was one thing having a perfunctory and thoroughly unsatisfactory wank in the shower thinking of Lila, but a completely different thing having her in his arms, soft and sated, wanting him.

"Rhys." She turned in his arms, sliding her hands up his chest. "You are wearing far too many clothes."

Her fingers worked shakily at his buttons and he let her, running his hands over her back restlessly. Once she had gotten rid of his shirt, she reached for the button of his jeans, glancing up through her eyelashes at him to check. Nodding, he squeezed her ass impatiently. Her hand slipped in through his open jeans and it was heaven when she gripped him through his pants. A moan escaped his lips, but this time, he didn't grab her hand to stop her.

"Lila," he growled. "If you keep doing that, I'll come in your hand."

Her lips pulled into a slow smile as she removed her hand and turned to the bedside table, wiggling her ass as she pulled out a condom and gave it to him. She climbed on the bed and lay down for him, spreading her legs.

Wild blonde hair splayed across the pillow, nipples hard and wetness glistening on her core. His dick twitched proudly at the proof that she wanted him again.

Fuck, she was beautiful.

Climbing to kneel between her legs, he said, "Like this? You want it like this?"

Hooded eyes blinked slowly and her chin moved in a jerky nod.

"Show me," he said, gripping the base of his swollen dick.

Leaning forward, she took his cock out of his hand and rubbed it through her wet pussy, coating him with her juices.

Fuck.

Notching him at her entrance, she lay back, pulling him down with her. Smoothing her hair back from her face, he dropped kisses over her cheekbones and slid his tongue over her lips. She moaned and lifted one leg around his waist, squirming for him to enter her. He grinned against her mouth at her eagerness.

Canting his hips slowly, he sank into her. A breathless moan came from her, and fuck, it was good. She tightened her leg around him and buried her face into his neck, her breath hot against his skin.

He held himself back. She wasn't some quick fuck. He wouldn't just get dressed and go. No, he wanted to savour every inch, every second of their first time together. Pulling back nearly fully out of her, he slid back in as slowly as he could, grinding his hips against her where they joined, pressing on her clit as he pushed himself deep.

"Rhys," she gasped into his neck. "More."

That's all she needed to say. His self-restraint snapped and his hips drove harder and faster into her. Fingers dragged down his back and held on to his ass, as he pulled her leg higher, giving himself better access.

"Fuck, Lila," he said, because he couldn't hold back anymore, there was no stopping this. "I'm going to come."

Her pussy tensed around him and that tipped him over the edge. With an urgent few pumps, he cried out as he came, Lila's teeth dragging against his neck.

Fuck.

"Lila, I'm sorry, I—" he swallowed, trying to catch his breath. "I'm sorry I didn't last longer, you're just too... I was just too..."

She silenced him with a kiss.

"Rhys, that was amazing," she said, hands resting behind his head. "You don't need to worry."

He dropped his forehead to hers, closing his eyes and dragging in deep, warm breaths.

"Fuck," he whispered. Rhys slid out of her. "Let me deal with this," he said, motioning to the full condom. Lila lay back with a smile on her face, eyes dropping closed.

He hurried in the bathroom, but stopped to wet a flannel

to take to Lila, and grabbed a glass from the windowsill to fill with water. To take care of her.

When he got back to her room, she was under the covers, dozing. He slipped in beside her and slid the flannel down her body.

"What are you doing?" she mumbled.

"Cleaning you up," he whispered, dropping a kiss at the corner of her mouth.

"Are you staying?" she asked, eyes still closed.

"I would like to," he hesitated. What if she didn't want him to? God, they'd just had sex and all he wanted to do was hold her, but he was so unsure. Sex was the easy bit. "I can go if you'd prefer?"

"No, stay," she said, turning and snuggling into his chest.

"Okay," he said with a smile, slipping his arms around her.

This evening had gone much better than he had expected. Everything he had read, everything he *knew*, told him that there would be no first date sex. He had been more than prepared to kiss her on the cheek, say good night, wait three restless days and then call her to see if he could take her out again. Well, probably not three days.

Lila hadn't been wearing knickers. He had told her he wanted to fuck her and she hadn't worn knickers.

Christ.

He hoped she let him fuck her again, because now he'd had a taste of her, he wasn't going to be able to let her go easily. It was more than that though, he'd had a taste of her cookie-flavoured life and he wanted to be part of it. Rhys wanted to share his time with haphazard, multicoloured Lila. Protect her. Care for her.

He hoped she'd let him.

CHAPTER 15

Limerence (noun) lim·er·ance

1.a. state of mind resulting from romantic attraction,
characterized by feelings of euphoria, the desire to
have one's feelings reciprocated, etc.

LILA

Rhys woke her up in the early hours of the morning for slow, sleepy, warm sex, and again at nine for more. He was insatiable and she loved it.

Jason had always been perfunctory and as regular as clockwork. Well, it made sense, because he was getting his kicks elsewhere with Leanne and probably a whole host of other women throughout their relationship. But she didn't care.

Rhys made her feel desired, beautiful and needed and that's exactly how she wanted to feel after a night of sex. Because that's what it was. A night of sex. Otherwise, her heart couldn't take it. They were friends, yes. Friends who'd had sex one night.

"Lila, would you like to go out for breakfast?" Rhys asked, kissing the groove of her collarbone.

"Sure, where do you want to go?" she asked, absently pulling her fingers through his hair.

"Where do you like?"

"Um," she said, crinkling her nose. "Don't know. Where do you like?"

"There is an amazing brunch place called Crwst in Cardigan, West Wales, but a four- and-a-half-hour drive is a little far for bacon." He looked at her pointedly. "So, where do you like?"

There was a beautiful little French-style cafe on the other side of town. It served the most delicious patisseries, the sweetest hot chocolate she had ever tasted, and she felt like Audrey Hepburn any time she stepped into it. But it was too sappy for Jason, too chintzy and quaint for Jasmeet, and didn't have enough space for Maddy's buggy. There was only so many times she could go there by herself before the staff started giving her pity macaroons.

Rhys would hate it. It was full of *stuff*, colourful and bright, and the tables were close together and small.

"Let's go there," he said, decisively.

"But I didn't say anywhere."

"You were thinking it."

How did he know her so well? Yes, she had been thinking of a pain au chocolat and an almond croissant. And possibly the sweetest raspberry tart to finish.

"No, it's okay," she said. "You won't like it."

"Maybe I will, maybe I won't." Rhys raised an eyebrow at her. "But you will."

Lila's heart swelled as he kissed her cheek and scrambled out of bed.

"Do you mind if I have a shower?"

"Of course, help yourself," she said. "Towels are in the cupboard."

She watched the muscles of his bum move as he headed out of the door. He threw a wink over his shoulder at her. Rhys was so different from the first time he had accidentally on purpose slept over. He had been so bristly, so awkward, hiding his body. Now, it was as if a switch had been flipped in him. Once they'd done all the things that they were supposed to do – going on a date, holding hands, leaving her on the doorstep, having sex all night – he was relaxed and calm and downright hot. She enjoyed Relaxed Rhys. Enjoyed him a lot.

As much as she told herself she didn't want a relationship, she did want someone to wake up with, to go to French brunch places with her, to sit with through Susie Dent. She liked being excited when Rhys texted her. She liked telling him random things and him enjoying hearing her talk. She liked learning about Henry II and Welsh words.

Lila liked caring for people and prickly, soft-centred Rhys, needed caring for.

Would a relationship with Rhys be the worst thing in the world? Perhaps not. Perhaps it was exactly what she wanted, what she *needed*. But she wasn't even sure if he wanted a relationship and that was certainly not a conversation she was going to broach, because how awkward would that be? Oh sorry, going for brunch was actually just a way of saying thanks for the great sex, see you at work. And then she would have to see him *at work*, knowing that he had rejected her after literally shagging all coherent thoughts out of her head.

So no, she would not be bringing up that conversation. If he did, she could be breezy and bright and *oh yeah, sure, I'm happy with a one-night thing, that's fine. See you at work, bestie!*

Her face fell at the thought. Nope. She was one hundred percent not happy with a one-night thing. She didn't want to go back to just being friends and seeing him at work. Yep, she wanted Rhys for more than one night and for more than his excellent tongue and dick.

She was in real trouble with this beautiful man who cared about what she thought and cared about what she wanted.

She wanted Rhys as a boyfriend.

Oh fuck.

RHYS

Well, the coffee wasn't bad, and neither was the plain croissant he had, but the pastel-coloured chairs were uncomfortable and the little round table was too small for his coffee, two plates of pastries and Lila's teacup and teapot (obviously). She was remarkably pretty in a clingy flamingo-print dress, and bee-stung pink lips. He was so lucky to be here with her.

Mostly, though, she looked thoroughly delighted that they were in this tiny cafe with overpriced bottled water.

"This is my most favourite place. This pain au chocolat is beautiful," she said, a crumb dropping from her lips.

Rhys reached across the tiny table and linked his fingers with hers.

She glanced at their intertwined fingers and a frown flashed across her face. Was she embarrassed? Did she not want people to know they were together? *Were* they together? Usually, that conversation would have to be after date five, but everything was so topsy-turvy with Lila that perhaps it was a conversation to be had now. When they first started their agreement, she mentioned that she had sworn off all men. Perhaps that was still true. But perhaps, just *perhaps*, he had done enough that she wanted him in her life. Proved that he cared.

Hopefully.

Besides, he wasn't ready to go home.

"Lila," he started, unlinking their hands and dabbing his mouth with a napkin. She sighed, her shoulders dropping, but plastered a kind smile on her face.

"Rhys."

"Can I spend the day with you? Do you have other plans?"

Lila blinked in surprise.

"Because if you have other plans, then don't worry."

"No, I just thought," she hesitated, some internal debate going on inside her. "I thought you'd want to go."

Rhys watched Lila tear apart the remnants of her pain au chocolat.

"Want to go? No. Lila," he said, reaching across and tipping her chin up so she was looking at him. His heart stuttered. She was vulnerable and worried, a small crease in between her eyebrows that he'd never seen before.

"Lila, I would like to spend the day with you. I'd like to spend every day with you. I would very much like to have a relationship with you, call you my girlfriend, but I know you've sworn off men. You can call us whatever you'd like, but I would like to be in your life, as more than a friend." He dropped his hand to his coffee cup. "But only if you want to. I don't want you to do something just because you think it will make someone else happy."

Well, it was not the most flowery of speeches, but it did the job. Accurately conveyed his feelings. What he hadn't banked on was the pounding of his heart against his ribs, the dryness of his mouth, the nearly imperceptible tremor in his hand as he sipped his coffee. He was fucking nervous about what she would say. What if she said, *thanks for the dick, see you at work?* Then that was that, he would see her at work and be whatever she wanted him to be. Just a work colleague, if that's what she wanted.

He wouldn't pretend to himself that he wouldn't be hurt. Because he would be terribly hurt. But that was something to deal with if or when the time came.

"You want to be in a relationship? With *me*?" She was pretty incredulous.

"Yes," he answered. "That's exactly what I want."

Another sip of coffee and a non-threatening smile.

"You don't have to answer me now," he said, placing his coffee down on the table. "We can spend the day together, or if you feel you need some time to yourself, I'll go home."

Rhys watched Lila's throat bob in a swallow and clenched his fist under the table. He was not ready to say goodbye just yet. Not at all.

"Um." Her tongue stroked across her bottom lip. "I, uh—"

"I'll tell you what, Lila," he said, kindly. "I'll go home. You have a think about what's best for you. Call me when you want to."

Lila adjusted her teacup, the clattering against the saucer betraying her nerves.

"Why do you always make things my choice?" she blurted.

Rhys's head tilted and he frowned.

"Because it is," he said simply. "It's up to you who you spend time with, who you're in a relationship with and I don't want to take away any decision from you."

"Oh." She focused on her torn-up pain au chocolat.

"I think that you're so busy trying to please everyone that you don't do what you want to do, things that make you happy. And I like seeing you happy."

Her eyes flicked to his.

"You like seeing me happy?" Her voice was small, tentative.

"Yes." He grinned, because that was an easy question. "I like the way your eyes sparkle when you're surprised. I like your satisfied smile when you taste a particularly good cookie. I like your grin when Richard Gere does something stupidly romantic."

"You do?"

"Yes, I do." he said firmly. "But—"

Lila's shoulders sank, but he pushed on.

"But, I don't want you to think about me. I want you to think about *you*. Whether you want this. Whether you don't want this. This is entirely *your* decision and I will be happy that you've made it for yourself."

Inside, he was screaming *Pick me! Pick me!* but everything he said was true. It was her decision and he would not take that away from her. He was worried that if he didn't give her that specific choice, she'd go with the flow because it was what *he* wanted, which is precisely what he *didn't* want.

Rhys wanted her to be with him because she wanted to be.

Lila's mouth dropped open ever so slightly, her soft lips desperate to be kissed. He could kiss her, he *wanted* to kiss her, but this wasn't the time.

They sat for a beat in silence. She wasn't going to say anything. Fuck, she needed time. Fine. Time he could give her. He wouldn't like it, but he could.

"Okay, I'll talk to you later. Call me when you're ready, okay?"

He took one more slurp of his actually quite delicious coffee and stood, throwing on his jacket and forcing a smile for Lila. How did she manage to smile all the time? Especially when he wanted to shout and demand and, most of all, scowl. But he wouldn't, not with her.

The stupid ring of the bell as the door swung shut behind him grated on his last nerve. He was definitely doing the right thing, he knew he was, but his jaw ticked with tension. Rhys did *not* like decisions about his life being left to other people, he didn't like giving up control. But she needed this control and he wanted her to have it. It was just difficult giving it.

It was colder today and he zipped up his jacket and turned up his collar against the wind. Dodging annoyingly happy couples out for a Sunday morning stroll, with pushchairs and children, was obviously not what he wanted to be doing right now.

Fuck.

Lila's surprised face, the O of her plump lips, the awkward way she'd picked at her food. Yeah, he'd fucked this up good and proper. He should have left well enough alone. Lila had said that she wasn't looking for a relationship and here he was, just like Jason, running roughshod over her decisions. Stopping in the middle of the pavement, he pinched the bridge of his nose. For fuck's sake.

"Rhys!"

Whipping around, his eyes focused on her, because they always focused on her. Sidestepping a dog on a lead, Lila was a little manic, with her floral coat flying around her, wisps of her hair caught in the wind. She really needed a better hairspray or hair tie or whatever.

"Rhys," she wheezed, hands on her knees as she caught her breath. "I cannot believe you made me run. I don't run."

A wry smile tugged at his lips. *Evidently.*

"Well?" she said, hands on her hips. "I've run *all this way.* Aren't you going to kiss me?"

"Is that what you want?"

It had to be her choice. It had to be what she wanted, not just to make him happy.

She stood up to her full height (which wasn't very tall at all), flushed either from the 'exercise' of running twenty metres, the bite of the autumn wind, or from asking him to kiss her.

"I, Lila Cartwright," she put her hand on her chest, "take you, Rhys Aubrey, to be my boyfriend."

A smile spread across his lips, because Lila was nothing if not dramatic. He couldn't bring himself to care that people were giving them funny looks or tugging their children away from their spectacle.

"But," she jabbed him in the chest with a finger, "we are not *calling* you my boyfriend. It's too much for me, I can't have that label. I know you need that clarity, the specifics and that's fine, but after…"

Lila trailed off, an uncharacteristic line again between her eyes, pleading with him to understand. Which he did.

"Yes." Rhys worked his hand at gently unclenching her small fist and flattened her palm against his chest. She took a tentative step forward.

"And," her voice was almost a whisper. "You have to be careful with me. You can't hide things from me. I make my own decisions."

Jesus, Jason had really done a number on her. What a prick. "Yes. Of course, yes."

He reached for her, sliding his fingers into her hair at the nape of her neck. Her hands slid up his chest and over his shoulders.

Kissing Lila was the best thing. Softly, with promise. The rumble of traffic didn't exist anymore, neither did the woman tutting loudly about their PDA, or the crying child in the pram. The only thing that was real was the softness of Lila's lips against his, the way her hair caught in his fingers.

"Yes," he said.

LILA

They spent the rest of the day together. Rhys introduced her to his dreary, immaculate grey flat and she fully understood how her house both horrified him and filled him with some strange sense of wonder. Like a bruise that you couldn't stop touching.

It was depressingly cold in his flat. Functional and perfect, but just so... impersonal. The sofa was more of a punishment for believing you could sit down rather than a hug made of fabric and there were certainly no blankets to be seen anywhere. It was even tough on her skin as Rhys bent her over the arm of it to thrust into her, gripping her bum hard enough to leave a mark.

He hadn't been able to keep his hands to himself as he showed her his black and white galley kitchen, pushing the fabric of her knickers aside so he could gently massage her clit, pressing his front to her back. He had made her come with a sharp pinch to her nipple.

She hadn't been this horny, or felt this *wanted* since – well, ever.

Rhys circled his thumb on the softness of the inside of her wrist, his fingers slid down the back of her arm, kisses dropped behind her ear.

"Can I pick you up in the morning for work?" Rhys asked.

It was Sunday night and they were back at her house, and she was close to falling asleep in the blanket cocoon Rhys had made for her on the sofa. She hadn't asked him to stay and he hadn't assumed. Gentle, careful and slow. That's what she kept repeating to herself. Don't rush, don't go all in, because what if, what if, what if. It already felt that they were free falling too fast to grab onto any tree branches on the way down, probably because of all the time they'd spent together getting ready for his family thing.

"You don't have to." She leaned in to kiss him quickly on the lips.

"I know. But if you'd like me to, I would like to as well."

Rhys was so aware of asking her, not demanding or assuming anything.

"Well, in that case, Dr Aubrey, yes, you can pick me up in the morning. But," she hesitated, a wry smile on her lips, "won't people think that we've *spent the night together*?"

His eyebrow quirked upwards.

"Miss Cartwright, are you teasing me? Because if you are," Rhys stepped forward with narrowed eyes and bent to whisper in her ear, "I'll have to punish you."

His hot breath glided across the shell of her ear before he grazed her ear lobe with his teeth.

Lila could not get over the fact that his mouth was so… so… *filthy*, and in more ways than one. Every time he said something about how pretty her pussy was, or how hard he was for her, what he'd like to do to her, it was a jolt straight to her core. Then he'd grin wickedly, knowing precisely what he was doing to her. Never, *ever*, had anyone wielded words to make her skin tingle and wetness seep between her legs, and she loved every syllable of it.

"For clarity, Lila," he stepped back and smirked at her blushes. "I'd happily tell everyone how much I enjoy spending the night between your legs, but I don't think you'd want me to."

"Rhys!"

"Can you be ready by 8? 8.15?"

"I'll try for 8," she said, because he was usually already at his desk at eight, if not before, and compromise was the key to success here.

Rhys winked at her (actually winked) before getting into his swanky car. After he left, she threw herself on the sofa and dragged the blanket around her. It smelled of his clean, fresh washing powder and the forest-y tang of his bodywash and, like a complete weirdo, she huffed on it like an addict snorts up Tipp-Ex.

Her phone blinked accusingly at her from the squidgy ottoman.

Jasmeet, Girls Group Chat

are you dead? i haven't heard from you all weekend

I'm not dead! Sorry Jas! You okay?

The phone rang in her hand.

"Lila, I'm dreading going back to work tomorrow, just dreading it. My headteacher texted me this afternoon to say that she needs a meeting with me first thing in the morning and it's not going to be good, is it? Otherwise, she wouldn't have texted me."

No 'hi', 'hello', 'how are you', just straight into it, which meant Jasmeet was panicking.

"Firstly Jas, calm down. Okay? Take a breath," she said gently, smoothing the blanket over her legs. "Secondly, that's really unprofessional and you should talk to HR about it."

"HR?" Jasmeet snorted. "You think we have HR?"

"Okay, well someone higher that your Head. It's not within working hours and it's ruining what's left of your weekend."

And hers, the high from Rhys's words fading like the promises of a political party the more Jasmeet poured her drama into her ear. Not that she minded, not at all. Jasmeet needed her.

"And thirdly, whatever it is, you can deal with it. You're a fantastic teacher, you're an amazing person. You know your stuff, okay? You're good."

Lila kept her voice soft, because tough love was something that didn't work on Jasmeet at all. At. All.

"I am. Aren't I?"

"Yes," she said decisively. "One hundred and ten percent."

"You can't get higher than one hundred percent," she said absently.

"You know what I mean," Lila said, flicking through Netflix. "Seriously, Jas. Don't let this worry you any more tonight. I know it's hard but do something to take your mind off it. Do you want to come over?"

Lila immediately regretted the words leaving her mouth. It wasn't that she didn't want Jasmeet to come over, but... actually, no. It was exactly that. She was in a perfect little post-Rhys bubble and she didn't want to be disrupted. Yes, she loved Jasmeet, but if she came over then they would spend all evening dissecting every conversation she'd had over the last week, trying to work out what the meeting could be about and how Jasmeet would deal with it.

It would be draining.

"Would you mind, Lila? I mean, I'm stressing myself out over here."

"Where's Dan?"

"Oh, he's out with Rhys. He called a few minutes ago and wanted to go for a drink, so Dan has gone. He invited me, but it seemed like a boys' thing."

"You could have gone. He wouldn't have invited you if he didn't want you to go."

"I suppose so," Jasmeet said. "I could text him, see if I could go. That would stop me stressing."

"Yeah, it would."

"Are you sure you don't mind? I mean, I just said I'd come

over." Well, not exactly, but okay. "Why don't you come as well?"

"I'm already in my pjs," she lied.

"No, no I won't go. I don't want to be too clingy. Do you think I'm being clingy?"

In the end, Jasmeet didn't turn up on Lila's doorstep, but she did stay on the phone until halfway through *Risky Business,* going through every possible conversation that could be had tomorrow at 8.15am.

Rhys

Night, see you in the morning. 8am, yeah?

Yes Mr Aubrey Sir! Enjoy your night with Dan? :)

Rhys

How did you know I was with Dan?

I have my ways.

Rhys

Jasmeet told you.

Ha! Yes, she did.

There was a lot of flashing dots before:

Rhys

Cool.

That's not what you were going to say!

Rhys

No, I was going to say something about missing your tits, but decided to do it in person tomorrow morning.

She blushed, even though there was no one there to see.

Well, you'd best come over at 7 then

Rhys

On the dot.

You're bright red, aren't you?

Rhys

Yes, I am.

I fucking love that.

Night Rhys

Rhys

Night Lila

CHAPTER 16

Demarcation *(adjective) de·mar·ca·tion*
1. The action of fixing the boundary or limits of something

RHYS

Seven o'clock couldn't come soon enough. Rhys had deliberately not seen to himself in the shower that morning and he arrived at Lila's with a semi just from the thought of her curves. She'd already text him that the key would be under the mat and he was to let himself in and come and find her.

Fuck, he hoped she was as ready as he was.

His shoes were off and he was already unbuttoning his shirt halfway up the stairs when he noticed steam curling around the open door to the bathroom.

Lila, his *girlfriend*, was in the shower. Waiting for him. His dick was now painfully hard and he hurried up the last of the stairs, stopping to hang his shirt and trousers over the banister and to tug off his socks and pants, before stepping into the steamy bathroom.

Lila's body was hazy through the obscure glass shower screen, her hair piled on top of her head. Pausing for a moment, he just watched her allowing the hot water to stream against her chest, down her body, his hand going instinctively to his cock. He must have made some kind of noise, because she whirled around, catching sight of him through the glass.

Lila slid the shower door open, her eyes going straight to his dick, tongue darting out to wet her lips. He ran his thumb across the pre-cum already seeping out of his slit, his hand pumping his shaft a couple of times at the sight of water dripping off Lila's hard nipples.

Two urgent strides and he was with her, under the spray of the water. A bruising, urgent kiss and the sweet torture of her hard nipples against his chest had him wishing he had helped himself this morning, because he wasn't going to last very long with her. He *never* lasted very long with her.

His hands slipped up her ribs and to her chest, twisting ruthlessly at her nipples before releasing and soothing them with a gentle brush of his thumb. One hand kept working a nipple, whilst the other dove between her legs.

"Shit, Lila," he moaned into her mouth. "You're so wet. You're always so ready for me."

"Rhys," she panted, bucking and jerking against his two thick fingers that were relentlessly pumping her pussy. "I want you. I can't wait."

She grabbed a condom from the shelf where her bodywash stood and ripped it open with her teeth, her wet fingers shaking and slipping against the foil. He angled his dick away from the spray and sucked at her nipple as she rolled the condom on with unsteady fingers.

"Lila, if you want my dick, you're going to have to ask for it," he said into her chest, nipping at the nipple he'd been sucking on.

"Rhys," she gasped, hands at the back of his head. There was a hesitation and he bit again, this time the underside of her breast and she shuddered, her pussy tightening on his still pumping fingers. "Rhys, I need your dick in me."

"Good," he said, pressing her back against the cool tiles of the shower enclosure. He hooked one of her legs over his arm and she reached between them to guide his cock into her. Using both hands made her breasts press together and he couldn't help but pinch one nipple, then the other, earning himself beautiful gasps from her throat.

He thrust in, one long, hard thrust that had him buried in her up to his hilt.

"I'm not going to last very long," he panted, bracing one arm above her head as he lifted her leg higher, pressing himself deeper.

"Neither am I," she said, her eyes fluttering closed and head falling back against the white tiles of the shower. Rhys angled her so the shower water fell between them, hitting her sensitive nipples, running down the valley of her chest, collecting where they were joined, splashing where he drove deeper into her.

She cried out as she came, her nails digging into his shoulders, standing leg trembling so hard he was vaguely worried they'd slip and fall. Two more thrusts and he was with her, the veins standing out in his neck as he spilled inside her.

Lila's leg slipped from where it was hooked over his arm and she fell against him, boneless and spent.

"Fuck, Lila. That was—" He swallowed, catching his breath. "That was amazing."

"Mmm." Her voice vibrated against his chest and he looked down, running his hands over her skin.

They stayed like that for a while, breath slowing, arms around each other while the water cascaded over their skin.

"Lila," he whispered, eventually. "We've got to go to work."

"Two more minutes," she said, her breath minty sweet across his lips.

Rhys was late for work. Well, not *late* late, but late for him. And he didn't mind one little bit.

LILA

The way Rhys played her body with his fingers, his tongue was nothing short of magnificent. She had no idea that sex could be like that and that her orgasms could literally have her seeing stars. He was a maestro and she was his instrument .

It didn't seem to be one-sided. Rhys shuddered when she nipped at his nipple, moaned when she scratched her nails over his scalp, couldn't wait to be inside her in any way possible; his fingers, his dick, her pussy, her mouth.

"Lila? Did you hear me?" Sue popped her little erotic daydream bubble for the fourth time that week. "What is with you at the moment?"

"Sorry Sue," Lila said, snapping a smile into place. "World of my own."

"I was just saying that the PhD students need enhanced access to the Moodle so they can set work for the undergrads? Can you sort it please?"

"Yes, of course," Lila noted it down on the pink heart-shaped pad next to her.

Sue turned to leave.

"Oh Sue, while I've got you," Lila said, standing. "I sent you my application for the Lexicography Masters course. I just need you to forward it on with your approval."

"I'll have to check to see if I received it," she said, dismissively.

"I had a delivered receipt when I sent it last week. I'll resend it again now for you." Lila bent down and tapped on her keyboard to forward the email. "It's due tomorrow by five o'clock. If you could have a look at that, I'd be super appreciative."

"Hmm, yes," Sue said, glancing towards the door before raising her eyebrows to Lila. "PhD access to Moodle."

"On it," Lila said, with her most professional, reassuring smile.

Sue swept out of the room, her chintzy perfume trailing

in her wake. Sue had been less than excited about this course for her. It was like she couldn't quite work out why Lila would want to take the course. *That* was why she hadn't told anyone what she wanted to do. The judgment, the assumption that she couldn't do it. Or why she would want to do it in the first place.

People didn't outright put her down, but it was the head tilt and the sympathetic smile that said 'good for you, giving it a go, don't worry if it's too hard'. Or Jason's 'be careful you don't overstretch yourself, *you know how you get.*'

This course wasn't about proving anything to anyone. It was about *her*. What she wanted. And she wanted this course. So there.

She'd finalised the flier for next week's student/lecturer mixer by adding a couple more star bursts, and sent to the whole of the History Department. It was good for the students to see the lecturers as actual people, not just teachers. It was also good for the lecturers to see the students as not just numbers, a chore to deal with so that they could do their research. A mix of terrible sangria, crisps and popcorn in bowls, fun party hats, a chance for people to mingle early so the students could go out after and the lecturers were in time to go home for tea.

Lila was bent over the bottom drawer of the filing cabinet in the far corner, trying to work out what kind of filing system her predecessor had used for the module information (answer: a rubbish filing system) when a phone pinged in her office, but it wasn't hers. She looked over her shoulder at Rhys, leaning against her office doorframe.

"Oh, hi," she said, straightening up and turning to face him. How had he snuck in without her noticing?

"Hi." There was something about this Rhys – with his eyes growing darker and the way the muscles in his jaw tightened, looking all hard-edged and dangerous standing in her soft, cosy, colourful office – that was insanely attractive. She couldn't help but notice how his grey trousers and crisp white shirt completely contradicted the shabby, tasselled cushions piled on the sofa where he'd held his seminars, and yet he didn't look out of place. His presence was electrifying.

His eyes leisurely traced from her eyes to her lips, then lower, caressing down her neck, across her collarbone to her breasts. His tongue darted out to wet his bottom lip, and she swallowed, her breath turning shallow. This man, with his dark, hungry eyes, was making heat coil low in her belly and her nipples harden against her lacy bra.

"What are you doing?" she whispered.

Rhys let his gaze linger on her chest, lips turning up in a smirk because he could obviously see how turned on she was, and just by him looking at her. This man was seduction itself, and she felt desired and worthy, a heady combination that made her feel flushed and beautiful.

"Looking at you." His voice was smooth and low, muscles in his jaw flexing with restraint. "I haven't been able to concentrate on anything this morning."

Lila swallowed heavily. "Oh?"

"Emails, marking essays, my Fellowship application, prepping for my meeting with Professor Painter," he said, shaking his head slowly. "Not dealt with any of it."

"Why?" It was little more than a wispy breath.

He closed the door to her office with a soft click and prowled forward, steps slow and measured, his erection bulging hard against his trousers, and oh my God, that was all for *her*. Being the object of his obvious lust heightened the tightness in her belly and the heaviness in her breasts. She squeezed her thighs together.

"Because I know you're here, wearing that sinful green bra that barely holds your tits in, and I've been thinking about all the ways I could make you come." He stopped half a step from her, resting one hand on the filing cabinet behind her, and the other on the windowsill, caging her in. He bent closer, and she was surrounded by his masculine scent and it was all she could do not to bury her face in his chest and huff on him like an addict.

"Rhys," she started, but her voice trailed off when his hot breath puffed across her neck. This was dangerous, his filthy words making her so hot, desperate for him.

"I could work my way under that long skirt, push your knickers aside and fuck you with my fingers," he whispered, lips just a fraction from the burning skin of her neck. He held himself back, deliberately staying just a breath from her, waiting for her to come to him. "Or, I could bend you over the back of the chair and make you come on my cock."

Oh my God.

A raspy, pleading noise came from her throat and she pressed her thighs together harder.

"Someone could come in," she breathed. Rhys trailed his nose up her neck, leaving a trail of delicious shivers in his wake.

"There's no one there, it's lunchtime. And I don't care," he whispered, pressing hot kisses to her neck. She tilted her head to give him better access, and threaded her fingers in his hair. He didn't care, and she wasn't sure she did either. "I don't think it would take much, would it? You're already wet for me." It wasn't a question.

Yes. Wet and ready for him.

"I—" she started, but the words wouldn't come.

"It wouldn't take me long, I've been thinking about your pussy all morning." He pulled back to look at her, desire vibrant in his eyes.

He hadn't been able to concentrate because he had been thinking about *her*, and that made her feel beautiful and powerful. She reached for the button of his trousers, and he hissed out a breath. Slipping her hand inside his boxers, she gripped his hard length, sliding her hand up and down. His jaw muscle pulsed and his eyes fluttered shut briefly, the arms caging her in shaking with tense control.

"Bend me over the back of the chair," she breathed

across his lips and his eyes snapped open, darkening with primal need.

He grabbed her waist, spinning and pressing her against the chair. Lila moaned as he pushed up her skirt, hands shaky and urgent against her skin. Rhys cupped the hot wetness between her legs and the noise she made was more animal than person.

"Lila, you have to be quiet," he ground out, pulling her underwear to the side and swiping his fingers through her sex, and she bit her lip, hard. "Fuck, you are so ready for me."

There was a tearing of a wrapper and a quick fumbling behind her, and then he was back on her, positioning the head of his cock at her entrance. She pushed her hips back, desperate for him. It took one thrust for him to be deep inside her, and the delicious stretch and fullness of him was nearly too much.

"Fuck Lila, you take me so well," he rasped as he withdrew and slammed back in. This wasn't slow and sensual, it was hard and fast, his fingers digging into her hips, driving into her faster and faster. The moans she was trying so hard to keep in became louder, and she couldn't bring herself to care because the heat of her orgasm was building so quickly, so intensely.

"I fucking love the sounds you make," he said through panting breaths, "but I'm going to cover your mouth. You want me to stop, you tap my hand."

She nodded and his strong hand closed over her lips. His other arm wound around her hips, dragging her back towards him so he could get deeper, the wet noise of flesh on flesh the only sound other than their harsh pants. Even with the submissive position she was in, the hand over her mouth, him taking and taking, she felt safe and in control. She had the power.

"Give it to me, come on my cock." His voice was low and strained.

The danger of being caught, the eager, frantic pounding of his cock and his words brought her to the edge, and one more deep thrust had her clenching hard around him, her cry muffled by the hand clamped across her mouth.

"Fuck," he hissed, driving into her one final time, before collapsing over her, his hand slipping from her lips. "Fuck, Lila. You are so good."

Lila tucked her hand into the crook of his elbow as they headed towards her bench, smiling up at him like he hadn't just railed her over the back of the chair in her office. Sitting, Lila took her lunch bag and handed him a chicken salad sandwich.

"Can I take you home after work?" he asked.

Rhys was just, well, he was just the sweetest guy (most of the time). *Can I take you home after work*? He asked her every day. Thing was, she wasn't going to be able to get home without him, because he was driving her in to work after staying the night. Except on kickboxing nights with Dan, which Lila forced him to go to, he went home and she called her parents, happy to listen to the trials and tribulations of wine tours. They even asked her how she was now and again, and she could actually tell the truth. She was happy.

"Hmm." She tapped her chin. "What if we go to yours?"

"But my flat is so… so…" Rhys frowned, looking at the lake, "dull. I much prefer your house. I much prefer you."

"You can drop me home. But you've got kickboxing tonight." She poked his chest.

"Dan's not going. I'm not going." There was a distinct whine to his voice.

"That's not how that works," Lila said with a reprimanding smile. "You need to do the things that make you, you."

And she needed to put in some boundaries to stop her from falling, falling, falling. Because it would be easy to fall for Rhys and she was just so wary and nervous of losing herself again. Technicolour Lila had been hard fought for.

"You make me, me."

Obviously, Rhys had other ideas because that guileless honesty squeezed her heart.

"Rhys." She shook her head with a smile.

"What?" He took another bite of his sandwich. "It's true. I've never felt freer, more like myself. That's all because you've showed me a better way to live my life. How to actually enjoy it."

He was so matter-of-fact, like it was so obvious, but it wasn't. Not for her. Emotion clogged her throat because she finally felt needed. No, that wasn't the right word. She felt *wanted*. She had been convenient for Jason. He just needed her financially to support his dream. Rhys didn't need her, he *wanted* her. And that made her feel like she was free falling without a parachute; exhilarating and terrifying.

"Kickboxing," she croaked out. "You've got kickboxing tonight."

"Fine," he grumbled and linked their fingers together.

It was so calm, so easy and best of all, she wasn't worried that something she said or did was wrong. He wanted her for her, not for what she could do for him. Tears pricked at her eyes and she looked away, trying to blink them away.

"What's wrong?" Rhys tugged at her hand. "What's the matter?"

"Nothing's wrong. I'm just..." She rubbed a finger under her eyes. "I'm happy."

"Oh, okay." An awkward, crooked smile pulled one side of his lips and he squeezed her hand. "I'm happy too."

A blush flared across her cheekbones. The way he was looking at her was soft and warm, and no one had ever looked at her like that before. Gosh, her poor battered heart was working overtime. The subject needed changing before either of them said something that she wasn't ready to hear or say.

"I've handed my application in to Sue. She just has to sign it and submit it." It felt so good to be getting somewhere. "When are you handing in your Fellowship application?"

"That's brilliant, Lila." He kissed the back of her hand. "Tomorrow. Definitely."

"Good." Lila handed him a cookie from her lunch bag. "I'll cook you a celebratory dinner."

Rhys grinned and leaned closer to whisper in her ear.

"I'd rather have you for dinner."

A shiver ran through her as his hot breath ran down her neck. Already needing her again was *hot*.

"Rhys," she hissed, glancing around quickly. "You can't say things like that! Not here."

"Don't pretend you don't love it." Rhys sat back with a smirk. "Besides, I've just fucked you in your office, when anyone could have come in."

The thought of the past fifteen minutes made heat coil again low in the base of her stomach. How much she wanted him was worrying, and exactly why it was good to have some separation.

Lila poked his hard thigh in reprimand and Rhys leaned forward to grip her chin, before planting a solid kiss on her lips.

RHYS

Kickboxing was hell. Not just because Dan wasn't there, but because he wanted to be with Lila. He completely got what she was doing, he really did. But he didn't like her feeling she had to protect herself from him. Because she didn't. Not at all.

Things like this should be straightforward. He liked her, more than liked her.

Fuck, who was he kidding? Rhys was in love with her. Desperate, stomach-churning, sleep-depriving, all-encompassing, love. And he was more than fine with that. Lila didn't want his money, didn't want his name or his connections. She didn't need anything from him at all. Except

264

his patience, and perhaps his mouth, and he was more than happy to give her that any time she wanted.

He grinned and aimed another long reverse punch at the poor skinny guy he was partnered with today. If he wasn't going to have her tonight, then he'd have to get rid of his energy somehow and if it meant taking it out on this guy, then so be it.

Lila's eyes softened and warmed for him, and for him alone. Her blushes, her smiles, her orgasms – they were all for him. But her hangover from Dr Dishcloth Douche-Twat meant she was holding back from diving into anything super-serious. Because that's what it would be, that's what it *was* – serious.

Him and her, together. A partnership. There were no other women, no post-Lila. Not for him. There was a black ball of anxiety sitting low in his stomach. What if he wasn't good enough for her? He was highly strung, difficult, not in touch with his emotions. He was sharp and particular and obsessive. The last thing he wanted to do was tarnish her shine. Because he knows that's what he'd do if he was too… *him.*

"Hey man, go easy," his partner said, stumbling back after a particularly good front punch.

"Sorry."

Head in the game, Rhys.

The Fellowship application was ready and waiting for a press of the send button. An email that should have dictated the rest of his life, but it no longer did. The Fellowship application should have been the absolute pinnacle of his academic achievement, should have been the only thing he could think of, where all his ambition, drive and thoughts were.

If he didn't get the Fellowship, he'd have to return to Dallimores, sell his soul for a corporate office and a suffocating tie and be back under his father's thumb. But this time, with all the considerable weight of familial disappointment pressing down on his shoulders, pushing him underwater. At least, that had been the deal.

If Lila could rebuild her life, reassemble herself after her gas-lighting wanker of an ex-boyfriend, then he could, as a thirty-two-year-old man, choose what the hell he wanted to do with his life. Why did he need to go back to Dallimores if (when) he didn't get the Fellowship?

Answer: he didn't. He had a decent job that enabled him to do his research. He had a rented flat that was affordable on his salary, good friends (well, Dan), and best of all, Lila.

Eventually, his father would get over himself. Elin was much more suited to corporate life. Somewhere along the line he had just stopped caring what his father thought. A father should be supportive of his choices, even if he disagreed with them. It wasn't like he was selling his soul to the devil to be able to play the blues. No, he was simply researching Henry II and his sons. Just because his father didn't *understand* his passion, did not mean it wasn't valid.

Rhys did not need his father's approval.

"Hey man, good class," he said to his skinny partner after the class. "Sorry if I got a bit carried away."

"No worries," he said. "You here next week?"

"Yeah." Rhys stuffed his towel back into his kit bag.

"See you then." The guy clapped him on his shoulder and with a smile, off he went.

Rhys pulled out his phone as he headed to his car.

Elin

When are you bringing Lila for dinner with me and James? I like her.

You'll have to invite us first. And we're busy.

Elin

I'll get my PA to sort something.

Dan

Sorry couldn't make it tonight. Class okay?

Yeah, went with a new guy. He was good.

Dan

Look at you, branching out, making new friends.
How's Lila?

She's fine.

Dan

Double date?

No.

Dan

Jasmeet will organise it with Lila.

It wasn't that he didn't want to see Dan or his sister, but he was too selfish to share Lila. He would, because he knew she'd like it. The rest of the world was out there, but he was here in his little bubble with Lila. His girlfriend. Who he wouldn't call his girlfriend and who he would be gentle with, because she'd asked him to.

"Call Lila Cartwright," he said to his car as he pulled out of the car park.

"Hey, you finished? Was it okay not going with Dan?" There was the tell-tale noise of her snuggling down into a blanket on the sofa.

"Yeah, it was fine. A new guy said he'd see me next week." Rhys indicated left to his flat.

"What? Are you making… friends?" She would be sitting there, her hand on her chest and eyes teasingly wide. A rumble of a laugh came from his chest.

"People want to see us," he said.

"That makes no sense to me."

"My sister has asked us round for dinner. Well, she's asking her PA to sort it out and Dan has asked for a double date. Have you told Jasmeet about," he hesitated fractionally, "us?"

Because there was an 'us', he was just unsure how she wanted to frame it.

"No, I haven't found the right time," she said.

"What about your parents?"

There was an uncomfortable silence from the other end of the phone.

"I was just wondering," he said.

Logically he knew that Lila telling people about their official relationship status was a big step, and *logically* he was fine with that. It was him she called, him she kissed, him she gave her smiles to. But also, something hot clutched at his stomach. That's what you did. You told people about your boyfriend. Or whatever she wanted to call him.

Was she not telling people because she was embarrassed of him? There was a moment of disbelief that this beautiful butterfly of a woman would ever want to be with someone like him; highly-strung, set in his ways, poor personal skills. Perhaps she wasn't telling people because she couldn't bear people to know that she was with someone like *him*.

"Rhys, it's so difficult to get a word in edgeways with anyone half the time, I haven't been able to tell anyone," she said. "Besides, I'm not sure people would be that interested, they've got better things to worry about."

Fucking Jason breaking her down. Fucking Jasmeet and the other one, Maddy, for making her feel less than. Fuck her parents for not seeing how much she needed their attention.

Seren had never been embarrassed by who he was – in fact, she would tell anyone who would listen that she was engaged to the Dallimore heir. But Lila wasn't Seren, and he never wanted her to be. If it was up to him, he would shout it to anyone who listened, but it wasn't. He had to be slow and safe for her, and if she needed time to realise that she wasn't a burden to other people, then he would give it to her, no matter how much he had to push down his feelings of inferiority.

"Lila, you are worthy of people's time. You are worthy of everything you want."

The line was silent, apart from a little sniff.

"I can come over, if you'd like?" he asked gently.

"Okay, if you want to."

"Lila, I always want to."

"Yeah, I would like that."

Rhys went all the way round the roundabout and headed for his girlfriend, who was sorely in need of care.

CHAPTER 17

Indignant *(adjective) in·dig·nant*
1. feeling or showing anger because of something unjust or unworthy

LILA

Sue's office was milky-tea bland. The artwork on the walls looked like someone had vomited abstract lines and circles onto a canvas and entitled it 'Corporate Art for Offices'. There were no books, just folder upon folder upon folder on her shelves. Where Lila's smaller office was welcoming and cozy, Sue's seating area was barely used, demonstrated by yet more folders stacked up on her sofa.

Standing awkwardly in front of Sue's desk because she hadn't been invited to sit, was not one of Lila's favourite pastimes, especially when she was at a loss as to what to say. Dumbfounded was not the word, and Sue didn't even seem to care as she clicked away on her computer, eyes certainly not on Lila and her imminent breakdown.

"Was there anything else?" Sue peered at her from behind her computer, her mouth pursed together like a cat's bum.

Was there anything else?

Well, actually Sue, yes there was. That you are a condescending prick who couldn't manage a conker-finding expedition in the bright depths of autumn? Yes, that was something that she *could* say. She wouldn't, but she could.

"No," Lila choked out.

Sue sighed. "You're not going to let this affect your work, are you?"

If she was a phoenix, Lila would have blazed and died right there and then. Since *when* had she ever let *anything* affect her work? Going above and beyond was in her DNA.

"No, it won't," she said, the back of her throat burning to keep tears from filling her eyes.

"Okay then."

Lila knew a dismissal when she heard it and if she stood there any longer, she'd turn into a statue that Sue would move around her office like the Corporate Art.

"Okay," she whispered, swallowing down her emotion.

As soon as she closed Sue's office door (Sue had an open-door policy, but without the 'open door' aspect), everything she had worked so hard to keep down in the last three minutes flooded out of her. It was a good job Sue called Lila to her office every forty-five minutes to 'convert this to that PDF thingy' or 'where did I save this?' or 'how can we stop the starlings nesting outside my window?', because Lila's mind had absolutely zero spatial awareness as she barrelled down the corridor, face wet and vision blurred with tears.

"Uh, Miss Cartwright. Are you okay?"

Students waiting outside of her door were usually a welcome sight, but now? Not so much.

"Oh, hi Kerry." She hiccuped. "I'm okay. I'm sorry. What can I help with?"

Lila rolled her lips together, but nothing she did could stop the tears running over her cheeks.

"Oh uh, nothing," Kerry said. "I'll come back."

Usually, Lila would make a fuss and insist she come and sit on her sofa, pressing a hot cup of sugary tea into her hands and have her spill all her worries into the cookie tin. But not today.

"Okay," she whispered with a small, defeated smile. She ran.

Lila carefully closed the door to her office and took herself over to her sofa, shoving a cookie from the tin on the coffee table into her mouth. How could Sue do this to her?

Five minutes. That's all she'd allow herself and then she'd power through the rest of the day and collapse into a messy heap when she got home. It felt more like eight minutes when she was interrupted.

"Lila?"

Wiping her cheeks, she found a smile hidden deep and looked up at Rhys. He was dishevelled in the best way, probably from having power-walked his tight little conker butt to her office. One look at Rhys and her precarious smile fell into a grimace and the tears started again. She buried her face in her hands. Christ, she was pathetic.

Three long strides and he was sat beside her, pulling her into his chest and smoothing her hair away from her face, letting her tears drench his shirt. When her sobs subsided, she sat back and offered him a little smile.

"Sorry, I've got your shirt all wet," she said, dabbing at his chest with a tissue from the coffee table.

"Lila, what's happened?" he asked, stopping her hands with his.

Trying to postpone the inevitable, or distract him so he wouldn't make her tell him, she asked, "How did you know I was upset?"

"Kerry came to tell me."

Wow, Kerry had built up enough courage to go and see Rhys to say Lila needed him. And Rhys had remembered her name.

"Oh," Lila whispered.

"Do you want to tell me?" Rhys asked softly.

"It's not that important." She shook her head and sat up straighter.

"Right." Well, that was a disbelieving look if ever she saw one. "I would like it if you told me"

That's all it took. Lila opened her mouth and it poured out.

"Sue 'forgot' to send in my application. I had to push for her to sign it and I told her a million times that it had to be in yesterday by five o'clock, that was the deadline and she 'forgot'." Yes, air quotes.

"You don't think she forgot?" Rhys narrowed his eyes.

"No, she didn't forget," Lila spat. "She didn't want me to do it. She didn't think I could do that and my work." Lila waved an arm at her office. "Sue actually said '*I hope this won't affect your job*', because I was a little upset that she hadn't handed it in."

"She was definitely supposed to?"

"Yes! You need to get a signature from your line manager and they are supposed to forward the application on to the relevant department. It's all in the staff handbook." She reached under the coffee table for a floppy, dog-eared copy.

"No, it's okay, I believe you." He stroked a thumb across her cheekbone. "I believe you."

Lila nodded, her shoulders slumping.

"So, I've missed the application deadline. I won't be doing my course this year, all because someone else didn't believe in me, or didn't want me to do it." Lila shoved another cookie in her mouth, because cookies made everything better. "It's a sign," she said, mouth full. "I shouldn't do it. I can't do it."

"No."

She took a deep breath.

"Oh, well. Never mind. I'll be okay." She smiled, but it hurt. "I'll just have a couple of wallowing days and then, you know, back to Happy Lila."

"No." Rhys shook his head, his lips turned down.

"What do you mean 'no'?" Because that's what generally happened when she was disappointed. A couple of days of ice cream, then back to normal.

"I don't want you to go back," Rhys said, a line creasing between his eyebrows. "Tell her that it's her mistake and that she has to fix it."

"Maybe," she said with a conciliatory shrug. That's what

people wanted, wasn't it, her to agree with them. She thought Rhys was different, but she was too emotionally exhausted to argue with him. It was so easy for him; see a problem, find a solution, do it. But that's not how it worked for her, she couldn't switch her emotions off and the fear that churned in her stomach when she had to make demands for herself probably wasn't something he'd ever experienced. She could go to bat for any of her students, she could stand up for her friends, but herself? That was a struggle, because what if Sue *was* right and she wasn't good enough to do a Masters? What if she wasn't capable enough to go after her dream?

"Go and see her this afternoon and tell her she needs to speak to the Admissions Officer and explain her mistake."

Amanda, the Admissions Officer who was waiting for her application, would be another person who thought she didn't have the ambition or plain ability to get anywhere in life.

"I said 'maybe'." Lila stood up and closed the cookie tin, taking it back to her desk.

"I'm sorry, Lila," he said. "I'm sorry. You do whatever you think is best. I'll support you either way."

She pushed her lips into a poor semblance of a smile. Whilst all he could probably see was an easy problem to get over by just having a conversation, it was much more than that to her. He needed to respect her choices, her wishes, how *she* decided to deal with it. Which may be by doing nothing for a day or two, wrapping her head around the situation, building herself back up just a little, then going into battle. God, she hated battle.

"Would you like me to cook something tonight?" Rhys stood and reached for her hand, rubbing his thumb over her knuckles. "How about that creamy pasta you like?"

"Comfort Carbonara?" This time, her smile was more genuine. He'd remembered. "I'd like that."

"Okay."

RHYS

The anger in his veins burned ice cold.

"I'll pick the ingredients up. Can I drive you home?"

He forced his voice to be calm, forced his hands not to shake as he cupped her face and kissed her gently on the forehead.

"Rhys, you don't have to ask anymore," she said wearily. "You can take me home."

A frown flickered across his face. That's what he wanted, to not have to ask to take her home every day, but also, he didn't want it because she was so worn down by that fucking cretin, Sue, that she'd do whatever he said.

"Lila," he tilted her face up to his, her eyes puffy and red. "You don't have to humour me."

"I want Comfort Carbonara and I want you to take me home." Lila wrapped her arms around his waist and rested her cheek on his chest. He splayed one hand across the centre of her back and the other nestled in the hair at the back of her head. She needed him and he was more than happy to give her exactly what she needed.

The phone on her desk rang, jerking them out of their little reverie.

"Thank you," she said, with such trusting sincerity it made his blood burn in his veins. He wanted to rage at the world which had made her believe that she wasn't worth caring for. She offered him a wan smile before sitting at her desk and answering the phone.

He kissed her on the cheek and headed out of the door and to the department kitchen.

Fuck.

The anger was burning him inside, forcing his pulse higher and higher. His hands balled into fists as the kettle boiled for his black coffee. The corporate businessman in him reared its ugly head. Sue was unprofessional, inappropriate and truly a bad manager. He'd had run-ins with her before, but nothing he couldn't handle. It took a bit of force, a bit of guile, a bit of hard-nosed pressure for Sue to do the job that she was paid to do. He'd met people like her before and he could deal with them in his sleep.

So why couldn't Lila? It was so easy, all she had to do was talk to Sue, point out her obvious mismanagement of this situation, and all her troubles would be fixed. Rhys forced himself to breathe evenly and think.

Lila was soft-hearted and had low self-esteem, so that was probably a tough thing to do for her. Really tough. The worst thing was that she didn't want his help. He could have this nipped it in the bud in ten seconds flat, but he wouldn't, because she didn't want him to. Even though it killed him inside.

"Hello, Rhys." Sue bustled into the office, huffing and puffing, setting her mug next to his. "Mine's black, two sugars."

Fucking hell. The world could piss right off with this test of his willpower and self-restraint.

"I am having the worst day," Sue said, leaning her portly ass against the small kitchen cabinets. She was obviously wanting some kind of response.

"Oh?" he said, his voice clipped.

"I've just had to tell Lila to buck her ideas up and not let disappointment affect her work. It's so tough getting people who are resilient, you know?"

Resilient. Buck her ideas up. Disappointment.

Rhys made a non-committal noise at the back of his throat, because if he said *words*, he would say much more than Lila wanted him to. How fucking unprofessional of Sue to be gossiping about Lila's work which, he might add, was pretty damn good.

"I mean, she's good. She is. But she couldn't possibly keep everything running and do a Master's course as well and it's not like I have time to do her job as well as my own."

"Isn't personal development part of the University's guidelines?"

"Yeah, but not at the expense of a well-running department. Come on, Rhys, she wants to do a Linguistics Master's? Lila Cartwright couldn't linguistic her way out of a paper bag." Sue gave a very not attractive snort laugh.

What did that sentence even mean? Either way, Rhys got the derogatory drift. The vein in his temple pulsed and his jaw ached from clenching it.

Nope, no. Cannot do.

He could not stand there and listen to this dreary old woman who sat on her arse all day, having Lila do her own job *and* Sue's job so she would look good, crow about how she was stifling someone's dream, all because she knew full well she wouldn't be able to cope without Lila.

That's what he heard when Sue opened her stupid, insipid, manipulative mouth.

"Sue." His voice was cold and quiet, a trick he had learned from his father.

Don't shout, boy. Don't let your emotions get the better of you.

Rhys folded his arms across his chest and pinned her with his eyes. He waited just long enough for Sue to shift on her feet, looking slightly uncomfortable.

"Firstly, do you feel it appropriate to discuss a colleague's professional development, and your opinion on the same? And to do so in such a public setting?"

"Uh, well, it's just you and me, Rhys."

"Yes it is, and I find it highly inappropriate."

Sue blanched. Her shoulders stiffened.

"Secondly, your inability to grasp why someone would want to take a course to further their career, to possibly branch out into something new, demonstrates your extreme lack of motivation and ambition. Frankly, it's embarrassing the scorn you show for anyone who does demonstrate such qualities."

Fuck, this felt amazing.

"Thirdly, your vindictive and soulless managerial skills have ensured that Miss Cartwright can never progress, because you will constantly keep her under your thumb doing both her work *and* yours, when she is capable of so much more than you ever will be."

Sue spluttered, her face an interesting puce colour.

"However, now that you have some apprehension of these defects in both your personal awareness and professional skill level, I feel sure that you will discuss the matter of the late submission of the application with the appropriate Admissions Officer and secure an extension to allow Miss Cartwright's application to be considered."

"How did you, how do you—"

Rhys cut her off with a wave of his hand. This was not her show.

"If that is not the case, then I'm sure that the Vice Chairman and the Head of HR, both of whom I am well acquainted with, will be very interested to hear about the vicious and spiteful way in which you manage your hardworking staff members."

Sue looked like her brain was ready to explode. He would lay a bet that in all her years, no one had *ever* spoken to her like that. Well, she fucking deserved it.

It wasn't how you managed people – fuck, it wasn't even how you treated people, and then she had the gall to come in and gloat about it in a public environment to someone who had literally nothing to do with the situation. Nope. Not today, Satan.

Sue said nothing. Her mouth opened and closed like a schoolchild caught in a lie. Rhys waited. Emotions flew across her face and there was no way he cared enough to work out what they were. He was in the right here and Sue was definitely slap-bang in the middle of 'wrong'.

"Uh, well, I uh…"

Sue finally gave up and threw her hands in the air before storming out of the room, hissing profanities. If he was petty and petulant (which he was not), then he would have asked her to repeat herself and then reported her to HR for the use of foul language in the workplace.

And then he would have taken her coffee to her, white no sugar.

What a twat.

LILA

There had been so many RSVPs to the meet and greet. It was amazing that people wanted to come. Well, perhaps it was the promise of a glass or two of dodgy sangria, some plain tortillas and the garlickiest guacamole she could make. Students, lecturers, admin staff; lots of people would be stopping by, so much so she'd had to move it to one of the bigger seminar rooms. Even people from outside the department had got wind of it and wanted to come. Excellent.

She'd persuaded Rhys to come and help set up (i.e., told him he had to) and prepared tinny mariachi music to play from her little portable speaker. Bunting had been found in the stationery cupboard and Rhys's pert little bum was in particularly good form as he stood on a chair to pin it across the wall.

"Dan's coming," Rhys said over his shoulder as he stretched to stick the last plastic triangle to the corner. "That's all right, isn't it?"

"Yeah, course it is." She liked Dan and it was good to form relationships with other departments. Not to mention the fact that he was Rhys's best (only?) friend, and her best friend's boyfriend. It would be good to get to know him better. "The more the merrier."

Rhys stepped down and looked like he had something else to say, probably something about telling Dan about their 'status', but wisely kept his mouth shut. It wasn't that she didn't want people to know, it was just that she didn't want the fuss, the exclamation, the judgment behind the eyes that someone like Rhys would want a mess of a person like her. It was just better to let people notice organically. Easier.

She thought she'd been happy before, but what she really wanted was someone to share her life with, someone who would support her and respect her. Finding that in the most unlikely of places (a very stroppy, highly strung academic) just made her grin. She hadn't even been looking. The swearing off all men tactic had gone spectacularly badly in the best way.

Rhys stepped down from the chair narrowed his eyes at her.

"What are you smiling at?"

"Hmm, just… things," she said, resting her hands on his chest. "I'm happy."

Happiness flashed across Rhys's eyes and a soft smile pulled at the corners of his mouth.

"Good," he said. "I am too."

Rhys was happy with *her*, no changes needed. Warmth spread through her chest.

"Oh, uh sorry, Miss Cartwright." DeVon cleared his throat behind them. "Has it started yet?"

"DeVon," she said, stepping away from Rhys, whose hand lingered on her waist. "Thanks for coming. Help yourself to a drink, some nachos."

"Okay," he said, heading for the lukewarm sangria. "The others will be here soon."

The absolute worst outcome for a party was if no one actually turned up. Or one person came and stood there awkwardly until they could feasibly leave the room.

"Good," she said.

Forty minutes later, the room was full of plastic cup-holding students and lecturers, and a couple were already a bit worse for wear. Someone had produced some face-paint from somewhere, and Lila was busy drawing rainbow moustaches and Taylor Swift hearts on people, which were getting progressively wonkier after two glasses of what had turned out to be quite strong sangria (good job Rhys had driven that morning). Dan was her current victim.

"Let me take a picture for Jasmeet."

Lila pulled out her phone and Dan grinned at her.

"I look sexy, don't I?" he asked with a wink.

"Yeah, sure," she said, laughing. The glitter pink neon heart stood out nice and bright around his eye.

"Hey, I hope you're not flirting with my girl," Rhys said, slinging his arm over her shoulder. See! They didn't have to put an announcement in the paper. *Organic*. No big deal. But the flutter in her stomach as the words *my girl* rolled around her head made her hot and flushed. And, good Lord, that little bit of possessiveness was *hot*.

Lila swallowed hard before saying, "Your turn now, Rhys."

"Oh no, I don't think so." Rhys looked absolutely terrified, holding his hands up defensively.

"Go on, mate," Dan said, swigging his drink. "Do what you're told."

"Please?" she whined, opening her eyes dramatically wide. It took a couple of beats, but Rhys's jaw relaxed and his muscles flopped in defeat.

"Okay, fine, but nothing as much as," he gestured vaguely to Dan, "that."

She could work with that.

Rhys sat and she stepped between his thighs. Gripping his chin, she bent slightly to sweep some dark blue face paint across his top lip, shaping it into a thick, bushy, Tom Selleck moustache.

She stood back and admired her handiwork.

"God, Rhys, I have never been more attracted to you," she said, laughing. He looked *dashing* with that moustache, which was more teal than blue, sitting proudly on his top lip.

She knew she shouldn't compare Rhys with Jason, but she wondered at how easily Rhys, who obviously hated having his face painted, had done it for her because *she* liked it, and how Jason wouldn't even let her have the remote control.

"Good," he said, brushing his lips against her ear. "I'll keep it on when I eat your pussy later tonight."

Good Lord. He'd said that in the middle of a work event.

"Rhys!" she hissed, slapping him on the shoulder.

"I don't know what you said and, judging by how red Lila is, I don't want to either," Dan said, cringing at them. Well, that made her even more red. Could the earth just swallow her up please? Rhys's wide grin said he couldn't care less what anyone thought.

Lila surveyed the room. More people had arrived, some left, but the sangria was going down steadily, the nachos were nearly gone and students and lecturers were chatting and laughing, which was exactly the point. Her history lecturers were even chatting with members of other departments. She clucked like a proud mother hen.

This was a success.

Except for Sue, scowling in the corner with a half-filled plastic cup, a contamination zone of a good metre around her. Fine, if she didn't want to engage, that was on her.

Lila laughed at a joke one of the students cracked and caught Rhys's eye across the room. He was chatting to Dan and a couple of other students.

Chatting. With students.

It wasn't so long ago that he barely tolerated being in the same room as them for his actual job and look at him now. Chatting. Making small talk. Smiling. At people who weren't her or Dan. Lila smiled to herself. Even with that ridiculous moustache, he was so handsome.

Professor Painter, one of her senior lecturers and Rhys's Fellowship admission sponsor, poked his head in the door, his eyes searching the room until he found Rhys. Rhys clocked him and waved him over. After being introduced to Dan, the two exchanged whispers and she watched, horrified, as Rhys handed his drink to Dan and followed Professor Painter out of the room.

"Rhys," she called, but her voice was drowned out by mariachi music and laughter. "Rhys!"

By the time she'd elbowed her way to the door, Rhys had disappeared with Professor Painter.

"Dan," she turned to him. "Where did Rhys go?"

"He said that guy, Professor Painter, wanted him. There was someone Rhys had to meet?" Dan shrugged.

Rhys had to meet someone, with Professor Painter, his Fellowship admissions sponsor. With a blue moustache on his face. Oh God.

"Didn't you tell him about the moustache?" she asked, trying to keep the bite out of her voice. Seriously though, Dan should have warned him.

"Oh shit, I forgot it was still there. I kind of got used to it," he said, apologetically.

Lila pressed her hand to her forehead.

"Lila." There was a tap to her shoulder. "This is great!"

Turning, Amanda the admissions officer was smiling widely at her, nachos on a paper plate in one hand.

"Oh hey, Amanda. Thanks for coming," she said automatically, her mind still on Rhys and his blue moustache.

"Of course. Hey, between you and me," Amanda leaned forward conspiratorially, "congratulations. The acceptance letters are going out tomorrow."

Lila looked at her blankly. "Letters for what?"

"For the Master's course, silly." Amanda crunched a nacho.

Lila's head was spinning with Rhys and his stupid blue moustache. Why had she done it? Presumably he'd just forgotten it was there, but now he was talking to Professor Painter and a mystery person, looking absolutely ridiculous. She shook her head and tried to concentrate on Amanda.

"The course that I missed the deadline for?"

"Mmmhmm" she said, crunching a nacho. "Well, Sue

called and said it was her fault that your application was late and practically begged us to let you on the course."

"Sue? *My* Sue?"

That didn't sound like the grump in the corner. Whatsoever.

"Yeah, your Sue. Anyway, congratulations!" she said with a grin, before turning away and disappearing into the crowd.

Sue. Her fault. Begged. *What?*

Lila pushed her way through the crowd to where Sue was perched on a tall stool, perma-scowl front and centre on her face. People were avoiding her, and frankly Lila would too if she wasn't confused, grateful, flabbergasted.

"Sue, did you—" Lila swallowed. How was she going to put this? Oh well, just press forward. "Did you call Amanda and get me on the Linguistics course?"

Sue pursed her lips so tightly her face looked like a cat's arse. She rolled her eyes and put her plastic cup extremely carefully down on the windowsill. Crossing her arms in front of her, Sue perused her stonily.

"What else was I supposed to do when your boyfriend threatened my job?"

"*What?*"

"And that's a new development, I see. You and Rhys. I'll have to check the staff handbook on that."

Of course, Lila had already done that. There was no rule about dating a co-worker.

Sue stood, somehow looking down her nose at her even though she was three inches shorter. "Rhys threatened my job if I didn't get you on that course. He threatened my *livelihood*. I can't believe you'd stoop so low, Lila. Getting your *boyfriend* to do your dirty work."

Lila shook her head. "What?"

"Rhys might like that fake innocence, but I can see right through you."

Sue stormed past her, bashing her shoulder as she pushed past her.

What?

Lila's phone buzzed in her hand and she swiped at it absently.

Jason

> Money transferred. The full amount of the loan. After everything between us, I cannot believe you got your bloke to email me with ultimatums. Fuck you Lila, fuck you.

First Sue, now Jason.
What the hell had Rhys done?

CHAPTER 18

Compunction *(noun) com·punc·tion*

1. anxiety arising from awareness of guilt

2. distress of mind over an anticipated action or result

3. a twinge of misgiving

RHYS

Rhys's top lip fucking hurt. The bastard face paint was coming off slowly and leaving in its place a massive fucking red mark where he'd rubbed furiously at it.

It was worse than that though. He'd *forgotten* about the meeting. He'd missed the email, or he'd read the email and it hadn't sunk in, he hadn't put it in his diary, he'd just… been distracted and had completely forgotten. He had *never* forgotten anything as important as this. Never.

He'd sat there, bumbling through a half-prepared and half-remembered speech about what an honour and a privilege it would be to be part of the Historical Association, about his research, his planned papers, his book proposal. With a massive fucking blue moustache painted on his face.

How could Dan have let him just walk off with it on his face without saying anything? It wasn't Dan's fault though. It was his own for letting Lila paint his face. Lila's fault for actually doing it. Why did she have to be like that? All fluffy and insistent that he join in, be part of the 'History Department community' when he was quite happy by himself.

Now his chances were ruined. He would never be taken seriously with a poorly worded, rambling speech and a fucking bushy blue moustache on his face.

Fuck.

Bracing his hands on the sink he glared at himself in the mirror. This 'informal chat' would influence the panel and he would be a fool to think otherwise. He'd been on enough interview panels, had enough fucking experience to know that connections, relationships, networking fucking *mattered*.

Rhys had let his mind go. He'd been so absorbed with Lila, so loose and free with his time and mind that his focus had gone.

Slamming the bathroom door behind him, Rhys stormed back to his office. There was absolutely no way that he was going back to that stupid fucking Mexican party with warm sangria and tinny music that put his teeth on edge.

He was vibrating with anger, his hands unable to stay in his pockets, legs unable to let him sit still. All the frustration burst out of him and he smashed his fist hard into the side of the filing cabinet.

"Fuck," he shouted.

The pain shot up his wrist into his forearm, but he didn't care. He didn't care about the blood pooling on his knuckles, staining into his coarse, awful beige carpet.

Somehow, some way, his father would hear about this and that would be yet another negative mark against him. Turning up unprepared to what was essentially an interview with fucking face paint on. There was no way he would ever live that down.

He moved over to the window and leaned his elbows on the sill, holding his head in his hands. None of this was going to be fixed any time soon. In fact, it may have ruined his chances with the Historical Association.

Forever.

All because *Lila* had wanted to be in his life. All because *he* had wanted her to be in his life.

His door opened and the smell of vanilla wafted in.

"Not now, Lila. Not fucking now," he growled, not turning.

"Yes, fucking now, Rhys," she snapped. "What have you done?"

"What have *I* done?" he said, voice so low he nearly didn't recognise himself.

His muscles tensed and he turned, every fibre of him shaking with control. That's how he should have been these past months. Controlled and disciplined. Not fawning like a lovesick puppy over cookies and a pretty face.

Lila's eyes were blazing bright with anger, spots of red high on her cheeks. If possible, her hair was even more crazed than it usually was.

"Yes, Rhys," she said, matching his tone. "What have *you* done?"

"What I've done, Lila," he said, pressing his hands to the desk and leaning over it, "is managed to absolutely fuck up my chances of ever being accepted into the Historical Association because *you* managed to screw me over."

"Screw you over? What, with the face-paint?" she said, taking a couple of steps towards him. "You're a grown up, you make your own decisions. Besides, it wasn't *me* who let you walk out of that room with it still on your face. That was Dan."

Another step towards his desk.

"Why did you even need reminding? It's not like you're a four-year-old who needs your face wiped by your mother."

"Lila, this is my life *ruined*." A warning in his voice, because she really didn't want to push him now and he could not even begin to comprehend why she didn't even seem to care.

Lila rolled her eyes and flapped her arms. What was she, a fucking bird?

"Don't be so dramatic, Rhys," she said, her voice too loud

for his office. "Your life is *not* ruined. It wasn't even the formal interview, and you—"

No, no way. She didn't get to dictate this discussion, if it could even be termed as such with their voices definitely the wrong side of quiet.

"Dramatic? I'm not the *dramatic* one in this relationship. A relationship, I might add, that has caused me to completely ignore my responsibilities. *You* have made me lose all sense of what I'm supposed to be doing, my reason for being here." It all became clear to him, so clear that he could see the unfocused, irresponsible, failure of a man that couldn't make a success of anything. The man that *she* had turned him into. "I've been with you, or thinking about you, when I should have been preparing for the Fellowship application."

Rhys dragged both hands through his hair.

"What the fuck have I been doing? How did I let myself get this distracted?" he muttered.

"Hang on a minute, Rhys—" Lila put her hand up and took a little step forward, but he battled on.

"And you're so ashamed of me, so embarrassed to be with someone like me, that you couldn't even bring yourself to tell your friends or parents that we're even in a relationship." That hot sting that he'd tried to douse burned extra hot in his stomach. "That's how invested you fucking are."

"You know that's not true," Lila whispered, shaking her head.

"Miss Cartwright." She looked as if he had slapped her, but he didn't care. "You are unwanted in my office. Get. Out."

Rhys forced his hands into his pocket and ground his teeth together, waiting for her to leave so he could do some damage control with Professor Painter. But she didn't go. Instead, her shoulders tensed and she took a deep breath, collecting herself.

"I don't give a shit whether you want me here or not, Rhys Aubrey-*Dallimore*," she snapped. "I am not leaving until you tell me why you interfered with my life when you promised, Rhys, you *promised*."

Lila's voice broke a little on that last word but he was too far gone to care.

"What are you talking about, Lila?" He shook his head, shaking his words out of his brain. "I have to deal with this absolute fucking shit show and I don't have time to deal with whether your wool is all knotted or your favourite blanket has a stain on it."

Lila's eyes hardened and her entire body stiffened.

"I guess I was wrong." Her voice was quiet. "You haven't changed a single bit. You don't give a shit about anyone but yourself and I can't believe I ever thought that you could."

"I've got no idea what you are talking about and quite frankly, I don't give a shit." He sat down and scanned his computer screen, waiting for the inevitable 'I'll get your office ready for you' email from his father. Because his father would know, he *always* knew. Rhys wondered if his father would go so far as bugging his office.

Rhys clicked the refresh button on his email. Nothing yet.

It was silent, but there was still the sweet smell of vanilla standing in front of him.

"I can't believe I ever thought you were different to Jason," she whispered. "Fuck you, Rhys."

Rhys snapped his eyes to her, confused. Like Jason? He was nothing like that absolute sweat stain. He'd think about that later.

The door slammed shut and he was left with no unread emails and fading vanilla. Heart slowing somewhat now he'd exploded, he tapped his fingers on his desk, waiting for his father. Retrieving his phone from his pocket, he lined it up next to his keyboard on the desk.

Refreshing his email again, a message from Elin's assistant popped up asking if he and Lila would be free next Saturday for dinner. Yeah, no, he couldn't think about that right now, not when all this Fellowship stuff was going on.

Besides, he wasn't sure that he actually wanted to spend time with Lila right now.

"Fuck," he whispered, because that wasn't true.

It wasn't true at all.

She had just been a convenient punch bag in a convenient place at a convenient time. An easy target. What had he done?

Shit.

His email updated with something from his father's assistant, but Rhys didn't bother to open it. He was on his feet and wrenching open his office door.

Dan, with a Taylor Swift heart around his eye, was heading in his direction, brow uncharacteristically low over his eyes.

"Dan, I can't deal with you now," he said, aiming to push past him. "I need to find Lila." He needed to fix it, to apologise, to hold her.

"No, the last thing you need to do is find Lila," Dan said, shoving him hard in the chest. "What the fuck is wrong with you, Rhys?" he hissed.

"Dan, I know—"

"Do you? Do you actually know? Because she's in her office with Amanda, bawling her eyes out. Absolutely fucking distraught." Dan shook his head in disgust. "I've called Jasmeet to come and get her, because she can't even drive in this state."

"Look, I'll talk to her. I'll fix it, it's just been a bit of a shit hour and a half."

"No fucking way will you talk to her. She hasn't said it, but I *know* this was you, Rhys. I know you and I know how you get. I know how to deal with you, I can tell you to back off. I know when to take things seriously and when not to. But her? Your 'girl'?" Dan pointed down the corridor. "You don't get to treat her that way."

Rhys opened his mouth to say something, *anything*, to defend himself. But what was there to say?

"There is absolutely no way you're talking to her again today." Dan sighed and passed a hand over his face. "She was good for you, Rhys. She pushed you to think about how you treat people, how to enjoy life. You were really happy, for the first time since I've known you."

"Dan, I—"

"I bet you ran roughshod over her, didn't you? Wouldn't let her get a word in edgeways because *your* shit is always so much more important than anyone else's, right?" His voice was low, disappointment leaking out of each syllable.

"That's not true and you know it," Rhys said, pointing a shaking finger at Dan.

"Do I? Really?" Dan snapped. "I care about you, man, but you have fucked up big time here. So big, that I can't even deal with you right now."

"Whatever, I need to see her." Rhys moved to push past Dan again.

"You need to listen to me," he said, his voice tense but so calm. How could he be so fucking *calm*? "You don't get to see Lila. Not now."

Dan just didn't get it. He *needed* to see her, make things right. Shake her devastated, broken look from his mind and just hold her. Apologise and apologise and apologise again, because it would never be enough.

Dan put a firm hand on his shoulder and gave him a pointed stare. Rhys looked back at his friend for a long moment, before his shoulders slumped and he felt his soul sinking. Dan was right, this was not the time. He left Rhys standing in the corridor outside of his office, alone with nothing but dread and guilt.

LILA

It might not have been professional, but Lila took the next day off work. Jasmeet had stayed over, holding her whilst she had spiralled and sobbed herself to sleep, left her a plate of heart-shaped pancakes and a freshly brewed pot of coffee (both now cold) and a note apologising for not being able to call in sick, but that she would call on her break and at lunch and be over as soon as school finished. Jasmeet being the best person she could ever wish for made Lila feel even worse because she'd been so hard on her lately.

In her mind, she knew that Rhys's forgetting his meeting wasn't her fault. But perhaps, in some small way, it was. She *had* monopolised his time. They'd been together nearly every night. Something would have to give if he was spending so much time with her, and this is what it was. He'd missed the email, probably because he'd been screwing her in her office.

It must have been devastating for Rhys, realising that he had sat through that meeting, so important to him, with a blue moustache on his face. He was so anxious about the Fellowship anyway, let alone making what he thought was a fool of himself at an informal chat. Being how he was, it would play on his mind. He would find it incredibly difficult to reconcile that he hadn't put his best face forward.

She could almost see his point of view. Almost.

You know what, she wasn't going to take any responsibility for his petty, childish, absolutely vile behaviour. It had been an informal chat. It certainly wasn't the end of the world. He hadn't even bothered to check on her after he had… well, said what he had said. Shouted, in fact.

None of this was her fault. None of it.

Lila scraped her hair back from her face and wound it up with a hair tie. Her eyes were crusty because she'd barely slept and when she had it was fitfully, what with Jasmeet snoring, the never-ending tears, and Rhys's horrible words going round and round in her head, merging and morphing together.

Miss Cartwright, you're unwanted.

She pressed a hand to her chest, because that was an awful, awful thing to say. Yeah, he had said *in my office*, but he might as well have said *in my life*, because that's what that amounted to, wasn't it? She'd done exactly what she had promised herself not to. After working so desperately hard to put her life back together, to put *herself* back together, she'd let a fucking man take her apart again.

A distraction, that's what she'd been to him. Distracting him from more important things, like that godforsaken Fellowship and proving to his father that he was a success. Yeah, she was a people pleaser, but here was Rhys, dancing to his father's tune, jumping through his father's hoops, just so he could do what he wanted with his life. Well, he'd have one less distraction now.

"Enough," she said, pressing her fingers to her puffy face.

Jasmeet

text me when you wake up. love you

I'm awake. I'm going to wash my face, make tomato soup and drink hot chocolate. Thank you for staying with me last night, love you too. Xx

Nothing from Rhys. Not that she wanted to talk to him, but just some acknowledgment, some sign of any guilt about the way he had treated her, would have been nice. But he wasn't nice, was he? He was blind to anyone and everyone else. Selfish and blind.

That was that. End of.

She washed her face with cold water, bringing down some of the puffiness around her eyes, and headed downstairs. Completely unsure as to what to do with herself, Lila put her stained blankets in the washing machine. She liked her blankets. They were *not* stupid. Well, maybe they were just a little bit, but she liked them and that was all that mattered.

It was four o'clock before she sat down to figure out some sort of plan.

The anger was still there, simmering like her tomato soup,

but it was the disbelief that clawed at her the most. She couldn't believe that Rhys had not once, but *twice*, undermined her, meddled in her life without so much as a 'if you don't mind' or 'thought I'd run this past you'.

He'd put her job at risk. The job that she enjoyed, a stepping stone to where she wanted to be. She would have talked to Sue, would have got it straightened out. She didn't need a White Knight stepping in and wielding his massive... ego around.

That brought her on to Jason. How dare Rhys go behind her back to demand that Jason gives her back the entirety of the loan that they took out *jointly*. Truthfully? She had felt a little bullied into it, but a signature on the bottom of the page was a signature on the bottom of the page. She was a big girl. She knew what she was getting herself into. Although she would be lying if she said that having the full amount of the loan wouldn't be a wonderful addition to her bank account.

She could pay for the course upfront rather than have a payment plan, and she'd have a nice little savings pot as well.

Regardless, Rhys had broken his promise to be gentle with her, to not behave like an absolute douchebag. He'd broken her trust.

He'd broken *them*.

Logging on to her work laptop, she ignored the fact that Rhys was showing as 'online' on Teams and had been since six that morning. Nope. Not her issue.

She clicked on Sue, took a deep breath and videocalled her.

"Lila," Sue said, answering quickly. Her face was still pinched.

"Good afternoon, Sue," Lila said. "Firstly, thank you for letting me take a mental health day today."

"That's fine. You wouldn't have asked if you didn't need it." Sue's face softened a little.

"I just want to apologise," she sighed. "I didn't ask Rhys to talk to you and I certainly didn't ask that he threaten your job. I'm sorry."

God, why didn't her words work? She loved words, why couldn't she find any?

"Lila, you don't need to apologise, Rhys already has," Sue said, leaning forward towards the computer screen. "What he said made me think and actually, I would like to apologise to you."

Ah, so this must be an alien that had been put into Sue's body, because Sue, *apologising*?

"I felt you were far too valuable to let you go for a few hours a week. After a surprisingly productive conversation with Rhys this morning, first thing I may add, it made me realise that I was holding you back rather than helping you progress, like a good manager should."

Well. That was a surprise.

"Sue, I—"

"I really am sorry, Lila. I'm going through..." Sue hesitated. "My husband and I are separating, and I've obviously taken things out on you." The words were rushed and clipped, evidently not something Sue wanted to share.

"Sue, I'm ever so sorry to hear that." Gosh, what an awful thing for her to be going through.

"It is what it is," Sue said, forcing a tight smile to her face. "Lila, I want you to take Monday and Tuesday off as well, have a nice long weekend, pamper yourself. You've got more than enough lieu hours, but I won't be putting them through and it won't go on your sick record."

"I don't know what to say."

"Say 'goodbye Sue, I'll see you Wednesday'."

"Okay," Lila nodded with her first real smile for a few days, albeit small. "Bye Sue. See you on Wednesday."

Sue ended the call, leaving Lila staring at her laptop. Huh. That was a turn-up for the books. Whatever Rhys had said certainly hit the spot. But that did not excuse him. Not even in the slightest.

Lila pulled her phone out.

> Jason, I'm sorry. I didn't ask Rhys to talk to you, or do whatever he did. I will transfer your half back.

It didn't take long before Jason texted back.

Jason

> Rhys has already emailed me explaining that he did it without your knowledge and apologised. Don't worry about it, I've done a lot of thinking and you should keep it all. It's yours.

> Don't be silly. Text me your new account details.

Jason

> No, Li. It's yours.

Lila's finger hovered over the little green call button on Rhys's contact. If it were anyone else who had done this, she would have called to thank them. But no, this was Rhys. Rhys who had interfered with her life, had been vile to her and, yeah (she was big enough to admit it) broken her poor heart. Putting it right was the absolute least he could do.

So she was not going to call to thank him. She wasn't going to contact him at all.

In fact, she was going to sit on the sofa, watch her films, eat tomato soup and wait for Jasmeet to get home so they could lament the state of her life.

RHYS

I'm bringing Jasmeet, and we're only staying for one.

They were late. Rhys sighed and put his phone face down on the table. Dan was still mad at him, or disappointed. But at least he had agreed to meet up for a chat, which is why he was sitting in the expensive wine bar in town, in the hope that his students would prefer to go somewhere a lot cheaper.

After drinking way too much over the weekend, Rhys was thankful that they served non-alcoholic beer. He hadn't slept, he hadn't shaved, he'd just wandered around his grey box of a flat emptying the fridge of beer and pouring it down his neck. Both Dan and his mother had called, Elin had texted, but he hadn't bothered answering. There was only one person that he wanted to speak to, but he couldn't bring himself to be rejected by Lila not answering her phone or ignoring his messages.

Rhys had contemplated going to her place, but that was too much. She would not appreciate that. So he didn't.

That devastated look on her face when he called her 'Miss Cartwright' and told her that she was unwanted in his office – it was seared on his eyelids and he saw it every time his eyes closed. He'd essentially said that it was her fault that he'd dropped the ball on the Fellowship application, when that was patently not true. It was him. It was all him. But it wasn't just that, it was what he had said to Sue, what he had said to Jason. Sure, it was to make her life better, but it was precisely what Jason had done to her, precisely what she had asked him *not* to do. And he hadn't listened. He had overridden her, thinking *he* knew better.

He'd broken them, and he didn't know how to fix it.

There was a small whirlwind as Jasmeet flung her coat

298

over the back of one of the uncomfortably high seats and smashed her handbag on the table.

"We're not staying long," she announced, Dan following close behind. "If it were up to me, we wouldn't have come at all."

He deserved that.

"Thanks Jasmeet, Dan." He nodded. "Do you want a drink?"

"White wine," Jasmeet said, positioning herself on the chair.

"Lager," Dan mumbled, as he took a seat next to her.

They sat in an uncomfortable silence whilst the drinks were brought over.

"So?" Jasmeet said, raising her eyebrows at him. "What do you have to say for yourself? Because I have spent the last few days trying not to let Lila spiral into a grey pit of depression and self-loathing. And that is *your* fault."

Fuck. He passed a hand over his face. God, he was tired.

"Do you even understand what you've done?" she said. "Do you understand that underneath all of the sparkles and rainbows, there's a fragile person that *you* have destroyed, after promising that you wouldn't?"

She sat back and waited, face stony.

"Is she all right?"

"Is she *all right*? No, she's not fucking all right, Rhys," Jasmeet hissed. "Not only did you say the most terrible things to her, you interfered in her life. You didn't trust that she could sort out her own shit and you went behind her back, threatening Sue's job, talking to Doctor Dickhead. She asked you not to do that but you did. You treated her like she was some pathetic kid who couldn't take care of herself. You put yourself as more important than her, overruled what she wanted, ignored her choices about *her* life and then said that she was *unwanted*. Fuck, Rhys."

"I'm sorry, I—"

"Oh, he's sorry," Jasmeet muttered under her breath.

"Jas," Dan said, "let him speak."

"Fine." It was more of a challenge than anything. "Go on then."

Rhys took a breath.

This was awful. This was more awful than the realisation that hit him smack in the face when Lila slammed the door behind her and left his office. The realisation that he had destroyed their relationship, that he had destroyed *her*. Not realising at the time was half the problem and he couldn't have stopped himself because he didn't know what he was doing. He wasn't aware of how his words were landing, just that his life was in ruins because of that stupid fucking moustache.

"There is nothing I can say to make up for what I've done," he started. "Nothing, and I hate myself for it. I hate what I said, I hate that I treated Lila like that. I hate that I—" his throat thickened and if he wasn't careful more fucking tears would come. Rhys swallowed. "I hate that I put myself before her. I never wanted to do that."

"Yeah, well," Jasmeet said, sipping her wine.

"I've tried to fix it with Sue and Jason, but I can't bring myself to talk to her. I don't know what to say. I don't know how to apologise."

"Can't bring yourself to talk to her? This isn't about fucking *you*, Rhys. This is about her and how she's feeling. Do you think she wants to hear from you?"

"No."

"No, she fucking doesn't," Jasmeet sighed. "But that doesn't mean that you shouldn't try to call her, text her, anything. She thinks you've wiped your hands of her. Fixed your mess and moved on."

Rhys pressed the heels of his hands into his eye sockets. Hard.

"Do you love her?" Dan asked bluntly.

"Of course I fucking love her," Rhys snapped, louder than he wanted to be. He was so far gone for her, and had been for so long. "I am literally nothing without her."

There was silence around the table.

"Does she love you?" Dan asked. How the fuck was he supposed to know that? He desperately hoped she did. Rhys shrugged.

"Jas?" Dan asked.

Rhys turned hopeful eyes onto Lila's best friend. If there was anyone who knew what Lila was thinking, how she was feeling, it was Jasmeet. Perhaps even more so than Lila herself.

"She hasn't said."

"But what do you think?"

"I think you've got an awful lot of ground to make up," Jasmeet said, her mouth pinched. "I just don't know. Could go either way."

Rhys nodded and stared at his drink.

"I've got my first therapy session on Wednesday. I've booked three a week for the foreseeable future."

"Yeah?" Dan said, surprised. "Good for you, man."

"I've got a lot to work through."

That was the biggest understatement he had ever made. His father, his self-worth, his obsessive need to succeed. He should have gone to therapy a long time ago, turned himself into someone worthy of a woman like Lila.

"You shouldn't go to therapy for her, you should do it for yourself," Jasmeet said, not unkindly but there was no warmth in his words.

"I know, and I am. But she's shown me what life can be like. The threat of losing her, then *actually* losing her, put my entire life into perspective. I will do anything, *anything*, to make it up to her, to make her happy. Even if it's not with me, I just need her to be happy."

Jasmeet took a long look at him, obviously trying to see into his soul. He'd bared it all to them and he just hoped that it was enough.

"Fine."

"What does that mean, Jasmeet?" he asked quietly.

"It means that I believe you're trying to better yourself. It means I believe that you understand what you've done."

He let out a relieved breath and let his head hang.

"But that doesn't mean that I forgive you or that I like you. Because I don't. At all."

"Yeah, I get that."

"You're a dick, you know that right?" Dan said, a smile pulling at his lips.

"I know. I know I am."

"If you really do love Lila, you're going to have to prove it, Rhys." Jasmeet finished her wine in one large gulp and stood, hooking her handbag over her arm. "Dan?"

"Yeah, coming," he said, pushing his half-finished beer to the centre of the table. "Kickboxing tomorrow? I'd really like to hit you."

Rhys smiled, the first one since Thursday evening, and nodded.

CHAPTER 19

Crestfallen *(adjective) crest·fall·en*
1. dejected, dispirited, discouraged
2. having a drooping crest or head

LILA

Professional, professional, professional was the chant that went through Lila's mind as the lift opened on the first floor of the History Department. This was her job, she was professional and she could cope with addressing Rhys in a professional manner.

Not screaming or shouting or crying or curling up in a little ball under the table. She was a big girl and she could be *professional.*

There was a vase of fresh flowers on her coffee table and she hung up her coat on the stand in the corner. *Things would be okay,* she kept telling herself.

"Lila?" Sue poked her head around her door. "You good?"

"Oh, morning Sue," she said, pasting a smile on her face. "Yes, all fine. I really appreciate the time off. Thank you."

"Not at all." Sue came fully into her office. "Look, I know things might be difficult today. If you need anything, please do come and see me, okay?"

There were so many unsaid words there, but it was an olive branch. One that she grabbed onto with both hands.

"Thanks, Sue, I will. I'm sure it will be fine. Rhys and I are both professionals."

Sue nodded, not looking convinced, but wisely kept her words to herself.

"I'll let you get on," she said, leaving her room.

Lila was expecting eleven billion emails in the Departmental inbox, but Sue had obviously kept on top of them and she was grateful. A letter sat on her desk, her name handwritten across the large envelope. What if it was from Rhys? Perhaps it was a printed PowerPoint presentation of how she should get stains out of her blankets, or a step-by-step guide to unwinding knotted wool.

If it was, she could shred it, but she did have to check because if it was something from a student, her professional mindset would be ruined if she chucked it before she could read it.

Ripping the envelope open, she grinned. A wide, proper grin. It was her acceptance letter from Amanda on the Lexicography course and she hugged it to her chest tightly. Never mind that it only happened because Rhys had threatened Sue, she wasn't going to dwell on that and she certainly wasn't going to let him take any credit for her being accepted on the course. It was all her. It was the beginning of her dream to work in lexicography. She tucked it in her handbag for further discovery at lunch.

The morning passed slowly, perhaps because she was constantly on the lookout for stupid Rhys. Her head snapped up at every person who passed her office and because she was on the main thoroughfare, it meant that she was constantly looking at the door and, consequently, not getting an awful lot of work done. And getting a bit of whiplash.

Just checking in, I'm fine.

text me if you need ANYTHING and i'll call you back asap

Okay, love you xx

Jasmeet had been the absolute best person she could think of, staying with her, checking in, but realistically, Lila needed to put this in perspective. She'd been through a breakup before and that's exactly what this was. A breakup with a man who didn't deserve her. That's what she kept telling herself.

This was *not* her fault.

So why hadn't he come to apologise? Why hadn't he been in contact since the whole debacle of Thursday? It was both gratifying that she didn't have to see him or deal with his attempts at reconciliation, but a little part of her wondered why he hadn't bothered. Not even to say sorry.

Lila took her lunch outside to the lake. It wouldn't be long before it would be too cold and windy to sit outside. Today, the clouds hung low and threatening over the dark water.

She looked through the course paperwork. The modules were absolutely perfect. The History of Etymology, The Sociolinguistics of English, Forensic Linguistics. All practically perfect in every way.

It was time to share her excitement.

Girls, I'm doing a thing, look!!

She sent a selfie of her holding the paperwork by her face with a grin. Not that she looked *great*, but at least she looked better than she had at the weekend.

Lila popped in her headphones, scrolled to a podcast and gobbled down her sandwich. She wasn't one of those women who forgot to eat when they were sad. Oh no, she was an 'eat your feelings' kind of girl, as demonstrated by the three empty tubes of Pringles and the two empty tubs of ice cream in the bin at her house.

Engrossed in her podcast (and concentrating on not slipping over), she didn't notice the warm brick wall in front of her until she walked into it.

"Oh, gosh. Sorry," she said, looking up.

Rhys, smelling of his stupid beautiful body wash.

She took a step back.

"Hi."

He sounded like he had swallowed rocks. He looked tired. Pale, wan and tired. Smaller than usual.

"I'm sorry for ambushing you, but I didn't want to talk to you in your office, I wanted to do it somewhere where you'd feel comfortable and had the ability to walk away if you wanted to."

Well, that was kind of considerate. But still, nope.

"But, I really hope you don't," he said quickly, probably noticing that she was poised to run. Or walk quickly. "Walk away, that is."

Lila clenched her jaw together. He didn't get her words.

"I would like to apologise to you and explain." Her eyebrow raised of its own accord. "I don't want to make excuses. There are no excuses for what I said, but please let me talk to you."

Let him talk to her? Uh, no. Lila stepped to the side to bypass him.

"Thank you for giving me the option to walk away, Rhys."

He visibly deflated and her heart melted a teeny-tiny bit. Okay, so perhaps that didn't come out as kindly as she thought it did. She was genuinely thanking him, because it was quite thoughtful to give her an out of this really rather terrible interaction.

"We will talk at some point," she said, because she did want to hear what he had to say, but not right now. He looked up at her like a little puppy, wide-eyed and hopeful. "But it will be on my terms and when I want to."

"Yes, yes of course. Whatever you need, whatever you want," he said, shuffling forwards slightly. She matched him shuffle for shuffle, because the last thing she wanted was for him to touch her right now. He must have got the point, because he took a step back. "Thank you."

"Yeah, well," she mumbled.

Putting her headphones back in so she wouldn't be tempted to talk to him anymore, Lila kept her eyes facing forward because if she looked back, she would crumble. He looked so desperate, so alone and her deep-seated desire to make everything all right reared its ugly head.

Instead, she hot-footed it back to her office and sat down behind her desk, busying herself with work. There was more than enough work that she could throw herself into, setting right all the stuff that had gone undone under her predecessor.

Her phone rang, interrupting her podcast.

"Just checking in, you okay?" Jasmeet rushed out. "I'm on lunch, can't be long."

"Yes, all fine thanks," she said to the most wonderful best friend in the world.

What had she done to deserve such a good friend? Yeah, there were times when Jasmeet could be self-centred and dismissive, but couldn't everyone when they had stuff going on? Hadn't she been when Jas had that stuff going on at school? The main thing was she was right there when Lila needed her, holding her whilst she cried.

"Do you need me tonight, because I really have to do some washing," Jasmeet said.

"No, I'm good, Jas. Thank you so much, I really appreciate it."

"That's what best friends do, Lila!"

"Quickly, how's your Headteacher? I'm sorry I haven't asked, I've been..." How had she been? A bit crap, really.

"Lila, don't worry. I get it," Jasmeet said softly. "You know that meeting? I got my union rep to come and she ripped the Head a new one. I'm getting another teaching assistant, and the Head has taken a personal interest in Devil Child."

"Excellent! That's really good, Jas," Lila said.

"Okay, got to go. Love you!"

"Love you too."

Maddy, Girls Group Chat

Are you okay? Jasmeet said what happened. xx

I'm fine, Mads. How's Ellie? How's Ruby?

Maddy, Girls Group Chat

Glad you're okay. They're good! Ellie is rolling over and Ruby is up for promotion and I'm not looking forward to going back to work. xx

Oh gosh, is that soon? I'm so sorry, I've kind of lost track of time.

Maddy, Girls Group Chat

Not for a while, but still. It worries me that I won't be here for her and Rubes. xx

Oh Mads, I feel for you.

Maddy, Girls Group Chat

Can we meet on Saturday at 11.15 at the Costa down the road from me. I really need some Lila advice! xx

Lila started to type out an 'of course, whatever you need' message but stopped herself.

Actually, no.

> I'm sorry Mads, I'm not really in the right headspace for that right now. Perhaps another time?

Maddy, Girls Group Chat

> Okay. Let's make it another time. Call me if you need me, I'm here for you. xx

> Are you?

She'd sent it before she thought. Christ, was it too late to delete it? Yes, the three dots were flashing that Maddy was typing.

Maddy, Girls Group Chat

> I'm hurt that you're questioning that. I've just had a baby, Lila. I've got other things going on.

> I know, I shouldn't have said that. I'm really sorry, I wasn't thinking straight. So sorry.

Maddy, Girls Gr

> Fine.

Shit.

RHYS

It had been just over two weeks.

Rhys had taken to finishing at six, because he didn't want to run into Lila. Well, of course he did want to run into Lila, because he desperately wanted to see her and check that she was doing okay. He didn't because she said they'd talk

309

on her terms and he didn't want to bulldoze her. He settled for bringing the biggest, brightest flowers in for her office every day. Even though he wasn't sure whether that was a bit creepy, he did it anyway. The florist had suggested big, fat orange roses for today because she was out of proteas.

The email from the Fellowship, had come through confirming his attendance at the pre-interview day dinner the evening before, and there was a personal message from Professor Painter.

Huh, that was different. They were actually *impressed* by the blue moustache stunt. Apparently, it showed that he 'didn't take himself too seriously', that there was 'some joy in him' as well as a hard-nosed passion for Henry II. They were 'looking forward to seeing him and introducing him around'.

This was the dream. The thing was, he wasn't sure he even wanted to go. There was so much more he wanted to do and the Fellowship was no longer the be all and end all. Fuck, he didn't even know if he wanted to apply to it at all. It was a stuffy, elitist club that reminded him of his father and his cronies. Did he want it because it was tangible, physical proof of his success that he could wave in his father's face and say 'SEE!'? Or did he want it for himself?

He was obviously still in the running for the Fellowship, but he couldn't bring himself to be excited about it. He'd never get through the interview stage, his body of work just wasn't big enough. So why was he putting himself through it? Rhys sat and typed out a withdrawal, apologising for wasting everyone's time, and said he would reapply in a few years' time, when he had more publications and perhaps even a book. Rhys smiled. What a load lifted from his shoulders. He didn't realise how much that had been weighing on him until it was gone.

Elin

Why haven't you got back to my PA about dinner?

Rhys, do give me a call. Would like to chat with you.

Ah. That wasn't *really* from his mother. That was his father trying to sound out what had happened with the interview. How his father knew absolutely everything he would never figure out. Perhaps he had some kind of corporate 'fixer'. But why would his father even bother wasting his time on that? Just to prove to himself that Rhys was some kind of loser, unable to make it in academia and therefore needing his help to be successful in life. God, what a pathetic little man his father was sometimes.

Fuck this shit. He was going to deal with this once and for all.

He scrolled to his father's contact and pressed the green button, but he could hear the phone ringing outside of his office. Was his father *here*?

The door flew open and Llewellyn Dallimore, brown sheepskin coat and all, strolled into the small room. He took up too much space, making everything look like Lilliputian furniture.

Fuck. His father was here.

Rhys took a fortifying breath and tried to keep his emotion off his face.

"*Shwmae*, my boy."

"*Tad. Prynhawn da.*" *Dad. Good afternoon.*

"It's hardly the afternoon, Rhys," his father replied in English.

"Yes, well. Near enough." Rhys stood and put his hands in his pockets, feigning a nonchalance that he certainly did not feel. "Can I do something for you?"

Llewellyn Dallimore peered at the family photograph on top of his out-of-shape filing cabinet and made a derisory noise in the back of his throat.

"I heard that you've had a bit of a set back with the Fellowship interview." He turned to face Rhys and rocked forward on his toes. His lips curved in a smug smile and Rhys curled his hands into fists in his pockets to stop him from smacking it off his face.

"How did you know?" he asked.

"I know everything, boy," his father said. "You'll be back in Dallimores before Christmas then. I've got your office all picked out. It's near mine."

Rhys cringed. That sounded fucking awful. "No."

"No?"

"*Dim, diolch.*" *No, thank you.* "I won't be coming back to Dallimores."

Llewellyn Dallimore puffed his chest out and tilted his head back so he could stare down his nose at his son.

"That wasn't our agreement, *bach.*" *Boy.* His father's voice was low. "A Dallimore always sticks to his word."

What was this? Game of fucking Thrones?

"Yeah, well," he said flippantly. "I'm not going to spend my life doing something I don't want to do. I like it in academia. I like it here. My success isn't measured by whether I get a Fellowship or not. I'm measuring my success in happiness."

"What does that even mean? What's this nonsense you're saying? Measuring your success in *happiness*?" His father was baffled, and positively disgusted by Rhys's words. "Oh, I see, this is that girl Lila, isn't it?"

"Don't, Dad." Rhys warned, but his father carried on regardless.

"She's filled your head with rainbows and smiles. She has no idea what it means to be a Dallimore and she never will. She's not good enough for you, Rhys. She doesn't have the right mindset."

Rhys's blood burned in his veins. It was one thing to insult him, he'd gotten used to that lovely little nugget of parenting, but to insult Lila? No. Absolutely not.

He snapped.

"Stop." He leaned across his desk, veins bulging in his arms. "How dare you speak about Lila like that? How absolutely dare you? You're right. She doesn't know what it means to be a Dallimore and I thank my fucking stars every day that she doesn't."

"What is that supposed to mean?" His father matched his tone, coldly furious. "Think now, before you speak again. Think on what this family has given you."

Rhys didn't need to think. He knew exactly what he wanted.

"You think she's not enough for me? She's more than enough, she is everything. It's me who isn't good enough for her," Rhys said, louder than he would have liked, but his father fucking pissed him off. "I love her and I will *not* hear anything against her. Do you understand?"

Rhys's heart beat solidly in his chest. He had never spoken to his father like this before, but an attack on Lila deserved a well-rounded and swift defence.

"You *love* her?" his father spat. "She's not like Seren. For God's sake Rhys, she's *Saesneg!*"

"Oh for God's sake, Dad!" Rhys shouted. "It doesn't matter if she's English! Christ, it wouldn't matter if she was green or had no teeth, I'd still fucking love her."

For once, Llewellyn Dallimore was lost for words. His mouth opened and closed like a sock puppet with no voice. Finally, he raised an arm to point at him, finger shaking with rage.

"*Byddwch yn difaru hyn, bach,*" *You'll regret this, boy.*

"Dad, the only thing I regret is letting you dictate my life for so long." And how he'd treated Lila, but he wasn't about to open that little can of worms for his father. "Also, stop calling me fucking *bach.* I am *not* a boy anymore and you don't get to treat me like one."

"You are a boy until I tell you otherwise, Rhys," his father said. "I will cut you from this family."

Rhys scoffed and shook his head.

"Dad, I hope you don't do that, for Mam's sake, but if that's what you feel you have to do, fine." Rhys put his hands back in his pockets. "I'm done with this discussion."

"We are done with this discussion when I *say* we are done with this discussion." His father's voice shook with anger.

There was a knock at the open door.

"Um." Lila stood there, mouth open in a little O, eyes wide in shock. "You're very loud, and people are still here."

"*You*," his father seethed at her, his face puce.

Rhys was out from behind his desk and across the small office before his father could say anything else, placing himself in front of her.

"*Tad*," he warned, this time in Welsh. "*Ei amser i chi fynd.*" *It's time for you to go.*

Looking like he was about to explode, Llewellyn Dallimore sneered one more time at Rhys.

"You're making the wrong choice, *bach*," he said, pushing his way through the door and storming down the hallway.

Rhys watched him go, not regretting one little thing. In fact, his shoulders felt lighter than they had for an awfully long time.

Lila touched his arm gently and he turned to face her. God, she was beautiful.

"Are you okay?" she asked.

He actually was.

"Yeah, I am," he said. "Why are you still here? Are you all right? I'm so sorry, my father is…" So many words, none of which would do him justice.

"He is, isn't he?" she said, wringing her hands in front of her. "I stayed late because I wanted to come and talk to you, because the flowers are great but I don't have any more vases at home and then your father came and you were both very loud and we could all hear. We could hear what he said, what you said." She looked up at him through her lashes. "And I'm a bit flustered now, so I think I should probably go."

But she didn't make any move to leave.

"Lila, I'd obviously like to talk to you, but I'm not going to force you. Like I said, it's your decision," he said, rooting his feet to the floor, "but before you do go, can I just tell you a few things?"

She nodded, a pink blush high on her cheeks.

"I've realised that I need help to sort through all my emotions and I've started therapy because it's unfair on you to be that sounding board for me." He paused briefly before continuing, "and apparently, the blue moustache worked because the Professor Painter wants to introduce me around on the meet and greet evening, but I'm not going to go."

"Wait, what?" she said, a frown creasing her forehead.

"It was a pin that my father put in the calendar. Professor Painter hinted strongly in his email that although they were impressed, I don't have the body of work. Which I knew. I've withdrawn," he said. "I'm not ready and I don't want to put myself through the stress of it, nor do I want something I haven't yet earned."

"But Rhys…" she said, unsure of what she was supposed to say.

"I'll apply again, but when I'm ready, not to prove something to someone else." He started to reach for her, but held himself back.

"You've made me want to be a better person, Lila. You've shown me what it's like to be happy."

"Rhys—"

"And I'm doing the therapy for me and it's helping. I feel so much lighter."

Lila nodded, not meeting his eyes. "I'm glad for you."

"Lila," he said softly, "look at me."

She raised her eyes slowly, until they met his.

"Are you all right? I'm sorry about what my father said. He doesn't speak for me, he never does."

She waved her hand dismissively in front of her. "Oh no, I don't care about what your father said."

"Then what is it?" he asked. There had to be something

because the frown was still across her forehead and the pink blush was flooding her face. She took a breath, then another.

"You love me?"

Was that all? He relaxed and smiled.

"Of course," he said. "How could I not?"

LILA

Lila was up in the air looking down on herself talking to Rhys. He was so calm and serene, so relaxed, especially after what had just gone down between him and his father, because quite frankly, that had been *bad*. But Rhys looked cleaner and freer than she had ever seen him. He was obviously tired, the skin around his eyes betraying him, but he was looking at her with clear, bright eyes.

"Oh," she said. What else was she supposed to say?

How could I not?

Rhys's mouth spread into a smile.

"I wasn't going to tell you now, and definitely not like that. I wanted to give you some more time and I don't expect you to say it back. Not at all. I'm just comfortable and happy that you know."

"Oh," she repeated. Who was this Rhys, all loosely strung and laid-back?

"Do you want me to walk you to your car? It's getting dark," he said.

"Um…" Surprisingly, she did. She really did.

"I don't have to," he rushed to say, "it's just the lighting isn't great in the car park."

"Yes." Lila swallowed. "Yes, okay."

Rhys nodded and pinched his lips together, probably trying not to grin like the Cheshire Cat while she went to get her stuff. He met her by the lift. Standing in a confined space with Rhys 'how could I not' Aubrey with his relaxed (muscular) shoulders, his pert (perfect) little tush and the smell of his bodywash around her, was a little bit like hell.

Hell, because she had *missed* him.

Even after what he had said and done, she missed his arms around her, the grumpiness of him in the mornings, the put-upon way he took a cookie after pretending not to want one.

Rhys had tried to fix things. Indeed, he *had* fixed things with Sue and Jason. He was going to therapy, he had respected her wishes and stayed away until she came to him. He was respecting her wishes now, in this lift, by not pressing his luck because she was a captive audience. Rhys could go on and on and on and beg and plead and explain and justify and lie, if he wanted. But he'd chosen not to, because he respected her.

Lila hugged her bag to her chest and stared at her shoes. She was boiling hot and could feel every strand of fabric against her skin. It was his closeness, his control, just *him*.

Do something for yourself for once.

Lila looked at him out of the corner of her eye, but he was nonchalantly staring at the doors, hands in his pockets. Looking damned smug.

The door pinged open and he gestured for her to go first.

It was definitely cold tonight and Lila pulled on a pink crochet hat, which matched her coat. She was a massive pink raspberry with black-tight-ed legs for a stalk.

They walked in silence to the car park, although he could have been talking about how he had a newfound love for Richard Gere and she wouldn't have been able to hear him over the whoosh of blood in her ears.

"Here we are, Petunia," he said, tapping the top of her little blue car.

"Yeah," she said, adjusting her bag on her shoulder.

"Listen, Lila—" he started, but he wasn't going to get any more words out because she launched herself at him, throwing her arms around his neck and pressing her lips tight against his. He stumbled, but righted himself quickly, pressing her back against the little car, his mouth opening eagerly to lick his tongue into hers.

Lila had *missed* this. Damn it, she'd missed *him*.

As much as she wanted to take him home, to fall into him completely, she couldn't and she knew she couldn't. Pressing her hands to his chest, she pushed against him gently.

"Rhys." She was breathless. He pulled back and searched her eyes urgently.

"What's wrong? I'm sorry, I—"

"No, no, nothing's wrong," she said. "I just, I can't."

Hurt flickered in his eyes, but he stepped back and ran his hand across his mouth.

"I'm sorry, I shouldn't have." What? Kissed him? Thrown herself at him? Given him hope that she wanted him back? All of the above.

"No, no, I'm glad you did," he said, lips pulling into a tight smile that certainly did not reach his eyes. "I've told you before, Lila. You never need to apologise for kissing me."

Lila's breath caught in her throat at the memory of being his fake girlfriend. There was nothing fake about the way she was feeling now, but it was too much for right now. Too big, and she was not ready to deliver herself to him all wrapped up in a pretty bow.

"Okay, um. Thank you for walking me to my car," she said, fumbling with the door handle.

"Any time, Lila," he said. "Anything you need. You just, uh, need to tell me. I think it's pretty clear to everyone who has eyes what I want."

The unspoken word was *you*, and she flushed.

"But I don't want to push you. I want you to make your own decision, to want to be with me because you want to. Not because *I* want you to," he said. "I'm not like him, Lila, and I'd like to be able to prove it to you."

"Those things you said, Rhys." They went round and round in her mind every night before bed, stirring up the feelings of 'not good enough', 'will never be good enough'. So much for not talking about it.

"You'll never know how much I regret them. I was frustrated, angry, stressed and you were the closest, so I took it out on you. I shouldn't have." His voice cracked slightly. "Lila, I'm so sorry for hurting you. I have never been more sorry for anything in my entire life."

"You went behind my back and threatened Sue's job, Rhys. You went behind my back and contacted Jason about our loan. You *interfered*, and that was exactly what I specifically asked you not to do," she said, throat burning. "You told me I was unwanted, that I was a distraction."

He cringed, despair and regret clear on his face.

"I said those things. I know I did. But you have never been unwanted, you are never a distraction. I was wrong to say those things, I was wrong about so much. I should never have blamed you, none of this is your fault." His voice cracked dangerously and he took a shaky breath.

Lila held herself back, because all she wanted to do was to smooth his frown, to pull him to her and make it all better. But she couldn't, she *wouldn't*. She had to put herself first, and if that meant not fixing this situation with Rhys, then so be it.

"What I did with Sue and Jason was wrong. I fully admit that. I'm not going to say 'but', because it was wrong of me to do so. Completely wrong." He blinked rapidly. "I was trying to make things better for you. But you're a grown woman, you don't need me to fight your battles for you. I should have supported you in how you wanted to deal with matters rather than taking things into my own hands."

"Yeah, you should have," she said, tart and bitter.

"I know that now. I think I even knew it when I was doing it, but I couldn't stop. I just wanted you to not have to deal with people who were trying to bring you down." He shook his head sadly. "I never thought I would be one of those people."

He was raw, in pain, self-reflective, so different from the

assured, cocky, ego-driven 'I'm always right' Rhys that he was before she slipped on those leaves all those weeks ago.

"Sue does need some management training though," she mumbled.

A little smile pulled at the corner of Rhys's mouth.

"I miss you, Lila."

She nodded, fiddling with the strap of her bag, not ready to give him what he wanted. What would that say about her? Some pretty words and a searing hot kiss against Petunia, and she was anyone's? Yeah, no.

"I've got to go," she said, gesturing vaguely towards her car.

"Okay," he said. "I know I have no right to ask, but will you let me know you get home okay? I worry."

Lila rolled her eyes and nodded. "Sure."

"Night, Lila."

"Night, Rhys."

I'm home now.

Rhys

Good.

I meant everything I said tonight.

I know. I also meant it, I don't have any more vases.

Rhys

All I'm hearing is that you need me to buy you more vases.

That's not what I meant.

Rhys

I know.

CHAPTER 20

Onesie *(noun) one·sie*

1. *a bodysuit for an infant having a snap closure at the crotch and not covering the legs*

2. *a one-piece garment for adults usually with long sleeves and pants and sometimes with a hood*

LILA

"I don't know," Lila said, wrapping her wolf blanket around her tighter.

"But you love karaoke," Jasmeet said down the phone, "and you need to get out. When was the last time you went out?"

"I go out every day."

"Work or the supermarket does not count. When did you last go out and have fun?"

"I take your point," she said. "But I'm in my Oodie and my blanket and I'm just about to start *Ten Things I Hate About You.*"

"It's half three, Lila," Jasmeet huffed. "I'll pick you up at seven. Maddy and Ruby are coming."

"Maddy *and* Ruby?"

"Yeah, both of them. They've got a babysitter for the evening."

"So, I've simply *got* to go because Maddy and Ruby have deigned to grace us with their presence?"

"Don't be hostile, Lila," Jasmeet said. "You think they want to do karaoke? They're going for you. I think Maddy is feeling bad because she sort of dropped off the face of the earth and she wanted to do something you want to do."

It would be so nice to see Maddy, to apologise for that horrible text message she'd sent. Maddy was going through so much, and Lila regretted not being a better friend.

"I don't know, Jas. I'm not very fun at the moment."

"Lila, we love you whether you're fun or not," she said. "I'll pick you up at seven. Be ready."

Jasmeet ended the call. For crying out loud, she had the entire evening planned. *Ten Things I Hate About You*, followed by *Bridget Jones*, approximately fourteen gallons of raspberry ripple ice cream, a pile of Wotsits bigger than her and then a sugar coma. Karaoke was not on the list.

Maddy

> I'm sorry, I've been awful. I'm just so wrapped up in the baby that I haven't really thought about anyone else. Please come tonight, I really want to see you. xx

She did love karaoke and it had been ages since she'd been. Perhaps she could do that song at the end of *Ten Things I Hate About You*? Well, she'd best watch it to make sure she knew all the words (which she did) and she'd still have plenty of time to get ready after (and make sure Wotsits crumbs were off her face). Besides, it would stop her moping about the house thinking about Rhys 'how could I not' Aubrey.

Rhys hadn't tried to minimise what he had done. He had taken responsibility for his actions, recognised they were wrong and apologised. She'd said that he was like Jason, but that wasn't entirely true. Everything Jason had done was for his own benefit, to keep her compliant and doormat-y.

Rhys had only been trying to get her what she deserved, what she wanted, even if he had gone about it in completely the wrong way.

But the cold, unaffected way he had said 'Miss Cartwright, you are unwanted in this office' still pinched at her bruised heart. Rhys had addressed that though, two weeks ago, after she'd practically climbed him like a tree and kissed his face off.

Acknowledged, accepted responsibility, apologised. All of the As (kind of). He was trying to better himself, he wanted to be worthy, and she desperately wanted to believe that he was. She was teetering on the edge of forgiveness, but if she went into it with any doubts, then any relationship they could have would be doomed.

She'd never be able to get those words out of her brain.

Lila just wasn't sure of him yet. Wasn't sure at all.

Ten Things I Hate About You went by rather quickly and by the time Letters to Cleo were singing on top of the school, Lila was actually quite excited about karaoke night. Jasmeet was right. They hadn't been for ages and she did love karaoke.

Okay, decision made.

It took forty-five minutes for Lila to shower, dress and do her make up. Tonight, it would be a fifties polka dot wiggle dress, red lipstick and straightened hair put back into a neat ponytail, with a lot of hairspray to keep it all in.

"Bitch, you look amazing," Jasmeet said, giving her a hug. "I'm so glad you're ready. I didn't want to have to forcibly dress you."

"You were right. I do love karaoke and it will be nice to go out."

"Yeah, good," Jasmeet said, swallowing. "Dan's in the car, is that all right?"

"What, that Dan's coming? Sure!" she said with a smile that she wasn't feeling. Great, that meant that she would be fifth wheel, stuck between Jasmeet slobbering on her boyfriend and Ruby and Maddy stressing about the baby. But never mind that, she would be out and doing something she loved with the people that she loved.

It wasn't long before she was seated in the pub with a large gin and tonic in front of her and an extremely drunken rendition of Journey's *Don't Stop Believin'* being belted out by a couple of swaying friends on stage.

Maddy was gripping her arm tightly.

"I'm just so sorry," she said. "I know I'm all baby-fied, but I should have been a better friend. It's just so hard and I'm struggling with this new life."

"Maddy," Lila said, her heart melting. "You don't need to worry. I'm the one who should be apologising, you've got all this change and I can't imagine how difficult it is."

"I love you, Lila. I'm so sorry," Maddy said. "Please forgive me."

"God, yes, please forgive her," Ruby said, rolling her eyes. "She hasn't shut up for the past week about it."

"Only if you forgive me," Lila said, hugging her friend. They had both been a bit stressed and a bit emotional. But she was glad she had put down some boundaries.

"Thank the Lord," Ruby said under her breath, before taking a big gulp from her pint.

"I'm going to go to the toilet," Dan announced, giving Jasmeet a kiss before leaving.

"Urgh, you two are the absolute worst," Ruby said, pointing a finger at Jasmeet.

"Uh, I remember when you and Mads got together, we couldn't go anywhere without your tongue down her throat," Jasmeet said.

"Ha, yeah," Ruby said with a smirk, "and in other places."

"Ew, Rubes! Shut up!" Lila said with a laugh.

"What are you going to do tonight, Lila?" Jasmeet asked, but she was distracted, her eyes flitting around the pub.

"He'll be back in a minute," Lila said.

"What, Dan?" she said, a frown flicking across her face. "Oh, yeah. Sure, yeah."

"Um, I don't know. I'm not sure I'm down for singing, I'm just having the best time with my girls."

"Cheers to that," Maddy said, raising her glass for a clink.

"They've finished, thank God." Jasmeet said, indicating the stage, which was no more like a tiny, raised platform which usually sported two tables.

"They were awful," Lila agreed, "but that's the fun of karaoke! It's for everyone, it's not meant to be *good*."

"Thank you Shania and Tanya," the compère said in that lilting way they all had. They must have all gone to the same compère school.

There was a tap on her shoulder.

"Hi, Lila." Elin, in a silk shirt that must have cost more than her entire wardrobe (obviously, not including The Dress. Or maybe including that, who knew?) and the skinniest jeans possible, was in the pub. At karaoke night.

"Oh good Lord," Lila said, standing. "What are you doing here?"

James appeared at her side with a drink.

"James, did they not have any Mediterranean tonic?" she asked, glancing briefly at the drink.

"Hi, Lila," he said with a floppy grin. "No, sorry."

Lila stifled a laugh as Elin sighed dramatically.

"I could *not* miss this. Not for all the Spanish mergers in the world," she said, sitting next to Jasmeet. Elin introduced herself around and Lila sank into her chair uncertainly. If Elin was here, there was a good chance that Rhys was here as well. Oh.

"Next up, with *Up Where We Belong*, is Rhys!"

She looked at Jasmeet, who had a grin plastered to her face, her eyes wild and bright. Lila's mouth dropped open. *Rhys*? Singing karaoke? The man who had said that his worst nightmare date would be karaoke was here? By choice?

Elin got her phone ready to record, as James put her drink in front of her.

Maddy squealed and clapped her hands together, then gripped her arm so tightly that it would probably leave marks.

"Look! Look!" she cried, pointing at the stage.

Lila flicked her eyes to where Maddy was pointing and oh good Lord in heaven.

What. The. Fuck.

The introduction music started and Rhys was shifting uncomfortably on stage. Uncomfortable, not only because he was doing *karaoke*, but because of the absolutely disgustingly beautiful tie-dye unicorn onesie stretched tight across his broad chest and thighs. He had the hood up, the unicorn horn drooping floppily to one side, his face wary and pink.

There was laughter throughout the pub, and Rhys's eyes flitted around uncertainly. Sweat beaded on his forehead and he rolled his lips together.

The piano music started and he breathed deeply through his nose. He was really going to do this. Rhys opened his mouth and a whisper of a voice came out. Then, falsetto, trying to get to the female part. Good lord, he was doing the Deborah Winger bit.

Pub goers cheered drunkenly, but Rhys ploughed on, his voice getting louder and more confident with the male part.

"Are you all right?" Jasmeet whispered in her ear.

"It's Rhys." Stating the obvious much?

"Yeah, he's up there for you. He's really trying, Lila."

"You knew?" Of course she knew, Jasmeet had orchestrated the whole thing. "You knew."

Jasmeet nodded. "Please don't be mad. I believe him and I don't want you to miss out on something beautiful because of how Jason treated you." Jasmeet looked at her, her eyebrows drawn close with worry. "He loves you, Lila. He really does."

Lila looked back at Rhys. He was fully leaning into the song now it had hit the chorus, his voice stronger and more confident. Completely out of tune and with a shaky hold on the timing, but stronger nevertheless. He'd certainly won over the pub because they were belting it out with him, drunken arms swaying in the air.

Elin handed her phone to James with instructions to zoom in and leaned across Jasmeet to her.

"Rhys has told me what he did and he's a fucking idiot," she said. Jasmeet nodded. "I know a people pleaser when I see one. If there's one thing I have learned from Rhys, it's that you have to live your own life. But if you tell him I said that, I'll never forgive you."

Lila couldn't find any words. "I, uh…"

"If you decide to be with Rhys, do it because you want to. Not because that will make him happy. Do it for you."

Elin sat back and rested her hand on James's shoulder, a smile on her face as she watched her brother.

Rhys was up there for *her*. He wasn't just words and bluster. He'd taken something that he knew she loved, which he absolutely hated, and he'd done it in front of people, wearing a too-tight unicorn onesie.

If he was willing to do this for her, he would do anything. How could she not.

Lila pushed herself unsteadily up from the table and weaved her way through the tables. Rhys dragged his eyes away from the words long enough to spot her coming towards him, and he messed up the next line because a heartfelt and breathy 'Lila' certainly wasn't part of the song.

She cupped her hands to her mouth and called over the cheers, "Keep going, Rhys!" He pulled his gaze back to the screen. Stepping up onto the stage with him, Lila entwined her fingers with his and leaned towards the microphone to join in. The crowd hollered, and she could hear Jasmeet's wolf-whistle from the back of the room.

Rhys turned to look at her, words no longer in his mouth and she smiled as the chorus came round again. He spread his hands across her cheeks, fingertips reaching round to the nape of her neck and turned her face to him. Lila reached up on her toes to kiss him.

"I love you, Miss Cartwright," Rhys breathed before he ghosted his lips across hers, to raucous cheers and wolf-whistles from around the pub.

"I love you, Rhys Aubrey," she whispered.

"Yeah?" he asked, an uncertain, vulnerable smile tilting his lips.

Gripping his arms, she kissed him back, not caring that they were on show for the world. It was just him and her, Rhys and Lila, Lila and Rhys.

"How could I not?" she said.

EPILOGUE

One year later

LILA

"No, Lila. I'm not having that there."

"But Rhys," she whined. "I really like it there. It's the best memory ever."

"Can't you put it in your craft room or something?"

"No, because I want to remember this for the rest of my life. So, unless you want an unhappy girlfriend in this sparkly new house, then it goes here."

"Fine," Rhys said, rolling his eyes and adjusting the frame.

Of course she'd cut a still from James's video of his infamous karaoke night, framed it, and *of course* she was hanging it above the mantel in the front room. And of course Rhys had pouted as soon as he'd walked in, but she didn't care.

"Can you taste this?" she asked, holding out the wooden spoon.

Rhys headed into to the kitchen area and put the white wine he'd bought in the fridge. He slurped the tomato-y sauce off the spoon. "Mmm, perfect," he said, kissing her hard on the lips.

"Rhys Aubrey," she murmured against his lips. "If you don't stop kissing me, no one will have any food tonight."

"I don't care," he said, taking the spoon from her and placing it on the side. "I really don't."

Lila smiled against his mouth and wrapped her arms around his neck.

After a few moments of his tongue massaging hers gently, Rhys pulled back.

"Thank you," he said, suddenly looking very serious.

"What for?"

"For letting me into your life, for letting me live here with you, in what will be a cosy, messy, beautiful house."

"It's ours, Rhys," she said. "Our house."

"Our house," he agreed. "But you decorate it."

"Oh God, yes. I'm not living in a grey box with an uncomfortable sofa. But I did let you have all your dusty books, *and* a filing cabinet."

"But you've decorated the filing cabinet."

"I have Lila-fied it."

"And I love it," he said, kissing her again.

They were interrupted by the doorbell.

"That'll be Jas and Dan. Maddy and Ruby are going to be late. Unless it's Elin and James?"

"No, they won't be early either," he said. "I don't care who it is. They can wait."

He kissed her again.

ACKNOWLEDGEMENTS

What an adventure this year has been! This is the second book of my double debut year and it's all been quite a whirlwind. There are so many people who have played a part in making this book a reality, so many people to thank! Firstly, Olivia, Lucy, Liza and the team at Serendipity and Legend Press – thank you so much for taking a chance on me and my little love stories! Bailey, obviously, for the most GORGEOUS cover! Hanne, Georgia and the team at W F Howes for making my audiobook dreams a reality.

Of course, my Super Agent Saskia, who is always in my corner, giving me notes like 'no, no, that's not how you spell… that' (YOU KNOW WHAT IT IS). Seriously, thank you for putting up with my 'oh and another thing' emails, and the panic and the crises (yes, plural) of 'but it's SO bad!'.

Thank you to my beautiful Ann who checked the Welsh for me, and thanks (you and Vic) for consistently laughing at my extremely bad pronunciation. I try so hard!

Thanks to Hunts Bookshop for organising the best launches ever, and generally being super supportive and nice to me!!

It's not been a great couple of months, and I'm so grateful to everyone who has checked in on me – thank you, it means the world to me. In no particular order:

- Paul, Kit and Owen – yes, your better halves are much better than you, but I love you guys anyway.

- Smut Club – the most beautiful cinnamon roll group

of ladies who never fail to make me laugh! I love you guys so much!

- Core Six – here's to more alcohol and book research trips!

- Karen and Al – thank you for the long chats, the dinners, the laughter, the visits!

- The Survivors – Vicki and Ann, you two are the bestest friends a girl could wish for and your voicenotes are the best antidotes for everything. I love you.

- Emilie Tumulty – my best across the pond writer friend! I CANNOT WAIT to see what 2026 has in store for YOU my love! You are DOING IT!!!

- Nadine, Paul, Hannah and Olivia – you have been so supportive and so good, and my kitchen roll, kids and I cannot thank you enough.

- My Ride or Die, my Superhero, my Powerhouse, the best woman I know – Gemma. Always in my corner, always my Best Woman. Love you.

- My in laws, who have always supported me and have been extremely kind – thank you very much, I always appreciate you. Please don't read the smutty bits.

- Mother and Father Cheese, Lizzi and Catherine – thank you for everything, all the support, all the checking in, all the believing in me. Thanks for doing the windows, Dad. Thanks for trusting my fashion choices, Catherine. Thanks for not disowning me for writing spicy scenes, Lizzi. Thanks for making me cottage pie, Mum. Also, Cheese Family, please don't read the smutty bits.

But most of all, the Double L's (or the Double U's because we're all winners!), Luke and Lauren for being the best children a mother could wish for. Love you, my babies. And no, you still can't read it until you're older.

However, the biggest thank you is to you, Dear Reader. You, who have picked up this book, given my little love stories a chance and are making my dreams come true.